Forbidden Passion

Fiona could not help staring at Dag, perusing his bare flesh as he had hers. So dazzling he was, this fiery sungod. The glow of the flames turned his long wavy hair to molten bronze and cast his strong, well-made features into dramatic relief. She watched the light warm his skin and make his blue eyes glow hot and wild.

Her breathing quickened. From the beginning, she had desired this man. It had not mattered that he was a Viking, her enemy. She had felt an intense craving to have him touch her. Awed by his fair coloring, his height as he towered over her, the strength and power implicit in his long limbs and sleek muscles, she had known instantly that this was a man among men. Deep down in her woman's soul, she recognized him as a male to mate with, to seek strength and protection from.

''Fiona,'' Dag whispered. He smiled at her, a brilliant smile of satisfaction and warmth. Fiona felt something stir inside her, something beyond the languorous bliss which enveloped her body. She lay her head against his chest. She had let this man meld his body with hers, dared to allow him to touch her heart. . .

DANGEROUS GAMES   (0-7860-0270-0, $4.99)
by Amanda Scott

When Nicholas Barrington, eldest son of the Earl of Ul-
combe, first met Melissa Seacort, the desperation he
sensed beneath her well-bred beauty haunted him. He
didn't realize how desperate Melissa really was . . . until
he found her again at a Newmarket gambling club—being auctioned off by her father to the highest bidder. So,
Nick bought himself a wife. With a villain hot on their
heels, and a fortune and their lives at stake, they would
gamble everything on the most dangerous game of all:
love.

A TOUCH OF PARADISE   (0-7860-0271-9, $4.99)
by Alexa Smart

As a confidence man and scam runner in 1880s America,
Malcolm Northrup has amassed a fortune. Now, posing
as the eminent Sir John Abbot—scholar, and possible
discoverer of the lost continent of Atlantis—he's taking
his act on the road with a lecture tour, seeking funds for
a scientific experiment he has no intention of making.
But scholar Halia Davenport is determined to accompany
Malcolm on his "expedition" . . . even if she must kidnap
him!

STORM MAIDEN

Mary Gillgannon

Pinnacle Books
Kensington Publishing Corp.

http://www.pinnaclebooks.com

PINNACLE BOOKS are published by

Kensington Publishing Corp.
850 Third Avenue
New York, NY 10022

Pinnacle and the P logo Reg. U.S. Pat. & TM Off.

First Printing: July, 1997
10 9 8 7 6 5 4 3 2 1

Printed in the United States of America

My Viking

He says he's Irish
But I look into those eyes
Blue as the North Sea
And know he's an immigrant
Like all the rest.

I see him
A few centuries ago
Riding his bird boat
Seaspray halo
Gold-red hair glinting with the sunset
His bones are as white and strong
As the seafoam
His smile a bright fierce
Sea monster of passion.

He's come
To plunder my heart
Ravage my soul
Take me away to sleep
In the Northlands
Where the gods still thunder
And we can dream in endless twilight.

Chapter 1

Ireland, A.D. 805

At last they came to kill him.

Relief filled Dag Thorsson as he saw a gleam of light in the tunnel beyond the small underground chamber where he was imprisoned. If he went down fighting, he would know a hero's death and join his companions in the gleaming halls of Valhalla. He had no weapon, and his sword arm was useless, but he would do damage with his left arm, shackled though it was.

He blinked and tried to move. Fire seared through his arm, and he gasped as the pain robbed him of breath. Gritting his teeth, he watched the light. His suffering was almost over.

That had been his chief fear, that he would rot here, slowly wasting away without food or water in this dank, dark hole. His injuries made him lapse in and out of consciousness. He was no longer able to separate the agonies of being awake from those of his dreams. The idea of dying alone and helpless terrified him, for what would happen to his spirit then? Would it be trapped on this eerie green island? Would his soul remain entombed forever under these ancient, musty stones?

He shuddered and focused his eyes on the light, willing what strength he could into his stiff, aching limbs. He tried to lick his lips, but his tongue had swollen in his dry mouth. Struggling to keep his aching head upright, he raised his good arm as far as his chest. For all his resolve to fight, every movement made him dizzy.

The light came closer. He could see the shadow of the torch-bearer wavering and flickering on the far wall of the chamber. He blinked. The shape of the silhouette reminded him of a woman, and a horrible fear assailed him. What if the thing nearing him were not human at all, but one of the fairy creatures said to inhabit the misty isle? Dread clutched at his chest. He could not fight a spirit; it would carry away his soul. Never would he reach Valhalla. Never would he see his companions again.

The thing approached, slowly, stealthily. Dag's breath caught in his throat. It *was* a woman! A small, delicately built woman with flowing dark hair. Fear squeezed his chest even more tightly. A fairy! He had heard the isle was overrun with them— tiny creatures, surpassingly fair. They bewitched a man, carried him off to live in their underground kingdom. Time passed differently there, so if a man escaped, he would return home to find he had been gone for years, that his children's children's children now walked the earth.

Dag dropped his arm in defeat and closed his eyes. His muscles had no power against this thing. He would use his mind instead. He would try to will it away, to make it disappear. He concentrated, but his head ached and his thoughts were anxious and fragmented. It was no use. He was not strong enough. His spirit was too battered, too close to death to fight this enchantment. He gave up and opened his eyes to face his destiny.

She was remarkably beautiful. She had fastened the torch onto a holder on the wall, and the light illuminated her form quite clearly. He could make out the lissome curve of her mouth; the fine, graceful bones of her cheeks and brow; her strange, light-colored eyes. She was almost as small as he'd imagined—her head reached no higher than his chest. She wore a tightly fitted green kirtle, the shade of spring foliage. The color would allow her to disappear like a shadow into the verdant Irish woods. Her hair looked black, fine and silky and reaching nearly to her hips.

He was convinced now that she was a fairy. No mortal woman would deign to descend into this damp, stinking hole, certainly not one so exquisite. If his captors meant to keep him alive, they would send a slave with food and water, not this elegant creature. She looked like royalty, a fairy queen.

She stared at him, her face uncertain, somehow tense. Slowly, she approached, warily reaching out her hand, as if attempting to gentle a wild animal. He stared back at her, utterly confounded by this spirit which did not act like a spirit, this woman who could not really be here, here in this *hel*hole.

She touched his chest, and his flesh shivered. He had no idea how to stop her bewitchment—if that were what she intended. He looked down at her hand, holding his breath. She had long, tapering fingers with carefully shaped nails. Not the hand of a mortal woman, unless an extremely pampered one.

He stiffened as her fingers stroked him. Why did she caress him? Was it part of the spell she wove? A man could surely lose himself in the beguiling loveliness of her face, the feel of her smooth fingers. But, having lost himself, what fate would he would endure afterwards?

Dag resolved to fight the soothing pleasure her touch aroused, concentrating on the burning pain in his arm, the agony of his battered body. The delicate fingers went away. When he glanced up, the woman's face wore a look of consternation .

She took a step back, then began to unwork the clasp of the ornate gold girdle at her waist. Dag watched her uneasily, determined to thwart her if she approached again.

The girdle fell to the filthy floor. His eyes widened as she slipped off her kirtle and stood before him in a short shift of white linen. His breath caught as she grasped the shift at the bottom and pulled upwards.

In the name of Freya—now she was naked! What sort of enchantment was this? He gaped at her, at her full, rounded breasts, curving hips, the silky black hair covering her woman's mound. The beauty of her form made terror beat through him.

She meant to seduce him, and a mortal who coupled with a fairy was doomed!

His shaft rose. Despite his weakness, the pain, even his fear, his body desired hers. She moved closer. Surprisingly, she looked anxious, almost frightened. He focused on her face, trying to forget the enticing vision of her naked body.

She was close enough to rub against him, but she did not—thank the gods. Dag swallowed and closed his eyes; he could fight her better if he could not see her. Time passed. He could almost hear the beating of his heart. Still, she did not move. Then he felt the sensation of her lips brushing against the bare skin of his chest. He shuddered. His whole body went rigid; his shaft throbbed. He squeezed his eyes more tightly shut.

Her fingers grasped the wrist of his wounded arm. He winced. If he held it bent and close to his body, his arm did not pain him so badly. But if he had to move it . . .

She pulled on his hand, drawing it toward her. Agonizing pain shot down his arm; blackness swirled in his brain. His legs turned to water under him. He swooned, twisting his weight to his good side, trying to protect his wounded right arm.

The blackness lasted only a moment. When he came to himself again, the woman no longer held his wrist, but he still felt her presence. He decided to feign unconsciousness. It was cowardly to avoid fighting something you feared, but this creature was unlike any danger he had ever faced. Mayhap she could not work her magic if he appeared insensible.

She touched him again, carefully examining his wounded arm. Dag remained still, praying to all the gods he knew. As her fingers probed the mangled flesh, he could not suppress his groan. At the sound, the woman's hand left him, and he heard her sharp intake of breath. He slumped lower, hoping the fairy would mistake his outcry for delirium. From the smell of the wound, it had already begun to putrefy. The fever would take him soon, if lack of water did not. If the creature knew anything of fleshly ailments, she would guess him near to death.

She touched his forehead with her cool fingers. Dag ceased to breathe. Then she spoke a few words, almost a curse. There were rustling sounds. He held his slack pose until he heard footsteps receding in the distance.

He opened his eyes to darkness, and shifted his weight on his trembling legs. She was gone; he was safe. He breathed a deep sigh of relief. Then an awful thought came to him. What if he had not been visited by a fairy, but a mortal woman had come to aid him? If he had coupled with her as she'd intended, she might have helped him escape, or at least brought him food and water. Now, he would die for certain.

Dag stared out into the blackness of his prison, wondering if he had lost his last chance for life.

Christ help her—even the pagan gods were against her! Fiona sighed in exasperation as she replaced the torch in the hallway of her father's feasthall. Her plan had seemed so brilliant, so certain to succeed. Now, remembering the Viking's swollen, ruined arm, her hopes crumbled to ashes.

The huge warrior had swooned at her touch; it was obvious he was dying. What a waste! she thought grimly. Such a splendid specimen of manhood, destined to rot in her father's souterrain. Her breath still caught at the memory of her first glimpse of the wounded warrior. So tall he was, so finely muscled. His long, wavy hair gleamed reddish-gold in the torchlight. His features—even distorted by suffering—seemed as fine and beautiful as if cast in bronze by a master artisan.

Pity filled her. The Viking was obviously burning with fever. She shuddered, thinking of the damp, cold walls of the underground tunnels of the souterrain, the rats and crawling things that inhabited the place. Without water, his end would come soon enough.

She sighed. If only she could help him. But that was foolish. He was her enemy. If he and the rest of his bloodthirsty kind had attacked her father's settlement, they would have shown no mercy. Rape, murder, robbing monasteries—atrocity came easily to the Viking race. She could not feel sympathy for such barbarians.

Indeed, that was the beauty of her plan. She'd meant to lose her maidenhead to the captured Viking and confront her father with the deed. Let him try to marry her off to the proud Sivney Longbeard then. No royal man would want her, not after she had been soiled by the hated Viking. Her father's plans to use her to form an alliance with the house of Mac Carten would be thwarted. A defiant smile rose to Fiona's lips, then faded as the gruesome scene in the souterrain returned to haunt her.

The man was obviously too weak and ill to be aroused. If she could not entice him, she would have to give up her plan to avoid the marriage her father had arranged to enhance his prestige and swell his ranks of warriors. She thought of her prospective bridegroom, and the gorge rose in her throat. What a contrast Sivney was to the Viking. One so tall and fair, the other stout and bowlegged, with rotting teeth and pitted skin.

Even worse than the dark-haired Sivney's looks were his lechery and crudeness. When his eyes rested upon her, Fiona could see the greedy hunger there. It repelled her, much more than the Viking's fetid wound and filthy appearance. The enemy prisoner's stink could be washed away, his wound cleaned and treated. But Sivney's foul nature was irredeemable. He prided himself on his crude habits, his contemptible appearance. He would not change for any woman, certainly not Donall Mac Frachnan's only daughter.

Fiona paused suddenly in the doorway of the bower where she slept with the other unmarried women. She had not considered it before, but the situation with the Viking was not hopeless. If she were to clean his wound and stitch it, then provide him with food and water, he might well recover enough to accomplish what she wished of him.

Swiftly, she calculated the time until the wedding—only a fortnight now, but that might be sufficient. The Viking was obviously strong, or he would have perished already. With a little aid, he might survive.

Fiona went to the wickerwork bed she shared with her foster sister, Duvessa. Sitting down, she began to plait her hair in preparation for her journey. If there were one person who could advise her on how to heal the Viking, it was her aunt, Siobhan. She lived in a hut in the woods a short distance from Dunsheauna, as Fiona's father's fortress was called. People sought out Siobhan to heal everything from toothaches to fevers. Although the holy men of her father's household called Siobhan a witch and considered her use of spells and potions blasphemous, Fiona could not believe there was anything evil in using herbs and simples to help people.

Her hair arranged, Fiona slipped off her kirtle and changed into a stained brown one. She had hoped the clinging green garment would help her entice the Viking, but obviously he had been too far gone to respond. Jesu, even when she stripped naked, he had still done nothing!

Fiona's cheeks flamed at the memory. The man had been aware of her nakedness, of that she had no doubt. She recalled his deep-set eyes perusing her, full of astonishment and some emotion akin to fear. But it could not have been fright which had made him regard her so warily. She had carried no weapon, made no move to harm him. Besides, even wounded and shackled, the Viking easily had enough strength in his magnificent body to overpower her.

Fiona fastened a simple bronze girdle at her waist and went to put her elegant green gown and the hammered-gold girdle in a chest in the corner. When next she saw the Viking, she would not need lavish attire, but some of her aunt's magical herbs—and a goodly amount of courage. The thought of what she meant to do made her heart pound. It was like ministering to a wild beast—once the remedy took, what was to keep the animal from attacking?

Fiona's heart raced faster at the thought of the Viking's long, powerful arms closing around her, his well-shaped lips pressed against hers. If he raped her, she would have the means to her heart's desire—an end to the betrothal to Sivney. But how could she be sure the Viking would release her afterwards? He might strangle her after he had his pleasure or use her to affect his escape.

Fiona shivered. Her plan was fraught with problems. Not only must she induce the Viking to ravish her, she must also flee safely afterwards. Then what would happen to him? Once her father knew how his plans had been ruined, Donall would express his frustration violently. It was sure to mean a beating for her, although her father was unlikely to hurt her badly. Even sullied and no longer desirable as a royal bride, she would still have place in his plans. The Viking, though, would be killed, mayhap tortured as well.

It was foolish, irrational, but Fiona could not stop the stab of pain that went through her at the thought of the Viking suffering more. If she tended his wounds and saved his life, he would no longer be the faceless ravisher she intended him to be. Indeed, she had begun to see him as more than a despised savage she could use as she wished. Having seen the recognition and pain in his eyes, she knew he was a man, a wounded creature to be pitied and aided.

"Too soft," Fiona muttered to herself. "Exactly like your mother. You'll never get anywhere in this life if you're so careful of others' feelings."

Her words drifted away on the breeze as Fiona left the women's house and hurried through the busy settlement. As she passed the feasthall, Tully, her favorite of Donall's hunting dogs, left his sleeping place in the shade and followed her. Fiona reached out to scratch the rough, curly fur between his ears.

They moved unnoticed through the gate. Once outside the palisade, Fiona glanced around quickly, then chose a half-hidden pathway that led into the tangle of gleaming green hazel and oak trees. Tully bounded after her.

She found her aunt at her hearth in the small stone hut, stirring a rich vegetable stew and humming. "Fiona!" her aunt cried. "How good to see you!"

Fiona returned her aunt's warm embrace, then sat down on one of the large, flat rocks that served as seating places in the crowded dwelling. As she gazed into the fire, she sighed in satisfaction. "I always feel so at peace here." Her eyes met Siobhan's. "What magic do you practice that my cares seem to drop away as soon as I cross your threshold?"

Siobhan laughed softly, a sound like the wind through the reeds. In many ways, her aunt reminded Fiona of an older, faded version of her mother. Siobhan was small and fine-boned, with dusky skin and large gray eyes. Her black hair was streaked with silver and fine lines creased her narrow face.

"And what cares do you have that need easing, my child?" Siobhan responded.

Fiona sighed again. "I face the same trouble as when I visited you at the beginning of the sunseason. I despise the man my father has chosen to be my bridegroom."

"Ah, the Mac Cartan chieftain. I remember your complaining of his foul breath and ill-favored visage. Have you not yet found something to recommend the man?"

"Nay. You told me to look beyond his disgusting appearance, but in doing so, I discovered only his greedy, grasping temperament and a taste for bestial pleasures."

Siobhan shook her head. "How fortunate I was to avoid marriage. Of course," she added, "my circumstances were much different from yours. I was not a princess. You have my sister to thank for your royal blood. Many times I warned her that marriage to a warrior king would be disastrous."

Siobhan visibly shook off the mood, and a warm smile chased away the lines in her countenance. "Of course, Aisling was happy, for a time at least, and she was blessed with you."

Fiona nodded, feeling an answering ache in her heart. Her sweet, gentle mother had died two years ago of a wasting sickness. Even Siobhan, with all her herbs and medicines, had not been able to save her.

"Enough of the past," Siobhan announced briskly. "How can I aid you? A potion to put your bridegroom to sleep on his wedding night? Something to shrivel his manhood?" Her fine features crinkled with mirth.

"If my plan succeeds," Fiona said grimly, "there will be no wedding night."

"Tell me." Siobhan settled opposite Fiona, her gray eyes bright. "Tell me your plan."

". . . and if I can heal the Viking and entice him to fornicate with me, my father will have to call off the wedding." Finishing her tale, Fiona sat back and waited for Siobhan's response. The older woman frowned, but she had not dismissed Fiona's scheme outright. There was hope.

Siobhan stood up. "How bad is the man's wound?"

"Almost two days now it has been untended, and he has been without food and water as well."

Siobhan shook her head. "Once the poison starts, it is difficult to stop. The wound must be cleaned, then stitched. Mayhap if you drugged him, but even then . . . if he is fevered and weak already . . ."

"You can show me; I know you can," Fiona insisted.

Siobhan abruptly faced her. "And after you have healed him and coaxed him to deliver you of your maidenhead—not that I think he will need coaxing, mind you—what then? You're father is sure to kill the Viking, after he tortures him, of course."

Fiona blanched. Her aunt had seized upon the very thing she did not want to be reminded of. "I . . . I . . . I don't know. Mayhap I could free him before I go to my father."

"Free him? A brutish fiend like that? Do you think he would go meekly on his way, content to return to his people with never a thought of vengeance against those who captured him and held him prisoner?" Siobhan made a contemptuous sound. "Fiona, sometimes you are as much a fool as your mother was."

"It may not work, but I must try." Fiona looked up, her eyes pleading with Siobhan. "You are a healer, sworn to aid all who seek out your skill; do you advise me to turn away from this man, to leave him to perish in my father's prison?"

Siobhan smiled, a quirky, mischievous grin that made her look like a young girl. "Of course I will aid you. You do not think I would pass up a chance to thwart the great Donall Mac Frachnan's will, do you?"

Fiona watched her aunt, uneasy with her mocking words. There had always been bad blood between her father and her mother's sister. The look of malice she saw glinting in Siobhan's eyes made Fiona's own guilt intensify. She did not hate her father or wish him ill; she only wanted to foil his wedding plans for her.

"Come." Siobhan gestured to the corner of the dwelling where she kept her herbs. "If I am to give you a quick lesson in healing a man's battle wounds, we'd best begin at once."

Chapter 2

"Fiona!"

Her father's sharp voice made Fiona jerk around as she hurried across the muddy courtyard. She quickly thrust behind her back the leather bag of healing supplies Siobhan had given her. "Aye, Father. You wish speech with me?"

"Daughter." Donall's eyes swept over her. "Where are you going in servant's attire?"

Fiona hesitated, then met his stern gaze. "I went to visit Siobhan." Let him dare to tell her she had no right to visit her aunt, her own blood kin.

"Alone?"

"Nay, Tully was with me."

Donall's stance relaxed, but his shrewd green eyes continued to pierce her. "What business did you have with your aunt?"

"I asked her to show me some of her healing methods. Since I am to wed a warrior, I need to know how to drain an oozing wound or make a healing poultice."

"Healing?" Her father snorted in disgust. "More likely you have obtained poison to help your bridegroom into the spiritworld ere you have to wed him."

Fiona set her jaw. Her father obviously knew how much she

despised Sivney Longbeard, but he intended to wed her against her will. "I would do no such a thing. You must know it, Father."

"I would hope not. Still, your sulky look reveals your feelings for Sivney have not softened." He sighed, and his scowl eased. "Come with me into my private chamber. We'll talk of this some more."

Fiona followed her father into the spacious sleeping area built into the back of the feasthall. The walls were draped with rich, vivid cloths, and woven mats covered the floor. Wooden chests bound with enameled bronze strips held her father's clothes and the gold and jewels Fiona would take as her dowry when she wed. A bronze ewer and priceless glassware from Brittany graced the carved table near the wickerwork bed. Fiona fidgeted. Her father had taken no concubine since her mother's death, and the fine ornaments that adorned the place remained as they always had, reawakening Fiona's dull, aching grief over her loss.

Donall saw her wistful look and nodded. "Aye, I still miss her, too. I've wondered sometimes if it would be better if I gave away her things. Perhaps you would like them as part of your dowry when you go to Rath Morrig?"

At the mention of the wedding, Fiona's mood again turned rebellious. She glowered at her father. "I've told you, I'm not going to Morrig."

Her father's jaw clenched; but when he spoke, his voice was surprisingly mild. "*Acushla,* I do not make this decision lightly. If I did not need Sivney's support, I would not think to give you to him."

"And how many cattle and bondsmen make up the price of my maidenhead?"

Her father's face flushed with anger, and the veins stood out on his forehead. "Would that your mother ever heard you speak so! 'Tis a fine and honorable match I have arranged for you. Sivney has vowed to treat you with utmost respect and honor."

"Oh, so 'tis only serving girls and sluts he cavorts with in his banquet hall! 'Tis pleased I am that his vow to you will save me from his coarse attentions."

Her father grabbed her wrist. "Do not speak so of your future husband."

" 'Tis true, though, isn't it, Father?" Fiona spoke his name acidly.

A stricken look crossed Donall's face. He dropped her wrist and turned away. Fiona noticed how much silver threaded his dark hair. Her father had aged greatly in the two sunseasons since Aisling died. An unwanted sense of compassion disturbed Fiona's thoughts as she realized how much her mother's death had affected him.

It vanished as her father spoke in his cold, imperious voice once more. " 'Tis my right to command you to wed this man, and you will do as I bid. Sivney Longbeard is a powerful, wealthy man. He will keep you safe. You'll want for nothing."

Fiona took an outraged breath. "Safety! Wealth! Is that what you think a woman should seek from marriage? What of fondness and affection? You and my mother married for love— and against the wishes of both your families as well. Why is it different for me? Why must you barter me off in a loveless marriage to a man I despise?"

Donall turned to face her, his eyes cold. "These are danger-ous times, daughter. You need a man to protect you. I knew I could protect your mother, else I would never have wed her." He drew back, his lean, still-powerful body rigid with tension. "If your mother were alive, she would be grieved to see you question your sire's wishes. You shame her memory."

Tears sprang to Fiona's eyes. How dare her father evoke her mother to hurt her! Anger and reason warred within her, making her shake. She wanted to shout at her father—to wound him as he had wounded her. She knew arguing would avail her nothing. Better to make peace with Donall so she could be about her business with the Viking.

"You are right, Father," she said with as much calmness as she could muster. "Only an ill-mannered, disrespectful daugh-ter would question her sire's wisdom in wedding her to a man she hates."

Silence fell on Fiona's ears as she walked briskly from the bedchamber. A twinge of doubt nagged at her. Most men would beat their offspring for speaking as she had. Donall had always shown remarkable forbearance in his dealings with her; it was almost as if he cared for her feelings. But that could not be, Fiona told herself. If Donall cared, he would not insist she wed Sivney.

She quickened her pace as she made her way to the main kitchen of the settlement. The evening meal had long since passed, and the place was vacant except for the ancient cook, Vevina. The old women said nothing as Fiona entered and went purposefully to the supply area behind the cookroom.

Fiona hastily wrapped a joint of beef in a piece of linen, then grabbed a chunk of hard white cheese to add to her provisions. Vevina stepped behind her. "Hungry are we, little Fi? I have some fine stew simmering."

Fiona shook her head. " 'Tis not for me, but Tully. The silly hound caught a thorn in her front paw. I'm taking her some healing ointment, and I need a treat to distract her." She pointed to the leather bag draped over her shoulder. "I'll also need fresh water to clean the wound."

"Tully, eh? I knew her for an awfully fancy beast, but I had not heard the chieftain be giving his hounds wine these days." Vevina gestured to the bulging wineskin tied to the bottom of Fiona's bag.

Fiona blushed, and her eyes met the cook's pleadingly. She could hardly pretend that the drugged wine Siobhan had given her was meant for a dog. Vevina gave a hearty laugh that made her massive belly jiggle and revealed the single ivory-colored tooth remaining in her broad mouth.

"Ecch now, your secret's safe with me, princess. No one could blame you for seeking out a little sport before your father binds you to that greasy cattleherder. Wait here while I fetch you and your lover a blanket for comfort." Vevina gave an exaggerated wink, then waddled off to the little cubbyhole behind the kitchen where she slept.

Fiona gave a sigh of relief. Vevina would not breathe a word of her secret. She had known the old cook since babyhood, and the huge, cheerful woman had always indulged her craving for sweetmeats; now Vevina obviously thought to indulge her tastes for even more forbidden pleasures.

Fiona shivered, a thrill of fear and anticipation shimmering down her spine. What would Vevina think if she knew Fiona's "lover" was really a Viking prisoner?

Vevina returned in a moment, and Fiona collected the rest of her supplies. Then she set off for the souterrain, weighed down by a caldron of water, the blanket, and the bag of supplies. Fiona's progress was slow, and her muscles tightened with apprehension as she neared the edge of the palisade. The entrance to the souterrain was located a few paces behind the granary. If anyone saw her, it would be difficult to explain her numerous burdens.

Fortunately, she met no one. When she reached the wooden door set in the ground, she put down her provisions and glanced around warily. It was almost twilight. It would not do to light the torch until she was well down in the passageway; someone might mark the glowing light and come to investigate.

She took a deep breath, shuddering involuntarily as she contemplated again entering the damp, gloomy hole. The place made her shiver, and not only because of the darkness and the crawling things that lived there. Her father's fort had been built almost on top of one of the old burial mounds of the Tuatha De Danaan, the original inhabitants of Eire, and the storage chambers of the souterrain made up part of the passageways of the ancient barrow. Although Fiona had never sensed spirits lingering there, the place still made her uneasy.

Now her dread was intensified by the fear that the Viking had roused and freed himself of his shackles. Her throat closed up at the thought, but she forced her fear aside and unfastened the souterrain door. Jerking it open, she maneuvered into the opening and found the crude stairway that led downward. She took a few steps, then fumbled for the torch and the flintstone tied at her waist. She struck the flint, and the passageway flared into light. The pitch on the torch caught quickly, burning with a pungent odor. She placed the lighted torch in a crack on the side of the stone stairs and went up to retrieve the rest of her supplies.

Sweat trickled down Fiona's brow as she moved gingerly down the steps and reached the floor of the main storage area. Come winter, these rooms would be full of cabbages, turnips, leeks, and apples; now, only a few weeks into summer, they stood almost empty. The Viking was in the farthest chamber. Fiona made her way to the room and paused in the doorway, wondering what her torch would reveal.

He was still there, his body twisted awkwardly as he sagged sideways in his shackles. His head hung forward, hiding the finely chiseled features and piercing eyes which had so struck Fiona when she first saw him. She approached cautiously, expecting him to raise his head and stare at her again. He did not move.

She dropped the full wineskin to the floor to make noise, then called out "Viking" in a loud voice. He did not stir. Fiona took a deep breath; it appeared the man was unconscious or dead.

She went to him and touched his arm. The heat of it made her draw back. Aye, he lived, but he was clearly ill with fever. It would take all her efforts to keep him alive. Fiona felt some of the tension leave her body. The chore of healing was much easier to contemplate than seduction.

She found the bracket in the wall and hung up the torch, than began to unburden herself, spreading her supplies on the dirt floor. Siobhan had laid out her tasks carefully. She must get the man to drink. First water, then the drugged wine.

Fiona filled an empty skin with water from the cauldron, then stood on tiptoe and aimed the skin at the man's mouth. She squirted some water between his lips. His mouth hung open, slack, motionless, and the water dribbled down on the filthy straw beneath the prisoner. She swore softly and lowered herself to the balls of her feet. How to make him drink if he was insensible? She searched her mind for some memory that would aid her. Sometimes newborn babes would not suckle at first, and Siobhan would stroke their throats. If it worked with a babe, why not a man?

Fionna again stretched up on tiptoe. With one hand, she dribbled the water toward the man's mouth. With the other, she touched his throat. His skin felt searingly hot. She stroked gently, trying to coax him to swallow. Abruptly, he coughed. The vibration echoed down her fingertips. She drew her hand away and concentrated on holding the waterskin.

He drank deeply, pausing occasionally for breath, his great chest shuddering. She was so close; every movement he made seemed to transfer to her own body. He smelled rank, sweaty, and sick. Still, it was fascinating to be so close to this foreign man-beast, akin to petting a wolf or a panther or some such savage-but-beautiful creature.

The skin emptied. The man took the last swallow and sighed, still seemingly insensible. Fiona took the waterskin away, then retrieved the one full of drugged wine. Siobhan had warned her that she must get the man to drink some of it before she attempted to clean the wound in his arm. Otherwise, he might thrash around and make it impossible to aid him.

Cautiously, Fiona lifted the wine to the man's mouth. He moaned, but allowed her to force the spout between his lips. The wine dribbled down his chin at first, then he mastered the technique of gulping it as she poured into his mouth.

Fiona's hands shook and her legs ached with the effort of standing on tiptoe. She began to worry that he imbibed too much of the drug. Weakened as he was, it would not take much to induce a deep and dangerous stupor. She tried to take the wineskin away, but as she lowered her arms, the man's shackled left arm jerked around to grasp her by the hair. Fiona gasped and dropped the wineskin. She struggled, but the man held her tightly pressed against him, his massive, fevered body like a banked fire next to hers.

"Swanhilde, Brunhilde—what art thou?" The Viking's deep, gutteral voice sounded thunderously in the low-ceilinged chamber. His foreign words meant nothing to Fiona, but the tone of his voice reminded her of an endearment. Was he dreaming; did he think her his lover?

Fiona fought to catch her breath. She should let him ravish her here and now and be done with it.

She relaxed in his embrace, letting her body meld to his. He mumbled something intelligible, then his fingers moved down to touch her breast. Fiona drew in her breath. No man had ever touched her so intimately. Even through her wool kirtle and linen shift, she felt the heat of his fingers, the deftness with which he teased her nipple to throbbing hardness. Her body went limp, tingling with wanting.

He mumbled again, then released her so abruptly she almost pitched to the ground. She caught herself as the Viking sagged backwards. The drug had clearly taken effect.

She felt frustrated, aching. She glanced at the Viking, half hanging on his shackled good arm, half braced against the wall behind him. The pure, clean lines of his handsome face and heavily muscled neck sent a thrill through her. If she could ever get him fit enough to manage it, she might actually enjoy losing her maidenhead to this wild barbarian.

Sighing, she turned back to her task, kneeling down and searching her bag until she found the large iron knife at the bottom. She raised it and again approached the Viking.

She had considered long and hard whether to undo the enemy warrior's shackles. If his arm were to heal properly, it would have to be cleaned and stitched. She could not accomplish that if his arm remained shackled. On the other hand, if she only desired the man healed enough to couple with her, simply giving him water and easing his fever would suffice and limiting his recovery might actually be wiser.

Nay, she could not leave him as a cripple, Fiona thought decisively. It would be a crime against the gods to doom such a splendid warrior to live out his life with a useless sword arm. Whether it was wise or no, she must do her best to heal him.

She carefully used the knife to pry open the shackle around his wounded arm. Before the damaged limb could hang slack, Fiona grasped the elbow of his injured arm and braced it against the man's body. The Viking groaned. Fiona took a deep, steadying breath and reached up to undo the other wrist shackle.

The old metal gave way against the pressure of her knife, and the shackle fell loose. Fiona shrieked as the Viking sagged forward, his dead weight threatening to smash her into the dirt floor. She grunted and pushed against him. Slowly, the unconscious man's body moved backwards. His back struck the dirt wall behind him, and he slid down.

Fiona took a deep breath, her whole body trembling with strain. She raised a hand to her sweaty forehead. Blessed Saint Bridget! It had been like trying to hold up a pile of rocks! She had yet to begin her real healing work, and already she was exhausted.

She leaned over to inspect her patient. He sprawled against the stone wall of the souterrain as if he had been thrown there. His legs lay at an angle to his body, his injured arm half buried in the filthy straw that covered the dirt floor. Fiona sighed. She needed space to work; she must move him so she would have a clean area in which to tend the wound.

Kneeling, she lifted the man's head. With her other hand, she thrust the dirty straw aside. She continued cleaning, exposing the floor beneath the man's upper body. Then she took the blanket, spread it out and tugged it beneath his head and shoulders. Still crouching down, she pulled the cauldron of boiled water near and began to clean the wound in the man's arm, attempting to keep the water from spilling on the blanket. The wound was not deep, but Fiona knew she must get every trace of poison out if it were to heal properly. She dug and probed, making the Viking groan even in his stupor.

Finally satisfied the wound was clean, she obtained the pack of healing herbs from her bag and sprinkled them over the gash. Then, patiently, tediously, she took a clean needle and some fine silk thread and stitched up the wound.

Afterwards, she leaned back on her heels to inspect her work. Siobhan would have made a better job of it, she knew; but for a first effort, she believed she had done well. If the healing herbs kept the wound from swelling with poison and his fever abated, the man would recover. Whether his sword arm would ever be the same was difficult to say. Ideally, the wound should be cleaned and the dressing changed every few hours; but if the man were strong and healthy enough, his body might fight the poison and heal on its own.

Besides, Fiona thought with a twinge of grief as she bandaged his arm, the Viking could never be allowed to leave his prison.

She glanced down at the rusted shackles still binding his ankles; she dared not remove those and risk his escaping, especially since she had yet to secure what she wanted of him.

She struggled against her feelings of pity and reminded herself that this man was her enemy; if he encountered her when he was healthy and free, he would no doubt fling her on the ground and rape her, then slit her throat and kick her aside as if disposing of the leavings of a meal. She dared not grow too enamored of this dangerous if tantalizing man. She must obtain what she wished of him, then forget his barbarically handsome countenance.

Fiona began gathering up the supplies she'd brought. The blanket and cauldron she would leave behind; if he roused, he might wish to use the cauldron as a chamber pot and the blanket to cover himself. She dumped the bloody water in a corner of the room and left the soiled rags there as well. The two empty skins, the healing herbs, and the knife she replaced in the bag on top of the cloth-wrapped meat and cheese. There had been no opportunity to offer the prisoner food, and it seemed likely that when next she saw him, he would still be too weak to do more than sip broth.

The torch sputtered as she went to retrieve it from the wall. But despite her fear of the flame going out and leaving her in darkness, Fiona could not resist kneeling down for one last look at the Viking. Her gaze caressed the graceful planes of his face, the high forehead, prominent cheekbones, and strong jaw. A curl of thick, bronze-colored hair dipping over his forehead softened his fierce visage.

Fiona reached out a trembling hand and brushed back the damp strand. A wave a longing went through her. The Viking was so fair, so compelling in appearance. Never had she seen a man so massively and yet so gracefully built. Observing the Viking's huge hand lying slack in the dirt, she recalled those long fingers fondling her breast. The memory made her shudder. What would it be like to wed a man like this, one so comely and strong?

Shaking her head, she drew back her hand. This man was

her enemy, her father's prisoner. She had wasted too much sympathy on him already.

Fiona crossed the shadowy chamber and entered the ancient, damp hallway. A cold finger seemed to trace its way along her spine as she hurried down the corridor and scrambled up the crumbling stairs to the world of light and life beyond.

Chapter 3

'Where have you been?'' Duvessa's whisper came hissing out of the darkness as Fiona crept into the bower they shared. Fiona sighed and began to wearily remove her clothes. From the moonlight shining in the narrow window in the wall, she could see her foster sister's slender form rising from the bed across the room.

"I couldn't sleep, so I went for walk and looked at the stars," Fiona answered.

"Alone?" Duvessa's voice was full of excitement as much as fear. "There might be Vikings out there."

"Donall's sentries guard the palisade; no one could get by without the alert being sounded."

"What about the spy discovered two days ago? He was a Viking, Dermot said; and where there is one, there are bound to be others. Dermot said your father increased the guard on duty at night; he must expect an attack."

Fiona resisted the urge to tell Duvessa that Dermot was hardly a reliable source of information. Although Duvessa's younger brother slept in the same dwelling as the soldiers, at eleven winters, he was not likely to be included in any serious strategy sessions.

"Father Fearghal says all Vikings are savages," Duvessa continued. "They delight in butchering monks and innocent babes—and ravishing Christian women." There was a noticeable thrill in her voice, despite the shocking aspect of her words.

Duvessa moved across the room and plopped down on a stool. Like Fiona, Duvessa was small; and her thick curly hair, unbound for sleeping, floated around her shoulders, almost overwhelming her slight form. By daylight, it appeared a deep red and was so wavy and unruly it took a dozen plaits to keep it confined.

"Are you still brooding over your betrothal?" Duvessa asked gently.

"Aye."

Duvessa sighed. "Your father must have good reasons for making this match. Mayhap it has something to do with the Vikings."

"Nay, it has to do with greed!"

Duvessa sighed again. "I hate to see the two of you like this. Your father loves you. He would not wed you off merely to increase his herds or to gain a hoard of gold. He must have some other plan, some secret goal he cannot speak of yet."

"At least you admit that my bridegroom leaves something to be desired," Fiona said hotly. "My father will not even admit how repulsive and crude a man Sivney Longbeard is!"

"But the Mac Cartan chieftain is powerful; it's said he can call up two hundred warriors with half a day's notice. If the Viking raids continue, we may need the forces of another strong chieftain to aid us."

Doubt weakened Fiona's anger. What if fear rather than greed motivated her father? Had concern over the Vikings driven Donall to plan this alliance with Sivney? She quickly dismissed the thought; if her father needed Sivney's men, he would have told her. Instead, he had shouted and raved and thrown her mother's blessed memory in her face.

Anger and indignation again flowed through Fiona's veins. She would not change her mind; she would find a way to defy her father's loathsome wishes.

"I need to sleep," she told Duvessa curtly. She went to the

bed and climbed in. Duvessa remained seated on the stool for
a moment, then got up and made her way to the bed.

Fiona lay still, wide awake. The image of the Viking filled
her mind. On the morrow, as soon as she could sneak away to
the souterrain, she would go to him again. If the herbs healed
his wound and his fever eased, he might be able to perform
the task she required of him. Fiona's body grew hot at the
thought. It would be better if the man were still weak, perhaps
even a bit delirious. There should be some curb to his enormous
strength, else he might think to overpower her and escape.

The idea of the savage Viking running loose in her father's
compound made Fiona's heart pound with fear. She had not
tamed the beast, and she dared not forget that. Mayhap tomorrow, if his arm had improved, she would attempt to refasten
the shackles binding his wrists. From what she knew of the
act, a man could couple with a woman standing up, and it
would be safer to keep the Viking fettered.

Duvessa made a small, sleepy noise. Fiona struggled not to
squirm on her bedplace and risk waking her foster sister. Her
flesh felt as fevered as the Viking's had, especially her breasts.
What madness was this that she desired her enemy's touch
with such longing? Surely it was punishment for her willfulness
and lack of obedience to her father.

Guilt tweaked at Fiona, dampening her desire but scarcely
bringing restfulness.

He climbed through a long, dark tunnel, but even as he
reached the end, there was no cessation of darkness. Dag woke
to the solid blackness of his underground cell. Pain still stabbed
down his arm, but it felt different, somehow milder, more an
ache than a burning. He shifted abruptly, realizing with a start
that his circumstances had changed. No longer was he shackled
to the damp wall; his left hand was free and his head rested
on something soft.

Slowly, he raised himself to a sitting position. The familiar
scent of rot and earth assailed his nostrils, and the pull of the
shackles on his ankles assured him that he remained imprisoned.

The moisture in his mouth told him he had been given drink; the stale taste suggested wine. He tested his wounded arm and found it bound near his body. With cautious fingers he explored the bandage. Someone had tried to mend him. The fairy?

Dag searched his mind, trying to recall something beyond the blackness and the pain. If the fairy had come and tended to him, he had no memory of it. But someone or something had undone his shackles and bound up his arm. The realization of his improved conditions did not reassure him. Even magical beings did not do things without motivation; if the fairy aided him, then she wanted something. What was it?

Remembering the sight of her delectible, naked beauty, Dag shuddered. It was obvious what she desired, and he would be cursed if his traitorous body did not want to give it to her. Thank the gods, the fairy had not been insistent. She could have used her fingers to entice him or rubbed up against him until he could not resist the lure of her nakedness. The fairy appeared too shy or inexperienced to pursue the matter beyond her first tentative invitation. She had left him, then apparently come back when he was unconscious and cared for the worst of his hurts.

Dag flinched again as an awful thought came to him. What if he had lain with the fairy during his delirium? He had no memory of her visit; how could he be certain he had not coupled with her while senseless? *Nei*, he would know. Some feeling of satisfaction would remain. A creature as exquisite as that would leave some impression upon his flesh, even if the memory of joining with her eluded his mind.

Relief flooded him as he began to investigate his new circumstances. The blanket under him was clean and soft but rather worn. His fingers searched the dirt floor further and encountered an empty cauldron. If only it were full, he thought regretfully as his stomach squeezed with hunger. Had she given no thought to feeding him? Mayhap fairies did not consider such mundane things.

He found nothing else. Apparently the creature had poured wine into his mouth, unbound his shackled wrists, treated his wounded arm, then disappeared. It was obvious she meant to keep him alive so she could attempt seduction at a future time.

Unless he escaped. Dag reached down with his good hand and explored the iron bands encircling his ankles. If such a slight being could release his arm shackles, then surely he could pry off his leg irons. His fingers searched the uneven floor. All he needed was a sharp rock, something to work the metal against. It would take time, but he could eventually get free.

Once he escaped the dank hole where he was imprisoned, he would wait until night and find a weapon to use in case he was discovered. For a warrior trained in stealth and spying, it would be easy to sneak out of the palisade. Ah, but that was what he'd thought when he first saw the Irish chieftain's fortress on the hill above the river and bragged to his companions that he could assess the strength of the place and be back in the longboat before dawn. His cockiness had led to his capture, or mayhap it was simply ill-luck that had resulted in his being trapped between the chieftain's returning war band and the fortress.

He had fought hard, but no man could outmanuever ten warriors at once. After one of them hacked his sword arm, leaving it bleeding and useless, they had surrounded him and forced him to the ground. Then the Irish warriors had kicked him, taunted him, spat upon him, and thrown him into this *hel*hole to rot. Except for the fairy's aid, he would likely be dead already.

Anger rose in him, hot and bitter. He would make the Irish chieftain pay for leaving him to such an ignominious, shameful death. As soon as he could free himself, he would find his companions. They would fire the chieftain's fortress. Everyone inside would die.

The fairy, he wondered—would she succumb to the flames as a mortal would? It would be a waste for such an exquisite creature to perish.

Dag shook his head sharply, trying to clear it. What was wrong with him? Why was he concerned for the fairy's fate? The thing she planned for him was worse than death. She meant to steal his spirit, to entrap him in her timeless fairy world.

She was a demon, as dangerous as an *undine,* the half woman, half fish creatures who lured seafarers to their deaths upon the rocky shores. The fairy represented a more terrifying doom than wasting away in the darkness. If she came back, he must feign unconsciousness and hope to avoid her alluring treachery.

Meanwhile, he would work furiously to free himself.

Sweat trickled down Fiona's brow as she made her way down the stone steps into the darkness. It was reckless to enter the souterrain door again during daylight. Even now, she could not be certain she had not been seen. She should not have returned so soon, but the image of the Viking would not leave her. She must reassure herself that he still lived.

A slight scratching noise made her halt, and her heart thudded loudly in her ears. What if the Viking had freed himself? Did she have the nerve to face him if he were unbound and alert?

She listened; there were no more sounds.

She crept forward, every muscle tense. As she entered the final chamber, she thrust the torch ahead, prepared to defend herself. The flame wavered with the motion, casting spooky shadows. Slowly, she made out the Viking's huge body lying motionless against the wall.

Panic made Fiona rush to where he lay. She dropped the supplies she had brought and hastily stuck the torch in its niche in the wall. Trembling, she knelt beside the man and touched his face. She exhaled her pent-up breath. He was warm, slightly fevered, but obviously alive. His breathing seemed slow and steady.

Her still-shaking hand moved to examine his wounded arm. It felt much less swollen. She could not be certain without removing the bandage, but it appeared to be mending. Relief raced through her. It was her first attempt at healing, and so far she had been successful.

She sighed softly. Hope remained for her plan. If only the Viking would rouse a little. Perhaps the drugged wine had affected him so strongly because he was weakened by the fever.

Her eyes perused his still face, and the strange fascination again crept over her—the irresistable urge to touch him. Her fingers hovered over his forehead, aching to smooth his thick hair away from his brow. Then she leaned closer, and her nose wrinkled with disgust. His smell had not improved after two days of lying senseless. If she meant to couple with him, she must do something about his odor. Now appeared to be the ideal time.

She glanced down at his long body. His filthy clothes smelled evilly. She would have to cut them off, then bathe him. But if she allowed him to lie in the soiled straw afterwards, he would only get dirty again. Fiona removed the old cloak she wore, swiftly deciding that it would serve as another blanket.

She stood, took a deep breath, then leaned over, grabbed the Viking's ankles and, grunting, dragged his lower body away from the wall as far as his shackled ankles would allow. Straightening, she took several deep breaths. Jesu, but the man was heavy!

She did not rest long, but began to kick aside the fouled straw which had lain beneath him. Once the dirt floor was exposed, she picked up her cloak and spread it out next to the wall. Then she grasped his ankles and dragged him back to his former resting place.

Fiona wiped the sweat from her brow and caught her breath again. The Viking had not moved a muscle during the ordeal but had lain as limp and inert as a sack of grain. It seemed odd he did not stir. Again, she leaned over and touched his forehead, searching for fever. His skin seemed only vaguely warm; it must be the wine which kept him senseless. Even so, she must hurry. If he roused and discovered her, she was not certain what he would do.

Her hand trembled as she pulled the small, sharp knife from the leather thong at her waist and began to cut off the Viking's tattered tunic. It was already badly torn at the neck, exposing much of his chest. She made a cut at the top, ripped it the rest of the way, then began to ease it off.

Under his left arm it seemed to stick. She leaned over and saw that the garment had adhered to a patch of dried blood. As gently as she could, she loosened the fabric and pulled it away from the jagged gash. She grimaced. Another wound. Indeed, now that his chest was bare, she could see a half-dozen ugly bruises and several deep cuts marring his fair skin.

Pity filled her. He must have been in awful pain the first time she'd come to him; it was well the wine had kept him unconscious and eased his suffering. She felt the familiar regret that the Viking's magnificent form should have been so battered and damaged.

She turned away and sought out the supplies she had brought. Unstoppering the jar of water, she poured the water into the cauldron, reserving a bit for the Viking to drink. She added a handful of medicinal herbs to the cauldron, then dipped a cloth into the mixture. With slow, gentle strokes, she began to wash the Viking's face.

Her hands trembled as she felt his smooth flesh beneath her fingers. She cleaned the cut on his forehead, then rinsed the cloth and rubbed it over the planes of his chiseled cheekbones and the stubble-covered squareness of his jaw. The torchlight made his sun-reddened skin gleam bronze and brought out the coppery highlights in his wavy hair and thick mustache.

She reached his neck, and her hands shook even more as she perceived the raw strength of the corded muscles in his neck, the breadth of his square shoulders. Steadying her hands, she rinsed the cloth and continued washing. Here, where it had been covered by his tunic, his skin was fairer, a creamy shade, darkened with freckles. A silky down of reddish-gold hair began at his neck and spread across his upper chest, then trailed down his belly in a line to his groin.

Awe and some other emotion she could not identify assaulted Fiona as she rubbed the scented cloth over his chest. The sensation of sleek skin over iron-hard muscles made her throat go dry. He was so beautiful, so pleasing to look at. The sight, the feel of him caused a dull ache to spread through her body. She could do this forever, stroking him, feeling his aliveness, the deep thud of his heart beneath his skin.

She forced herself to concentrate on washing. The dried blood that caked the gashes on his skin took some scrubbing. As her fingers rubbed at the wound on his lower chest, the

Viking took a sudden, sharp breath. Fiona froze, watching his face. When he made no other movement nor emitted any sound, she returned to her task. A deep bruise was visible around the cut; it seemed likely that the damage extended to the ribs beneath. Fiona left the injury alone and began washing beneath his left arm. He shivered slightly as the cloth touched his armpit, and Fiona again tensed. Most people were ticklish there, but if the man were truly unconscious, he should not feel it.

She sat back on her heels, observing the Viking closely. Could he be aware, but pretending unconsciousness? Nay, it was absurd to think so. Why would a man lie as if dead while a stranger bathed him?

She watched him a moment longer, then went on with her washing. After rinsing what she could reach of his other side and back, she glanced with distaste at the murky water in the cauldron. She should have brought more, but it was awkward to carry and would have been difficult to explain if anyone had noticed her. She would have to make do with what she had.

Fiona took a deep breath and glanced at the line of hair that ran down the Viking's flat, muscular belly and disappeared into the top of his trews. Her skin suddenly felt hot, and the weak, aching feeling inside her deepened. Despite the reek of his clothing, did she have the nerve to bare more of his breathtaking-but-frightening body?

Fool! she told herself. *You mean to have him couple with you—what difference does it make if you see him naked?* Fortified by the thought, Fiona sought out the knife and used it to cut the drawstring of his trews. Grasping the stiffened fabric, she slowly eased it down. She had not even gotten it past his hips when the trews fell from her hands and she gave a smothered cry.

Sweet Bridget! Fiona gaped at the large, erect phallus thrusting up from the Viking's thatch of reddish pubic hair. The man was as aroused and ready as a stallion in rut! Suspicious, she darted her eyes back to the Viking's face. His features were still, expressionless. Was it possible that a man's body could be primed for lovemaking while his mind remained unaware?

Fiona swallowed hard. Dared she continue washing him? At

any moment, he might throw off his stupor and grab her and rape her. But was that not what she wanted?

Her eyes again took in his engorged male organ. She had not thought men were so large. He seemed as huge as a stallion—and she was no mare! Would he kill her if he coupled with her? At the very least, it would be painful. She felt sweat dribble down between her breasts. She must be brave. Losing your maidenhead was said to hurt, but it could hardly be worse than bearing a babe. If a woman's flesh yielded to allow a babe through the birth passage, surely it could accommodate a man of almost any size.

Fiona bit her lower lip and stared. Men often referred to their phalluses as "shafts" and "swords." Observing one closely, she found the descriptions very apt. The woman's body acted as a scabbard—the sheath for the man's weapon. Fiona felt a blush firing her cheeks. She wanted to touch the intriguing sword of flesh rising from the Viking's belly. She wanted to know if it felt as smooth and warm as it looked.

She shivered with the thought and shot another glance at the Viking's face, relieved to see no hint of awareness in the man's impassive expression. Cautiously, she reached out her hand.

Silky. Hot. A faint smile curled Fiona's lips as she explored. The tip of his shaft was very soft. It tapered like an arrow point, then dipped in to meet his sleek, firm length. Beneath his shaft, his softly rounded testicles drooped downward.

Her fingers encircled him, gauging thickness, weight, warmth, experiencing the wonder of supple skin overlaying solid flesh. She imagined him inside her, filling the passageway to her womb. Her knees went weak and her insides clenched with yearning.

She paused, eyes closed, her senses intoxicated by the Viking's glorious hot flesh. What she felt was sinful. It was wicked enough to defy her father, worse yet that she might enjoy the wanton thing she intended. And there were other risks. What if the Viking's seed took hold in her womb? It would be disastrous to bear a half-Viking babe.

Fiona pulled her hand away and clenched it stiffly against her body. The further she progressed with her plan, the more addle-witted it seemed. She meant to couple with a barbarian, a savage, and she expected him to neither kill her nor impregnate her.

She stood. She should give up this folly, gather up her things, climb the crumbling steps, and bolt the souterrain opening behind her. Let the Viking rot.

Fiona leaned down to grab the handle to the cauldron. She paused. Her eyes sought the captive's sprawled form and perused his naked, gleaming flesh. A wild hunger unfurled inside her. One time—what could happen if she lay with him one time?

Her fingers released the cauldron handle, and she bent to kneel in the dirt at the Viking's side. She jerked the man's trews down to his hairy thighs, then paused. Because of the ankle shackles the man still wore, she would have to cut his trews to remove them completely. Finding her knife, she used it to sever the fabric, then alternately ripped and cut the garment the rest of the way down his legs. Grimacing, she threw the smelly trews aside. They were good for naught but burning now, and the man did not need clothes for what she wanted of him. Indeed, being naked might discourage him from escaping. To that end, she decided to take off his cowhide boots as well. She unfastened the leather strips from around his ankles and removed the boots.

Fishing her cloth out of the cauldron, she resumed washing the Viking. She went about her task rapidly; but even so, she could not avoid noticing the muscular shape of his long legs, the awesome size and perfection of the man's lower body. Every inch of him seemed as solid and strong as if honed of tempered iron.

Finished, she dumped the soiled water in the corner of the chamber, then returned to the captive. Although hardly clean, he no longer smelled of blood and sickness. She reached to feel his brow again and noted with approval that he seemed cooler, as if bathing him had eased his fever even more. There was nothing else she could do for him until he roused.

Would he rouse? If he had not stirred during all her washing and touching, why should she think he would ever awake? New anxieties crowded Fiona's thoughts. The Viking had suffered a head wound; could that be what kept him unconscious? She examined the gash on his forehead carefully. There was some swelling there, but not enough to seem dangerous. Except for his arm, the man appeared whole and relatively healthy. His breathing was even and deep; his color appeared normal. Every moment she was with him, she expected him to open his eyes and confront her. It was baffling that he did not wake.

She leaned over him and sighed. She could not linger here. It must be midafternoon now; if she did not appear by the time of the evening meal, Duvessa would grow alarmed and alert Donall to her absence. If her caresses did not rouse the man, it seemed nothing would.

Frustrated, Fiona studied the Viking. His shaft seemed incredibly stiff and solid. She wondered if she might be able to force it inside her body though the rest of him lay inert and insensible. If he tore her maidenhead, who was to know how it had been done?

She started to undress, then paused, suddenly feeling cold with guilt. Her whole plan was unscrupulous, she had accepted that. But to use a man's body while he lay wounded and helpless—something inside her rebelled. She defied her father because she did not think it right for him to treat her like a thing, a possession. Now she meant do the same to the Viking, to exploit him for her own ends.

But he was just a godless savage, an animal, she argued with herself; he had come here to kill and destroy. His feelings were beneath consideration.

Fiona shook her head. The Viking was not an animal. She had heard him speak, looked into his compelling blue eyes. He had a soul, and she would not trade his soul's freedom for her own.

Her hands left the girdle at her waist. She would come back tomorrow. Surely by then, the man would waken.

Fiona retrieved the cauldron and her leather bag. She would leave the water jar and the food. If the Viking woke, he would need refreshment.

She took the torch from the niche in the wall and left the

captive. Halfway to the doorway of the chamber, she turned once more, unable to shake the sense of connection she felt with the wounded man. She had tended him, bathed him, touched him as intimately as a lover. Although she did not know his name or the slightest thing about his life, she could not help feeling that there was a bond between them. A bond that would not easily be broken.

Chapter 4

Dag exhaled a groan. He had survived, but only barely. To lie still and lifeless while the fairy tantalized him with her gentle, teasing fingers—Thor's hammer, what agony! At any moment he had expected to lose control and twist her body under his and thrust into her until he exploded with release.

Obviously, that was what she wanted. She had removed his clothes and washed him to prepare him to mate with her. It was a wonder that she had not also undressed and mounted him, her slender thighs parted over his groin, her small sheath pressing down on his flesh.

He clenched his teeth. Thank the gods she had not tried that! All his resolve would have been undone. A man could stand only so much. If she were a toothless old crone, he would have found it easy to resist. But he had seen her; he knew exactly what loveliness she possessed.

He shuddered again, then moved his hand down to his shaft. With swift, rough strokes, he brought himself to climax in seconds. As the last tremors of satisfaction pulsated through him, her image filled his mind—so fey, so delicate, so unearthly beautiful.

He sighed, the tension flowing from his body as he wiped

the sticky seed off his belly with the edge of the cloak beneath his hips. The woman was an enigma. The way she'd touched him, the tenderness and patience with which she'd cut off his garments and bathed his body—she had treated him as a lover would. Could it be she sought his heart as well as his seed?

The thought unsettled him. He did not know what to think of the beautiful creature who had tended his hurts and inflamed his passion. She felt real, a fleshly being rather than a supernatural one. Except for the oddness of her appearance in his dank prison and her extraordinary beauty, he would have assumed she was mortal as soon as he laid eyes on her. He had been delirious then, his wits confused by pain and exhaustion. Now that he was alert and aware, he knew his rescuer to be as mortal as he was.

He frowned. That fact did not resolve the puzzle, only worsened it. Why would an obviously highborn woman tend a prisoner? More baffling still, why would she seek to seduce a bloodied, fevered warrior? Such a woman could have her pick of lovers. What had he to offer her?

It made no sense. The woman did not seem wanton, but frankly innocent. He would swear she had never known a man's body before his. Her touch had been hesitant, curious. Indeed, it was the very wonder with which she explored him which had aroused him so unbearably. To have a virginal beauty like that caress him with such reverence—he had gone near mad with pleasure.

Only by summoning up every scrap of determination he possessed had he resisted. Fear drove him at first—the dread that she meant to steal his soul and entrap him in her fairy world for eternity. Once he no longer suspected her of magic, he realized there was another reason to control his urgent lust. This woman affected him, so deeply it was frightening. He could not risk that she might involve him in some other dangerous fate.

He must keep his wits about him. His shackles had loosened; a few more hours work and he would be free. The pleasure of dallying with a beautiful woman could not make up for the threat to his life nor cause him to forget his responsibilities to his sword brothers.

Dag sighed wearily, thinking of the ordeal ahead of him. He was weak from lack of food and water. If only there were a drop or two left of the water she had bathed him with. He sat up slowly and reached out his good arm to search the dirt floor around him. His fingers encountered the smooth surface of a pottery jar, and his heart leapt as he heard the slosh of water when he lifted it. He raised it to his lips and drank it dry.

Tossing it aside, he again searched his surroundings. A small bundle lay next to where the water jar had been. Dag picked it up and inhaled the intoxicating odor of food. He unwrapped the cloth and began to greedily gnaw the hunk of beef. Finishing in moments, he stuffed the large piece of cheese into his mouth and swallowed it in one bite.

Dag smiled. Hardly an extravagant meal for a man who had not eaten in days, but it would serve. Already he felt stronger. The fairy woman had thought of everything. Although he did not expect to see her again, he would not soon forget her. No matter what happened, from this day forward, no matter how dire his circumstances, he would think of her and summon back his hope and courage with the enchantment of her memory.

The shadows grew long as Fiona raised the door of the souterrain and peered out. This side of the palisade seemed strangely quiet, and her instincts warned her that something was wrong. She climbed out of the cavern and began to run. She hurried past the storage buildings and deserted shops to the large timbered feasthall in the middle of the encampment. Except for a few bondswomen going about their duties, the place seemed deserted. Fiona's alarm increased.

She checked the women's house. Empty. She ran faster. Her breath came in gasps; her body felt clammy with sweat by the time she saw Duvessa in the open area near the fortress gate. Her fiery-haired foster sister stood among a group of free-woman, talking intently.

Fiona dashed up. "What's happened, Duvessa? Where is everyone?"

Duvessa reached out and hugged her. "Fiona, I'm so glad

you are safe! Lisconnar was attacked and burned last night by Vikings. Your father fears we are next.''

"Nay!" Fiona protested. "A handful of Vikings would not dare attack an armed settlement like Lisconnar. The barbarians seek out easy quarry; they strike unprotected villages and holy houses, not strongholds of Irish warriors.''

Duvessa shook her head. " 'Tis true. One of the survivors came to warn us.''

Fiona's stomach—already twisted in knots—clenched even tighter. "Where is my father? Where are the other men?''

"They went to watch along the river for Viking dragonships.''

"But if there are Vikings near, my father should be inside the gates!''

"Donall hopes to lie in wait for the enemy and attack first.''

" 'Tis madness.'' Fiona groaned. "If the Lisconnar warriors could not repel the raiders, my father does not have enough men to defeat them either!''

"Your father means to try,'' answered Sybil, Duvessa's kinswoman and wife to Niall, one of Donall's oldest and fiercest war companions. "He said he would not wait meekly for his fate.''

Fiona shook her head in dismay. The other woman had not seen the Viking in the souterrain; they did not know what monstrous warriors Donall and his men would face.

Duvessa put a gentle hand on Fiona's arm. "Come, join me in the feasthall for a bite of freshly baked bread and honey. You look half dead.''

Fiona sighed and followed her friend.

With the warriors gone, the feasthall was quiet. Near the huge hearth, two hunting hounds snarled over a bone while a group of boys too young to join the warriors or stand guard played a game of draughts in the corner. Seeing Fiona and Duvessa, one of the boys left the game and hurried over to them.

"Thank the saints, Duvessa found you,'' Duvessa's russet-haired brother Dermot said to Fiona, his voice cracking slightly. "You've heard, haven't you, about the raid at Lisconnar?''

"Aye, I've heard," Fiona answered absently.

"You should not be so careless about leaving the palisade," Dermot continued. "You might have been carried off or killed."

Irritation gnawed at Fiona's distress. Now freckle-faced boys barely out of their mother's lap saw fit to warn her of the Viking menace.

"Fiona was never outside the fortress," Duvessa informed her brother. She jerked around and gave Fiona a sharp look. "Which reminds me—where *were* you all day? I vow I did look everywhere for you."

Fiona could not hide the flush she felt creep up her neck. If her foster sister knew the shameful things she had done—and with one of those accursed Vikings no less! "I . . . I was down in the souterrain," she answered hesitantly. "Vevina told me I might find some apples there left from the fall crop."

"Apples! You spent all day in a stinking, spider-infested hole looking for apples? I don't believe it!"

Fiona opened her mouth to defend her lie. She was cut off by Dermot's shocked exclamation. "The souterrain! But that's where they put the Viking prisoner! Did you see him, Fiona? Does he still live?"

"I saw nothing," Fiona answered sharply. "He *must* be dead, for I heard nothing either. If they put him in the end chamber, I would never know it; I did not search so far."

Fiona averted her face from Duvessa's probing, thoughtful look and cursed herself for her foolishness. Even if the Vikings did not raid Dunsheauna, she would have to live forever with the knowledge that she had saved the life of one of the murdering monsters. It was traitorous, apalling.

"I'm going for the bread," Duvessa said.

Fiona took a seat at one of the board tables and placed her hands in her lap so no one would notice how they trembled. She had to get away, to return to the souterrain and make certain the prisoner remained secure.

Looking up, she saw Dermot sit across from her. Her sense of guilt intensified. *Did he guess she had aided the Viking?*

Fiona shivered. She should take her knife and kill the prisoner now. No one would ever have to know what she had done.

Nay! a voice inside her protested. *If you cause the Viking's death, the guilt you bear will be unendurable.* Fiona twisted her hands in her lap. The man had stroked her breast and whispered endearments to her in his delirium. Killing him was beyond her. But she must make certain he did not escape. At the first opportunity, she must slip away and visit the souterrain again.

Duvessa returned with the bread and honey. Fiona stared at it, unable to eat.

"What's wrong?" Duvessa asked. "Do you fear for your father and the other men?"

Fiona nodded.

"They will have the advantage of surprise," Duvessa reassured her. "And they are brave warriors all. The Vikings will not get the better of them."

Fiona closed her eyes. If only she could believe her foster sister's words.

Fiona lay on her bed in the bower, feigning sleep. Her father and the other men still had not returned. Fiona felt cold all over, but she would not squirm and risk waking Duvessa. She cast a wary glance at her foster sister. Duvessa appeared to be asleep, but Fiona did not trust her. There had been a canny look in Duvessa's eyes when she'd suggested they seek their beds. Fiona did not put it past Duvessa to pretend to be dreaming, then follow her as soon as she left the bower. *Patience,* she told herself, *you must wait a little longer.*

Outside the bower window, open to the breeze, the night sounds of the fortress echoed softly. Fiona tensed, again thinking of her father and his war band patrolling the forest beyond the shelter of the palisade. Would dragonships sail up the river this night? Would they arrive with hordes of Vikings—all as huge and strongly built as the one in the souterrain?

Fear for Donall made her stomach clench. She did not want her father to be hurt or killed. He was a good man and, for the most part, a fond and loving sire. The troubles between them had begun only recently.

Looking back, Fiona could see how much he had changed after her mother's death. He had become so caught up in his own grief that he no longer cared for anyone else's feelings. He was brutal about enforcing his authority—to the point that Fiona had heard grumbling among his soldiers. She had also been outraged by his suddenly autocratic attitude. No longer did he discuss things with her; he ordered her to do his will. The conflict between them had culminated with his plan to wed her to Sivney Longbeard, and she had seen it as further evidence of his disregard for her feelings.

Fiona bit down on her lower lip. Although she still despised the thought of marrying Sivney, at last she could see her father's motivations. He was afraid for her, for all of them.

"Oh, Da, I was wrong," she whispered to herself. *"I should not have tried to thwart your will. I should have helped you think of another plan to bring us warriors."*

Fiona's mind reviewed the neighboring chieftains, trying to think of one who could strengthen Dunsheauna's defenses, yet not repel her as a husband. She sighed. It was difficult to face the thought of marrying men who were neither young nor handsome. Naggingly, the image of the Viking filled her mind with his strong, well-made body, his compelling face.

Fiona shook off the thought. He was probably a cruel, stupid beast, and besides, he was her enemy. There could be no future between them. She could not forget her duty to make certain he remained imprisoned.

Duvessa muttered something in her sleep. Fiona waited until her foster sister's breathing deepened again, then rose from their bed and crept to the doorway. The night air felt cool on her skin as she slipped out the entrance of the women's dwelling. She wore only her thin linen shift; to dress would take time and risk waking Duvessa.

She hurried through the fortress, her footfalls light and rapid on the damp grass. Under her breath, she prayed the rest of the fortress slept as soundly as Duvessa. It amazed Fiona that the other women were not panicked with fear as she was. To them, the idea of a Viking attack must still seem unreal. They trusted Donall and the other men to protect them.

Reaching the souterrain entrance, Fiona glanced around, then lifted the timber door and climbed inside. Halfway down the stone stairs, she found the torch and lit it.

The interior of the souterrain seemed utterly quiet. She crept forward, dreading what she would find. What if the Viking had roused? Could she bear to look into his eyes, then turn away and leave him to die?

He's your enemy! Fiona reminded herself. *If he came upon you outside the souterrain, he would rape and murder you.*

But what if he had gotten free of his shackles already? Fiona's heart hammered in her chest at the thought. Would the Viking consider sparing her because she had aided him earlier? Or would he kill her on the spot? Her broken body might be found days from now when they thought to search the souterrain.

Fiona tightened her grip on the torch. If she had to, she would use it as a weapon. She would not die meekly.

The doorway of the last chamber loomed ahead. Despite the chill in the tunnel, Fiona felt sweat bead her forehead. In a moment, she would know the Viking's fate—and mayhap her own.

The light from the torch flickered and wavered, casting wild shadows against the rough stone walls. The chamber was empty!

Fiona stood frozen. Panic gripped her as she wondered if the Viking waited in another part of the souterrain. Could she have missed him? She had passed a half-dozen nooks and niches where someone could hide in the shadows. She must search them. She could not climb the stairs to the outside world without knowing for certain if the prisoner had escaped.

She cautiously retraced her steps, shining the torch into every turn of the tunnel, every corner of the four main storage chambers. Nothing. The Viking was gone.

Fiona took a deep breath. He was outside now, somewhere. He had no clothes, but he would not be overly cold on this summer night. From what she'd heard of them, some Viking warriors even did battle naked. Berserkers they were called—

men so mad with battle lust that they entered combat naked and sexually aroused.

Fiona's throat closed up at the thought, and she hurried up the souterrain stairway as fast as her legs would take her. Reaching the outside, she took a deep breath of fresh air. Her heart had almost begun to slow when a harsh cry rang out behind her.

Chapter 5

The sound rose in ragged crescendo, then died with a horrible gurgling moan. Although she had never witnessed such a thing, Fiona imagined a man having his throat cut and drowning in his own blood.

She swallowed hard, and her eyes raked the darkness as she sought to gauge the source of the sound. It seemed to have come from the perimeter of the palisade. Had they been attacked? Why had no alarm been raised?

Another tremor of foreboding raced down her spine as she turned away from the souterrain. She must make certain the men remaining in the fortress knew of the danger.

She ran toward the main entrance of the palisade, reaching it in time to see the sentry scrambling to close the heavy timber gate. A man doubled over nearby, retching in the dirt. When he finally raised his wild-eyed, bloodied face, Fiona recognized Dubhag, one of the youngest of her father's men. He stared at her, speechless and stricken.

Fiona gave a choked cry. Dubhag stumbled toward her, like a wraith come up from the underworld. "Fiona . . . lass . . . I'm sorry. There was nothing I could do . . . dozens of Vikings."

"My father?" Fiona breathed.

Dubhag shook his head, his youthful features raw with grief. "I'm sorry, Fiona. 'Twas a slaughter. They only allowed me to live so I might come and warn the rest of you."

"Warn us?" Fiona's body felt cold, her senses dull. This could not be happening. It must be a dream, a terrible dream.

"The Vikings mean to kill every living soul in Dunsheauna. There is no escape. . . . They taunted me . . . told me to come and warn everyone that 'Death walks on the nightwind tonight.' "

Dubhag's face contorted, and he bent over and began to retch again. Fiona opened her mouth to cry out her father's name in grief. Then she smelled fire, and her scream died on her lips. Duvessa, Dermot—she must get them to safety!

She whirled away from Dubhag and the sentry, who had also smelled the smoke. He began screaming "Fire! Fire!" at the top of his lungs.

Fiona's unbound hair whipped behind her as she jerked her shift up to her thighs for speed. Never had she run so fast, but it seemed to take hours for her to reach the women's house. She plunged into the doorway and nearly trampled the group of women waiting near the entrance, their eyes wide and frightened, their faces pale. Some of them held crying babes and sleepy children.

Fiona ignored everyone else and sought out Duvessa. "It's a raid," she gasped. "We must find Dermot and seek shelter."

"Where? Where will we be safe?" Nessa, an older woman who had served Fiona's mother in her day, clutched Fiona's arm, her aged features etched with terror.

"The souterrain," Fiona answered firmly. "If we can get inside before the killing starts and the fires spread, we might survive."

"Fire?"

Fiona met Duvessa's horrified gaze and nodded. "The Viking bastards—they mean to burn us alive."

The room suddenly erupted with screams and crying.

"Silence!" Fiona shouted. As the woman quieted, she turned determined eyes on them. "If we panic, there is no hope for us. Duvessa and I will get Dermot and the other boys. The rest of you, hurry to the souterrain. We will meet you there."

"But it's naught but a dank hole in the ground!" one of the younger women, Ismey, wailed.

"Dark, cool, underground—the perfect place to wait out a fire," Fiona answered, her voice sharp. "Now, all of you—go!"

Fiona's courage ebbed as she and Duvessa neared the building where the soldiers slept. Her spirits sank utterly as they entered and found the place deserted.

"Too late," Duvessa whispered. "Dermot would go with the men; he would die as the warrior he will never live to be."

"Nay!" Fiona answered, her voice harsh with frustration. "I will find him!" She turned to Duvessa, eyes blazing. "Go to the souterrain with the others. I will find Dermot and meet you there."

"Fiona, please!" Duvessa begged. "Save yourself. You are the last of the line of Deasúnachta. You must not go to your death because of my brother. 'Tis too great a sacrifice!"

Fiona shook her head, tears filling her eyes. She had failed her father, but she would not fail everyone she cared about. If there were a chance to rescue her foster brother, she must take it.

"Go," she insisted, giving Duvessa a shove out the doorway. "I will be right behind you, I promise." Duvessa gave her one last agonized look, then took off in a fleet-footed run. Fiona muttered, "Don't fret for me, sister. I vow that tonight I am too angry for any mortal man to kill."

Dark shadows flitted past her. A shriek of pain sounded in the distance. Fiona crouched in the doorway of the feasthall and tightened her sweaty fingers on the handle of the dagger she had taken from the men's lodge. So far, she had seen no sign of Dermot or any of the Irish defenders. She had no idea if they had already been captured and were being tortured by the Vikings or had managed to escape the fortress.

Either way, she was ready to admit defeat and join the other women in the souterrain. She wondered if she had waited too long. Vikings swarmed the settlement, carrying torches, setting fire to the buildings one by one. She had retreated here, trapped. It was only a matter of time before they set the feasthall ablaze. Then she would have to run, out into the darkness, like a desperate hart driven before the hounds.

She took deep breaths, trying to calm herself, to prepare herself for one last dash through the maze of supply buildings and shops that lay between her and the souterrain door. Reaching down, she grabbed a handful of dirt and smeared it over her white shift, then smudged her face as well. She was small and agile; if she could avoid the blaze of firelight, she might not be detected.

With one last gulp of air, she began to run. She dodged and swerved, grateful that she knew the dark pathways so well. Twice she had to duck back into the shadows while a Viking passed by, but each time the man went on as if he had seen nothing. The gods were with her tonight, Fiona thought grimly. Or mayhap she was already dead and did not know it. She might be a wraith, gliding soundless, invisible past her enemies.

Her hand twitched on the hilt of the blade she held as another Viking warrior moved past her. How she wished she had the strength to take one of them down, to stab one of the Norse devils in the back and watch him die like the filthy pig he was.

The man vanished into the shadows. As soon as he was gone, Fiona stepped from her hiding place and began to run. Her lungs ached from the acrid smoke and her body trembled with fear, but she was so close, she would not lose courage now. The souterrain entrance lay a few paces ahead beyond the granary. Thank the saints, the Vikings had not yet fired the grain supply.

Fiona slowed as she reached the back of the granary. She peered around it, her eyes straining to see the wooden door in the earthworks that marked the souterrain entrance. She saw it, then sucked in her breath in dismay. A huge Viking stood between her and the doorway. His back was to her, but she could make out the glint of his helmet as it reflected the blaze of the fires, the apalling breadth of his back and shoulders, the corded muscles of his massive arms. Compared to him, even the Viking captive would seem small.

Fiona set her jaw. No matter that he was a giant—she must distract him. He was much too close to the souterrain entrance; even if it were too late for her to seek shelter herself, she could not risk his discovering the women and children hiding in the tunnels beneath the earthworks of the palisade.

Picking up a rock, she threw it far to the left of the Viking. He whirled and took a few hesitant steps in that direction. His massive, helmeted head jerked this way and that as he tried to ascertain the direction the rock had come from. Fiona crept back behind the granery wall.

When she again dared to look, the Viking had moved away from the souterrain entrance. Fiona took a deep breath and began to inch steathily toward the doorway, her eyes still on the Viking. She had covered half the distance when the man turned toward her. Fiona froze. If she made a dash for the souterrain door, the warrior would pursue her and discover the hiding place. If she ran in the other direction, he would be on her in seconds.

Fiona gripped her knife in trembling fingers. If she were going to die, she would not die fleeing but fighting.

The Viking approached her with an easy, casual stride. Fiona flexed her legs and shifted her weight from one foot to the other, mimicking the movements of the warriors she had watched in combat games.

When he was only inches away, Fiona lunged. With lightning swiftness, the Viking's hand closed around her wrist and jerked her hard against his bulky chest. The breath left Fiona's body in a gasp as the knife slipped from her numb fingers.

Fury burned through her. She gritted her teeth and began to thrash against the Viking, kicking and clawing. The man gave a deep, rumbling laugh, and his free hand reached for her shift and tore it down the front.

Tears of fear and rage burned Fiona's eyes. The Viking meant to ravish her, and she was helpless to stop him. She paused in her struggle, trying to think. He would have to put her down to mount her. Then she would have another chance. If only she had not dropped the knife.

The Viking grabbed her other wrist and lifted her far off the ground so she dangled close to his leering face but far enough from his body that she could not kick him. His guttural, mocking voice rang in her ears, and she guessed he was assessing her body beneath the thin, torn shift.

She gritted her teeth, struggling against a rising tide of humiliation and terror. Never would she weep or give in to helpless despair. She would fight him again as soon as he put her down.

A deep voice sounded to the Viking's left, and he relaxed his grip, seemingly startled. Seeing her chance, Fiona managed to give a weak kick in the direction of his groin. Her captor grunted, but did not release her. The stranger's voice came again, harsh and commanding. The Viking's only answer was another grunt.

The other man moved closer but was still out of Fiona's line of vision. When he spoke this time, there was no mistaking his anger. As the Viking responded, sudden awareness dawned on Fiona. The two men were arguing over her, no doubt over who would have the privilege of raping her first.

Sheer outrage made Fiona's body go rigid. Then she screamed her fury and twisted violently in the giant Viking's grip. He spoke sharply and shook her. When she continued to struggle, he let go of one of her wrists and used his free hand to strike her on the side of the head.

Fiona's vision dissolved into piercing, savage stars.

"If you've killed her . . ." Dag's voice trailed off in teeth-clenched anger. "I told you, she saved my life. I don't want to see her hurt!"

"The little bitch came at me with a knife," Sigurd Thorsson answered in an irritated voice. "I wasn't going to hand her over until I was certain she wouldn't cause you trouble. After all, you're still as sickly as a puking dog. Here . . ." He thrust the limp woman toward his brother. "Have your Irish witch. She's too fierce for my taste anyway."

Dag suppressed a groan as he grabbed the unconscious woman around the waist and heaved her over his left shoulder. Sigurd was right. He still felt shaky and woozy. Damn the Irish for leaving him to die. If it had not been for the woman, he would be a rotting corpse by now.

A feeling of mingled resentment and gratitude swept over him. The maiden had saved his life, and he owed her hers. But what in Thor's name was he going to do with her?

Dag adjusted his burden and began to walk through the fortress. Around him, fire raged, sending up billows of smoke into the midnight sky. A horse's whinny of fear caught his attention. Dag turned toward the sound, frowning. Sigurd had told him that the Irish nobility used horses to draw their wicker-work carts for ceremonial events. The local chieftain must be wealthy enough to afford such luxuries.

The horse screamed again. Dag's limbs went rigid. He hated to see animals suffer. Mayhap if the animals were only penned, not enclosed in a stable, there was a chance he could free them so they could flee to safety. He walked swiftly toward the sound, panting with the weight of the woman.

At the eastern edge of the palisade, he found two light-colored horses and a smaller, darker one milling around in a small pen. The shed next to the pen was ablaze, and the flying sparks and the smell of smoke had panicked the horses. Dag quickly found the pen gate and jerked it open. The animals ignored the opening and continued their frantic circling. Cursing, Dag slid the woman off his shoulder and onto the ground. Then he charged into the pen, waving his arms and shouting. The terrified animals veered away from him. Making his way to the back of the pen, he was able to drive them toward the opening, and they finally ran through the gate.

Dag leaned against the timbers of the pen, gasping from exertion and the smoke eating into his lungs. He could do nothing else to aid the fleeing animals. They would have to escape through the palisade gate or run through a gap in the burning walls, else they would die from the smoke. At least now, they had a chance.

A man's scream in the distance made Dag jerk around, and a sudden twinge of guilt went through him. He had sought to save the Irish chieftain's horses, but no man or woman would survive this night's work. Anyone found inside the palisade would be slaughtered, then tossed into the flames. As much as he told himself the Irish deserved their fate, a part of Dag could not help pitying them. His gaze turned to the woman lying senseless on the ground. The people dying around them were her kin. What would she think of him when she woke?

Shaking off the thought, Dag retrieved the woman and began to make his way toward the fortress entrance. When he reached it, he saw that the timber gate was gone, utterly consumed. As he moved through the gaping opening in the fiery ring of the burning palisade, a man caught him roughly by the arm. "What goes here?" the man growled. "Sigurd said we take no prisoners."

Dag turned and met the coarse-featured, filthy countenance of the warrior Brodir. "I owe this woman a blood debt. I would have perished in the Irish chieftain's prison if not for her aid."

Brodir furrowed his leathery brow and his deep-set eyes glinted with malice. "A man cannot owe a blood debt to a woman. You mean to take her for a slave, and Sigurd has forbidden it. He says we have no room or supplies in the ship for captives."

Dag's temper flared. Would but he had both hands free and uninjured—he would challenge Brodir for his insolence! But he was weak and tired, and the ship lay some distance away. Instead, he said, "Seek out Sigurd if you don't believe me. He'll tell you that he has made a gift of the woman's life to me."

Brodir's mouth twisted resentfully, but he moved out of Dag's path.

The fresh air cleared Dag's aching lungs and helped revive him as he began the journey through the darkness to the Viking ship, *Storm Maiden*. His broken rib still pained him and his injured arm throbbed. Thank the gods that the woman was so small and light or he could never endure her weight on his bruised shoulder. He considered putting her down and leaving her in the damp grass. *Nei*, he would carry her a little farther; he did not want to risk her being found by one of the other men. The sight of his brother handling her still filled him with wrath.

The recollection of the woman's gentle touch also remained bright and sharp in his mind. She had given him his life; despite Brodir's words, he knew he owed her protection.

He shuddered as a skein of mist floated across his path. With the heat and light of the fortress behind him, it seemed he entered the fairy realm. The very air of this isle felt alive, like a clammy hand against his skin. Near the river, the mist thickened, and Dag's pulse accelerated. He still feared the spirits haunting this place. And tonight he walked alone, injured, his own spirit weak. He would be easy prey for a wraith or phantom.

With superstitious dread, he clutched the Irish maiden's body more closely against his chest. The feel of her flesh warm against his own helped ease his fear. Although not a true fairy, she was of this place; mayhap her presence would keep him safe.

The moon moved from behind a cloud, and, ahead, he caught a glimpse of the curved prow of the *Storm Maiden* rising from the river. Dag sighed with relief. This was the world he belonged to—the realm of wood, water, metal, and men, not the strange, misty pathways of this spirit-plagued isle.

Two men had been left behind to guard the ship. As Dag approached, one of them shouted a challenge: "Who goes?"

Dag relaxed further at the sound of Rorig's familiar voice. " 'Tis Dag," he answered. "I left as the fortress burned to ashes and the Irish curs lay in the death straw."

"Sigurd?"

"He comes soon. He and the others are gathering what booty they can claim from the licking flames."

The other sentry stepped forward. "What do you carry? I heard Sigurd say 'no captives.' "

Dag grimaced. Would he have to defend his right to keep the Irishwoman to each of his brother's men? As exhausted as he felt, it seemed a daunting task. Why had he not left the woman before he reached the river? He had saved her life— what more did he owe her?

"This woman kept me alive during my imprisonment. Sigurd has agreed to spare her life in return."

"That he spares her life does not mean he will allow you to take her back to Engvakkirsted. Sigurd warned all of us that this was not a slave run. We must be satisfied with jewels and gold and naught else."

Angered by Kalf's arrogant answer, Dag stepped toward the ship. The woman was his, and he would do with her as he wished!

"Hold!" Kalf moved to block his advance. "We guard the ship, and I say that you do not bring her aboard."

Dag's fingers itched for the axe at his belt, but he could not reach it with the woman slung over his shoulder. Releasing his grip of the woman's thighs, he let her slide down his body. When he had settled her limp form on the ground, he pulled out his war axe and brandished it.

"You seek combat with me, Kalf?"

The warrior took a step backwards. "You're injured, Dag. Sigurd would not wish to return and find me fighting with his wounded brother."

"Neither would Sigurd wish to return and find you bleeding in the rivermud, but it matters not to me." Dag shrugged in nonchalance, although the motion pained him dearly. "If you would keep me off the ship, you must dodge Blooddrinker's fiery kiss."

Kalf took the measure of the axe's gleaming blade, then stepped aside. Dag reslung his axe in his belt and stooped to pick up the woman. Pain screamed down his body and his knees nearly buckled, but he managed to heave her over his shoulder once again. He suppressed a groan and began wading out to the ship. By the time he reached it, his breath came in gasps and sweat poured down his forehead.

He dropped the woman over the side, none too gently, then dragged his trembling body in after her. The sway of the ship soothed him, but he still felt sick onto death. For a moment he lay there, breathing heavily, then he began searching the hold where the supplies were stored, hunting for a skin of water. Finding one, he unstoppered it and gulped the contents down. He let out a deep sigh and lay back in the gently rocking craft.

He closed his eyes, halfway to oblivion. As he sank toward

sleep, the image of the fairy woman floated before his eyes. He saw her as she had first come to him, her midnight hair swirling around her hips, her skin golden in the torchlight, her face both uncertain and proud.

With a sigh, he rose from his resting place. Groping in the darkness, he finally located the woman's limp form. He felt for her pulse; the tension in his body eased as he found it. His hand explored further and found the swelling lump on the side of her head. His brother had a heavy hand; the woman would have a fierce headache on the morrow.

His fingers touched her face, and he recalled the delicacy of her features. She was like a bird, an exotic lovely bird. His hand slipped further down, caressing her slender throat. Her skin was so soft. He could not resist the lure of her silken warmth. Holding his breath, he allowed his fingers to glide beneath the woman's ruined clothing. His hand closed over a full, lush breast.

The Goddess Freya, but she was beautiful! He could not see her, but his fingers experienced her perfection. What would it be like to lie with her, to feel her fine-boned softness yielding beneath him? The thought made Dag's head swim and his body throb with desire.

A second later, he pulled his hand away. Fool! That was the danger of women; their beauty made a man blind to their other weaknesses. Did he not know that they were all vain, petty-minded, and incapable of loyalty? And this woman, she was no different. She had aided him—her enemy. No matter that she'd saved his life, he could not help but suspect her motives.

Dag frowned as he recalled the woman's rich attire the first time she'd come to him. Why would a fairborn woman seek to couple with a prisoner? . . . unless she meant to defy the man she belonged to.

A sense of disgust crept over him, and he eased farther away from the woman, glad that the darkness hid her extraordinary charms.

Chapter 6

Fiona woke to shards of light piercing her skull like a band of nails around her forehead. She lifted her head and fought back the wave of nausea that threatened to overwhelm her, then touched her hand to her throbbing temple. She must have bumped herself there—or been struck. With sudden, awful clarity, she remembered the huge Viking. She opened her eyes and suppressed a scream as a vision out of a nightmare swam into view.

Vikings! She was surrounded by Vikings! A dozen of them crowded her vision, their huge, sweaty shoulders flexing as they rowed, the sun gleaming on their fair hair. Beyond them, a ship's prow rose high above the horizon. Fiona shrank back into the corner where she lay among wooden chests and bulging sacks. She was a helpless prisoner on one of the Vikings' monster-headed ships!

Cold terror filled her body, blotting out the pain of her head. There was no escape. They had kept her alive so they might ravish her repeatedly. The image of a dozen naked, grinning Vikings coming toward her made Fiona's limbs go rigid. Better to jump off the side of the ship and sink into the sea. She gained control of her trembling body and rose, determined to seek out death by drowning before her nerve gave out.

She had barely taken two shaky steps when she heard a man's voice behind her. She turned, responding to something familiar in the guttural tones, and her gaze met cold, gleaming blue eyes.

Fiona's heart twisted in her chest in recognition. It was the Viking from the souterrain! He watched her, his face as unfeeling and impassive as when he'd lain unconscious, but his eyes blazing with intense emotion. Although she tried, she could not read any sense into the turmoil of his gaze.

She put a hand to her head, abruptly aware of how shaky and sick she felt. Her vision dipped and swayed as though the ship itself had tilted upside down. She sat down where she stood, her legs useless. The blue-eyed Viking took a step toward her, and a look of concern crossed his face. Then it was gone, and he glared down at her. Fiona felt too sick to care. Her head throbbed as if it were being pounded, and her stomach felt none too steady.

Rough hands pulled her up, and she felt a skin being pressed to her lips. She drank greedily and her disorientation eased. When she could see clearly, those wintery-blue eyes again gazed into hers. The Viking's left arm cradled her shoulders, and she could feel the strength of his muscles and the warmth of his body. The sensation evoked a pang of memory. A few days ago, she had held this man's head as he drank. A few days ago, she had caressed his sleek shoulders and marveled at the muscled heat of his chest.

Tears filled Fiona's eyes. Now everything was changed. Because of this man, her father was dead, her kinsmen and loved ones murdered. She had been a fool to succor him. Better that she had let him die in his dank prison.

The Viking seemed to guess her bitterness, for he released her. She fell back limply onto the bottom of the ship. The impact made Fiona's head throb anew, and she closed her eyes, seeking the comfort of oblivion.

When she next awoke, her first sight was of a bright, red-and-white-striped sail billowing out from the tall mast of the ship. Fiona sat up and saw that the Vikings around her no longer rowed. Most of them slept, curled up awkwardly between the large, heavy chests that lined the deck; a few men remained alert, busy adjusting the sail. Deciding that she was not in immediate danger of ravishment, Fiona stood unsteadily. Someone had thought to cover her with a cloak, and she picked it up and wrapped it around herself, hiding her torn shift.

Her gaze took in the long narrow ship crowded with her enemies. Panic started to set in again; she fought it. She had survived, so far relatively unscathed. It was senseless to throw her life away.

She turned. Behind her, in the stern, stood the bronze-haired Viking from the souterrain. He appeared to be steering the ship by means of a rudder mounted at the rear of the hull. He did not see Fiona but stared off toward the starboard side. She followed his gaze and felt a sick ache in her belly. In the distance, a blue-green shape floated on the horizon. Eire—her homeland, her people. Would she ever see Duvessa again? And what of her aunt? Had Siobhan—hidden away in her little hut in the woods—survived the Viking attack?

For a moment, grief struck Fiona another blow and she had the urge to leap over the side of the ship to drown her pain in the depths of the gleaming blue waves. Then her reason reasserted itself, that and a cold, hard anger. If she died, there would be no one to avenge her father's death. No one to make the Vikings pay for the destruction they had so casually wrought.

Fiona braced herself against the wicked sway of the ship and made a vow. "Da," she whispered, "I shall avenge you. Somehow I will make up for what I have done."

Tears streamed down Fiona's cheeks; she brushed them away. She could not afford the luxury of self-pitying sorrow; from now on, she must concentrate on survival.

She glanced back at the Viking at the rudder. His very existence infuriated her. She had cared for him and saved his life, and he had repaid her by killing her kin and burning her home, then taking her prisoner. For such treachery and betrayal, he deserved to die a gruesome death.

Fiona sighed. She could not kill him herself, especially weak-ened as she was. Her head still ached; her limbs were stiff. Worst of all, she had a terrible need to relieve herself. It was a petty problem, but on a ship full of lecherous Vikings, real enough.

Her eyes perused the craft, searching for some sort of shelter. There was a leather tent near the bow of the ship, although it was too small for even her to stand up in. Fiona guessed that it must be the sleeping area of one of the Vikings or it might be used to protect valuable goods from the weather.

She gauged the distance to the tent, wondering if she could make her way there without attracting the notice of her captors. If there were a jar or vessel inside, she might use it in private, then empty it over the side of the ship.

She took a step, but as the ship swayed, she lost her balance and found herself smack on her bottom. She grimaced at the sting of solid timber against her flesh, then tried once more to rise. Bracing herself against the roll of the vessel, she took several more wobbly steps. With her eyes focused on the pitching ship bottom, she did not see the man step in front of her until his bare, sweaty chest loomed inches away from her face. She raised her eyes and stared into the leering countenance of an unknown Viking.

The man responded to her horrified gaze with a harsh laugh, then lunged for her. Fiona shrieked and stepped backwards, losing her balance. As she was tossed to the ship's bottom once again, her captor grabbed at her clothes, tearing off the cloak and very nearly yanking off her shift as well. Fiona clutched the ruined garment to her body, closed her eyes, and screamed again.

She heard harsh, angry voices, then the smack of a fist against bare skin. When she finally summoned the courage to open her eyes, she saw two men standing over her—the bronze-haired Viking and, next to him, the gigantic fiend who had attacked her in her father's fortress. She looked from one to the other, speechless with mingled terror and relief.

The huge man turned to his cohort and spoke abruptly, then walked past Fiona. As his bulky form moved out of the way,

Fiona caught a glimpse of a third man, the one who had grabbed her. He sprawled on the deck of the ship, rubbing the side of his head and looking dazed. Fiona felt a grim satisfaction. She knew exactly how the monster Viking's blows felt, and she did not sympathize with the man's misery one whit.

Dag glowered at the woman lying at his feet. "Take her," Sigurd had ordered him. "Sink your shaft between the little witch's white thighs before the other men start snarling at each other like hounds fighting over a bitch in heat. If you think you owe her privacy, seek your pleasure in my tent. But make certain she screams a little. I want no doubt in any warrior's mind that I have given her to you and she is yours to do with as you will."

Take her. *Ja*, he wanted to do exactly that. He would make certain she knew who her master was, inspire enough fear in her weak woman's heart that she would not dream of defying him. It would be sweet indeed to enjoy her exquisite body. He could not blame Brodir for wanting her. With that thin, filthy gown outlining her breasts and hips, 'twas a wonder the other men had kept off of her this long.

He watched her stare up at him with those strange, pale-green eyes. He had not known what an unusual color they were until he'd seen them by daylight. An otherworldly hue—the color of a murky, moss-bottomed pool. If he had seen them clearly when he lay in his delirium, he would have been even more certain that she was not a mortal woman. But mortal she was; he could see the terror in her eyes, the desperation. He meant to use that fear to bend her to his will.

He reached down to grab her hand and jerk her to her feet. She swayed and fell against him. The feel of her body along the length of his made fire burn his flesh. Slowly, he stroked his hand down her back, then eased it lower to cup a round, firm buttock. She stiffened against him and tried to draw away. He pressed her closer and brushed the fabric of her shift smooth so he might feel her more intimately.

He felt her heart pounding beneath her fragile ribs. He moved his hand lower, between her thighs. Let her know his absolute power over her, let her try to fight him.

She tried to wrench away, but he held her tight against his hips and brought his mouth down to hers. For a moment, her body quieted and Dag forgot everything except the taste and feel of her. He closed his eyes, lost in the sensation of her mouth beneath his.

Suddenly, she fought him again, her body twisting frantically in his arms. Dag pulled his mouth away and tightened his grasp. The woman continued to struggle. He gazed down at her, at her wet, rosy lips and flushed cheeks. Her furious eyes burned a vivid, jewel-like green.

He took a deep breath and tried to clear his mind. A cacophony of whistles and crude taunts made their way to his ears, reminding of his purpose. He meant to conquer this woman, to convince her that he was her master. With his good arm, he lifted her up and slung her over his shoulder, then pushed past his leering comrades.

It was impossible to maintain his grip on the woman as he bent over to enter his brother's tent. He released her, then once inside, leaned out and got a grip on her shift. The garment began to rip. He grabbed another handful and jerked her into the tent.

She sprawled half-naked next to him, looking dazed. One breast and both slim legs were bared to his view. The aching heat rose in his body, and his mind seemed to go blurry. Dag reached out and ripped off the ruined remains of her clothes. The sight of the silky, black triangle at the juncture of her thighs inflamed him. His breathing grew heavy and labored as he moved toward her.

Fiona watched the Viking advance, all fiery-blue eyes and bare golden skin. This was the vision of her erotic dreams, but gone horribly awry. The Viking and his kind were responsible for her father's death. She could almost imagine blood dripping from his hands and smell the awful odor of smoke filling her nostrils. Her home, burned. Her people, slaughtered. And all because of this dread Viking.

She backed away. He was her enemy. Once, foolishly, she

had gone to the souterrain, defying her father to seduce this man. She had been a child then, naught but a stupid child. Now she was a woman, hardened by grief and despair. This time she would not submit meekly to this destroyer of her life, her home.

Fiona paused in her retreat, facing the Viking with grim determination. He might be twice her size, but she knew where his weaknesses lay. She would aim her blows for his injured right arm, his broken rib.

He was upon her so quickly she had no time to strike at all. In seconds, his thighs straddled her hips and his left hand grasped a handful of her hair. She writhed beneath him, helpless.

But he had miscalculated as well. With his good hand occupied in keeping her upper body still, he had no way to undo the drawstring that held up his trews. Realizing his dilemma, he cursed, then gingerly lowered his wounded arm to his groin. As he fumbled with the drawstring, Fiona watched in satisfaction. The use of the stiff, sore muscles in his injured arm caused him significant pain. With luck, he might tear the stitches out and bleed to death, she thought spitefully.

The garment finally fell away, revealing the man's engorged phallus. This time, Fiona felt no fascination or desire. She gave his member a look of revulsion, then gazed straight up at the Viking and spat in his face.

His eyes darkened with rage, and Fiona felt a belated tremor of fear. She was completely vulnerable to this man; to taunt him was madness.

Their eyes locked, her contempt meeting his fury. His grip tightened in her hair, and for a moment, Fiona thought he meant to twist her head around until her neck snapped. Then his fingers relaxed. He released her hair and slid his big body off of hers. He paused a moment, still kneeling, then grasped his swollen shaft in his left hand and began to rub it with short, rapid strokes.

He leaned back and closed his eyes. In what seemed like seconds, his features contorted and he exhaled in a gasp. A glistening white liquid spurted over his fingers.

He opened his eyes, caught his breath, then reached over to

wipe his hand on Fiona's torn and filthy shift lying nearby. He moved awkwardly to the entrance of the tent and paused there. His trews still gaped open, exposing his male organ. But it was not that which drew Fiona's eyes, but the murderous expression on his face.

She edged backwards, sure he meant to come back and kill her. He did nothing, merely turned and pushed his way out of the tent.

Harsh laughter echoed through the tent's leather walls at his reappearance on the ship's deck, and Fiona felt a sickening wave of shame. The Viking obviously intended for the rest of the men to think he had raped her.

A delayed reaction to the fear and shock she had endured set in, and Fiona began to tremble violently. Clutching her nakedness, she tried to calm herself. She was whole, safe. She had survived the Viking's attempted ravishment. There was hope that the worst horrors were behind her.

Another stab of terror went through her. What if the Viking changed his mind and came back? Or what if he decided to give her to the other men? They might be lined up outside, ready to take a turn with her. How would she survive if she were raped repeatedly?

You must, a voice inside her said. *You must survive or your father will have died in vain.* The thought gave her courage. Someday, if she managed to stay alive, she would return to Dunsheauna. If Duvessa and the other women lived, there might be some hope of rebuilding the settlement. The dynasty of Deasúnachta need not perish altogether. But to ensure that, she must keep her wits about her.

Fiona got to her knees. It was self-defeating to dwell on the tortures the Vikings might inflict upon her. She could not afford to be immobilized by fear; she must see about surviving as a captive, and her most pressing need was for a means to relieve her bursting bladder.

She crawled toward the rear of the tent, planning to search for a vessel which could serve as a chamber pot. A slight sound at the entrance of the tent made her whirl around. Her heart leaped into her throat at the sight of the giant Viking's head thrust through the tent opening.

Fiona grabbed for her shift and held the tattered remnants over her nakedness. She feared the giant meant to be the next to attack her, and she had no wish to further incite his lust. The man crawled through the opening, surprising Fiona that he actually fit into the small space. He crouched down and regarded her.

"I see you are whole and unhurt. I did not think my brother would use you harshly. He is not known for hurting creatures weaker than he."

Fiona gaped at the man, too stunned at hearing him speak in the Irish tongue to comprehend what he said.

"How . . ." she whispered. "How do you come to speak Gaelic?

"I wintered a few years ago at the Norse garrison at Dublin," the man answered. " 'Tis a skill I have, to learn the speech of foreign lands—a useful aptitude for a trader . . . or a warrior."

The man's earlier words suddenly sparked Fiona's awareness. Brother—he had called the blue-eyed Viking 'brother.' She observed the man's features carefully. The giant was dark; the other Viking, ruddy fair. This man wore a full, curly beard of black with reddish tones, while his brother's jaw had been clean shaven, his mustache of coppery gold. The giant's features were heavier, as befitting his massive size, but both Vikings had straight, finely molded noses, high cheekbones, and deep-set eyes.

"What do you mean to do with me?" she asked, then held her breath. Would it be easier to endure if she knew what was planned for her? Or more difficult?

The huge Viking's eyes narrowed. "Your fate is up to my brother."

"Does he recall that I saved his life?" Fiona asked boldly. "That he would have died if not for my care?"

"If your kinsmen had not cruelly left him to perish in a hole in the ground, there would have been no need for you to aid him. Among my people, it is considered a grave insult to refuse a dying warrior the chance for an honorable death."

Sensing the contempt in the Viking's gaze, Fiona recalled stories she had heard regarding the Northmen's warrior code. They believed death in battle conferred immortality to their souls. By not allowing the Viking warrior to fight to the death, her father had shamed him. "Is that why you killed my father and burned the fortress?" she asked. "You sought revenge for your brother?"

There was a flicker of surprise in the Viking's eyes. "The chieftain—he was your father?"

Fiona nodded.

"Your father was brave," the Viking answered harshly. "He did not wait for death, but went out into the darkness with his men. Of course," the Viking continued, "bravery counts for naught against men such as us. My warriors were filled with blood-lust when I told them of the treasure they would find within the walls of your people's fort. They could scarcely wait to torch the palisade and begin ransacking the buildings."

Fiona's grief turned to fury as she imagined the Viking savages pawing through the wealth her family had accumulated over generations. "And were they satisfied with what they found?" she asked bitingly.

The Viking smiled. "My men were disappointed to find no women to enjoy, but they discovered booty aplenty. The exquisite silver casket of jewels I found in the large sleeping chamber off the main hall was in itself enough to justify our trouble."

Hatred filled Fiona. The Vikings had stolen her mother's beautiful things. They had no right! She wanted to lunge at the dark Viking and scratch out his eyes! She thought better of it. He could break her in half with one hand; she would be a fool to attack him.

The man's eyes swept over her face. "The wealth of your father's fortress belongs to my men now, and you belong to my brother. I have given you your life in exchange for your aid of him. If you are wise, you will seek to please him, and your life as a slave will be much easier."

He reached into his tunic and drew out a gaudy garment. Fiona's eyes rounded as she recognized the blue kirtle as Duvessa's.

The Viking thrust it toward her. "Put this on. My brother is still weak from his wounds, and I would not have him hurt protecting you. Also, bind your hair back and keep your eyes to yourself." As she took the kirtle, he continued to regard her thoughtfully. "When he first saw you, my brother thought you were an enchanted being—he feared you meant to steal his soul."

The Viking's jaw clenched. "Myself, I am not superstitious. I think you are nothing more than a conniving, spoiled wench who is accustomed to using her beauty to get her way. Beware, little Irish wench—do not think to use your 'fairy' wiles upon my brother. I might forget that I have agreed to spare your life."

With that chilling threat, he crouched over and prepared to leave the tent.

"Wait," Fiona cried. "If he is to be my master, at least tell me your brother's name."

The Viking's expression was cool, but there was pride in his voice as he spoke. "His name is Dag Thorsson, and I am Sigurd. We serve a jarl in the Norselands. We sail there now."

Sigurd left, and Fiona clutched the kirtle to her chest. What a terrifying man! Yet, oddly, she felt she could deal with him. Mayhap it was because he used her language and spoke so bluntly. With the Viking Sigurd, at least, she knew where she stood.

But his brother . . . Fiona shivered. Her fate depended upon a man she had sorely provoked just moments before. What would Dag Thorsson do with her?

Chapter 7

Dag stood at the tiller and guided the ship as his brother saw to the woman. His wounded arm throbbed, contributing to the foulness of his mood. The other men busied themselves polishing their weapons and examining their booty. Across the deck, the flash of armbands and brooches, of rich fabrics, of polished blades and metal-ringed body armor testified to the wealth of the Irish.

Dag watched the scene resentfully. The other men would return home with treasure; he had naught to show for the trip except a scornful wench who defied him and spat in his face. His kindness had cost him dearly.

He stiffened as he saw Brodir stand and approach the stern, a gold object dangling from his scarred, filthy hand. Although Brodir was a kinsman of sorts by the jarl's second wife, Dag had no liking for the warrior.

"The woman . . ." Brodir's mouth curled lasciviously. "Did she please you?"

Dag's muscles tensed further. Did Brodir guess the woman had fought him? Had he come to gloat? Dag answered coolly, "I've had much better. She is a foul-tempered bitch."

Brodir laughed. "Mayhap you prefer your women willing,

and the Irish wench obviously was not." His leer broadened. "Myself, I like a woman who fights. It deepens my pleasure to feel them thrash beneath me, to hear them scream." His thin mouth twitched. "I admit, sword brother, that I forgot myself when I touched your property. I'm here to make amends." He held out the gold object. Dag recognized it as the enameled belt the woman had worn the first time she'd come to him in the underground prison. "I would like to trade. This girdle for the woman."

Dag stared at the elegant object thoughtfully. Brodir offered to pay him to take the Irishwoman off his hands. Why should he not accept?

He glanced up at Brodir's harsh face, observing the malicious glint in his eyes, the cruel slant to his mouth. A wave of revulsion passed through Dag. He did not want to see the Irishwoman tortured and used. Her helplessness aroused his urge to protect, to preserve something lovely and fine from the brutality of life.

"Not enough?" Brodir's eyes narrowed. "I have plenty other booty. What will you take for her? Name your price."

Dag shook his head. "The woman is not for sale." He raised his eyes meaningfully to Brodir's. "At least not to *you*." A sense of uneasiness assailed Dag as he saw Brodir's face darken with anger, but he could not help himself. He resented the other man's use of the term "brother," his false camaraderie.

Brodir tightened his grip on the girdle until the soft metal bent and the fragile artistry of the enamelwork distorted. In seconds, he reduced the beautiful object to a shapeless lump of metal suitable only for melting down and selling by weight. Dag's jaw tightened as he watched Brodir stalk off. The man did not deserve the Irishwoman; he had no more appreciation of her beauty than he had of the priceless artifact he had so casually destroyed. If Dag sold the woman, it would at least be to someone who knew her worth.

He looked up and saw his brother manuever his bulk across the crowded ship deck. Dag glanced suspiciously toward the tent. What had transpired between Sigurd and the woman? His gaze met his brother's, and some of the tension left his body.

Sigurd was the most honorable of men; he would not bed a woman after ordering that no other man should touch her.

Sigurd nodded in greeting and assessed Dag. "Your arm pains you?"

"Aye, I twisted the muscles while grappling with the woman."

Sigurd's brows raised. "She struggled?"

"*Ja.* Some."

"I doubt she fights you again. I have made it clear that she serves you and she has no choice but to accept her lot. Only your protection saves her from being ill-used by the rest of the men."

Dag nodded, but remained unconvinced of his captive's compliance. Sigurd's sensible words might sway a man, but woman were more difficult to predict, especially this one. Even naked and vulnerable, she had dared to spit in his face. What an impulsive, hot-tempered creature she was.

"If she were mine, I think I would throw her overboard," Sigurd added.

Dag's gaze jerked to his brother's face.

"I suspected the woman of treachery, but her deceit is worse than I imagined. She informed me that the Irish chieftain was her father." Sigurd's jaw tightened. "Betraying her sire—what a shameful thing. If she were a man, I would make certain she suffered an unpleasant death for her perfidy."

Dag felt his belly clench. The woman was every bit as cold-hearted and calculating as he had feared. *And he had pitied her!* Anger swept through him.

"I'll do it, if you don't want to," Sigurd offered. "I'd be happy to cast her to the fishes. It would make one less mouth to feed on the journey home."

It was the sensible course of action. Sigurd would dump her overboard, and her compelling mien would vanish beneath the cold blue waves forever. He would never have to see her again, to deal with her sinister enticement.

Dag glanced at his bandaged arm. The woman had saved his life, healed his wounds, caressed him with gentleness. The memory of her soothing hands would never leave him. He could not banish the sense of obligation he felt toward her.

"*Nei,* I don't want her killed," he said.

"Why?"

He did not want to answer his brother's question, to face the weakness inside him, the urge to tenderness he had fought all his life. "It may have been evil for her to aid me, her father's enemy," he finally responded. "But because she did so, I am beholden to her for my life."

Sigurd looked skeptical. Dag realized he must think up some sensible motive for sparing the woman's life. His companions would be appalled if they knew he could not kill the woman because of how he felt about her. To them, she was a piece of property, and naught else. Considering her as property made him think of something. "The woman is the only thing of value I obtained during the raid," he told Sigurd. "I am loath to see costly booty tossed overboard."

Sigurd snorted derisively. "Costly? She will cost you, of that I have no doubt."

"I can sell her for a fine price at the slave market at Hedeby. Many come to Hedeby with their belts heavy with gold. I would not go home empty-handed."

Sigurd jerked his head toward the tent. "What sort of a price will you get for *that?* She's much too small and delicate to work as a field slave. Looking at her smooth, white hands, I doubt she has the training to serve as a kitchen thrall either. The best slaves are sturdy, plain, and stupid, and she is none of those things. With her sultry face and slim body, the woman is worthless except as a bed thrall."

Dag thought quickly. "*Ja,* exactly," he answered. "I would sell her as a bed thrall."

Sigurd raised his brows. "Throwing her overboard would be kinder. You've been to Gorm's slave market, seen how he displays the women near-naked and lets any man with gold have a sample of their bed skills. The man's crudeness is offensive even to me."

Dag felt sick at he thought of the fat, toothless slavemaster thrusting between the Irishwoman's creamy thighs. He could no more sell the woman to Gorm than he could throw her into the sea.

"You could let the other men have her now." Sigurd nodded to the men sprawled across the deck. "They would all pay for a turn at her. Especially Brodir; he's always eager to have a new woman to mistreat. You would get your gold and save us a trip to Hedeby."

"The woman is worth more than that." Dag struggled to keep his voice impassive as he envisioned the woman being passed from man to man. "I would not have her rare beauty destroyed by these louts. I doubt they would pay enough either."

"If you don't think your fellow warriors can meet your price, wait to sell the woman until we arrive home," Sigurd suggested. "I'm sure we can find a neighboring jarl with enough gold to satisfy you."

Dag realized suddenly that gold had nothing to do with his plans for the Irishwoman. He simply did not want another man to have her. The thought unsettled him even more.

"Why not keep her for yourself?" Sigurd asked, echoing Dag's uncomfortable musings. "You can always sell her later, when you tire of her."

Dag glanced down and pretended to examine the ragged bandage on his wounded arm. "She is fine to look at, but not exactly to my taste. I prefer my women big enough that I don't have to worry about crushing them beneath me, and also more Norse-looking."

"Like Kira?"

Dag's jaw clenched involuntarily. Kira had played him for a fool; it was because of her that he mistrusted women so much.

"*Ja*, like Kira," he answered.

The two men stood silent for a moment, both watching the pattern of waves as they swirled past the boat. Dag contemplated how to escape the burden of the Irishwoman and yet keep her from any other man. "I could sell her as a gentlewoman's servant," he suggested, "to help some jarl's wife with the spinning and weaving and such."

"Are you sure she knows such things? She seems like a pampered, useless creature to me."

"She must have some skill, else she could not have sewn up my arm. And there is always her healing knowledge to recommend her. She cured my fever as well as tending my arm."

"You think she is a wise woman?"

" 'Tis possible, isn't it?"

"Every wise woman I've ever seen was an ugly, old hag." Sigurd gave Dag a searching look. "You make no sense. First, you speak of selling the woman as a bedthrall, then you decide she would better make a gentlewoman's helper. I begin to question whether you want to be rid of her after all."

"Of course I do. It makes my skin crawl to remember how she first appeared to me. I told you I thought she was a fairy, an enchanted being come to steal my soul."

"But now that you have bedded her, you surely can't think that. She's only a slave, an odd-looking, unusually comely one, but still a slave. If you don't want to kill her, you must get some good of her somehow."

Dag's jaw tightened. The Irishwoman certainly had him trapped.

"Does this have something to do with Kira?" Sigurd asked.

Dag looked at his brother, startled. "Why should it?"

"You've been strange about women ever since Kira decided to wed with Snorri."

"Strange? How have I been strange?"

"You refuse to wed or even take a woman to your bedcloset for more than one night."

"Why should I wed? Unlike you, I will never be Jarl of Engvakkirsted, or anywhere else for that matter. I have no need of an heir, and that's the purpose of taking a wife." Dag did not like the bitter sound of his words. Truthfully, he had no desire to be jarl. In his mind, the power that came with the position did not make up for the responsibilities. Once his brother was jarl, he would no longer have the freedom to go *aviking* every sunseason. He would be busy at home, negotiating alliances and settling disputes.

" 'Tis not that I envy you your lot, brother," Dag added quickly. "I merely point out the differences in your life and mine. A wife would only be a burden to me."

Sigurd nodded. "I have fared better than most—Mina is efficient in all things and demanding in few. But it would please me to see my younger brother wed."

"We stray from our topic of what to do with the Irishwoman," Dag said. "In truth, I worry about the grief she would cause me if I keep her. When the ale flows and the warriors' blood runs hot, every man in the longhouse will want her, and I don't need the trouble of being her defender."

"Then heed my advice and dump her over the side of the boat," Sigurd growled. "She's only a woman."

They were back to where they had begun. Dag tried to think of another plan to protect the woman, yet banish her from his sight. He could not sell her, yet being responsible for the untrustworthy bitch made him distinctly uneasy.

Sitting down on his sea chest, Dag let Sigurd take the tiller. His arm ached, and he felt tense and restless. Despite using his hand to relieve his lust only a short time ago, his shaft was hard and ready once more. Damn the alluring witch! He had only to close his eyes against the sea glare and he saw the image of her naked body—the supple curves, the contrast between her creamy skin and ebony hair.

Dag glanced toward the prow and cursed again. The woman had left the tent. She was dressed and her hair demurely braided, but that hardly diminished her allure. The snug gown only reminded him of the lush curves beneath, and nothing could reduce the impact of her exotic face. Such pale, wild-looking green eyes, dark brows, and crimson-tinted lips—she was like a siren, luring a man to an unbearably pleasurable doom.

He watched her glance around warily, as if she might flee back to the safety of the tent. He prayed she would.

"Ho, lass!" Sigurd's voice boomed over the deck. Dag's body went rigid as out of the corner of his eye he saw his brother beckon to the Irish wench. Thor's fury! What did Sigurd mean to do?

Fiona stiffened as the dark Viking signaled to her. She had

found some water to wash her face and arms, and Duvessa's kirtle covered her decently; but despite being better prepared to face him, she did not want to be anywhere near Dag. A quick glance told her that he was seated close to where his brother steered the ship.

"Come," Sigurd called insistently. "My brother has need of you."

Aware that she had no choice, Fiona stepped gingerly among the clutter of sea chests, booty, and men. She kept her own gaze fixed on the gently swaying deck. Not all of it was to keep her balance; she also feared to meet the lustful looks that followed her.

She neared the stern of the ship and avoided the fair Viking's gaze and met Sigurd's. He reached out and grasped her shoulder, thrusting her toward the other man. "Make yourself useful and look to my brother's arm, wench. See that it heals so it is as it was before."

Dag did not look up as Fiona reached for his injured arm. Pretending a calmness she did not feel, she unwrapped the bandage and examined the wound. The stitches were still intact, despite the Viking's rough treatment. The angry redness around the sword cut had faded, and there was no other sign of infection. Fiona could not help feeling a sense of satisfaction. Without her aid, this man would have died; her skill and patience had not only saved his life but preserved the use of his sword arm.

She raised her eyes to the dark Viking. "Tell your brother that his injury heals well," she said. "In a few days, I will remove the stitches."

Sigurd grunted in apparent satisfaction, and Fiona refastened the bandage, then released the Viking's arm. She took a half step back, feeling the man's hot gaze on her body. She longed to seek shelter in the tent, away from his disturbing presence, but she was not certain she had leave to go.

Sigurd spoke a few words in Norse to his brother. There was a mocking, playful cadence in his voice, and Fiona was not surprised when the other Viking did not answer. After a moment, she began to walk away.

She gasped as the man called Dag reached out and caught

her skirts. She whirled around, and his icy-blue eyes impaled
her. His gaze raked over her, like hands caressing her body.
His silent scrutiny unnerved her.

The Viking spoke a few words to Sigurd. The big man
nodded, and Fiona looked at him in puzzlement. "He asks
why you saved his life." One of Sigurd's dark brows shot
up speculatively. "Why would you aid one of your father's
enemies?"

Fiona stood utterly still, racked by conflicting emotions so
powerful she did not know whether to sink to her knees weeping
or dissolve into wild laughter. This man asked why she had
aided her enemy so that he might burn her home and destroy
her life? There was no answer she could give them, no answer
that would not make her shatter into pieces with shame.

She swallowed. "I will not tell you."

Sigurd, appearing puzzled, translated her words for his
brother. Without even looking at Dag, Fiona could feel his rage
building. She stepped back, but not quickly enough. The man's
broad hand flashed out and struck her a stinging blow to the
cheek. Fiona nearly toppled with the force of it; but even as
she struggled to maintain her balance, the Viking righted her,
then withdrew his hand as if her flesh burned his.

Fiona met his horrified gaze in amazement. What was wrong
with him? Why would he hit her one second, then help her
stand the next? The Viking's wits seemed as addled as hers.

She began to shiver, overcome by the fear, anger, and grief
that had battered her since she'd awakened. Sigurd appeared
to curse, and she sought his eyes, wondering if he knew what
ailed his brother. His cold look said he did not. She worried
that he might strike her as well.

Dag heard Sigurd growl something in Irish, and the woman
moved away, her blue dress swishing.

"I ought to have you ravish her again to discover whether
you hate her or care for her," his brother said.

Dag gave him a threatening look, and Sigurd grunted. "So,
that would not help it either, eh? By Frey's power, what ails
you? I've never seen such looks as you give the woman—they
are potent enough to melt glaciers and set the North Sea boiling.

Are you sure you were not hit on the head when you were taken? Your mind does not seem right anymore.''

Dag shook his head. He had not been struck down, yet his wits were clearly awry. The woman had defied him outrageously, yet when he'd dealt her the appropriate punishment, he'd felt terrible guilt. What power did she have over him?

The uneasiness in his gut deepened as he took the tiller from his brother.

Chapter 8

When Fiona awoke, she was certain it was night. No light shone around the edges of the tent, and the harsh voices of Sigurd's men had quieted. Her stomach burned with hunger, and she wondered if anyone meant to give her food. A shiver of dread went through her. She was so alone, so helpless. If the fair Viking turned his back on her, there was no one who cared if she lived or died. Except mayhap Sigurd. She did not think he would starve her. More likely, he would tire of her angering his brother and throw her into the sea.

As if her thoughts had conjured him up, Sigurd suddenly appeared in the tent opening. She knew it was he because of his massive size.

"I see the fine Irish lady is awake." The contempt in his voice did not reassure her. "Get up," he ordered. "You cannot sleep here. My men think I have favored you too much already."

Something came sailing toward her. Fiona put her hands up before it hit her in the face.

"A bedsack," Sigurd said. "Take it to the far side of the ship, near my brother. I would order you to share his, if he would stand for it." He laughed. "It will be entertaining to see how long he persists in his stubbornness."

Grunting, Sigurd pushed his bulk into the tent. Fiona scuttled away from him as he settled into the pile of furs she had just abandoned. Her heart racing, she made her way toward the tent entrance, dragging the bedsack after her.

The sea air was cool, and she shivered violently as she left the tent. Above her, a veil of stars glittered across the heavens, and the soft sound of snores greeted her ears. She took a deep breath and began to edge past the sleeping Vikings. Harsh anxiety filled her as she neared the stern of the ship. Dag hated her; his brother had said as much. Yet, she was to lie near him, for protection.

She could not see him, but it seemed she was near the sea chest where Dag had sat earlier as she'd tended his arm. Surely this was close enough to satisfy Sigurd.

Shaking out the bedsack, she lay it down on the hard ship bottom, then found the opening and crawled in. The bedsack was made of otter furs stitched together; it smelled musty and old. She rubbed her arms and squirmed around trying to generate some heat so she could be comfortable.

The strange sounds of the sea disquieted her. The creak of the mast, the whipping noise of the sail, the splash of waves against the keel of the boat—they all reminded her of the foreign, threatening world she now dwelled in. Her life had been spent in the timeless, soothing realm of Eire, a land of warm mists, gentle hills, and water-smoothed stones whispering of the past. All that was behind her now. The Viking world was filled with the sting of the sea wind, the blinding glare of the waves, and the sharp odor of stale fish and sweaty men.

She thought with longing of the warm snug bed she had shared with her foster sister. Burned. Destroyed. Her father, little Dermot. Dead. Murdered. Duvessa, Siobhan—perhaps alive, but lost to her forever.

Fiona's throat burned and tears seeped into her eyes. She had not known until now how much she had to lose.

Memories of her father swam before her closed eyelids. She recalled his teasing her as a child, gently tugging her dark braids and calling her little darling—*acushla*. There had been a gentleness in Donall, a tenderness that most warriors lacked.

Mayhap that was what Aisling had seen in him, why she had left the world of trees and spirits to wed a Christian warlord.

Fiona had never appreciated her father; now it was too late. Or was it? The priests said a man's soul went to heaven when he died. Was her father there now? Could he see her and understand her troubles? If only he could tell her what to do. This time she would listen. She would not be so stubborn and willful.

She choked back a sob. Her former life was ended, gone as if it had never been. The concerns and troubles that had once obsessed her seemed hopelessly petty now. To think she had been consumed with loathing at the thought of marrying Sivney Longbeard. She had not known then what true misery was. Although Sivney might be disgusting and crude, he would never have denied her physical comforts. He would have protected her, even pampered her. Now she was to be reviled, treated as if she were no more important than a dog.

The harshness of her new life had only begun. She knew the Northmen used slaves to do the hard labor on their farmsteads. Would that be her fate—cursed to a life of endless servitude in the fields? Or would she be used as a bedslave, a vessel for the Vikings' lust, then tossed aside when she lost her looks or her body thickened with a Viking offspring? Once she had dreaded the thought of lying beneath Sivney's repellent body; now she might be forced to endure the attentions of many men.

Fiona let loose a sob, her throat choking with grief and despair. She had been a fool of the worst kind, a spoiled, misguided child. She had failed her kin, her father.

The terrible pain of regret pierced her, and she could hold back no longer. As the Viking ship sailed into the darkness, she wept bitter, hopeless tears.

The woman wept. Dag could hear her ragged breathing, detect the rhythm of her quiet sobs. He hardened his heart against the pitiful sound. She was naught but a deceitful, wicked creature. He had been taught from childhood that loyalty to kin was more important than life itself. In the eyes of his people, her aiding him was unforgiveable.

Why had she done it? Had she pitied him, wounded and helpless in her father's prison, and decided to heal him because she could not bear to see him in pain? Dag could almost understand such feelings; he had always found it difficult to ignore suffering. As a boy, he had sometimes tried to mend wounded animals he found, despite the ridicule of the other boys who thought such sentiments a sign of weakness.

But empathy could not be all of the Irishwoman's motivation. She had not only tended his wound, but attempted seduction. What drew a highborn woman to a foul underground prison, there to strip naked and try to entice her father's enemy?

It did not make sense. First, she betrayed her father by trying to seduce the enemy, then, after he saved her from rape and murder, she violently rejected him. If the woman were truly selfish and unprincipled, she should be eager to please the man who rescued her. Instead, she had spat in his face.

Another thought came to him, taunting him with its implications. By now, the woman knew that this was Sigurd's ship, that all the men served him. Did she imagine herself as Sigurd's concubine? Her slender neck draped with jewels, her soft, swanwhite hands free from all work except soothing her master's sore muscles and fondling his manhood?

The image infuriated Dag. How like a woman to seek out for her master the man of highest status. Had not Kira done the same?

He thought bitterly of the woman who had shared his bedcloset the previous sunseason. Kira—with her wheat-colored hair, her dark eyes, her full, swaying breasts. The image still aroused a pang inside him, but whether it was a pang of longing or hatred, he no longer knew. He could not forgive her for choosing another man to wed, especially an old man with a thick belly and crooked teeth.

Dag wondered how a woman could prefer such a man to him. As a tall, well-made warrior, he had always had his pick of bed partners, and he knew that women followed him with their eyes when he passed by. Ah, but that was for bedding, not wedding. Kira had told him frankly that she must think of her future, of her sons' future. Snorri ruled a fine steading, owned rich lands, and had a reputation as a shrewd trader. A woman must marry for security, Kira had said. Her father, of course, had agreed.

Sigurd always assured Dag that he was better off without Kira. What man wanted a woman who cared nothing for him, only for his wealth and status? Still, it had hurt his pride, and his heart. He had cared for Kira, and she had spurned him. He would not make hat mistake agan.

Dag started slightly, realizing that the Irishwoman still wept. Her sobs were louder now, harsh and wrenching. The sound reached inside him, twisting his guts. No matter that she might be treacherous, he could not forget that she had succored him once, gently tended his wounds, bathed his filth, brought him food and water. Because of her, he was alive; yet, how had he repaid her? He had led Sigurd and the other men to her father's fortress; there they had killed and burned and looted, destroying all the woman must have held dear.

The unwelcome guilt returned. He had saved the woman's life, but for what? Now she was a slave, destined for a life of travail and servitude. Better that he should have left her among the smoking ruins of her father's palisade. Some man would have come to her aid then; someone would see that she did not starve. He need not have brought her on the ship and made her his captive. Now, it was too late.

Dag sighed. If only she had welcomed him into her body. He had half thought she might. The one kiss they had shared had been full of promise. If only she had offered him a little of the fire that burned between them in the darkness of the underground cavern. If only . . .

Abruptly, he turned over. He could not afford to feel pity for this foreign woman. What she had suffered was no worse than what many women endured. Life was harsh. The Irish chieftain had been a weak leader and so he had died. His daughter had lost her protector and been enslaved. The strong prevailed; the weak died or were subjugated. No one could alter that truth.

Why, then, did it not feel right this time? He had half cringed as he'd watched Sigurd and the other warriors cut down the Irish chieftain and his men. They'd deserved to die for what they'd done to him, but even so, he had felt no satisfaction at their deaths.

Dag's nagging uneasiness increased. He must not be so foolish as to doubt the warrior's code he had honored all his life. It was the woman's fault. Because of her, he could no longer see the Irish as faceless enemies to be casually slaughtered.

Throwing off the bedsack, he rose abruptly and went to where Rorig manned the rudder. "I'll take my turn now," he told the younger man. Rorig nodded and went off to sleep.

Dag inhaled the night air deeply. His arm pained him and he was tired beyond reason, but it was wiser to keep busy than to lie on the deck struggling for sleep. He looked up and scanned the night sky, orienting himself to navigate the ship. He sighed with relief as the familiar energy and expectation renewed him. The sparkle of stars above him, the rush of the waves beneath the keel, the thrumming sound of the sail in the wind, the sensation of power and freedom he felt in guiding the ship— this was what it meant to go *aviking*. Not for him, the safe, settled life. This was his destiny, to sail the wild, restless sea until She took him in.

The wind shifted, and he used his left hand to steer the ship back on course. The *Storm Maiden* felt supple and graceful, responding at his touch, thrillingly acquiescent and eager—as a woman should be. Dag frowned as thoughts of the Irishwoman relentlessly returned. Would she ever yield to him? And if she did, what would it be like?

Fiona woke with her stomach burning and her limbs stiff and aching. She raised her head and blinked against the sea glare. It had not been a dream; the Vikings had not vanished in the night. This was her life now—the rocking ship, her grim, unfriendly captors, a dozen physical discomforts to occupy her mind.

She rose and looked around. Dag sat on his sea chest a few

feet away, his back turned. His brother stood in the rear of the boat, guiding the tiller. The rest of the Vikings sprawled over the ship, dicing, polishing weapons, and engaged in other idle pursuits. Some of them, Fiona noticed, were eating. Her stomach growled enviously.

She sighed. Although she was very hungry, she could do nothing for that. Better to think of the things she could remedy. Slowly, she made her way past the men to the tent. She heard a few low words as she passed and decided it was advantageous that she spoke no Norse. As it was, she felt like a mouse prowling past a sleeping cat; at any moment, she expected one of the Vikings to pounce on her.

In the tent, she began her personal tasks. She felt much better this morrow, less panicked. Giving vent to her grief had helped; from now on, she would not waste time on tears, but focus on her goal of vengence.

"Make me brave," she whispered as she redid her braid. Eyes closed, she reached out for her father's spirit. "Help me survive this," she entreated.

As soon as her hair was finished, she glanced toward the tent doorway. She could delay no longer, else Sigurd might come to throw her out of his tent.

Cautiously, she went out. Her heart jumped in her chest as she saw one of the Vikings blocking her pathway. He was young and not nearly as ferocious-looking as the rest; with his dark-red hair and light eyes, he could almost pass for Irish. He was not leering either, although his expression was bright and avid.

She squared her shoulders and made as if to push past him. He surprised her by holding out a piece of salt fish, then said something coaxing in Norse. Fiona glanced nervously at his face. Dare she take the food? What might he expect in return? She was so hungry. If she did not eat soon, she would be too weak to fight any of them.

Impulsively, she reached for the fish. The Viking's eyes gleamed with enthusiasm. She took a bite, then another. Her stomach gurgled with relief.

A low, angry voice startled her, and Fiona glanced past the

auburn-haired Viking to see Dag moving toward her. His jaw was tight; his blue eyes flashed with fury. He said a few harsh words to the young Viking, then grabbed Fiona by the arm and jerked her away. Too shocked to do otherwise, she scrambled after him, trying to keep her feet under her as he pulled her along the deck. When they reached the stern, he flung her down and straddled her, muttering harshly in Norse.

Fiona could only gape at him. She watched as he left her to search the nearby supply stores. When he returned with a barrel, some instinct told her to beware; she rolled away just as the Viking emptied a barrel of salt fish on the deck and narrowly missed showering her with reeking brine.

Something inside Fiona snapped, and she began to shriek. "Wretched cur! Bastard! Filthy Viking scum!" The curses poured from her mouth. None of them seemed vile enough for the scowling madman who loomed over her. He deserved to feel pain! To bleed!

Fiona struggled to her feet, avoiding the slimy puddle spreading across the deck. Her eyes examined the cluttered area, seeking something she could use as a weapon. She grabbed a piece of wood that looked like the broken handle of an axe and brandished it at the Viking. He watched her, his eyes narrow and hard. Fiona remembered the battle axioms Dermot used to quote: *Don't look before you strike; your opponent will guess from your eyes where you mean to land the blow.* She tried to think how to follow the advice.

Her concentration was disrupted by a smothered, snorting sound nearby, and she looked to see that Sigurd had dropped the tiller and doubled over, apparently so convulsed with laughter that he did not trust himself to steer the ship. His huge face was crimson with mirth, and it took him some time to collect himself enough to speak.

"Thor's hammer! I've never seen the like!" he choked out as she stared at him. "My brother attacks you with fish, and you—a mere gnat of a woman—you think to wound him with a splinter of wood!"

Sigurd sputtered with laughter once more, and Fiona could hear the rest of the Viking crew guffawing. She felt her face turn crimson and fought back tears of rage and helplessness. But never would she weep. Sigurd and the rest of them would only find that more amusing. Frustrated, she threw the piece of wood at Dag, aiming for his face. He ducked as it went sailing over the edge of the boat, then moved toward her.

Fiona's anger and humiliation dissolved into stark fear as he took hold of her wrists. He motioned with his head toward the mess of fish on the deck. He growled some phrase in Norse, then repeated it. Although Fiona knew not one word of his language, she clearly understood his fierce, eloquent eyes. "Eat or I will grind your face in it," they said.

Pulling away, Fiona leaned over and picked up one of the pieces of fish, then thrust it into her mouth. Grimly, she began to chew. She swallowed. The threat of tears subsided.

Standing a few inches away, Dag appeared to relax; his icy-blue eyes thawed. There was faint laughter among the other men. Fiona looked their way, suddenly remembering the young Viking. Harsh fingers closed around her chin and yanked her head around. Dag's forbidding gaze met hers. She found she could read his expressions easily by now. This one said, "Look upon the young Viking again, and I will cut out his heart."

Trembling, Fiona took another bite of the fish. She did not understand this man called Dag. *What did he want?*

As if reading her thoughts, Sigurd spoke. "Look upon your master, wench. Dag Thorsson is the only man allowed to feed you, to touch you, to look at you. Disregard that fact, and you will know the stinging reminder of my hand as well as my brother's. I warned you I would not have any of my men wounded in a squabble over a slave."

Fiona took a shaky breath and closed her eyes. She had entered a realm of madmen. If she did not keep her wits about her, she would never survive.

When she opened her eyes, Dag still stared at her in that wary, ferocious way of his, as if he wanted to spit at her and swallow her whole at the same time. He gestured again to the pile of fish on the deck.

Dutifully, Fiona knelt and picked up another piece. Although she felt less like eating than she ever had in her life, she stuffed her mouth and began to chew. She would not starve herself merely to spite this Viking madman. She would endure; that was the only hope for revenge.

When she was finished eating, the Viking held out a skin. She took it and drank the stale water greedily, seeking to wash away the strong taste of the fish. As she lowered the skin, the Viking made a satisfied sound. Then he fetched the barrel and motioned to the deck, indicating that she was to clean up the mess. With a glare at her sullen master, she bent and did so.

Dag watched the woman pick up the fish. It had pleased him to see her eat and drink. It did not please him to see her soil her hands in fish oil. He wanted her hands clean and soft-scented, to touch him, to stroke his flesh as she once had. The memory sent a thrill down his body, and he struggled to keep his face impassive, his demeanor commanding and cold.

He shot a quick glance at his brother, who still appeared amused. "At last you treat her like slave." Sigurd nodded approvingly. "The wench has a rebellious nature. If you mean to keep her, you must not let her forget that you are her master."

Dag nodded. His brother spoke the truth. The only way to deal with such a scheming creature was to subjugate her completely, to make her so fearful she would never dare to defy him.

"If I were you, I would take her to the tent and finish things," Sigurd said. " 'Tis obvious you burn for her, so why not slake your fever between her thighs? Sate yourself this time. Do not bring her out until you are completely satisfied with her compliance."

Dag took a deep breath. Mayhap his brother was right. He should have raped the woman when first she'd challenged him. Instead, he had given in to his weakness. He must make her realize the power he held over her. He owned her; he could do anything he wished with her.

The thought made his shaft harden. He turned to stare at the woman. She paused in her task and watched him with wary eyes. Dag allowed his glance to explore her exquisite features, to peruse every supple curve of her body. She reacted quickly, her cheeks flushing, her eyes flashing with resentment. He felt her defiance, but it did not anger him this time. Instead, it inflamed his desire all the more.

Then, abruptly, he remembered what he wanted from the woman—and it was not for her to be broken and weeping. He wanted her as she had been when she'd come to him in his prison—exotic, seductive, eager. He remembered how she had stripped naked and offered herself. The promise in her enigmatic green eyes had had nothing to do with rape, or fear.

Dag shook his head. Nothing else would satisfy him but that she would look at him that way once again. Nothing.

He turned away from the woman, focusing his eyes on the distant horizon. "Find some tasks for her," he told his brother. "She is too foul-tempered to suit as a bed thrall. I would have her trained for something else."

"As you wish, brother. I have a spare sail that needs mending. Perhaps a few days of plying a needle on rough, heavy *wadmal* will dampen her fiery temperment."

Dag gazed again at the Irishwoman, meeting her defiant look with a penetrating one of his own. "Ask her name, Sigurd. Now I know her only as Mac Frachnan's daughter."

Sigurd spoke. The woman answered in clear ringing tones. "Fiona," she said. "Fiona, daughter of Donall Mac Frachnan, chieftain of the Deasúnachta."

Dag took in her haughty expression, the regal set of her slender shoulders. Fiona. Fairy queen. Irish princess. Untouchable, enthralling.

Chapter 9

Fiona paused in pulling the iron needle through the tough fabric of the sail and looked toward the prow, where Dag and his brother stood talking near the tent. Since her fight with Dag in the forenoon, he had ignored her completely. She was on fire with curiosity and half-dread as to what he meant to do next.

She returned her attention to her sewing, chewing her lower lip uneasily. It hardly seemed possible she was to be spared ravishment. She had always heard that Viking men were beasts, used to venting their lust wherever they willed. Yet the man called Dag had not raped her. What was the reason for his forbearance?

She glanced up again, this time regretting that she had no knowledge of the Norse language. If only she could get an inkling of what the two Vikings talked about. Dag's gaze briefly met hers, and a shiver of foreboding swept down her spine. Did they discuss her future? Although she had no idea how far they had travelled, she knew the ship sailed north—away from Eire and presumably toward the Vikings' home. Would she be sold to another master there?

The thought made Fiona's stomach tighten. If she had to be

at the mercy of some barbaric Northman, the one called Dag was her first choice. For all his hostility, he had not beaten her nor let his foul companions ill-use her. It was obvious he protected her from the other men, even Sigurd.

Again, she met the Viking's gaze. His blue eyes bored into her, probing and wary. When he turned away, a thought came to Fiona, filling her with excitement. What if the man felt guilty for capturing her? Despite his bestial Viking background, he might be unable to deny his obligation to her for keeping him alive and healing his arm. There was a chance he could be persuaded to release her once they reached his homeland. Fiona's heart raced at the thought.

She stood quickly, before her resolve could fail, and made her way toward the prow. At her approach, the two men stopped talking and stared at her. Fiona looked at Sigurd and said, "I wish to know your brother's plans for me."

Sigurd cocked a dark brow, then turned to Dag and translated. Fiona focused her gaze on Sigurd. There was silence for a time, then Dag spoke. Sigurd repeated his answer in Gaelic. "He says he does not know yet."

Fiona dared to glance at Dag's face. It was controlled and impassive, except for a strange glint in his eyes. Fiona took a deep breath. "When we reach land, I would be happy to go on my way and not trouble you further," she told Sigurd with dignity.

Sigurd laughed. "And how long would you last, a lone woman, leagues and leagues from your homeland? I trow that inside of an hour, you would be begging my brother to take you back under his protection."

Fiona flushed. There was sense in Sigurd's words, but she would not admit defeat. "I do not need your brother's *protection.*" She spat out the word.

Sigurd glared at her. "My brother's protection is all that keeps you alive . . . and unmolested."

His gaze swept over her body meaningfully, and Fiona felt her color deepen. Sigurd spoke the truth. Without Dag, she was terribly vulnerable to the lustful inclinations of the other Vikings. To reach her homeland safely, she must have the means to purchase passage on a merchant ship, where she would be less likely to fall prey to rapacious warriors. Of course, she had no wealth now; the Vikings had stolen it all. She regarded Dag resentfully. Because of him, she was an impoverished slave. But he owed her—without her, he would not be alive.

She faced Sigurd boldly. "I saved your brother's life. In turn, he owes me a boon. I ask not only for my freedom, but also enough coin or wealth to secure safe passage to Eire."

Fiona allowed herself to glance at Dag, her heart pounding. Even to her own ears, her request sounded laughable, but she would not back down.

Sigurd's eyes narrowed, then he translated for his brother. Fiona watched Dag carefully. He spoke harshly to Sigurd, and Sigurd nodded. "My brother says he owes you nothing. If not for him, you would have perished with the rest of your kin. He has already given you your life in exchange for his. Any debt that might have existed has been repaid."

Fiona felt her heart sink at the Viking's arrogant response. What had she expected? She had attempted to bargain with a Viking as if he were a man of honor, but he was only a brutal barbarian who preyed on the weak and helpless. She stiffened her spine, allowing and the anger and hatred to seep through her and fire her courage.

"Very well," she said. "You may release me at the first port we arrive at, and I will make my way on my own. If any ill befalls me, it will be on your brother's conscience."

Sigurd translated for his brother in a low, gruff voice. Dag's eyes widened, apparently in amazement at her audacity, then his expression again became grim and fierce, his voice as frosty as the winter wind.

Sigurd rendered Dag's response in Gaelic. "You misunderstand my brother. He has given you your life in exchange for your aid of him, but he said nothing about your *freedom*. Once we arrive in our homeland, your circumstances will remain the same. You will be his *slave* . . . and subject to his will in all things."

Despite the fact that Dag's answer was much as she anticipated, panic beat through her. She had dared to hope her circumstances were not as awful as they appeared; now her hopes were crushed. Defiant words rose to her lips. What did she have to lose by telling the wretched Viking scum exactly what she thought of him?

Their gazes met and held. Something in Dag's expression made the curses stall in her throat. There was a look of regret in his blue eyes. Could it be that be pitied her?

Fiona felt as if the Viking stared into the very depths of her soul. She wondered what he wanted of her; then, suddenly, she knew. He still lusted for her. She had been stupid to use guilt to attempt to coerce him into freeing her. She possessed a bargaining tool which had a much better chance of swaying the stubborn Northman, if she had the courage to use it.

She licked her lips in a way she hoped was provocative, then spoke, her eyes on Dag's face. "If I am a slave, then I must have some sort of value, a price if I were to be sold. Mayhap there is a way I could *earn* my freedom."

She looked to Sigurd, waiting for him to translate. He did not, only pursed his lips speculatively. "What sort of payment were you speaking of?"

Fiona swallowed and regarded Dag again. "What if I were to lie with your brother—*willingly?* Would that not be worth something to him?"

Sigurd snorted, then translated her words. Fiona kept her gaze fixed upon Dag. She saw his look of surprise before it was replaced by a calculating expression. Fiona's confidence soared.

Sigurd's voice was rich with amusement as he translated Dag's answer, "My brother wishes to see proof of your willingness."

Fiona stiffened. Of course, the Viking would expect proof that she would keep her part of the bargain. What should she do—pretend to entice him in front of the other men? The idea outraged her, yet she dared not show reluctance. If she were to have any chance of negotiating her freedom, she must be exceedingly clever.

Vowing to herself that she would rather kiss a cow's rear

end, Fiona stood on tiptoe and reached up to pull the Viking's face down to hers. She pressed her lips to his.

He did not not embrace her or otherwise respond, and Fiona released him and sank down again on the balls of her feet. She felt herself tremble. Was that enough? Somehow, glancing at Sigurd, she did not think so.

He raised one of his brows and said something to his brother. Dag answered. Sigurd's face was lit by a mocking smile as he announced Dag's decision. "He is not satisfied. He demands further proof."

Fiona gritted her teeth. Once she had stripped naked in an attempt to tantalize the Viking into coupling with her. She could hardly do that now. What other means could she use to indicate her submission? She thought of Scorcha, one of the kitchen servants who was said to lie with any man who asked. Scorcha was extremely proud of her ample breasts; she said no man could resist fondling them.

Fiona reached for the Viking's hand, then closing her eyes, brought it to her breast. She arranged his fingers so they enclosed her flesh and held her breath.

Nothing happened. Fiona opened her eyes to see the Viking watching her. His eyes seemed bluer now, slightly glazed, but his mouth was still drawn into a grim line. Aggravated to the point of desperation, Fiona put her hand over his and guided his fingers to stroke her breast. As he began to rub her nipple, Fiona felt streaks of pleasure race down her body. She froze. It was one thing to feign willingness, another to actually respond to his caresses.

After a moment, Dag pulled his hand away. Fiona almost sighed with relief. Then she looked at Dag and realized her ordeal was not over yet. The Viking's expression was as harsh as if carved out of stone. He did not intend to make this easy for her.

She turned to Sigurd and said impatiently, "Ask him if he is satisfied." Sigurd repeated her question; Dag shook his head.

"My brother says you are a poor liar," Sigurd reported. "No matter what you pretend, your body reveals your unwillingness."

Fiona's throat went dry. What more could she do? Finding her voice, she said, "There is no privacy here. If he were to take me into the tent, I promise I would not fight him."

Sigurd gave a hearty laugh, then reached out and grabbed Fiona's long braid, half-jerking her off her feet. "Silly little minx—why should he barter with you at all? You have naught to offer him that he cannot simply take any time he wishes. Your body is *his*. Why do you pretend to give it to him as a gift?"

Fiona snatched her braid from Sigurd, a horrible realization dawning. Dag had never meant to consider her offer. It was all a game, a wretched game to humiliate her. She felt her face grow crimson and her hands curled into fists. Without looking at Dag, she stalked away, grateful she had mastered the art of moving gracefully on a ship.

"What did you say?" Dag demanded of his brother. "Why is she walking away?"

"I told her the truth. Her willingness is irrelevant. She is a slave."

Dag surpressed a groan of frustration. The Irishwoman had offered herself to him; she had promised to submit. Then Sigurd had ruined it. He wanted to strike his brother, to pound his stubborn, stupid face. Of course, he did not, although Sigurd guessed at once something was wrong. "By Thor's hammer!" he muttered. "You wanted to test her. You wanted to see her grovel."

"Nei."

"Why are you angry? Why do you look as if you could throttle me?"

Dag did not answer. Strangely, he had not enjoyed seeing the Irishwoman defeated; yet, he wanted nothing in the world so much as for her to yield to him. He shook his head, trying to clear it. "It was wrong to trick her. I should not have pretended I might free her if she pleased me."

" 'Tis not wise to offer a slave hope," Sigurd agreed. "It only makes them more manipulative and treacherous, thinking they can improve their lot."

Dag nodded. Unwillingly, he found his eyes drawn to Fiona's

slender form. She stood pressed against the ship's curving prow, as if retreating as far away from him as she could without jumping overboard. He wondered if she had ever contemplated throwing herself into the sea to escape her fate as a thrall. She was so proud, so wild and lovely. Like a bird, an exquisite, thrilling bird that he held in his hands, feeling its rapid heartbeat, the fear and desperation that made its perfect feathers shudder. *How did a man possess something like that and not destroy it?*

He moved toward her, hearing the mutterings of the men as he made his way past their clutter and dice and board games. She did not turn at his approach. He stopped inches from her and stared at the strands of hair which had escaped her braid and now danced wildly in the breeze. She was so small, seemingly fragile; he could encircle her slim neck with one hand or encompass her waist with two. With a twist of his wrist he could kill her.

Yet, despite her delicacy, there was a fierceness about her that he had never seen in a woman before. She had defied him repeatedly, dared to demand her freedom. Even her attempt to barter with her body was an act of daring rather than a concession to the power he held over her.

Her courage both tantalized and frightened him. She was a slave, and yield, she must. If she did not, he would have to break her spirit. The thought repelled him.

She turned suddenly and, seeing him, gasped. For a moment, he observed fear in her eyes, then the shield of anger was drawn once again. She spoke in low, furious voice that left no doubt as to her indignation.

Without thinking, Dag reached for her. She went rigid. He gripped her arms fiercely, wanting to kiss her, to bury his frustration in the lush warmth of her body.

She jerked away and spoke, her voice bitter and resentful. He met her green, cat-like stare. *Yield*, he told her silently. *Yield and I will think of a way to spare your wretched pride.*

Tension rose like a mist between them, and he was vaguely aware of the laughter and gibes of the men. He thought of making her submit to his much greater strength, then took a deep breath instead. He had tried force, and it had not worked. There must be some other way to gain her compliance.

He stared at her awhile longer, then turned away and made his way back to the prow where his brother stood.

"What a stupid wench," Sigurd proclaimed. "To ask you for her freedom and a share of your booty. Did she really imagine that you would return her to Ireland and restore her position as princess?" He snorted derisively. "I have never heard of a Norseman freeing a foreign slave. She is lucky you let her live, let alone deal with her so kindly."

Dag considered his situation carefully. By the customs of his people, the woman was his property. As long as he owned her, he would be responsible for her behavior, and he could see that she would not submit easily, but continually test him. He must rid himself of this intolerable burden, but how? He would not sell her to Brodir, nor any other man.

The solution came to him like a bolt of lightning from Thor's domain. "I've decided," he told Sigurd. "I will not sell her, but will make a gift of her to your wife, Mina."

Sigurd gaped at him. "Why would you do that?"

"I told you that she is not suitable as a bed thrall. What other use is there for her except as a noblewoman's servant?"

Sigurd frowned. "Earlier, you argued for her life, saying that you intended to earn gold with her. Now you want to give her away. You make no sense, brother."

"You said that she was mine to do with as I wished. This is what I have decided."

It was obvious to Dag that his brother was not pleased with his decision. After regarding him with narrowed eyes, Sigurd announced, "I refuse the gift. I want no part of what is between you and the Irishwoman."

Dag fought back his frustration and tried to sound reasonable. "She would be a gift for Mina, not you. You would not have to deal with her at all."

"But I will be charged with defending her, won't I? I don't want the trouble of protecting her."

"It would not be such a hardship, Sigurd. No man would dare to molest her if they knew she belonged to your wife, and

I would be doing you a favor by providing Mina with a skilled seamstress.''

"*Nei*, I will not allow it. You may order her to help Mina around the steading if you wish, but don't involve me.''

Dag frowned, dissatisfied with his brother's answer. If it became known that Sigurd would not protect the Irishwoman, she would be subject to all sorts of abuse by the other men and he would still be forced to take responsibility for her. His plan to rid himself of her had failed.

"There is another way, Dag," Sigurd suggested slyly. "You could always beat her until she learns meekness.''

Dag gave his brother a hostile look. Sigurd threw back his head and roared with merriment.

Chapter 10

"Halvveis Fjord," Sigurd announced, pointing toward the distant coastline. "The tide's running fast and the wind's from the northwest. Another league or so and we'll take the sail down and row in."

Dag nodded. In only a short time they would arrive at Engvakkirsted. He should feel pleased and excited, like the other men. Instead, there was a grinding unease in his belly. He blamed the Irishwoman. Ever since he had set eyes on her, his life had not been the same.

He glanced across the deck. Even from a distance, he sensed her turmoil. 'Twas no wonder, with Brodir slavering after her like a starving dog after a choice carcass. Dag longed to throw the leering bastard over the side of the ship, but, of course, he could not. To warn Brodir away from his prey implied Dag cared for the Irishwoman's feelings. That was unthinkable. She was merely a slave, after all.

"Brodir shows a great deal of interest in the Irishwoman." Sigurd spoke from his station near the rudder. "It might be wise to sell her to him so he will not cause trouble."

"I do not fear Brodir," Dag responded.

" 'Tis not only Brodir. This 'cat and mouse' game he plays

has aroused the other men's interest in the woman. I fear conflict will arise over her sooner or later.'' Sigurd gave Dag a warning look. ''I mislike a woman sowing dissension among my warriors, but the jarl will be even less tolerant. He once lived in *Jomsviking* camp, where they ban women from the settlement altogether. If the woman causes trouble at Engvakkirsted, Knorri will either order her put to death or sold.

Dag sighed. Sigurd always seemed eager to remind him of his alternatives, none of which pleased him. If only there were a way to keep the woman safe, and yet somehow be rid of her.

His earlier scheme returned to him. Giving the Irishwoman to his sister-by-marriage seemed the perfect plan. She would see that the woman was kept busy and out of his way. Mina, with her kind heart, would also seek to protect the woman from abuse. If only Sigurd would relent.

Dag let his gaze again stray to the Irishwoman. She stood below the ship's curving prow, gazing off at the misty landmass, her face full of foreboding. Fighting off his feelings of sympathy, Dag vowed that his responsibility for her would soon come to an end.

Fiona gazed over the bluish-gray waves with trepidation. Since sunrise, a landmass had been visible off the ship's starboard side, and from the excited atmosphere among the men, she could easily guess they had reached the cold, uncivilized realm of the Northmen.

She cast a quick glance back to the foredeck, catching a glimpse of the ugly Viking who had grabbed her the first day on the ship. She looked away quickly and drew the ragged cloak more tightly around her body. The man seemed to watch every movement she made. He did not speak to her or dare to come very near, but his lustful intentions were clear.

Always as he stalked her, he kept an eye out for Dag, as if assessing how far he could go before the bronze-haired Viking would interfere. So far, Dag had done nothing. He might shift his position so he could better observe Fiona and her tormentor, but he took no action against the foul-visaged Northman. Sigurd had warned her that his brother was all that stood between her and brutal rape, and Fiona could not help wondering what would happen to her when they arrived at the Viking settlement. Unlike on the ship, Dag would not be able to guard her every moment there.

Sigurd's harsh voice startled Fiona from her gloomy musings, and all at once, the deck of the Viking ship became a blur of activity.

The warriors, who had spent the sea voyage in the quiet pursuits of gaming, repairing weapons, and telling stories, abruptly came to life. They retrieved oars from the underdeck and shoved sea chests into place near the oar slots along the ship's steep sides. Dag and several other man went to work on the huge mast projecting up from the middle of the ship. Within a short time they had taken down the sail, then let down the collapsible mast altogether. Two dozen men took seats on the sea chests, pushed the oars through the oarholes, and began to row. Fiona watched in amazement; before her eyes, the ship had turned from a sailing vessel into one powered by men's muscles.

She was further awed as Dag and the other men continued their strange tasks. She moved past the mast to better watch as they dragged the huge, carved wooden head of a snarling beast out of the forehold and affixed it to the curved prow of the ship. Then they retrieved a large number of decorative shields from the storage compartment and, leaning over the ship's sides, fastened the shields at regular intervals along the hull.

Fiona's heart skipped a beat as she wondered if they were going into battle. She scanned the ocean's horizon thoroughly but saw nothing except the endless shimmer of waves and the blue-gray shape of land on their starboard side. Gingerly making her way across to the side of the ship, she peered intently at the nearing landmass. She saw no sign of enemy ships approaching from that direction either. Was it really possible the Viking's rigged their ship with such frightening gear for a peaceful landing in their own harbor?

She glanced at the Vikings' leader, Sigurd. He still shouted orders, but he seemed calm, even pleased. Fiona turned her attention back to the other men. While one group rowed, the other men began to strip their upper bodies bare of the ragged, filthy garments they had worn at sea and put on battle attire. Fiona watched as they donned leather corselets, gleaming breastplates, mail that shimmered like fish scales, and conical bronze helmets.

Fiona shivered as her companions on the ship were suddenly transformed into terrifying, supernatural beings. Her thoughts crept back to her last night in Eire, and she relived the horror of seeing the monstrous Vikings prowling among the buildings of her father's palisade, their armor and helmets casting grotesque shadows in the flame-lit night. She had forgotten whom she shared this boat with. All around were her enemies, depraved, bloodthirsty Vikings.

A deep quaver ran along her spine and cold sweat broke out on her skin. Once again, she had to resist the mad urge to hurry to the edge of the ship and throw herself over the side. She closed her eyes and prayed for strength.

When she opened her eyes, her heart again leaped into her chest. Dag stood facing her. The copper of his mustache and long hair and the sun-glossed ruddy-gold of his skin blended perfectly with the polished bronze surfaces of his breastplate and helmet. He looked like a god—a fiery, golden sungod. Fiona stared, unable to take her gaze from him.

Spokes of white flashed through his azure eyes, echoing the cold, frothy tumult of the sea. But there was yearning within their frigid depths as well, an aching hunger that made Fiona's body respond with an answering shudder. For a moment, she wanted to reach out to him, to caress the fierce, lovely lines of his face and body as she once had. Then he spoke. "*Engvak-kirsted,*" he said.

Fiona's heart sank. They had reached his homeland. Now Eire was well and truly lost to her.

He turned away and nodded brusquely to the nearest rower, indicating to the man that he would take a turn at the oars. Fiona watched him, struggling to recapture her hatred. The Viking had brought this despicable fate upon her. If not for him, she would be safe in Eire and her father would be alive. *Ah, but you would be married to Sigvey Longbeard,* her inner voice added. She had sought to change her fate, and so she had. Mayhap, as the pagan lore warned, it was wiser not to meddle with the plans of the gods. What had she wrought by defying her father's wishes?

Bright sunlight reflected off the armored shoulders of the rowers. Fiona took a seat at her place in the far starboard quarter of the ship and watched the dazzling show of Viking manpower. She did not want to look at the shoreline looming ever nearer. She did not want to think about what was to become of her.

The grunts and pants of the rowers soon gave way to another sound—the dull thunder of the Vikings shouting as their countrymen on shore came into sight. Fiona ducked her head, determined not to face her future until she had to.

Dag leaned forward and concentrated on rowing. Any moment Sigurd would give the word that they were close enough to shore to let the ship glide to the dock. Then they would wade in to greet their families and friends before unloading the ship.

He wondered why he felt so grim. Was it because, unlike Sigurd, he had no wife and children to greet him? It had never bothered him before. He had been content to be home, to see familiar faces and sights. Mina usually brought his dog down to the dock, and Ulvi, the huge deerhound he had brought home from a raid on the Orneys, would be waiting for him with furiously wagging tail and slobbering, eager mouth. That had always been enough of a greeting for him before this.

"Engvakkirsted! We're home, men!" At Sigurd's bellow, Dag released his oar and stood up to peer at the shore. His eyes scanned the crowded dock. He saw Mina and Ingolf and Gunnar, Sigurd's two boys, but there was no sign of Ulvi. Frowning, Dag swiped at the sweat trickling down his brow.

Around him, men scrambled to retrieve their choicest booty before wading in. Dag's eyes went to the Irishwoman. She appeared terrified. Her lips moved, likely in prayer, and her eyes stared straight ahead, as if she could not bear to face their arrival in his homeland. The sight of her irritated Dag. Because of her, he had no spoils to carry ashore. As he had told Sigurd, *she* was the only treasure he had stolen from Ireland; and at this moment, she seemed more of a burden than an asset.

Dag glanced toward the crowded dock. Several dinghies were being launched to offload cargo from the ship and transport it to shore. He could wait for a dinghy to take the woman or wade in like the others. A quick look at the woman decided him. She would not arrive in her new home like the haughty queen she thought she was; instead, he could carry her ashore like the worthless baggage she had turned out to be!

Leaving his seat on the sea chest, he went to the Irishwoman and gestured for her to gather up her things. She apparently did not know what he meant, for she simply gaped at him. Too impatient to wait, Dag grabbed her about the waist and half-carried her to the side of the ship. He left her there, then with a graceful vault, slid over the side into the water. Gritting his teeth at the cold, he shouted up at the woman in the ship, indicating that she should jump down to him. She stared at him, looking stricken and making no move to obey.

All around him, men dropped into the water and began to splash toward shore. Dag felt his armor absorb the chill of the frigid water. Aggravation surged through him. Damn the woman! He should have thrown her over first. If he had to climb back into the ship and get her, he would make sure she swallowed plenty of seawater before they got ashore!

He took a breath and once more looked up at her, trying to force his voice to sound coaxing. He held up his arms again. He intended to catch her and keep her from getting soaked. Was she too stupid to see he meant to aid her?

He saw her eyes widen in startled awareness, then a determined look crossed her features. She scrambled nimbly up and perched on the edge of the ship's timbers. Then, with a beseeching look at him, she jumped. Dag deftly caught her about the waist, then swung her over his shoulder.

He slogged the few paces through the freezing water toward the dock, glad she was such a small woman. The icy water sucked at his boots and trousers, reminding him that he was back in the North, where the coastal waters never warmed. Panting heavily, he reached the dock and flung his burden onto the wet timbers. He climbed up after her, then paused a moment, breathing hard.

"Uncle, what did you bring me?"

Dag looked up into the piercing blue eyes of Gunnar, his eldest nephew.

"Greedy child," he answered with a growl and a feigned cuff at his nephew's skinny shoulder. "Is that any way to greet a wounded kinsman back from war?"

"You were wounded?" The boy's eyes rounded in awe.

"Ja." Dag sat up and held out his right arm. He had begun to use it normally and no longer needed to keep it bandaged, but the scar was still an ugly, livid reminder of the seriousness of the wound.

Gunnar sucked in his breath in wonder and envy. "How many Irishmen did you kill?" he asked breathlessly.

Dag glanced toward his captive, lying in a disheveled heap a few feet away. It was well she did not understand the boy. He shook off the unwelcome stab of guilt and answered his nephew. "It took ten men to take me down, and I'm certain at least two of them suffered mortal wounds."

The boy's eyes widened even more, if that were possible, and he sucked in his breath with a satisfied sound. "You'll tell us all about it, won't you, Dag?" The boy glanced at the slender, fine-featured woman who had come to stand beside him and added hastily, "Tonight, around the feasting fire, of course."

Dag got to his feet and gave his sister-by-marriage a careful hug. "Greetings, Mina. I see you have your hands full with the boys these days. And another one on the way." He glanced down at her swelling belly. "By Thor's Hammer, my brother plants his seed well. For all that he is gone from home so much, he keeps you busy birthing sons."

"Ja," Mina agreed matter-of-factly. "For all that he is gone . . ." She shrugged.

Dag did not know how to respond to Mina's indifferent

reply. He could not quite fathom his brother's marriage. Sigurd seemed content, and he and Mina did not appear to argue much, but Dag was not sure how things were between them. If he had a wife, he would like her to act more fond of him.

He glanced quickly at the Irishwoman, who had apparently shaken off her terror and gotten to her feet. She stood watching the other people on the dock with a look that mingled wariness and curiosity. What would she be like as a wife? he wondered. She might be a shrew and a nag, but he did not think she would ever be indifferent to him.

He dismissed the absurd musing and grasped Mina's arm. Although larger than the Irishwoman, his sister-by-marriage still only came to his shoulder. Her small features and skimpy, dark-gold braids gave her a youthful, almost childlike appearance. Dag had to remind himself that at twenty-five winters, she was as old as he. "I've brought you a slave," he told her as he guided her over to the captive. "She's an Irish princess. Too slight and well-bred for kitchen work, but I thought she could help with the sewing and weaving."

They paused before the Irishwoman. Mina exhaled softly with what could have been either a sigh or a sound of pleasure. "She is very beautiful," she said, turning toward him.

Dag shrugged. "I'm sure I could get a good price for her at the Hedeby slave market."

Mina's voice was gentle. "Then why don't you?"

Dag took a deep breath before answering. "The truth is, I owe her my life. When I was scouting upriver before we attacked, the Irish took me captive. My sword arm was wounded badly. The woman cleaned it and stitched it, else I would have died."

"Why would she aid *you*, the enemy?"

"I don't know. Sigurd asked her, but she would not say." The familiar anger rose at the memory, sharpening his voice. "It matters not why she did it, only that I am alive because of her competence with healing herbs and fever brews."

"She's a wise woman?"

Dag shook his head. "I doubt she's a trained healer. She seems too young, and she hardly has the gentle nature of a wise woman." He jerked his head toward Sigurd, supervising the unloading of the dinghies. "Ask your husband. He'll tell you she's a fiery little wench, as likely to try and scratch out a man's eyes as to aid his wounds."

Mina's mouth twitched. "So, you want to give her to me, to assist me in my sewing work."

Faintly embarrassed, Dag pressed his lips into a thin line, but was saved from responding by Sigurd's appearance. The big man blustered up, brushing packing straw from his hands. He leaned over and kissed Mina briefly, then turned to Dag. "I suppose you're already pressing my wife to take charge of your captive."

Dag opened his mouth to argue.

"Mayhap we should wait to have this discussion," Mina said. She cast a glance in the Irishwoman's direction. "If I were ever made a slave, I would prefer not to have my future debated in front of me as if I were naught but a pig or cow."

"She doesn't know what we're saying," Dag argued. "She speaks not a word of Norse."

"Oh, she knows," Mina said firmly. "While she may not understand our words, 'tis clear she is half-sick with fear over what we will decide for her future."

Dag looked at the Irishwoman and realized that Mina was right. The captive woman's skin appeared as pale as bleached linen, her slim form taut with tension. Her astonishing green eyes reminded him of a cornered wildcat, regarding her surroundings with frantic alarm. Reluctantly, Dag allowed himself to feel pity for her.

"We should all go into the longhouse and discuss this over a horn of ale," he said. "You want me to help you finish unloading, Sigurd?"

The big man shrugged. "We've done enough for now." He leaned down and hauled Ingolf up on one of his shoulders. When Gunnar clamored for a turn, Sigurd lifted his elder son with his free hand and helped him find a perch on the other side. Thus laden, he started toward the longhouse. Mina trailed after him.

Dag waited, uncertain what to do about the Irishwoman. He was frankly sick of carrying her around like a sack of grain, but he was not certain she would come otherwise. He jerked his head toward the path to the steading, indicating she should follow him. Her eyes flared with a rebellious look, then she broke her rigid stance and approached him. Dag turned and started down the path, mentally urging the woman to follow him so he would not have drag her. The soft sound of her footfalls on the dirt pathway reassured him that she came.

Chapter 11

Fiona followed the Viking, apprehension weighing down her every step. What was to become of her? It was clear the Viking and his brother could not agree. She was not certain which man's judgment she feared the most. Sigurd appeared cold and unfeeling toward her, but not necessarily unreasonable, while Dag's attitude ran hot and cold from one moment to the next.

And now there was another person involved. Fiona frowned, trying to gauge the Viking woman's reaction. She appeared to be someone of wealth and substance. The two young boys favored her, suggesting she was Sigurd's wife, although his manner toward her had not been overly affectionate. Some marriages were like that, Fiona knew. If she had wed Sivney, certainly she would never have been able to manage a show of fondness toward him in front of others.

Beyond a low turf wall, a complex of timber buildings loomed ahead of them. She raised her eyes toward the soaring, darkly forested hills beyond the settlement and a new wave of homesickness crept over her. Such a harsh, lonely place to live. For all that it was summertime and the valley green and lush with plantlife, the place seemed cold and unfriendly. She could already imagine the wind sweeping fiercely down from the north, the ridges of the valley frosted with glittering snow. There was none of the softness of the Irish landscape, the gentle mists moving in and out among the rolling hills and gnarled, ancient forests.

Recalling the violent, warlike gods she had heard the Northmen worshiped, Fiona shuddered. She did not belong in this place, but she must adapt if she were to have any hope of returning to Eire. Quickening her pace, she hurried after the bronze-haired Viking. For all the turmoil he had brought her, his presence was somehow familiar and reassuring.

As if sensing her anxiety, Dag turned and looked back at her. Fiona steeled her expression to coldness once more. He scowled back at her, and her insides twisted. She should hate him, but more often than not, she could not manage it. Mayhap it would be better if he did sell her to another warrior, one she could despise unreservedly.

The Viking stopped and waited for her. Fiona hesitated, then walked to where he stood. When she came to him, he took her arm. His fingers were warm on her flesh as he led her along. Fiona repressed the urge to jerk away from his grasp. She reminded herself that she must try to appear docile. She was a slave now, and disobedient slaves were treated poorly by all masters.

They reached a very large timber building built in the shape of an overturned ship. At the Viking's urging, Fiona entered through the carved doorway. She froze on the threshold. The entire chamber was filled with Vikings. They all talked at once, and the cavernous dwelling echoed with the din of their harsh-sounding language. The man behind her gave Fiona a gentle shove, and she half-stumbled into the room.

A few people turned to look, but most ignored her. Fiona saw numerous women among the brawny warriors, as well as many light-haired children. The children were appealing, at least. Their fair hair and rosy cheeks made them seem angelic. The warriors did not seem immune to their charm either. Like Sigurd, they allowed their offspring to climb all over them and examine the loot they had brought home.

One small boy with a dirt smudge on his cheek clutched a

heavy bronze dagger in both hands and threatened a massive warrior with the weapon. The Viking laughed and leaned down to adjust the boy's hold. Fiona swayed slightly, feeling sick. She recognized the dagger by its gaudy red-and-gold enameled hilt. It was Etain's. For all she knew, it was still stained with her cousin's blood.

She shook her head, trying to regain her composure. The Vikings played with their children and hugged their wives just like normal men. How, then, could they be such beasts, such bloodthirsty, evil demons to the peoples they preyed upon? She glanced at Dag. He watched her impassively. When she swayed again, he led her over to the hearth in the center of the room and helped her sit down on one of the benches arranged around the fire.

Fiona took a seat gladly, feeling that her legs might collapse at any moment. She sat quietly for a moment, then turned at the sound of a voice next to her. A girl with startling curly red hair held out a beaker of ale. A wave of aching longing swept over Fiona as she accepted the beaker. The serving girl reminded her painfully of Duvessa.

The red-haired girl returned her gaze. Fiona noticed that she wore a rough, brown kirtle and a plain strip of leather held her chopped-off hair in place. Her humble attire suggested she was a person of low status, probably a slave. Fiona felt encouraged by the thought. This girl might also have been stolen from her homeland and brought here to serve the hateful Vikings. With that vivid hair, it was even possible she was Irish.

Fiona glanced around for Sigurd, then spoke clearly in Gaelic. "Good day, lass," she said. The girl's blue eyes widened slightly, then the look of awareness faded. After giving Fiona another careful glance, she hurried away.

Fiona stared after her, puzzled. Did she recognize the sound of the Celtic tongue, but not understand it? She might be a Pict or Cymry from Albion. For that matter, the woman could have been abducted from any of hundreds of isolated islands scattered along the Viking route between Eire and the Northlands. They had all been settled by Celtic peoples who spoke languages slightly different from Gaelic.

Fiona chewed her lip in consternation. If only she could communicate with someone, someone besides Sigurd, that is. If naught else, she must learn the Norse language so she would have a means to speak with the other slaves. If they knew her plight, they might aid her in her plan to return to Eire. She took another sip of her ale, considering who might consent to teach her Norse.

She glanced quickly at Dag, then chastised herself for her foolishness. Her Viking captor appeared to avoid contact with her; it did not seem likely he would agree to spend the time necessary to teach her his language. More likely, she could learn from one of the women. Dag was talking to one now, a tall, buxom creature with shiny yellow braids that came nearly to her knees. A stab of jealousy struck Fiona. Was this the sort of women the Viking fancied? No wonder he had not insisted on bedding her.

For the first time in her life, Fiona felt self-conscious of her dark coloring and small stature. She looked nothing like the Viking women. Everything about her must seem as foreign and strange to the Northmen as they did to her.

Fiona watched as the yellow-haired woman left Dag and came over to the hearth and filled a wooden platter with some of the flat, brown cakes warming there. The woman wore a plain wool garment with a simple neckline. Over that was a more elaborate green gown with a bright border of embroidered red and yellow flowers around the skirt and straps that fastened above her breasts with large polished oval brooches.

Gaudy, but not terribly flattering, Fiona decided. She was fortunate to possess Duvessa's blue kirtle. Although slightly snug across her breasts and hips, it was comfortable. From what she could see of it, Viking women's attire was anything but; it would be horrible to endure those heavy brooches hanging down all the time. Did Viking women really do their work dressed so foolishly?

Fiona's curiosity about Viking women was piqued further when the one who appeared to be Sigurd's wife came over and spoke to Dag. The two of them stood only a few feet away from Fiona, and she was able to study the woman's garments closely. Sigurd's wife's gown and overgown were similiar to the yellow-haired women's, although looser and dyed in much more subtle hues. Her fastening brooches were smaller and of gold rather than silver. Between her breasts dangled a strange necklace strung with metal objects. Fiona leaned forward, trying to ascertain what they were. When the woman turned sideways, Fiona recognized that the looseness of her gown was intended to make room for the child growing inside her.

Fiona had barely absorbed this information when the woman walked off. Returning her gaze to Dag, Fiona was startled to see a stricken expression on his face. She stared at him, wondering what was wrong. An older Viking came up and began a conversation with Dag, and his expression quickly returned to normal. Fiona watched him in puzzlement. For a moment she had seen a look of deep grief on Dag's face. Had she imagined it?

Fiona took a drink of ale. When she looked up, the old Viking speaking with Dag was staring at her. The man turned back to Dag, and Fiona sprang to alertness. Was the man bargaining with Dag to buy her? She noted the Viking's sagging, weathered skin, the way the muscles in his bare arms hung stringy and wasted. The gorge rose in her throat. Even marrying Sivney Longbeard would have been better than sharing that old man's bed!

Fiona took another sip of her ale, feeling sick. The fatigue and despair caught up with her, and she leaned forward, suddenly faint. A strong arm wrapped around her shoulders, supporting her back. She stiffened immediately and prepared to struggle. Dag's voice spoke low and harsh in her ear. Unable to understand his words, instinct made Fiona acquiese to the Viking's implicit demand. She let herself go limp and did not even attempt to resist as the Viking picked her up and slung her over his shoulder once more.

She must make a pretty sight, she thought bitterly as Dag walked quickly across the crowded room. With her bottom and legs hanging over the Viking's shoulder and her long hair trailing down his back, she retained about as much dignity as a bleating sheep being carried to slaughter. Fiona's defiance returned, and she resentfully kicked the Viking in the chest. Quick as lightning, his hand came up to give her bottom an answering smack. Fiona gritted her teeth. Someday she would fight him and win! Someday she would finally get the best of the arrogant bastard!

The Viking ducked as he passed through a low doorway, then bent over to drop her on a raised, box-like bed. Fiona sat up and tried to catch her breath. The tiny room was cold and dark; she could barely make out the Viking's shadowy shape at the end of the bed. She watched him warily, trying to guess what he meant to do next. If only they could argue, rail at each other. Anything would be better than this mute, frustrating battle between them.

Dag stood panting, trying to regain control. Must the Irishwoman continually fight him? She was the most frustrating creature he had ever encountered. Could she not see that he tried to protect her?

He turned from the bed, reluctant to stay in his bedcloset any longer. There were too many memories. He remembered Ulvi waking him with her wet, sloppy tongue on his face. Her warm, solid shape nestled beside the box bed, guarding him, patiently waiting for him for rise. *Ulvi was dead. Never would he see her again.*

The pain of his loss felt like a knife in his belly. Bless Mina for taking him aside to tell him. If she had blurted it out when he'd first arrived on the dock—with the Irishwoman, his nephews, and Sigurd watching—how would he have hid his anguish? Sigurd cared little for dogs, except for hunting purposes, and the boys had long spent their grief by now.

Only Mina understood. He had seen the sheen of tears in her eyes when she told him that Ulvi had died from eating bad meat. An accident, she said, something no one could have prevented. Guilt roiled in Dag's guts. Ulvi had not died immediately. She had suffered, and he had not been there to soothe her, to look into her dark eyes and reassure her.

He sighed heavily, preparing himself to go out into the crowded hall. Behind him, the woman made a small sound.

What would she think of him if she knew he was sick with grief over a dog?

Dag squared his shoulders. She would never know—no one would. A warrior could not afford to be soft and vulnerable. He would hide his grief as he had hid all his deeper feelings since he was a boy.

He turned, his eyes adjusting to the dim light. He could barely make out the Irishwoman, sprawled on his bed. The image evoked a throb of longing in his loins. He remembered the wonder of her silken flesh, the warmth of her skin, the taste of her lips.

He repressed the intense desire such thoughts aroused. The Irishwoman hated him, and he had no strength to endure another bout of grappling with her. She was clearly exhausted as well. He would leave her to sleep; she would be safe here. Later, after he had shared in the celebration, he would find a warm place to make his own bed.

He turned and left the bedcloset. As he stepped into the main longhouse chamber, the light and noise hit him like a blow. He paused a moment, orienting himself, then sought his brother at the raised table at the end of the room. Sigurd was deep in conversation with Knorri, their uncle and the Jarl of Engvakkirsted. At Dag's approach, both men raised their drinking horns in salute. Dag signaled one of the kitchen thralls to bring him a horn of ale and sat next to his uncle.

Sigurd began a detailed account of the events in Ireland. Dag tensed when his brother reached the part about his imprisonment; but to his relief, Sigurd made no mention of the woman. Dag silently thanked his brother for his foresight. If Knorri knew the woman was a traitor to her people, Dag suspected he would order her sold outside the steading.

As Sigurd continued his report, Dag found his mind wandering. He could not help worrying over the Irishwoman. How was he to explain why he had brought her back to his homeland? If he made her his bed thrall, no man would question his desire to keep a comely wench for his pleasure; but he had no intention of bedding the Irishwoman. She had made it clear she was unwilling, and that was not the way he liked his women. The memory of her seductive eagerness when she'd first come to him still tantalized him.

"You took only one slave?" Knorri's raspy voice jerked Dag back to awareness. "Why not more?"

Sigurd's voice was calm and reasonable as he answered. "I did not think there was room on the ship with all the plunder, and in truth, we encountered no women or young boys suitable for enslavement."

"We could use the help in the fields," Knorri groused.

"With the superlative booty we took, we can easily purchase all the thralls we need next spring," Sigurd responded. "Taking slaves is risky business; I would prefer to let other men take the chances."

Knorri muttered something under his breath, and Dag guessed that the old jarl secretly thought Sigurd's caution a sign of cowardice. It hardly mattered. Knorri might rule at Engvakkirsted; but on the ship, the men all recognized Sigurd as their leader.

"The black-haired creature I saw—is that the slave you mentioned?"

Sigurd nodded. Dag held his breath, wondering what his brother would say.

"The woman is Dag's," Sigurd announced loudly, as if to remind the men nearby of the fact. "She represents his share of the booty we took."

Knorri's grizzled brow furrowed. "How can a scrawny wench compare in worth to the gold and silver the other men flaunt?"

Dag licked his dry lips and prepared to respond. Sigurd answered first. "She is a beauty, for all her strange coloring. Brodir has already offered a good price for her."

Knorri looked vaguely around the room, then complained, "Damn my fading eyesight. I would like to admire her comeliness ere Brodir ruins her pretty features."

"I don't intend to sell her to Brodir!" Dag's words came out sharper than he intended, and he felt both Sigurd and Knorri's eyes on him. " 'Twould be a waste to sell her to a brute like him. She would die within days from his torture, and the steading would lose the benefit of any useful skills she possesses.''

''What skills might those be?'' Knorri asked.

''She seems to know of herbs and simples; and since she was a princess in her country, she is like to be an accomplished seamstress as well. I'm certain Mina could use the aid of another gentlewoman. She complained to me not long ere we left on the raid that most of the women thralls are too clumsy and heavy-handed for clothmaking.'' Mina had not addressed the words to him, but to Ingeborg, the smithy's wife, but Dag thought they lended weight to his argument.

Dag waited for Sigurd to protest against the plan, but he did not, only gave Dag a thoughtful, assessing look.

''Do what you will with the woman then,'' Knorri answered, obviously tiring of the subject. ''It matters not to me, as long as she does not cause conflict. I won't have the comaraderie between my oathmen torn apart by some cunning-faced bitch. Loyalty to the clan is more important than anything. Speaking of which, have you heard about this feud between the Thorkvalds and Agirssons?''

''*Nei*, tell us,'' Dag prompted, greatly relieved the jarl had dismissed the subject of Fiona. He could still feel Sigurd's warning eyes on him.

''It all started with a few raids here and there,'' Knorri said. ''Nothing serious. A few cattle stolen, a slave girl raped and left for dead. Then a sennight ago, someone burned out the Thorkvald steading.''

''Was anyone killed?'' Dag asked.

Knorri nodded. ''Thorkvald's wife and youngest son. Some slaves. The rest of the household climbed up in the loft and escaped by pushing out the ceiling and jumping down into the cattle byre.''

''Who would do such a thing?''

Across from Dag, Sigurd shrugged. ''There's been bad blood between the Thorkvald line and Jarl Agirsson's people for some time. I believe it started out in a dispute about grazing lands. That was years ago. I had thought the feud died out, but memories are long.''

"And land is scarce," Knorri said grimly. "That's what usually motivates murder. Jarl Agirsson has four sons, and not near enough land for all of them. I suspect the younger ones mean to secure their fortune any way they can."

"Will the Thorkvald family take their dispute to the *Thing?*"

Knorri snorted. "That's what should be done. Let the council determine wergeld for the murders and insist that the Agirsson's pay it. But 'tis not like to happen. Thorkvald has sworn blood vengeance. Before you know it, half the fjords of the Norselands will be ablaze as one murder leads to another."

Dag sighed. Once, talk of raids and counterraids would have invigorated him. Now it made him weary. He was sick of bloodshed for the sake of bloodshed. He had looked forward to a dull winter sitting cozily around the fire with a horn of ale in his hand.

"What? My little brother does not jump at the chance to avenge his kinsmen?" Dag looked up, startled, and Sigurd laughed and continued, "The Thorkvalds are kin on our mother's side, brother. No one would think it strange if we joined their raiding party."

"I don't savor the thought of waking up to find burning timbers above my head," Dag answered. "And you, Sigurd, have your sons to consider. Children are the first to perish if the raiding fever gets out of control."

"Have you lost your fighting spirit, brother?" Sigurd challenged. "It makes me wonder if that little Irish witch didn't do something to you after all."

"Enough!" Dag found himself standing, his body rigid, his sword arm at his belt, ready to draw his weapon and smite his brother's grinning face.

He took a deep breath and sat down. It was just Sigurd's way. He liked to find a man's sensitive places and poke at them. It served nothing to rise to his bait.

Knorri's faded blue eyes shifted between Dag and Sigurd. "You boys have always been comfortable together. I used to tell Groa that you were as close as if you had arrived in this world in the same birthsack." He sighed heavily, and his gaze became distant. "Don't let a woman come between you now.

Women come and go; all a man can count on is his sword brothers.''

Dag stood once more. His conflict with his brother unsettled him. Better to seek his bed before his temper frayed further.

He started toward his bedchamber, then stopped. The Irishwoman. He could not sleep there. He would have to seek out a bed in the cattle byre. At least the hay would be more comfortable than the *Storm Maiden's* hard deck had been.

He left the noisy hall and paused outside to gaze up at the sky. This far north, the nighttime sky was never fully dark during the sunseason, and the stars appeared only as faint specks amid the glowing heavens. He breathed in deeply, trying to find some satisfaction in being home. Nothing had changed at Engvakkirsted, but he felt different somehow. Was it really the fault of the Irishwoman, as Sigurd had jested? Had she done something to him? He held out his right arm and stared at it. Still stiff, but almost healed. Once he worked to get the muscles built up again, he would be able to use it as before.

''Thor's hammer, it feels good to be home,'' a voice said beside him. Dag turned to see Rorig, the youngest of Knorri's oathmen. A stab of guilt went through him. It was Rorig who had offered the Irishwoman fish on the journey home. He had reacted foolishly, with jealousy rather than gratitude, then later realized that the younger man had made the offer out of kindness.

''My apologies, sword brother, for the incident on the ship,'' he told Rorig. ''My anger was directed toward the woman, not you.''

Rorig shrugged and held out a skin. ''No harm done. If I had a woman like that, I would act like a dog with a choice bone myself.''

Dag took a gulp of the sweet, potent liquid that filled the skin, buying time before he spoke. Would he look more foolish if he denied that the woman meant anything to him or if he admitted it?

Rorig sighed. ''I'm glad you saved the woman. 'Tis witless of me, but while we were killing and burning, I could not help feeling pity for the Irish.''

Hearing his own thoughts said aloud rattled Dag, but he managed to make his voice harsh as he answered. "*Ja*, 'tis witless. A warrior cannot afford to feel pity. Any hesitation and you give your enemy a better chance of killing you. I trow you would forget your pity soon enough when you lay in the death straw bleeding your life away."

Rorig hiccuped and held out his hand for the skin. "I hear the wisdom in your words, Dag, but I do not *feel* it. There must be something besides this endless killing. As the youngest of sixth sons, I had no choice but to leave home with my sword and find a strong jarl to swear to, but I find I dislike the life of a warrior.

"What would you wish for instead?"

"My own land, of course," Rorig answered. In the glow from the northern lights, Dag could make out the troubled expression on the young man's features. "I would be a farmer rather than a warrior, if I could."

"Land must always be defended," Dag reminded him. "Even a farmer must keep his sword at the ready."

"I would not be a weak man, but neither would I be a man who makes his living by killing. I have no taste for raiding; I would do something else!"

Rorig's outburst struck an answering chord inside Dag. He, too, had tired of bloodletting. What was the glory in cutting down outnumbered, poorly armed men? In burning prosperous farmsteads? In slaughtering slaves and women? It left a man with naught but cold, gleaming treasure and ugly memories. There had to be a better life, but what was it?

Chapter 12

Fiona woke with a start. Someone was in the room with her. She could hear breathing, sense slight movements near the bed. Sitting up, she called, "Who's there?"

"You knew I was Irish back there in the feasting hall. Why else did you speak to me, call me 'lass'?"

"It's you, the red-haired girl. You understood me!"

"Aye, although 'tis not wise to be seen prattling together."

Fiona nearly fainted with relief. Here, at last, was a friend, an ally. "Are you a slave, too? How long since you were captured?" she asked eagerly, moving closer to the girl.

The girl struck a flint to light a soapstone lamp near the bed. She turned, and the lamplight illuminated her youthful features and the nimbus of curly hair around her face. "I don't remember how long I've been here. Five winters mayhap. I was merely a child when the jarl's nephew bought me."

"Bought you? You weren't captured?"

The girl snorted scornfully. "Not by Vikings. I was taken in a raid by the Ui Neill clan."

"Where are you from?" Fiona asked. "What part of Ireland?"

"Rath Coole, near the settlement the Norse call 'Dublin,' and you?"

"A place called Dunsheana, along the Shannon River."

"How did you come to be captured?"

Fiona's lips compressed with bitterness. "The Northmen attacked my father's palisade. They burned everything. The other women were able to hide in the souterrain, but I . . . I . . ." Fiona hesitated. How could she explain her need to try and save Dermot and the other boys, to somehow make up for aiding the Viking prisoner? "I was trying to find my foster brother when the Vikings found me," she finished.

The slave girl frowned. " 'Tis not like Sigurd to take slaves in a raid. He believes it easier and less risky to purchase them at the slave markets."

" 'Twas not Sigurd's decision. I was made a slave by the one called Dag."

"Dag!" The girl looked startled. " 'Tis not like Dag to take slaves at all." Her gray eyes peered at Fiona closely. "How did Dag come to possess you? Was he trying to save you from being killed by one of the other men?"

"In a way," Fiona acknowledged. "I helped him, and he . . . he returned the favor."

"How did you help him?"

Fiona took a deep breath. "My father's warriors captured Dag a few days before the rest of the Vikings attacked. He was wounded, and my father threw him into the souterrain. I took pity on him and aided him." The Irish girl gave her a startled look. Fiona suddenly realized how traitorous her actions sounded.

"I didn't free him or anything so foolish," she added quickly, suppressing the memory of removing the Viking's arm shackles.

"But obviously he got free."

Fiona nodded, unable to reply. What she had done sounded shamefully disloyal.

The Irish girl's gaze bored into her. "You and Dag are well-matched. His kindheartedness has more than once brought about the men's ridicule. He does not like to see any creature suffer. He's very fond of animals. For a while, he had a pet dog, let it sleep by his bed, and went everywhere with it."

Fiona's curiosity was piqued. "A dog? What happened to it?"

"Died in the spring. Some bad meat or something."

A Viking with a pet. The thought jarred Fiona's convictions about her enemy even more. Dag sounded almost like a normal man. Of course, she knew better.

"You're wrong," she told the Irish girl. "Dag is no better than the rest of his bestial countrymen. As soon as he got me alone, he tore off my clothes and tried to ravish me." She shivered at the memory.

"*Tried* to ravish you?"

"I fought him off," Fiona said proudly.

The Irish girl's eyes narrowed. "You are a slave now. The Northmen hold the power of life and death over each of us. 'Tis foolish to defy them or anger them, even one such as Dag."

"I will not submit meekly," Fiona protested. "I will go to my death cursing my foul captors!"

"Aye, you very likely will," the girl agreed. "I've seen it before. Those who will not submit do not survive. 'Tis your choice. Apparently you are braver than I. I have a strong desire to live, even if it means accepting my lot as a slave."

Fiona felt a chill at the girl's matter-of-fact words. Had she not vowed only a few days ago that she would do whatever was necessary to survive? Now she threatened to throw her life away in order to spite her captors. She must not forget her goal of someday returning to Eire.

"Aye, you are right," she said with a sigh. "I do not really want to die, either. My plan is to escape and make my way back to Eire."

The Irish girl shook her head mournfully. "I know of not one slave who has ever escaped. Better that you should earn your master's favor and win your freedom that way." While Fiona stared at her in surprise, the Irish girl continued. "Aye, it can happen. Sometimes a Northman will become so fond of a woman slave, he frees her and makes her his wife. You are comely enough that you might well win a man's heart—and your freedom."

"I will do no such thing," Fiona insisted. "I made a vow to my dead kin that I would avenge them. How can I seek revenge if I wed one of my enemies? Besides, I am poor at deception; my face shows everything I feel. I could never convince a Viking I cared for him when, in truth, I hate the whole race."

"A pity." The Irish girl shrugged. "If I possessed your beauty, I would use it to better my lot any way I could, even if it meant spreading my thighs for the old jarl himself."

Fiona shuddered. The girl was very young for such grim reasoning. "How old are you?" Fiona asked.

The girl frowned. "Mayhap fourteen or fifteen winters by now."

"Are there many Irish slaves here?"

"There are my two brothers, plus a half-dozen others. You are not like to meet them, though. They all work in the fields and seldom venture into the longhouse."

"That would make almost ten. If we all joined together and planned an escape . . ." Fiona mused.

The Irish girl gave her a stricken look and moved toward the door.

"Wait!" Fiona scrambled to the edge of the box bed. "Where are you going?"

The girl regarded her warily. "I told you, I have no wish to displease my Viking masters. I want no part of any plan for escape. 'Tis foolhardy to even speak of it."

"All right." Fiona sighed softly, wondering if in five years her outlook would be as resigned and hopeless as this girl's. "I won't speak of things that distress you. I would like to be friends."

The girl nodded. "I would like that also."

"What's your name?" Fiona asked.

"Breaca."

"I am Fiona, daughter of Donall Mac Frachan, chieftain of the Deasúnachta."

"Fiona of the Deasúnachta—a fine name," Breaca said, her voice soft with something like awe. "A name fit for a princess."

"I was," Fiona said bleakly. "I was."

* * *

He was burning. The blazing timbers of the longhouse showered him with sparks that smoldered against his skin. He tried to run, but the flames followed him. He saw the Irishwoman and shouted a warning. She turned, and her green eyes met his with a defiant look.

Dag shouted again. This time he woke himself up. Relief shuddered through him. There was no fire, merely the sun shining on his face through a broken patch in the byre roof. His skin was not burning, although the straw he was lying on made it itch mightily. And the woman. Mayhap she was not real either.

Dag sighed. *Nei,* he had not dreamed the woman. He remembered dumping her in his sleeping chamber. While he tossed uncomfortably on a pile of straw, she snuggled among the soft furs on his bed.

A tremor of sexual longing went through him as he envisioned the Irishwoman, her creamy nakedness spread out on the bedfurs, the silky patch of black curls between her thighs contrasting with her milky skin, the tantalizing pink tips of her breasts jutting upwards. He groaned. The bedeviling woman continued to torture him.

Getting up, he stretched, trying to ease the stiffness from his muscles. He could not wait much longer to settle his captive's situation. He must find Mina and win her aid.

As he had anticipated, his sister-by-marriage was already up and busy with household tasks. He found her near the hearth, ladling porridge into a wooden bowl for the boys' morning meal.

"Mina."

She nodded and went on with her tasks after he greeted her. "About the woman," he began. "I think she could be of use to you. You spend hours in the task of clothmaking. Certainly another pair of skilled hands would be welcome." Dag paused, reluctant to push too hard.

"Sigurd thinks you will regret it if I accept your gift," Mina answered in her soft voice. "He thinks you should keep the woman as a bed thrall."

Dag's jaw clenched. "I don't want her, no matter what Sigurd thinks."

"Sigurd said you would say that." Mina turned to look at him. "For your sake, I will agree to train her as a house thrall, but I can do nothing else. She needs a protector, and Sigurd refuses to take on the responsibility. If the other men harass her, you will have to be the one to defend her."

"Can she sleep with the other female slaves?" Dag asked. He would do anything to get his bedcloset back—and his life as well.

"If you wish it. Although it might not be the safest arrangement for a comely, young thrall."

Dag heaved a sigh of relief. "She's yours then. I serve as her protector, but you will order her life and keep her busy."

Mina nodded.

Dag turned and headed toward the corner of the longhouse where his bedchamber lay. He would not waste any time making it clear to the Irishwoman what her new circumstances were. Her life as a house thrall would not be idle, but it would not be overly harsh, either. Among the Norse, no woman's life was leisurely. Mina might rule as the mistress of Jarl Knorri Sorlisson's household, but she had little free time to enjoy her status. She was always busy.

Reaching the door of the bedchamber, Dag flung it open. Two pairs of startled eyes met his. Dag looked from the little red-haired thrall's face to the Irishwoman's. There was something conspiratorial about the way they stood near each other.

"You speak her language?" he demanded of the red-haired girl. She watched him warily a moment, then nodded.

Dag felt a spurt of resentment. It made him feel more frustrated than ever to think that a raggedy thrall could communicate with his captive while he could not.

He quickly quelled his irritation. The Irishwoman needed someone to share her thoughts with, else she would be miserable with loneliness. Besides, it would be less troublesome to com-

municate with the captive through a female thrall than through
Sigurd.

"Tell her that she is to serve Mina," he said to the girl. "Mina
will be responsible for her duties and her living arrangements."

The girl turned and repeated his words to the Irishwoman.
Dag saw Fiona look past him toward the main room of the
longhouse. Her expression was cautious, but not rebellious. He
inwardly heaved a sigh of relief.

Mayhap his burden for the foreign woman would finally lift.

"Take her to Mina now," he told the girl. "She will see
that she is fed and cared for."

The slave girl nodded. Dag darted one last look at the
Irishwoman's endlessly beguiling face, then strode out of his
bedcloset.

Fiona followed Breaca into the main room of the longhouse.
She was to serve a woman, and a gently bred one at that.
Observing Sigurd's wife closely the previous night, she had
been impressed by her quiet, efficient manner. It was startling
to imagine someone like her married to a lout like Sigurd.

The woman known as Mina looked up as Fiona approached.
A slight frown marred her face, then disappeared. She said
something to Breaca in Norse. Breaca quickly translated. "She
asks how much you know about clothmaking?"

"Some." Fiona met the Norsewoman's probing gaze. She
must please her new mistress, but it seemed better not to exag-
gerate her abilities. Although, like all woman, she had been
trained in spinning and weaving garments, in recent years, her
duties had been limited to supervising others.

Mina again spoke to Breaca, who translated. "She wants me
to take you to the bathhouse. After you are clean, she will find
some clothes for you and your hair will be cut to an acceptable
length."

Fiona's hand went to the long braid that hung over her
shoulder.

"Come," Breaca said abruptly and headed toward the door.
Fiona forced herself to follow.

"What is Mina like?" Fiona asked as the two women walked across the hard-packed dirt outside the longhouse.

"She is not cruel, but she demands hard work from her thralls. You would be better off if you had submitted to Dag and he had decided to keep you for his bed."

Fiona decided not to argue. She had no fear of hard work, and serving a woman was bound to be better than serving Dag. But her hair—did Mina truly mean to cut it off? She glanced at Breaca's butchered tresses and shuddered.

The girl turned to her. "If you were Dag's bed thrall, he would not cut your hair." Her eyes took in Duvessa's kirtle. "Like as not, he would let you keep your own clothes as well."

Fiona clenched her jaw. She would not let petty vanity weaken her resolve. Even so, she could not resist looking down at the soft blue wool she wore. The garment was the only thing she possessed which linked her to her past life in Eire. To give it up would be another painful loss.

Breaca led her to a timber building with smoke pouring through a hole in the roof. Inside, there was a large pile of rocks near a fire and several troughs full of water. Breaca gestured to a wooden bench near one of the troughs. "Take your clothes off and put them there."

Fiona removed her shoes and kirtle. Breaca watched, her blue eyes intent. Fiona had not been so acutely aware of her body since the Viking saw her naked. There was not lust on Breaca's face, but cool assessment. Fiona felt herself being inspected like a cow at a summer fair.

Breaca filled a pail with water from one of the troughs and dumped it over Fiona's head. Fiona spluttered and pushed her dripping hair out of her face. Before she could catch her breath, Breaca doused her again.

When Fiona was fully soaked, Breaca handed her a fistful of squishy soap that smelled strongly of pine. Fiona rubbed it over herself. Breaca rinsed her, then Fiona stood shivering until Breaca fetched her a rough cloth to dry off with.

Her bath finished, Fiona put on her kirtle again and combed her fingers through her hair. It felt wonderful to be clean, but underneath her satisfaction, anxiety hovered. How long would it be before she was forced to relinquish Duvessa's gown and have her hair hacked off?

Fiona followed Breaca back the way they had come. Before they reached the longhouse, Breaca veered off toward a squat daub-and-wattle building that stood near what was obviously a cattle byre. She led Fiona inside the dwelling and gestured to the rows of pallets spread on the floor. "This is where we sleep."

Fiona looked at the bare, gloomy chamber, the rude, uncomfortable-looking pallets, and the first glimmerings of doubt stirred in her mind. Could she endure the hardship which lay ahead?

She met Breaca's pitying gaze. "I warned you," the red-haired girl said. She took Fiona's arm and guided her back toward the longhouse. "At least consider what I suggest. If you are set against offering yourself to Dag, what about Sigurd?"

They reached the doorway of the longhouse and went in. Seeing Mina at the hearth, Fiona expected Breaca to end the conversation. Instead, she continued arguing her cause. "Sigurd will be jarl after Knorri dies, and 'tis not uncommon for jarls to take second wives. If you could snare his interest, you'd want for nothing. He dotes on his sons, too; if you birthed him a babe, he would certainly claim it."

"Sigurd?" Fiona smothered a laugh. "He hates me."

"What about Knorri, then? The jarl's been ailing lately, but he's still a man."

"He's *old*," Fiona protested. "I doubt I could even get his shaft to rise."

"But if you did, he would be exceptionally grateful," Breaca pointed out. "He's old, but he might live many more years. He could gift you with many things during that time, even your freedom."

Mina turned toward them, and Fiona flushed, thinking of the impropriety of their conversation. Thank the saints the Northwoman did not speak Gaelic.

*   *   *

Dag took a deep breath of fresh air before entering the stuffy longhouse. He went to the hearth and grabbed a piece of rye bread, then spooned some milk curds into a wooden bowl. Going to one of the board tables, he took a seat on a bench and began to eat.

Brodir sauntered over to the table, scratching his belly. "What have you done with the Irish bitch?" he asked. "Does she still sleep? Did you ride her so hard she cannot rise?"

Dag shrugged. "She's up and busy with the other women. Mina will be ordering her tasks."

"Mina?" Brodir's beady eyes narrowed even further. "You mean to make the foreign woman a house thrall? To set her to spinning and baking bread?"

Dag shot the other man a warning look. " 'Tis what she was trained for."

Brodir chortled. *"Nei,* that woman was made for bedding and naught else. What ails you, Dag, that you don't keep her as a bed thrall?"

A muscle in Dag's face twitched. This was what he feared, the other men's interest in Fiona. How could he warn off Brodir without again involving the Irishwoman in his life? "Mina will see to her," he answered firmly.

"And at night . . ." Brodir's eyes glittered with lust. "Who will see to her then? I warn you, Dag, if she does not sleep in your bed, I mean to have her in mine." The greasy-haired warrior rose and strode away.

Dag's stomach clenched. Not two hours had passed since he'd spoken with Mina, and already his plan was threatened.

He glanced toward the door and sucked in his breath in consternation. Fiona and the red-haired slave girl entered the longhouse as Brodir was leaving. Dag watched Brodir brush by the Irishwoman, nearly knocking her off her feet. The warrior reached out, as if to steady her, but instead of grasping her arm, his hand caught her waist, then skimmed upwards to grope her breast.

In a second, Dag was on his feet and heading toward the doorway. He saw the outrage and fury on the Irishwoman's face as her hand came out to strike at Brodir. She slapped him hard on the chin; Brodir laughed and released her. Before Dag could get there, Brodir slipped out the door, still laughing.

As Dag strode up, the Irishwoman fixed him with a defiant glare, her green eyes flashing fire. He returned her gaze coldly. Although pleased at her swift response to Brodir, he resented that he was again forced to concern himself with her welfare.

With only a few feet between them, he could smell the pine scent of Mina's special soap clinging to Fiona's damp hair and observe the pink flush of her clean, glowing skin enhancing her already formidable sexual appeal. He wanted her with a desire bordering on obsession—why should not the other men crave her as well?

"I warned you, Dag." Mina's soft voice came from behind him. " 'Twill not be easy to keep the men away from her. Mayhap after that wild hair is cut off, her appeal will be lessened."

"Her hair?" Dag turned to face his sister-by-marriage. "You mean to cut her hair?"

"I was just getting the scissors from the storage closet."

"Her hair is beautiful," Dag protested. "Why must you destroy her loveliness?"

"Really, Dag. Slaves do not have time to brush and plait their tresses, especially when they are as thick and long as hers. 'Twould be impractical to leave her hair long."

"Nei." Dag struggled to keep his voice calm. It was absurd that it bothered him to think of the Irishwoman having her hair cut. Mina was right. Once shorn of her glorious ebony tresses, the foreign woman would not seem so exotic and enticing. The men would bother her less.

"Nei," he repeated. He met Mina's glance. She looked impatient. "I know it's foolish, but I . . ." He took a deep breath, remembering the Irishwoman's tender care of his arm. He had said he no longer owed her a debt, but in his heart he felt differently. He had made her a slave, but he did not want to see her humiliated. Her long black hair made her look like a queen, and he did not want her haughty beauty diminished. "I owe her this," he said.

Mina gazed at him a long moment, then nodded. "As I said,

she remains your responsibility. I merely provide tasks to keep
her busy. What of her clothes? Would you have her churn butter
and bake bread in that frivolous garment she now wears?''

Nei, I would rather have her naked every moment of the day.
Dag suppressed the ridiculous thought. Of course, the woman
must have sensible clothes. He glanced toward the red-haired
girl, still standing by Fiona. The young thrall wore a shapeless,
brownish wool garment, no doubt the usual attire for slaves.
At least such a garment would hide the Irishwoman's delectible
figure.

''Whatever you think best, Mina,'' he answered.

His sister-by-marriage turned away, her irritation obvious.
Dag watched her beckon to Fiona and the slave girl, then lead
them toward the storage chamber in the back of the hall.

Dag returned to the table, his belly now too unsettled to eat.
If Ulvi were still alive, he would dump his food in the straw
and let her finish it off. Another pang of distress went through
him. Engvakkirsted was not the same without his dog.

Chapter 13

Wretched itchy thing! Fiona adjusted the platter of roast meat she carried and used her free hand to scratch at a place on her shoulder where her new slave's clothes rubbed. It might be looser and less confining than Duvessa's kirtle, but the coarse wool of the garment made it quite uncomfortable. The thick fabric was hot as well, especially in the closeness of the longhouse. Fiona could feel perspiration beading her brow and trickling between her breasts.

She paused, surveying the smoky Viking longhouse. The place reeked of ale and stale sweat, and if that were not disgusting enough, she had to endure the sight of the bare-chested Norsemen gorging on the roast oxen cut from the steaming carcass in the firepit and swilling horn after horn of ale. It reminded Fiona vaguely of the feasts in her father's hall, although certainly the Irish warriors who kept company with her father were never as coarse and crude as these men. The Vikings laughed raucously and constantly shouted challenges to each other in their barbaric tongue.

At least they did not sing. Breaca had told her that, unlike the Irish, the Norse were not known for their love of music, although they greatly honored their storytellers, called *skalds*.

Later in the evening, Breaca said, when the *skald* performed, the Vikings would grow amazingly quiet, listening like entranced children.

Perhaps then she could rest, Fiona thought wearily. Her feet and back hurt and her head ached. If she sat down for even a moment, she would surely fall asleep, despite the din.

Grasping the wooden platter in both hands, she proceeded to the table at the end of the room where the jarl sat in an ornately carved chair. Fiona shuddered at the sight of his leathery face crisscrossed with wrinkles, his iron gray hair thinned to wisps across his bare scalp. She could not help thinking of Breaca's suggestion that she entice him in order to gain better treatment. Nay, never would she do such a thing. If her lot became unbearable, she might try to win back Dag's favor, but she would die rather than bed old Knorri.

She moved behind the table and set the platter down in front of the jarl, acutely aware that Dag sat beside Knorri. Fiona could feel the bronze-haired Viking's hot eyes watching her, and the awareness of his gaze caused a strange sensation to fill her lower belly. Every time she glanced toward him, Dag's eyes were upon her. The intensity of his regard made her body feel hot, and the coarse wool rubbing against her nipples contributed to her distress.

She turned abruptly to head back to the cooking area for another platter. Mayhap Dag did not hate her, she thought as she moved among the crowded tables. After all, he had come to her aid when the repulsive Viking—the one Breaca called Brodir—attacked her. If she had not forced Brodir to release her by slapping him, she felt certain Dag would have intervened. He must still feel he owed her for her care of him.

Near the firepit, the Vikings had pushed the tables together, blocking her way. Fiona looked at the mass of flushed, sweating men and decided to go around the other way. As she turned in the awkward space, a man's hand reached out and grabbed her kirtle. Fiona shrieked as she recognized Brodir. He jerked her down into his lap. She struggled, crying out with rage and fear. Brodir laughed, his pig-like eyes raking over her. She reached up to strike him in the face, and he grasped her wrist and pulled it down with such force that tears filled her eyes.

Fiona glanced desperately toward the jarl's table, hoping Dag would see her and come to her rescue. Dag was turned away, apparently in deep conversation with his brother. Across the crowded, noisy longhouse, she had no hope of gaining his attention. Fiona twisted frantically as Brodir began to fondle her, his greasy fingers probing for her breasts beneath the rough wool. Desperation filled her. She had not endured a ghastly sea voyage and the shame of slavery only to be raped by a filthy Viking swine in front of his leering companions. She must do something!

She forced herself to go still and wait for her captor to relax his grip. If she had learned anything from her struggles with men, it was that she needed the advantage of surprise to have any hope of thwarting them.

Brodir's free hand roamed lower, seeking the bottom of the kirtle. Fiona's eyes darted to the nearby table, where an eating knife glittered among the refuse of bones. Elation raced through her; if she had a weapon, her struggle would not be in vain. She waited as the Viking tugged up her kirtle. His hand moved up her leg.

In one swift motion, Fiona leaned toward the table, grabbed the knife, then twisted around and jabbed at Brodir's face. He jerked back, and her blow caught him in the side of the neck. Brodir bellowed, then released Fiona and reached up with both hands to pull out the knife. Blood spurted everywhere. Fiona, squirming to avoid the spray, lost her balance and pitched into the edge of the table. The rough wood hit her sharply in the shoulder, and pain lanced down her arm. Momentarily stunned, she had no chance to flee before strong arms grabbed her.

Another Viking held her, his iron-like grip half-crushing the bones in her arms, his angry, flushed face glaring down on her. Fiona began to scream, her terrified cries adding to the uproar in the longhouse. She thrashed wildly, all rational thought gone from her mind. She did not want to die like *this*—murdered by a dozen mad Vikings!

The longhouse dissolved into a blur of shouting, angry men.

Fiona screamed and screamed, struggling frantically. She hardly noticed as another pair of strong arms wrenched her from the first man's grasp. She continue to flail as her new captor flung her over his shoulder.

Fiona found herself being borne to the corner of the dwelling. The noise and confusion of the longhouse receded. Her abductor ducked down to enter a doorway, then she was upended once more and flung onto a bed.

Gasping for breath, she stared up into Dag's livid face. Relief flooded her. He had protected her once again.

As he continued to glare at her, Fiona's sense of reprieve vanished. Dag stood over her, fists clenched, his jaw rigid, his eyes flashing cold-blue fury. If he would not kill her, he looked as if he wanted to beat her senseless at least.

Fiona heaved a sigh. Her body was bruised and aching, her throat raw from screaming. If she were doomed to die in this grim, foreign place, it might as well be by this magnificent warrior's hand. She lay back on the bed, her limbs trembling with fatigue. Let him do his worst; she had no energy left to fight.

She lay quiet, her light-colored eyes strangely tranquil, her slender arms stretched outward—as if she offered herself to him. Dag felt his anger depart as quickly as it had come. The woman was innocent; she had done nothing, nothing except defend herself. She could not know that the penalty for a slave attacking a Viking warrior was death. Would the jarl be lenient with her because she was a woman, and a beautiful one at that?

A shudder raced down his spine. That she was a woman made the insult worse. If Brodir died because of her attack, he would have suffered an ignoble death. Despite a lifetime of valiant fighting, his spirit would not be welcomed by the fallen heroes who knew glory in the great hall of Valhalla.

But Brodir would not die, especially if his wound were tended properly. He had survived a dozen serious sword and axe blows already; the man was as hard to kill as a thick-headed ox. But his hatred would not die, either. Brodir worshipped vengeance as the White Christ's followers worshiped their kindhearted deity. Even if the jarl spared the Irishwoman's life, Brodir would never stop plotting her punishment.

Dag sighed wearily. He had been wrong to think he could be rid of his responsibility for the Irishwoman.

There was a sound behind him. He turned as light from the doorway splintered across the dimly lit chamber. The red-haired slave crept into the room, her eyes wide. "You haven't killed her yet, have you?" she asked.

Dag shook his head. "How goes the mood in the longhouse? Has Brodir let off bellowing like a butchered pig?"

"*Ja*, although he still calls for the Irishwoman's blood. That one, he will not forget this."

Dag sighed again. "And the jarl—what says he?"

The girl shrugged. "Knorri reassured Brodir that you will see your slave punished appropriately. He also warned him that the woman was your property and yours to do with as you see fit."

"Of course," Dag answered bitterly. " 'Tis my *responsibility* to see her punished."

"How?"

The dread in the slave girl's tone unsettled Dag. Did she really fear he would kill the Irishwoman?

"Stay with her," he ordered the girl. "If anyone comes, run and find me."

"Where are you going?"

Dag paused in the firelight shining in through the doorway. "I must consult with the jarl."

As he entered, Dag observed that the hall had quieted. Near the firepit, Mina and Ingeborg tended to Brodir. At the front of the room, Knorri, Sigurd, and Veland sat talking and eating as if nothing had happened.

Knorri looked up as Dag approached. He frowned slightly but said nothing as Dag took a seat on the bench opposite. Dag recovered his drinking horn and, holding it out, gestured for a slave to fill it.

When he had drunk it down, he met Knorri's watery-blue

eyes. "I must consult with you, Uncle, regarding my thrall's disgraceful behavior."

Knorri grunted.

" 'Tis true she behaved outrageously, but considering that our ways are foreign to her, and she has been a slave only a short time . . ."

"You would make excuses for her?" Knorri interrupted. "A woman? A slave?" He snorted loudly.

"Why should the fact that she is a woman discredit her bravery?" Dag asked, trying another approach. "Can you deny that she fought well? If she were a man, even a slave, she would be lauded for her valor."

"*Ja,* lauded and then killed." The jarl's mouth set in a stubborn line.

Dag remained silent, trying to reason out another argument for sparing the Irishwoman. He glanced toward the firepit. Two slaves cleaned up the blood; Mina and Ingeborg argued with Brodir, trying to get him to remain still so they could bandage the cut. The warrior's face was flushed with anger, and he appeared to be cursing everyone and everything in sight.

Dag turned back to Knorri. "Brodir does not look to be grievously hurt. In a day or two, he will have nothing more than a small scar to show for the incident."

"Unless the wound festers," Knorri said, his voice cold. "If I lose a good warrior because of your thrall's foolishness, you will pay wergeld to me."

Dag set down his drinking beaker and used his finger to trace a pattern in the wood of the table. "If the Irishwoman tended Brodir's wound, you could be certain it would not fester. She is very skilled. Sigurd had her tend my arm . . . on the ship." He glanced up to see if Sigurd meant to contradict the misleading statement. "My sword arm was far gone with poison, but she saved it and cured my fever as well."

Knorri's eyes flickered with interest. "She is a wise woman?"

"I cannot say for certain, but she is skilled at wounds."

Knorri nodded slowly. "At the very least, we must have her look at Brodir's neck before we kill her. Knife wounds are dangerous; I would not lose a good warrior for scorning her skills.''

Dag grimaced. Knorri's talk of executing the Irishwoman made his guts twist. ''I don't want to kill her,'' he ventured. ''I owe her for aiding my arm.''

Knorri took a drink of ale, then loudly passed wind. ''She is a slave; she had no choice. Even if she saved your life, it would not be a worthwhile exchange. A woman's life is not nearly equal in value to a man's. If a horse should save your life in battle, do you owe the beast a debt?'' Knorri guffawed.

Why not? Dag questioned silently. Why could not an animal and a man's soul be bound together? He had saved Ulvi's life, and she would have been willing to do the same for him, if she still lived. He could not feel that animals' souls were so different than men's. And a woman—was not the Irishwoman's spirit every bit as valuable as his?

''On my honor as a warrior, I cannot see her put to death.'' He met the jarl's gaze firmly. ''She is my property, is she not? Surely you will not force me to kill a valuable slave, so long as Brodir recovers fully.''

''What about flogging?'' Veland, who had been sitting quietly nearby, spoke up. '' 'Tis a lesser punishment, but it might satisfy Brodir. He only wants to see her suffer.''

The image of the Irishwoman's slender back crisscrossed with scarlet welts flashed into Dag's mind. *Nei,* he could bear that even less than seeing her put to death. ''I fear such treatment would kill her,'' he said. ''She is a small, soft-skinned woman, unused to hardship. Even if flogging did not cause her death, it would ruin her as a thrall.''

''Why?'' Knorri asked. ''If, as Sigurd tells me, you mean to set the woman to baking and weaving for Mina, why should a few scars on her backside interfere with her usefulness?''

Dag felt a muscle twitch in his jaw. He had no explanation for his wish to spare the Irishwoman. It was weakness on his part, pure and simple.

Knorri gazed at Dag sharply. ''Feel you some affection for this woman, mayhap desire to beget children of her?''

Dag froze. What should he say? He did not want to admit

his feelings for the Irishwoman, but it might be the only way to save her. "She *is* comely," he admitted.

Sigurd laughed loudly. Knorri did not join in Sigurd's amusement. He frowned and said gravely, "If you care for her, I will respect your wishes. But do not forget that your first responsibility is to your sword brothers."

Dag released his breath in a sigh. Thank Odin, Knorri was so fond of him. The old man would never have honored the feelings of any man excepting his nephews.

"What of flogging?" Veland asked. "Have you decided to forgo that as well?"

"Dag is right," Knorri said. "Such harsh treatment might well kill her." He waved his gnarled hand dismissingly. "The woman will tend to Brodir's wound, and Dag will choose some appropriate punishment to subdue her spirit." The jarl paused and glared at Dag. "From now on, you must control her better. A slave who dares to attack a warrior—I will not allow it at my steading."

The jarl got up and began to walk unsteadily toward the longhouse entrance, likely intent on relieving himself. Dag heaved a sigh at the jarl's departure, then cast a look toward the door of his bedcloset. His jaw set. In his mind at least, the debt to the woman had been repaid. Would she ever appreciate how much he had risked to save her life?

Sigurd's mocking voice interrupted Dag's musings. "How will you punish her, brother?" he asked. "Or will you?"

Dag rose abruptly and followed the jarl's path to the door of the longhouse.

"You think they will kill me?" Fiona gaped at the Irish girl. "For stabbing a man who molested me? What kind of savages are these Northmen?"

Breaca shrugged. "I warned you that they consider slaves as little better than animals. In their eyes, Brodir had the right to rape you on the table in front of all. When you struggled, you broke their laws. When you stabbed him, you committed an outrageous crime."

"But Brodir had no right to touch me! Sigurd said clearly that I belong to Dag!"

"That is all that might save you. As Dag's property, your punishment is up to him. If he argues for your life, you might escape with only a flogging."

Fiona felt sick. All the times she had defied Dag—now, her life was in his hands. Would he see fit to spare her?

Fiona got up quickly, brushing down her kirtle. A plan whirled through her mind. She recalled seeing a forested area behind the steading when they first arrived. If she could escape from the longhouse . . .

"What are you planning?" Breaca asked sharply.

Fiona gazed at the Irish girl. Could she trust her? Truly, she had no choice. If she were to get away, she must have help. "I mean to run away. Will you help me?"

Breaca's expression grew grim. "You really are a lackwit, aren't you? You think you have merely to walk off? That they will not search for you and bring you back? A runaway slave is always killed, and not in a pleasant way, either. Even Dag could not forestall that verdict."

"What if they could not find me?" Fiona asked stubbornly. I may look pampered, but I have *some* survival skills. My aunt taught me to make a snare to catch small animals and also of wild plants that can be eaten."

Breaca regarded her dubiously. "You might survive, for a time. But then winter would come and you would either die of cold or be eaten by wolves. This is not Eire, Fiona. The air here may be soft and warm now, but the winters are brutal beyond your imagining."

Fiona began to pace, feeling desperate. Breaca's arguments were reasonable, but how could she listen? How could she remain here, helplessly waiting for death? Her Irish blood demanded that she fight to the end. She stopped pacing. "I need a knife, Breaca, or some other weapon. Would you be willing to get me one?"

Breaca exhaled in disgust. "I trow, you deserve to die, you are so stupid. If I were discovered carrying a weapon, I would be executed along side you. I do not like you that much, Fiona of the Deasúnachta, that I will recklessly throw away my own life to aid your honor." She approached Fiona, her voice intent. "You are not a warrior, Fiona. There is no need for you to go to your death fighting. Better you should use your womanly skills to persuade Dag that you are worth keeping alive."

Fiona began to pace again. It came down to the same dilemma—should she surrender to her enemy to save her life? Which was the more noble path? To die, having never submitted, or to do what was necessary to live and someday seek vengeance?

She whirled to face Breaca. "What if it does not work? What if I beg Dag for my life and he refuses me? Then I will have compromised my honor *and* lost my life."

Breaca rolled her eyes. "It will work. The Viking, Dag, is besotted with you. It is likely he would try to save your life even if you spat in his face."

Aye, Fiona thought, she had done that, and it had apparently not destroyed the Viking's concern. Mayhap Breaca was right, and the Viking warrior truly cared for her. She raised her eyes to the Irish girl. "What think you then, do I offer myself to him? Is that the way to win his favor?"

Breaca smiled. "Now, Fiona, you show some sense. Take out your hair." She gestured to Fiona's thick braid. "Then remove your clothes. When Dag returns, I trow he will do whatever he can to aid you."

Dag stumbled over the threshold of the longhouse, his head spinning. Rorig had joined him soon after he went outside, carrying another skin of the potent, sweet drink he had stolen from the Irish steading. The two of them had stupidly finished it off.

Now Dag's body felt heavy and awkward, and he would be miserable on the morrow. At least his mind was numb; that was the point of his foolishness. He did not want to think, to remember the trouble awaiting him in the longhouse.

He hiccuped loudly and crossed the main area of the dwelling. All around him, men snored and mumbled drunkenly in sleep.

The place was as filthy as the swine yard. Piles of greasy bones lay everywhere, and pools of ale dripped down over the edges of the board tables. Here and there puddles of vomit fouled the straw covering the dirt floor. Dag made a face, thinking of Mina and the other women having to clean up the mess. It was no wonder his countrymen were often accused of being filthy beasts. Certainly many of them acted that way when in their cups.

Nei, that was an insult to the animals, Dag thought groggily. Except for swine, most creatures did not wallow in their filth. Even wolves took care not to foul their dens.

Reaching his bedchamber, he pushed open the door. He was surprised to see the lamp on his sea chest still lit. He pushed into the room. The red-haired slave girl struggled to her feet from her seat on the floor. He had forgotten her; he had told her to stay and do something—what was it? Oh, *ja,* she was to get him if anyone came.

A fat bit of good that would have done, Dag thought sleepily. He was too drunk to fight; he could hardly have protected the woman if Brodir had come seeking vengeance. Thankfully, he had not.

A quick glance at the bed told Dag that the Irishwoman remained safe. She was tucked into the bedfurs with only the pale oval of her face visible.

He sighed and sat heavily on the box bed. The Irishwoman stirred; her eyes opened. Dag looked away. He would ignore her tonight. He had not the strength for fighting. On the morrow, somehow, he would deal with her.

He bent down and began to unwind the strips fastening up his boots.

"Would you like me to do that?"

He looked up. The red-haired thrall—he had forgotten her again.

"*Ja,*" he said wearily. He lay back while the slave undid his boots, then helped him off with his tunic. His head felt as if it were stuffed with wool. He jerked alert, suddenly aware that the girl had spoken again. "What?"

"I said, 'Do you want me to remove your trews?'"

"Oh, *ja*." Dag lay back again, scarcely aware of the girl's small fingers moving over him. Finally naked, he rolled into the bed. Meeting the Irishwoman's form beneath the fur covers, Dag pulled her close. In seconds he had begun to snore.

Fiona wriggled from the Viking's fierce embrace and glanced toward Breaca, standing by the bed. "Jesu, what do I do now?"

Breaca laughed. "Nothing. His shaft is as soft as a wet reed. He'll not be any use to you tonight."

"But how do I get him to ravish me?"

"You don't. 'Twill have to wait until the morrow."

Fiona sighed in frustration. By then her resolve might well have weakened.

Breaca moved toward the door.

"Wait!" Fiona called. "Can you not stay with me?"

"Why? There is only room in the bed for two, in several ways. I can't be here in the morning to tell you what to do. Some things a woman must manage on her own."

Fiona swallowed, feeling panicky. She had tried once to seduce the Viking, and failed. What if she should fail again? "Please," she whispered to Breaca. "At least stay the night. I'll give you one of the bedfurs. The floor here can scarcely be harder than the pallets in the slave shelter." She wrinkled her nose at the memory. "Certainly it is cleaner."

Breaca sighed and took the fur. "Sometimes you are the most helpless of creatures, Fiona," she said as she made a nest-like bed on the straw-covered floor. "If you were a pup, my da would have drowned you at birth for your puniness."

Chapter 14

His stomach was afire.

Dag rolled over on his side and groaned. Curse the Irish for their damned mead! Drinking ale or wine never made him feel so vile. If only he could go back to sleep. But something had awakened him.

He eased himself to a sitting position at the side of the bed. His head responded with a furious pain that made his ailing stomach seem almost bearable. Loki's balls! What had he done to himself?

A sound behind him made him stiffen; someone was in the room with him. His muscles tensed for battle, but the answering thunder in his brain made it impossible to turn quickly around. He slowly shifted his torso, keeping his head as immobile as possible. The other side of the room came into view.

The Irishwoman! She had slept the night in his bed, and he had not known it. He gazed at her, feeling more irritable than ever. What did she want now? Had she not already caused him enough grief?

She sat up. The bedrobe fell away, exposing her breasts. Despite himself, Dag stared. Sweet Freya, she was beautiful. But why was she naked? Why had she slept in his bed *naked?*

He watched her green eyes narrow enticingly, like a cat's. He sucked in his breath. Did she mean to seduce him? What miserable timing she had! At this moment, he was as like to puke on her as to pleasure her.

Besides, he could not help thinking why she did it. Was she grateful he had saved her spoiled little hide? Her yielding out of gratitude appealed to him as much as her yielding out of fear. He wanted to see desire in her eyes, genuine desire, not the false passion he observed now. Even as he watched, the sultry, provocative look faded and wariness surfaced.

He sighed. He did not wish to see her grovel, not his haughty fairy queen. Turning away, he went about the excruciating task of finding his clothes. He discovered them folded neatly on the chest and remembered the red-haired slave undressing him. At least she had left, like a decent slave should.

Grabbing his clothes, he slowly bent over and pulled his trews up to his thighs. His stomach lurched dangerously, and he wondered if eating would help. He pulled his trews on the rest of the way. Now for his boots. He bent down again and groaned as his head responded with a violent throb of pain.

He heard a rustling noise as the Irishwoman got out of the bed, then the soft sound of her footfalls on the rush-covered floor. When he raised his gaze, she stood in front of him. The sight of her naked belly met his eyes. His glance moved up, then down, inspecting the creamy suppleness of her form. He wondered what she wanted, then decided he did not care. His eyes feasted. It had been nearly a sennight since he'd enjoyed her thus.

Abruptly, she knelt and began to put on his boots. Her hair streamed over her slender shoulders like a cascade of dark water. Dag watched, entranced. After a while, she glanced up, an aggravated look on her face. Obviously, his feet were not cooperating, and she was unskilled at this. He wondered if she had ever dressed a man. He knew at least one that she had *undressed*.

The memory aroused him—painfully. It was difficult enough to endure the pounding of his head and the unsteadiness of his belly; now his shaft was hard and throbbing, too. He gritted his teeth until she finished. When she stood up and leaned forward with his tunic, he snatched it away from her. He tugged it over his head, not wanting to feel her soft hands on him.

Their eyes met. She appeared uneasy, frightened. He glowered at her. Troublesome wench. The grief she caused him—the embarrassing conversation with Knorri, the stupidity of getting drunk on mead, the multitude of difficulties awaiting him in the longhouse—she was the reason for all of it. And now she apparently wished to repay him with her wondrous body.

He was simply not up to it. Shoving her aside, he marched out of the bedchamber.

Fiona watched him, her heart sinking. She closed her eyes as tears of frustration crept from beneath her eyelids. Dag did not want her; he hated her. Why did she feel so miserable that he had not responded to her enticements?

She sniffed back a sob of self-pity as Breaca entered the doorway. The girl glanced at her in surprise, then made one of her frequent sounds of disgust. ''Fiona—you coward! You hide here simpering, as if tears could do you a bit of good. Get dressed. If you aren't out in the longhouse soon and ready and eager to tend to Brodir's wounds, it truly will go hard with you!''

Fiona's eyes widened. ''Brodir? What do you mean?''

''Knorri has decreed that you will treat his wound. Dag told him that you were a wise woman.''

''A what?''

''A wise woman, a healer.''

Fiona blanched. ''They can't mean for me to touch that pig-faced fiend. I won't do it!''

''You must and you will.'' Breaca's voice was hard. ''Dag has convinced the jarl to spare your life, but one of the conditions is that you will use your skill to aid Brodir.''

''I'll aid him,'' Fiona ground out. ''I'll slit his throat and put him out of his misery.''

Breaca rolled her eyes. ''Blessed Bridget, why do I try? There's no help for such a feebleminded creature.'' She turned to leave.

"Wait," Fiona called.

Breaca hesitated. Her shoulders heaved with a sigh. "What now?"

"I'll ... I'll do it ... if you think I must. It's only ... I have no herbs here, none of my aunt's healing potions. I'm not certain I know what to do."

Breaca shifted to face Fiona. "Pretend. Brodir's not like to die anyway. Thick-skulled oafs like him are hard to kill, more's the pity. All you need do is make the pretense of healing him."

Fiona nodded. She would not let her stubborn pride get in the way this time; she would do what was necessary to survive, even if it meant aiding that miserable wretch.

"Good." Breaca grinned in satisfaction. "Your obedience might save you. You owe your life to Dag. He argued with the jarl against putting you to death. I don't know what he said, but somehow he swayed Knorri." Her eyes flashed warningly. "I'm sure Dag promised you would be as meek and docile as a field mouse from now on. You might consider his honor before you let your temper get the best of you again."

"About Dag ..." Fiona began uncertainly. "Do you still think I should seduce him?"

Breaca shrugged. " 'Twould not hurt. He is the only ally you have."

Fiona bit her lip. "He turned away from me this morning when I tried ... tried to offer myself to him. Mayhap he does not want me after all."

Breaca laughed. "Even with men, some times are better than others. I imagine Dag is outside right now puking up his guts. I found out the fool shared a whole skin of mead with Rorig last night."

"He was drunk?"

"Aye. I imagine when he came to bed he was seeing two Irish princesses and unsure which one to fondle. And this morning— even stallions will not rut when their bellies ail. If you have any healing skill, you might mix a potion which will soothe Dag's stomach and cure his aching head. I'm certain he would be grateful."

Fiona frowned, trying to recall if she had ever heard of such a thing. Siobhan had never been keen on helping men, especially the sort that drank to excess. But there was always chamomile, effective for settling sick stomachs, and thyme, a common remedy for aching heads. "Does Mina have any healing herbs?" she asked.

Breaca shrugged. "Come, get dressed, and we'll ask her. I'm certain she will expect you to require some medicines to dress Brodir's wound."

Fiona made a face. Here she was, abetting her enemies. Would the spirits of her slaughtered kinsmen ever forgive her? She would not fret on it. They were dead and she alive—and she meant to stay that way.

Fiona carefully rubbed the healing paste over the wound she had inflicted on Brodir's neck, ignoring the almost tangible malice radiating from the man. The cut was actually quite shallow, disappointingly so. Breaca was right: he would likely heal without treatment of any kind. Even so, she must put on a good display, thoroughly smearing the greenish paste over the wound. The stuff smelled horrid, and she knew a sort of satisfaction in thinking that the other Vikings would avoid Brodir for a while.

She glanced up from her work, instinctively looking to the entryway. So far, Dag had been conspicuously absent from the longhouse. It was a shame he was not here to regard the sacrifice she made to save his honor, and her own skin. When she saw him again, she meant to cry peace and offer him a brew of the chamomile and thyme leaves Mina had given her.

Brodir grunted; Fiona returned her gaze to his neck. Aye, that should finish it. Too bad Mina did not have any fluxweed. It made a disgusting concoction which she could have made Brodir drink, and it truly was good for helping wounds heal.

She stepped back, relieved to be finished with her hateful task. Brodir glared at her, a look filled with such loathing, Fiona felt a tremor of forboding run down her body. She had made a dangerous enemy. But what else could she have done? She could not have let such a man rape her in the middle of a crowded feasting hall. It was possible Dag might have eventually come to her rescue, but she had not been certain he cared enough to spare her. At the time, she had had no choice but to defend herself.

She went to the firepit and washed in a pot of water warming there, eager to remove the stench of Brodir's blood from her hands. How strange it was. Brodir and Dag were countrymen and, judging from what she'd learned of the Vikings, kin as well. Like the Irish, Northmen allied themselves by the means of blood ties, and it was unlikely that any two men at Engvakkirsted were not related in some fashion.

But two men could hardly be so different as Dag and Brodir. One was clean and neat, the other habitually filthy. Brodir acted like a gluttonous boor while Dag apparently had strong concepts of honorable behavior. Breaca had said he was kind to animals; if that were true, even Siobhan might approve of him. She always said that a man's character could be judged by his attitude toward the beasts.

Fiona sighed. If she could, she would like to begin again with Dag. To forget what his people had done to her kinsmen and go back to that extraordinary time they had spent together in the souterrain. He had moved her then, inspired her tender thoughts and lustful ones as well. Now, she was not certain what she felt for him. He was her protector; she needed him to survive. Was that why she felt so drawn to him or was there something more? Could it be she had begun to forgive him for his part in her people's slaughter? Forgiveness—the Christian priests preached of it incessantly, but with little impact on the ancient Celtic values of revenge and retribution.

She turned at a sound behind her and saw Dag take a seat on the bench Brodir had vacated. He looked sick, his normally ruddy complexion a shade too pale, his blue eyes laced with red. Sympathy filled her. She went to him and tried to gesture that she would bring him something to drink. He watched her suspiciously. She touched her stomach and head, indicating that she knew he was hurting. His face remained wary.

Fiona sighed and went to get the brew she had made for

him. She *must* learn the Norse language; it was so frustrating that they could not understand one another.

Dag took the steaming beaker Fiona handed him and sniffed it. It smelled of earthy, dark things, but not unpleasant. He glanced at her face. Could she mean to poison him? *Nei*, if there were anyone she meant to murder, it would be Brodir, and he seemed well enough after her treatment, except for his foul temper. By now, the woman knew that he, Dag, had saved her life, and she likely did this out of gratitude. Miserable as he felt, he would not turn away anything which might reduce his distress.

He gulped down the contents of the beaker. It tasted strong, but rather savory. He looked up. The Irishwoman was smiling, an enchanting smile, a smile to steal a man's soul. For a moment he resisted, then he smiled weakly back. Their eyes locked; the first rays of understanding passed between them. He decided he must really learn some of her language; there were things he would say to her, things he would ask.

"Do you think she is a wise woman?" Mina's soft voice came from behind him.

Dag pulled his glance away from Fiona's. He shrugged in response to Mina's question. "Apparently she has some knowledge."

"Magic?" Mina asked solemnly.

Dag regarded his sister-by-marriage with surprise. He had hinted as much to Knorri and Sigurd, but was it advisable to ascribe supernatural powers to the Irishwoman? It might force his kinsmen to hold her in higher regard, but it would also irrevocably set her apart. The Norse respected wise women, but they did not associate casually with them. He did not want to doom the Irishwoman to always being an outcast. He knew from personal experience what loneliness being different could bring.

"*Nei*, I do not think so."

Mina frowned. "You must beware, Dag. I think the woman is deceitful. I heard her talking with her countrywoman, Breaca, and I understood a little of what they said. It seems the Irishwoman plots to win your goodwill by sharing your bed."

Dag opened his mouth to say he was well aware of the

woman's motivations. Mina stalled his words by continuing. "Knorri and Sigurd were also mentioned. While I care little if my husband beds a slave now and then, I would not see you hurt. If the woman is willing to offer herself to any man who gives her protection, you would be unwise to let yourself care for her too deeply."

Dag stared at Mina. His sister-by-marriage was not given to idle suspicions. "How could you know what they said?" he asked. "I was certain the Irishwoman spoke only her own language."

"I understand a bit of Gaelic," Mina answered. "At least those kinds of words." A slight blush spread across her cheeks. "Sigurd taught me. He likes that sort of bedplay."

"You mean she spoke of bedding Knorri or Sigurd? What did she say?"

Mina blushed more deeply. "I believe she said something about being able to make Knorri's old shaft rise."

Dag sucked in his breath. The scheming wench! She had rejected him on the ship, now she prepared to offer herself to the jarl!

His gaze sought the Irishwoman. She sat dutifully spinning wool with a hand spindle a short distance from the hearth. Looking up, she gave him a shy smile. The smile changed to bewilderment as he continued to glare at her. She flushed and put the spindle aside. He stared daggers at her as she got up and hastily left the longhouse.

Dag sighed. The fact that she fled his presence only confirmed her guilt.

Mina had moved away and was adding wood to the fire. "Mina," Dag called. "When did you overhear the Irishwoman talking to Breaca?"

"Yesterday, when they returned from the bathing hut."

Dag looked toward the longhouse entrance, remembering how the Irishwoman had offered herself to him that very morning. Did that mean she had changed her mind about enticing Knorri? Or had she turned to him because she realized that Knorri was not a man easily manipulated by a woman—and he was?

Bitterness filled his throat. A few moments ago, he had felt a special intimacy with the Irishwoman. Now his doubts were back. Could he ever trust such a fickle, inconstant creature?

"Dag, would you mind bringing in some more firewood?" Mina asked.

He looked irritably at his sister-by-marriage. There were shadows of weariness under her eyes, and she unconsciously held one hand to the small of her back, as if it pained her. He remembered suddenly she was with child, and his irritation vanished. "Of course, Mina," he answered.

"You should have more help," he said as he rose from the bench. "Where is Breaca?"

"I sent her to the brewhouse to aid Ingeborg. After that, she will churn the butter."

"Shall I call back the Irishwoman?"

"You don't care that she might marr her pretty hands?"

Dag grimaced. His sister-by-marriage was right; he had pampered Fiona too much already.

"She is a slave," he answered fiercely. "She will do as she is bid."

Another feast—did these gluttonous Vikings never tire of eating? Fiona sighed as she delivered a third platter of meat to the jarl's table. It was roast pork this time, served with lingonberry sauce. She watched Knorri stuff another knifeful of greasy meat into his mouth. Fat pigs—if they did not curb their rapacity, they would blow up like sheep bladders and find themselves too stout to wield their weapons.

Except Dag. She noted that he ate sparingly and with an easy grace she admired. He did not stuff his mouth with so much that he looked like a squirrel hoarding food for the winter, nor did he wipe his greasy hands on his tunic afterwards. His decent manners were a relief, especially now that she had decided to let him bed her.

If he still wanted her. The thought sent a shaft of anxiety through her. Dag had acted strangely throughout the feast, and, indeed, the whole day. He still watched her with gleaming, lust-filled eyes, but the spark of concern, almost tenderness, which she had observed earlier had vanished. Something had happened which made him hate her again. What was it? After she saw him talking to Mina, his expression had changed. What had Sigurd's wife said to him?

Fiona proceeded to the cooking area and filled another platter, this time with dark bread. As Fiona passed by, Mina glanced up and smiled at her. Fiona nodded stiffly and continued on her way. Mina did not seem to bear her any ill will. What could she have said to Dag?

Fiona took a detour to the side of the longhouse where Breaca was occupied filling endless alehorns from wooden casks. Fiona pulled the younger woman aside. "What does Mina think of me?"

Breaca gave her a startled look. "I think she is pleased for your help. I know the babe tires her. She seems paler than usual, and I often catch her rubbing her back. 'Tis early for her to experience such discomfort."

"When is the babe due to be born?"

"In the month of the Blood Moon. Sigurd worries because old Amir died last winter and we no longer have a wise woman at the steading. If the weather is bad when the babe comes, it will be difficult to get a midwife here in time."

Fiona opened her mouth to say she knew something about birthing babes, having helped Siobhan deliver at least a dozen. Quickly, she closed it again. If she earned a reputation for being a "wise woman," it might bring her trouble. People were often known to turn on a healer who failed. So far, she had not earned much goodwill among her captors.

"I'm sorry she ails," Fiona said quietly. "I cannot help liking Mina, although I fear she has turned Dag against me."

Breaca's blue eyes were instantly alert. "Why do you think Dag has turned against you? He saved your life, and at some cost to his pride."

Fiona shrugged. " 'Tis a feeling I have." She glanced once more toward the jarl's table.

Dag still watched her, his eyes a bleached, frosty blue that made her shiver.

Chapter 15

Dag watched the Irishwoman approach. As much as he despised the crude gown she wore, completely hiding her luscious curves, the way it covered her was for the best. She already attracted enough men's attention to anger him. Brodir watched her like a hungry predator, and Kalf and Balder, also. Even old Knorri could not keep his gaze away.

Dag glanced narrowly at the jarl, well aware of the lecherous expression in the old man's watery eyes. " 'Tis pleased I am that you advised me to spare the Irishwoman's life," Knorri announced as Fiona reached their table. "Now that I have seen her closely, I realize that she makes a fine serving thrall. Watching her entertains me. Tell me, Dag, are her breasts as full and high as they appear?"

Dag's muscles went rigid. What would he do if the jarl asked him to share the Irishwoman? "*Ja*," he answered gruffly.

"And her hips and thighs—are they as rounded and full as a man might desire?" Knorri probed.

"*Nei*, she still has a maiden's hips—slim and narrow." Actually, Dag thought her hips perfect, but he knew Knorri favored full-figured women. *Thank the gods.*

Knorri sighed softly at Dag's response. "Mayhap after she

has borne you a few babes, her hips will spread enough to
accommodate my thick shaft.''

Dag saw Sigurd stifle a smile. They both knew that by the
time the Irishwoman bore a couple of babes, Knorri would be
dead, or fully impotent. The jarl had not taken a women to bed
in two years. He said they were too much trouble; his warriors
suspected the old man did not want to risk failure.

Knorri beckoned to the Irishwoman. Dag shifted uneasily as
she approached. Would she insult the jarl? He could not save
her if she roused the old man's wrath.

The woman stood next to Knorri. He smiled at her, showing
his brownish but still healthy teeth. His gnarled hand reached
out for her. Dag held his breath.

The jarl touched Fiona's face, his weathered fingers tracing
the pure lines of her queenly features. ''Exquisite,'' he murmured. His hand moved down, smoothing the column of the
Irishwoman's neck, then lower. His fingers splayed across her
chest, groping for her breasts. He grimaced and jerked his hand
away. ''Damned scratchy wool! It's like sticking your hand
into a bramble bush.'' He turned to Dag. ''You fondle her
breasts and tell me if they are as soft as an old warrior's
dreams.''

Dag's eyes widened. Did the jarl mean for him to handle
the woman before everyone? He hesitated, his gaze focused on
Fiona. She stood very still, as if waiting for Knorri to grab her
again. When she glanced at Dag, he saw the fear in her eyes.
Why was she afraid? Did she fear his touch? Or Knorri's?

The jarl sat back in his chair and groaned. ''Cursed old
bones. I can't sit up swilling ale as I used to.''

''Tyrker promised to tell a fine story later,'' Sigurd reminded
him.

Knorri shook his head and rose stiffly from his chair. ''I've
heard them all before. I'd best seek my bedcloset—before I
have to be carried there.''

The old warrior tottered a distance, then turned and winked.
''Dag, don't forget to ride the Irish wench one time for me,
and tell me about it on the morrow.''

Dag nodded stiffly, greatly relieved that the jarl was leaving.

In the future he must contrive to keep Fiona away from the old lecher.

But was *she* relieved? He looked back at her. She had not moved, except to step back so the jarl could get by. Now she stared after Knorri, watching him wend his way toward the bedcloset where he slept alone. What was she thinking? Did she regret missing her chance to entice the old man?

A muscle twitched in Dag's jaw as he looked out at the rest of the room. Brodir and Kalf both watched the jarl's table, their gaze clearly centered on the Irishwoman. A possessive fury swept over him. The woman was his! Let every man in the room know it!

He leaned over and grabbed Fiona by the arm and wrenched her onto his lap. She squirmed. He hissed a warning and tightened his grip around her ribs. How dare she struggle! She had endured the jarl's handling; now she would tolerate his. And by Thor's hammer, she would act like she enjoyed it!

Fiona went still in the Viking's arms, her heart hammering. What had come over Dag? She had thought he meant to protect her, but it seemed he had other plans tonight. First, he had let that repulsive old man grope her, then he'd seized her as crudely as Brodir had.

Tears sprang to Fiona's eyes. She could feel his hand around her waist, as hard and unyielding as iron, and sensed the terrible tension in his body. His sudden anger baffled her. She thought she had done the right thing by suffering the jarl's ineffectual caress, but obviously she had not pleased Dag. She twisted to look at him and was stunned by the cold savagery in his eyes. A shudder went down her spine; dear God, what did he mean to do with her?

The longhouse quieted, and Fiona's heartbeat slowed to normal. A thin, fair-haired man made his way to the front of the room. He bowed before Sigurd and Dag, then took a seat before the high table in a carved chair one of the Vikings had brought for him. The room went utterly still, and the man began to speak.

So this was the *skald,* Fiona thought. A sense of reprieve

filled her. Mayhap Dag only wanted her to sit and be quiet while the man performed. That she could manage.

The *skald* told his story in a low and melodious voice, although in Fiona's mind, the coarseness of the Norse language spoiled the rhythm of his phrasing. Unable to understand a word, Fiona occupied herself with examining the man's appearance. He appeared much smaller than most of his countrymen, and his hair was so light a shade as to be almost white. His features were graceful, although fine lines etched patterns around his eyes and mouth. Occasionally, he gestured with his long-fingered, elegant hands. Fiona guessed that he described a battle or other violent scene.

Faint boredom crept over her, although the rest of the hall listened as if mesmerized. Dag shifted her on his lap, and she wondered if he, too, felt restive. His grip around her waist had relaxed; Fiona settled against him, beginning to grow comfortable. The warmth of the longhouse, the *skald's* lulling voice—Fiona wondered if she would be considered rude if she fell asleep.

Her lassitude vanished instantly as she felt Dag's hand move upwards to caress one of her breasts. The thick wool did not thwart him as it had Knorri. His palm firmly cupped her breast, then his fingers searched until they found her nipple. Fiona's muscles went taut, and she tried to wriggle from his grasp. Dag's other hand came up to hold her still. Even through the cloth, she could feel the heat and pressure of his hand. He toyed slowly with her nipple until warm arousal spread through her.

She felt her other nipple harden as her body reacted to his teasing touch. For a moment, she knew the urge to lean back and enjoy the provocative sensation. Nay, what if someone were to see him fondling her? She glanced at Sigurd, dreading that he might be aware of Dag's movements. Like the rest of the room, his attention appeared focused on the *skald*.

Dag's rhythm was soothing and inflaming all at once. He traced languid circles around her aureola till Fiona felt aroused to the point of pain. The unrelieved tension made her fidget, and she squirmed on his lap. She heard him suck in his breath, and she was suddenly aware of something rigid pressing against her buttocks. She felt a blush fire her cheeks and tried to remain still so as not to arouse him further.

Dag had other intentions. He pushed her forward on one of his thighs, then took her left hand and brought it around to touch his groin. Even through his trews, she could feel the hard bulge of his shaft as he held her wrist and made her stroke him. Fiona felt her face flame even brighter, but a part of her enjoyed what her hand was doing. She could not help remembering his shaft naked, silky and hot in her hand.

As she caressed him with more enthusiasm, she sensed Dag's growing discomfort. His breathing grew harsh and quick in her ear; his arm tightened around her ribs again. With a low curse, he removed her hand from his member and pulled her body hard against his chest. A slight smile curved Fiona's lips. Two could play this tantalizing game.

Her body felt wonderful, light and hot at the same time, and she wondered if Dag meant to take her to his bedcloset soon. Instead, he resumed touching her breast—the other one this time. In retaliation, Fiona used her hips to rub against his obvious erection, deliberately increasing his torment.

It was a mistake. Dag's right hand slid down to tighten around her waist, while his other hand began to pull up her skirt. Fiona's smugness faded. Handling her through her clothes was one thing, seeking out bare skin quite another. If Sigurd should look over, he would see her kirtle hiked to her knee. Fiona tried frantically to decide what to do. It did not seem possible Dag meant to hold her here and fondle her for all to see. Mayhap he was testing her, making certain she would not struggle if he took her to bed.

Would she struggle? Fiona was not certain herself. The Viking had made her hunger for him, and Breaca had assured her that it was wisest to yield to her master. But it was such a momentous decision. Once she yielded, she would truly be his slave.

He pulled her skirt higher, until her thigh was half bare. Fiona glanced nervously at Sigurd; he briefly looked her way, then returned his attention to the *skald*. Fiona took a shaky breath. The table blocked the view of most of those in the hall; if Sigurd did not notice, no one else would guess what Dag was doing.

Dag's hand slid under her skirt. Fiona gasped as his warm, callused fingers touched her skin and continued their upward path. She closed her eyes as she felt him caress her inner thigh. *Saint Bridget, please! Let him stop!*

To her relief, Dag twisted around on his chair so Sigurd could not see what he did. But he did not stop. Fiona began to tremble as she felt him caress her between her legs. She knew she was wet, appallingly so. He pressed his palm against her, as if calming her throbbing flesh, then he ran one finger between the outer lips of her womanhood. Fiona thought she would swoon; she leaned back against Dag, fearful that she might collapse into a quivering mass on the floor. He released her waist and adjusted her hips on his lap.

His whole hand cupped her now, his hot flesh against her wetness. She took a deep breath, then another. *When would he stop this torture?* His fingers parted her again. He slipped one inside her. Fiona went absolutely still. She was melting, her whole lower body turning liquid. Strange vibrations echoed through her, as though she were a harp he played. She wanted to cry out, to thrash wildly. She could do nothing or a whole feasthall of men would learn of her rapture.

He whispered something soft and tender in her ear, and his hand moved in a way that seemed to quiet the raging hunger growing within her. She suppressed a moan as he murmured her name, low and intimate. He stroked her slowly, deliberately, gliding his fingers gently across the inflamed, slippery place between her legs. Now and then, he would widen the opening and slide one finger into her feminine passageway. The pressure seemed to soothe her, and she could not help thinking of how his shaft would feel inside her, so hot and solid. The image made her grow even wetter.

He shifted his fingers, moving them upwards toward her pelvis. They found a place at the top of her cleft and began to move in slow circles. The resulting jolt of fire almost made her leap from his lap. As she heard his low chuckle behind her, she wondered—was he pleased to have found some magic place that, when he touched it, lightning streaked through her? She turned to look at him and saw no hint of confrontation in his eyes now, only the warmth of passion. His sensual mouth curved into a smile of pleasure.

Dag gazed at the woman on his lap, mesmerized. He had forgotten the *skald* and his sword brothers gathered around this hall. Nothing existed but this woman who filled his senses and made his body act of its own accord. He could not get enough of her warmth, her softness. She meant to yield to him, yield as he had imagined in his dreams.

He smoothed her skirt over her thighs and looked around the hall, wondering if any would notice if they left. Of course they would. Brodir and Kalf never took their eyes from the woman for long. But what did it matter? She was his thrall— why should he not claim her for his bed?

He eased her off his lap and stood. This was the test. If she followed him willingly to the bedcloset, he would know she had made her decision. What did he care that she might once have considered bedding Sigurd or Knorri? In the end, she would have chosen him.

She stumbled slightly as he guided her away from the jarl's table; he steadied her with his arm around her waist. The hall behind them was still, eerily so; only the *skald's* spirited voice broke the silence. She took a step and then another until they stood before the door of his bedcloset.

He helped her into the room and closed the door behind them. For a long time he simply stared at her—her lustrous skin, dewy and pink with arousal, her startling eyes, darkened now to a mysterious moss-green, her perfect mouth, stained the shade of lingonberry juice. She was spectacular, but her expression was vulnerable, shy. He felt uncertain how to begin.

He approached her and leaned over her. His hands glided over her shoulders and down her arms. Then he drew her arms up around his neck and kissed her.

He had wanted to do this forever, since that first time on the ship. To feel her soft mouth open under his, to tease her lips with his tongue, to explore the silky, honey-sweet warmth within.

Their tongues touched and mated. Dag smiled inwardly at her boldness. She was a greedy thing, eager for all the delights he could teach her. And there were more, so many more.

The kiss deepened. Dag felt her body meld to his; her pliant softness joined with his strength. He moved one hand down to cradle her bottom and lifted her up so her pelvis met his. Obligingly, she moved against him, her slim hips rotating over his swollen shaft. He groaned and groaned again. The woman was simply too arousing. He released her hips and, gripping her rough gown, began to jerk it up. When his fingers found bare, soft skin, he lifted her and pressed her hard against him. This time, *she* groaned.

He let her gently down and went to his knees, steadying her with his hands on her hips. Then he reached up and tore her gown down to her waist, burying his face in the softness of her breasts. Her scent tantalized him; the luxuriant warmth of her skin made him ache. He nuzzled both her breasts, then found one taut point and suckled. She cried out and her hips jerked. He deepened the pressure on her sensitive flesh until he had to strain to hold her writhing body. Then his mouth explored her other breast, tasting her fully.

Slowly, he released her. Tearing off the rest of her garment, he lifted her onto the bed. He arranged her bare limbs so her breasts were exposed, her legs splayed to reveal the glistening pink folds of her womanhood. Then he leaned over her, scrutinizing every inch of her beauty. He moved his hand between her thighs and fondled her, watching her face. It gratified him to see her eyes darken with passion, her lips part with ecstasy, her cheeks flush with rosy heat. Her body went suddenly rigid, her engorged nipples jutting upwards, her slender rib cage arching, her hips straining against his hand.

She sat up and grabbed his wrist, whispering imploring, desperate words. He kissed her, then stood to remove his clothes. He had barely removed his trews when she again reached for him, her hand closing around his shaft. He moaned and moved to settle himself beside her on the bed.

Her hand shook as she touched him, clumsy and tentative at first. The awkwardness of her maiden's touch aroused him even more. He tensed his muscles, struggling for control. He would not waste his seed this first time with her; he would plant it deep within her virgin thighs.

Mercifully, her hand left his groin and she leaned over him to caress the rest of his body. She twined her fingers in his hair, stroked his face and jaw, then swept her fingers lovingly over his chest and shoulders. He endured her caresses by taking slow, even breaths and remembering that he had suffered it once before. Then he had not known any hope of finishing their loveplay; this time he did.

She kissed him, her mouth sampling his body as his had hers. He shuddered as her warm lips moved over his neck and shoulders. She paused to draw one of his nipples into her mouth, and he felt a vague pleasure that startled him. In her innocence, she had discovered something no other woman had.

Her hot breath seared down his belly, tracing his body hair to his groin. She moved her face against his shaft, then kissed him. He thought she might take him into her mouth, but she did not. He breathed a sigh of relief; at this intensity of excitement, some pleasures were unendurable.

When she returned her lips to his throat and pressed herself against him, he decided it was time. He eased her on her back and kneeled above her. He spread her thighs again, then fondled her silken folds to gauge her readiness. She was very wet, and the way she moaned attested to her eagerness. But he worried he would hurt her. He eased a finger inside her, then a second. She cried out softly, as if in pain. He withdrew his hand, thinking they should engage in more loveplay.

But Fiona had other ideas; she reached for him and spoke in a breathless, urgent voice he could not deny.

Positioning himself against her slippery opening, he pressed into her a bare inch. She moaned, but did not cry out. He eased in deeper until he felt the barrier of her maidenhead. He gasped as the pressure of her tight passageway nearly undid him, then thrust in fully, driven half-mad by the urge to penetrate her warm, mysterious femaleness.

He heard her cry out and forced himself to remain still. The primitive desire to yield to his body's rhythm, to possess her with hard, swift strokes, pounded at his brain. But the feel of her beneath him—her slim body impaled by his strength and power—reminded him that he wanted their lovemaking to last, to satisfy her as it did him.

To distract himself, he began to whisper to her, knowing that she understood not a word. He told her how wonderful it felt to be inside her, how warm and welcoming her body felt. He told her how soft her skin was, how perfect her breasts, how beautiful her hair. How her lips made him want to kiss her endlessly. He told her how perfectly her buttocks fit into his hands and how lovely she looked between her thighs, the way the dark, silky hair over her mound curled like dark moss and her nether lips were like the petals of a rosy, dew-kissed flower.

He told her all the things he wanted to do to her, using crude and masculine words to describe her body and the pleasure he wanted her to experience in his bed.

She listened, and he felt her relax. He took a deep breath, sensing her trust, and began to move. His rhythm was slow and deep, not so savage as to hurt her, not so gentle as to deny his satisfaction completely.

He felt her stretch around him and quickened the tempo of his strokes. His control shattered. Fire erupted in his brain and shot down his body. He made one last lunge inside her and felt his seed explode against her womb.

When he became aware again, he quickly rolled off of her, fearful he had hurt her. Immediately, she cuddled against his chest, sighing softly. With his free hand, he pulled the bedfurs over them and settled her in the hollow his body formed when he curled on his side. It felt good to have her buttocks pressed against his thighs, her breasts soft and warm in his embrace.

He sighed. She was content, and so was he.

Chapter 16

The gods help her—how did this man fall asleep so quickly, as if he simply willed it? She would not sleep for hours, if ever.

Fiona wriggled away from Dag's embrace and moved her hand down to touch herself, exploring the strange, still-moist flesh between her thighs. She had barely been aware of this part of herself before, although she knew it for the place where a man planted his seed to make babies grow. Now it seemed the very center of her.

Cautiously, she found the slippery opening and pushed a finger inside as Dag had done. Her woman's place felt like a sheath, narrow and slick. It also felt sore. No wonder, after his big shaft had filled her. But she had wanted him to do it. There was something about the way he touched her, the feelings he aroused, which made her ache for their joining.

Fiona shivered. She did not like to think of the power this man had over her, the knowledge he seemed to have of her body that even she herself did not possess. For a time, she had lacked any control over her actions, responding blindly to some primitive force that drove her to mate like an animal.

At least Dag had been as helpless as she to control the

whirlwind that overtook them. She recalled his extravagant release, the way his neck arched and his body jerked as he cried out. The memory evoked an intense response that frightened her. She could not allow herself to feel tenderness toward this man. He was still her master, and she a slave. *She dared not forget that.*

She turned over, adjusting Dag's heavy arm so she was more comfortable, and tried to sleep.

He stirred, suddenly aware of Fiona's soft body pressed against his. Arousal, comfort, and doubt all warred for his attention. How long had it been since he had known the luxury of a woman's supple curves welcoming him in the morning? Kira, his mind reminded him; she was the last woman he had lain with all night.

His apprehension deepened at the thought. Would this woman disappoint him as Kira had?

She roused slightly, and one of her breasts rubbed against his arm, distracting him from his worries. He reached to smooth her silky hair away from her face. She was so lovely; he wanted her again and again. She turned to face him. As her eyes met his, he saw her surprise and confusion at finding him so close. He smiled at her.

He wanted to begin lovemaking again but felt uncertain how to proceed. The crude way he had seduced her the night before did not seem appropriate now. He could scarcely believe he had handled her so intimately among a roomful of men. At the time he had felt that she owed him her compliance to anything he asked, but he no longer knew the urge to act like a demanding brute. This time, he would not be so selfish, so unsubtle.

She sat up with a kind of moan, and his eyes went immediately to her groin. Realizing she was sore, he climbed out of the bed and went to his storage chest. On top, along with the lamp, he kept a beaker of water for drinking if he became thirsty during the night. Grabbing one of his old tunics hanging along the wall, he tore off a piece, then dipped the cloth in the water.

Returning to the bed, he motioned Fiona over to the edge. She slid toward him and sat there, looking hesitant. With swift efficiency, he knelt in front of her and pushed her thighs apart. She gasped as he brought the wet cloth against her body. He ignored her reaction and began to wash the dried blood and semen from her upper thighs and between her legs.

Although he tried to be gentle, she tensed as he rubbed her. He glanced at her face and decided it was mostly embarrassment which made her resist. He continued cleaning until, satisfied, he threw the cloth aside. She waited, motionless. Between her thighs, she looked rosy and swollen, and absolutely enticing. Following an impulse he had never felt before, Dag leaned down and kissed her, pressing his mouth against her silken folds. She jerked and tried to pull away. He held her tightly, his hands firmly grasping her hips.

She moaned frantically and grew moist and slippery as he tasted her. Salty and earthy—exactly as a woman should taste. He sensed the tension building in her body, felt her shudder. Her hips arched; the wetness seeped from her body. Exploring, he put his tongue inside her. Her hips thrashed and she cried out. He repeated the motion, probing her with light, fluttering strokes. She screamed, an uninhibited shriek of fulfillment.

He kissed her tenderly, waiting for the waves of her pleasure to subside. When he finally released her, her eyes appeared unfocused, her face flushed. She met his gaze, and he tried to smile reassuringly at her. She looked more uneasy than ever.

He ran his fingers down her long slim back, feeling his own desire. He must have her again before the day was over. If he brought her to climax again, mayhap she would let him satisfy his need to mate with her.

But that was for later. He could hear the men stirring in the longhouse, and he had promised the shipwright, Ranveig, that he would go out and look at timber for new strakes for the *Storm Maiden*.

He broke off the embrace, retrieved his clothes, and began to dress. Fiona pulled up the blanket to cover herself and watched him with a dazed expression. He wanted to tell her about his plans, to reassure her that he did not really want to leave her. Of course, he had not the words.

He gestured as he went to the door, trying to indicate that he was wanted in the hall. She watched him, seemingly bewildered. Crossing to the bed, he kissed her quickly before he left.

Fiona stared at the door through which Dag had left; she could not decide if she felt mortified or rapturous. Sweet Saint Agnes—she had never heard of a man kissing a woman *there!* Faint waves of completion still washed through her.

She stood up abruptly, seeking to banish the haze of satisfaction which clung to her. Turmoil immediately replaced contentment. How could she have let herself lose control so completely? She must not forget how she had come to be here, that the Vikings had taken her prisoner and killed her kin.

But Dag is not like that, a part of her mind told her. *He cares for you.* Fiona began to pace, torn by her conflicting thoughts. When the door opened, she whirled to face it, unsure whether she dreaded or longed for Dag's return.

Breaca's eyes met hers, and a slight smile turned up the corners of the slave girl's full lips. "So, Dag has at last mastered his thrall."

Fiona defensively wrapped her arms around herself.

"Where are your clothes?" Breaca asked.

"I'm afraid my kirtle is beyond repair." Fiona nodded toward the tattered garment lying on the floor.

Breaca picked it up. " 'Tis hardly worth mending. Mina will have to find something else for you to wear."

She left the room, promising to return with clothes in a moment. Fiona resumed her pacing. If Dag or Mina declined to provide her with garments, she would have none. She was utterly at the mercy of her captors; the thought unnerved her.

Breaca came back and handed Fiona another coarse brown kirtle. Fiona washed her face and put on the garment. "Come," Breaca said impatiently. "There is much to do. That you sleep in Dag's bed does not mean you are not required to work.

Fiona reluctantly followed the other woman through the long-

house and out into the steading yard. She did not want to meet
anyone, to face any of the Norse, man or woman. They would
see her submission to Dag as a sign of her acceptance of her
status as thrall. It was not, she told herself. She had wanted
Dag. She had allowed him to bed her because she desired him,
not because she had submitted.

A dark-haired woman thrall passed by them, carrying pails
of milk on a crossbar over her shoulders. She gave Fiona a
curious look, and Fiona immediately flushed. Did the thralls at
Engvakkirsted know that Dag had taken her to bed? Would
they despise her for giving in to one of their oppressors?

"Come," Breaca called sharply when Fiona dawdled. "Even
with Dag's favor, you will not be allowed laziness."

Fiona quickened her pace to walk beside Breaca. "I did not
let Dag bed me in order to win his favor," she said.

Breaca laughed. "Don't be witless, of course you did."

"Nay, I went with him because I desired him. I *wanted* him
to bed me."

"It does not matters why you did it, only that you have
finally come to your senses and decided to make use of your
beauty."

"But it does matter," Fiona protested. "I don't want you
to think that I have accepted being a thrall. I still mean to leave
this place and return to my homeland."

Breaca turned to regard Fiona. The cynicism in her young
face was startling. "Dream all you wish of freedom, Fiona,
but do not allow your bootless fancies to cause you trouble.
You are a slave now and will likely die a slave."

Although Fiona's whole being protested Breaca's words, she
realized it was pointless to argue. She silently followed Breaca
to a low timber building. Inside, bales of raw wool were piled
almost to the ceiling on one end, while several large looms
occupied the other. Two Norsewomen Fiona had seen in the
longhouse sat spinning the wool while Mina worked at one of
the looms. At Fiona and Breaca's entrance, Mina sighed and
stood up to stretch, then rubbed at the small of her back. Fiona
watched her intently. The Norsewoman seemed big for this

stage of pregnancy, and the dark smudges beneath her eyes testified to her fatigue and discomfort.

"Ask Mina if I may examine her. Tell her that I have had some training as a midwife." Breaca's eyes widened at Fiona's request, then she phrased the question to Mina. The Norsewoman hesitated, then nodded and stepped away from the loom.

Carefully, Fiona felt Mina's belly beneath her loose kirtle. It was big and hard; the woman carried no fat upon her body. Indeed, except for her midsection, she seemed to be wasting away. Fiona pushed at the smooth flesh beneath her fingers. The answering kick surprised and delighted her. She looked up and smiled at Mina. "Tell her that the babe seems strong," she told Mina.

Mina smiled back, obviously pleased. Fiona returned her attention to her examination. Gently pressing in a different spot, she was rewarded with another tremor of life. She glided her fingers upwards, seeking to feel through the distended skin and gain a sense of the babe's position. A flutter of movements met her fingers. Fiona furrowed her brow. From what Breaca said, three moon cycles must pass before the babe was due to be born, yet the babe was very active, and Mina very large. Sudden apprehension struck Fiona. What if the Norsewoman carried not one babe, but two?

Fiona raised her gaze to Mina's, wondering if she should say anything. Sharing her concern would not change things, and it might make the Norsewoman even more anxious.

Fiona removed her hands from Mina's belly. "Tell her that everything seems well, although I cannot tell for certain which way the babe's head is positioned."

Breaca translated. Mina responded in her soft voice.

"She says to ask you if there is anything she can take for the discomfort the babe causes."

Fiona shook her head. Most pain-killing herbs were too strong to give to a woman until she was actually in labor. "If she has any dragonwort, I could make her a draught which would help her carry the babe to term," she told Breaca. "The babe clearly saps her energy. She must save herself for the last difficult months.'' Even as she said the words, Fiona wondered if she should not make her warning more severe. As fatigued as she seemed already, Mina would scarcely survive a difficult labor.

Breaca repeated Fiona's words in Norse. Mina smiled faintly and gestured toward the huge pile of wool. Fiona felt a stab of sympathy.

Poor Mina. How could she rest when there was obviously so much to do?

"She should have more help," Fiona remarked to Breaca.

"She does, *now,*" Breaca answered. "Your main duty as a thrall will be to assist Mina in clothmaking."

Fiona looked with dismay at the pile of raw wool. It made her hands ache just to think of spinning it and her eyes hurt to contemplate its weaving. She had not appreciated her easy life in Eire.

"Ja, this one looks as if it would make a fine mast,'' Dag agreed. He splayed his hand over the bark of the enormous tree and tried to visualize the grain beneath, as Ranveig seemed able to do. It was no use. Although his strong arms and broad shoulders would be useful when it came time to cut down the huge timber, he had not Ranveig's skill at imagining a tree become a ship.

He grinned at the short, bowlegged shipwright. "I'll make a bargain with you, Ranveig. You build the ship—I will sail it.''

Ranveig grunted. "I merely wanted your approval. Sigurd would not come, and he says your knowledge of sailing vessels is as good as his."

Dag felt a twinge of surprise at his brother's praise. Sigurd often dealt with him in a slightly condescending fashion. It pleased him to hear his brother admit his worth.

"You have my approval, Ranveig. But I would go back to the steading now. I have some unfinished business that needs attending.''

Ranveig nodded absently and continued to stare at the tree.

Dag moved off into the woods, his heartbeat quickening at the thought of his "unfinished business." It was foolish of him, but he could not wait to see the Irishwoman again. His body still hummed from the pleasure of the night before, yet his greedy shaft was hard and ready for more. What excuse could he use to take the woman from her duties? Was there a tunic he could have her mend? *Nei,* better yet, he would say that he meant to begin teaching her Norse. He would have to take her someplace quiet for their lesson.

He smiled, thinking of exactly what words he would teach her first.

Fiona sighed and brushed a strand of hair away from her face. It was hot in the weaving room, and she had not had a respite since Mina had suggested that she and Breaca get some buttermilk from the dairy at midday.

Nearby, the Norsewomen talked quietly, but Fiona could not understand their words and their conversation did little to lift her boredom. She was alone with her thoughts—and troubling thoughts they were. She kept reviewing in her mind the events of the night before. At last, she had coupled with the Viking, and it had been as splendid as she had imagined. But guilt gnawed at her remembered pleasure. Dag was her enemy. Her mind knew that, even if her body would not accept the truth. How was she to endure living like this—torn between desire for her captor and resentment that he had such control over her life?

The drone of women's voices suddenly stopped. Fiona looked up and beheld Dag standing in the doorway of the weaving house. He seemed so big, his body blocking the light from outside. Fiona's throat went dry at the sight of him.

Dag spoke a few words to Mina. She raised her brows, then nodded, her face expressionless. Fiona's apprehension intensified.

Dag turned in her direction, and his blue-eyed gaze seemed to pierce her body with fire. He gestured for her to come with him.

Fiona breathlessly followed him out the door of the weaving house and past byres and storage buildings to the bathing hut. They entered the building by a different door than she and Breaca had used. Seeing the larger washing area, the many wooden tubs and benches, Fiona guessed this side of the shed was reserved for the jarl and his close kin.

Dag latched the door behind them, and Fiona felt a tremor of anticipation at once more being alone with this enigmatic, unpredictable man. What would he do to her this time?

Dag put more wood on the fire and pushed several large rocks against the hearth, then quickly undressed. Seeing his prodigious erection, Fiona shivered with sudden desire. So, that was what he intended.

He approached and gestured toward her clothes. Fiona took off her shoes and kirtle while Dag stared at her. He guided her to one of the benches. Cloths for drying off were piled on one end. Dag spread one across the wooden seat and sat down. He motioned for her to seat herself beside him.

She did so, her heart thrumming in her chest, all her senses acutely aware of the man inches away from her. The newly stoked fire behind them blazed into life, illuminating the room. Fiona could not help staring at Dag, perusing his bare flesh as he had hers. So dazzling he was, this fiery sun god. The glow of the flames turned his long wavy hair to molten bronze and cast his strong, well-made features into dramatic relief. She watched the light warm his skin and make his blue eyes glow hot and wild as if he were as fevered as when she had first beheld him.

Her breathing quickened. From the beginning, she had desired this man. It had not mattered that he was a Viking, her enemy. She had felt an intense craving to have him touch her. Awed by his fair coloring, his height as he towered over her, the strength and power implicit in his long limbs and sleek muscles, she had known instantly that this was a man among men. Deep down in her woman's soul, she recognized him as a male to mate with, to seek strength and protection from.

Dag reached out and touched one of her breasts. He said a word, then touched her other breast and repeated it. Fiona

looked down at his hand, surprised and a little disappointed to
realize that he meant to teach her his language rather than make
love. She spoke the word as well as she could. He nodded and
said it again. The second time she refined her pronunciation,
earning a warm smile from Dag.

Very deliberately, Fiona drew his hand to her breast and
gave him the Gaelic word. Dag's finger massaged her nipple
as he repeated it. Satisfaction swept through her, not merely
sexual, but pleasure that he was willing to learn her language
as she learned his.

Dag leaned down and touched her foot, giving her the Norse
word, then moved his hand upward to demonstrate the terms
for "ankle," "calf," and "knee." Fiona repeated them in a
breathless voice. Her body felt swollen and hungry, and she
could scarcely concentrate. She closed her eyes as he touched
her thigh and waited for him to move his hand to a more
satisfying position. When he did not, she opened her eyes
to see Dag regarding her with a teasing expression. Slowly,
deliberately, he put his hand on her wrist, apparently preparing
to begin his tantalizing upward route again.

Impatient, Fiona took his hand and brought his fingers to
her mouth. She said the Gaelic word for "mouth," then nibbled
on his fingers. Dag's eyes darkened with desire, and Fiona felt
a wave of gratification. Her Norse lessons would not last much
longer at this rate.

Abruptly, Dag stood and, taking her hand, brought it to his
erect shaft. Fiona inhaled sharply, barely remembering to repeat
the word for that part of him. His hand covered hers, urging
her to stroke him. Fiona gave a ragged sigh and complied.

She looked up and watched his eyes darken and his jaw go
rigid, then enjoyed the half-gasp, half-growl he made when she
rubbed her fingers lightly over the silky tip. She knew a taste
of the power he must have felt over her when he'd kissed her
intimate parts. He had made her helpless before his inflaming
and gratifying loveplay. Now he was near as defenseless.

Except, she did not know how to bring him to completion
as he had her. She was not certain she wanted to. Her own

body felt restless and wanting. Would he think her wanton if she let him know she did not want to wait to couple with him?

She released his shaft and stood to move her hand up to caress his chest and shoulders. Subtly, she moved closer to him so that her breast grazed his arm. He moaned, then grabbed her around the waist and kissed her—a deep, demanding kiss that made Fiona's knees go weak. As her stance faltered, his hands found her hips. He lifted her up and rubbed her aching groin against his. Fiona near exploded with the sensation of his hard flesh so near to her aching center.

When she was certain she could stand no more, he pulled them both backwards toward the bench and, sitting down, arranged her legs so she straddled him. With one swift, almost violent, movement, he lifted her hips and brought her body down upon his upthrust shaft.

Fiona screamed. For a second, she thought she could not bear it. Then she realized that the extreme pressure of his body inside hers felt wonderful. With her legs wrapped around Dag's strong body, his hard thighs supporting her bottom, she opened her eyes and looked up at her lover. His features were distorted, and she wondered if this position felt as intense for him as for her.

He took a harsh breath and lifted her hips, then brought them down. Fiona screamed again. The feeling of his shaft thrusting inside her made her almost mindless with pleasure. She clutched at Dag's shoulders, half-begging for mercy. He spoke harsh, emphatic words in his language, then rapidly repeated the motion.

Again. Again. Again. Again.

Fiona's thoughts shattered; her body burst into swirling flames. When she collected the pieces of her consciousness, she found herself lying on Dag's chest with both of them sprawled lengthwise on the bench. Beneath her cheek, her lover's heart thundered; his skin felt slick and hot. He groaned something in Norse, then reached up to smooth his hand down her back. Fiona felt tears creep from beneath her closed eyelids. The place this man took her to—surely it was paradise or heaven, the realm of the hereafter which they had caught a glimpse of.

"Fiona," Dag whispered. She opened her eyes and lifted her head. He smiled at her, a brilliant smile of satisfaction and warmth. Fiona felt something stir inside her, something beyond the languorous bliss which enveloped her body. She looked away from Dag's blinding grin and again lay her head against his chest. She had let this man meld his body with hers, dared to allow him to touch her heart.

His fairy queen—Dag sighed in satisfaction—he had possessed her, finally. She could not deny her helpless surrender in his arms. Her delicate body still trembled from the ecstasy he had given her. In the name of Freya, what sublime delight he had known himself!

He sighed again and caressed her hair, flowing over his chest like liquid silk. He wanted to kiss her, to seal the sweetness between them. She *was* enchantment and magic and endless beguilement, and he had drunk of it as if his soul were parched. Even if he woke up the next morning to find eons of time had sped by, it would not matter. At this moment, it seemed a fair trade—his soul for those moments of rapture when he'd burst into flames inside her.

He moved his hand to stroke her scalp, wishing she would raise her head again so he could gaze upon her exquisite features. He longed to look into the mesmerizing depths of her pale-green eyes and see his contentment reflected back at him.

When Fiona did not stir from his chest, Dag gently grasped her around the waist and helped her sit up. His fingers roamed over her arms, breasts, and belly possessively, assuring himself that she was his. There was so much he wanted to say to her— they had best resume their lessons if he were to learn the words before they both grew old!

He moved to a sitting position beside her and touched her lips, repeating the Irish word she had taught him. Next, he kissed her and spoke the word for "kiss." She repeated it, then gave him the Irish term.

He went on to naming objects in the room—bucket, cloth, bench, water, fire. Finally, when both of them were starting to grow confused, he left her and went to fill a large wooden tub with water. He put rocks from the fire in the bottom and waited for them to heat the water. When the bath was ready, he removed the rocks and helped Fiona into the tub. He helped her wash, then, after she had stepped out and begun to dry off, he climbed into the tub himself.

As he sluiced water over his chest and shoulders, he saw Fiona staring at him, her eyes appraising. He laughed and told her not to be greedy; there would be time for lovemaking later. Although she could not possibly understand *those* words, she apparently guessed his meaning for she blushed and looked away.

Dag laughed again. What a hot-blooded wench she was. Although surely sore and tired, she did not appear inclined to make him wait long to have her again.

After they had dried off and dressed, he unlatched the door and led the woman from the bathing hut. As they walked together back to the longhouse, Dag's mind whirled with the wonder of what he had experienced. Never had he known lovemaking so intense and satisfying. A part of him felt awed, another part apprehensive. Life had taught him that happiness and contentment were fragile things; it was dangerous to trust in them too much.

Chapter 17

The bakehouse was dimly lit and suffocatingly hot. With each breath, Fiona inhaled the moist, yeasty air and heard the monotonous sound of dough being pounded into loaves by the other women. She'd had a headache since she'd awakened this morning, and she suspected at least part of her ailment was caused by lack of sleep. Dag had made love to her much of the night. It had been explosive, intense, yet, for all the satisfaction that suffused her body, Dag's lovemaking had not banished the nagging doubts in her mind.

Fiona pushed the dough in front of her aside. She could not help feeling anxious and unsettled. Did Dag truly care for her or was his passion something that would wane as he grew used to her body? She shivered despite the heat. Was she a fool to trust her captor, to let him suborn her will with his magic caresses?

Someone spoke sharply to her in Norse. Fiona turned and tried to quench the resentment she knew showed on her face. Old Ymir, who supervised the bakehouse, gestured toward the neglected dough before Fiona, indicating that she should get busy. Fiona gritted her teeth and poked at the dough. It was not so much the work of a thrall she hated as always being inside. She longed for the scent of rain and growing things, the lulling green of the hills of Eire. There might be beauty in the Norse landscape, too, but she had not had a chance to experience it. She was constantly toiling in some dim, airless workhouse. Mayhap she should ask Dag if she could be a field slave instead. Surely it would be more interesting to milk cows or tend vegetables than this tedious work.

The sound of the other thralls kneading suddenly ceased. Fiona looked up and realized that Ymir had left the bakehouse. An odd sensation came over her, a wild, reckless feeling like a storm blowing in. She had a desperate need for freedom, to feel, at least for a time, like herself again. What would it hurt if she went outside for a moment?

She pushed aside the pile of dough and headed for the door. Outside, the breezeless air of the yard stank of manure and garbage rotting in the heat. Fiona wrinkled her nose and walked a few paces. She needed fresh air.

She moved beyond the byre, almost to the steading wall. With every step, her yearning grew greater, and with it, the awareness that she might be punished if anyone saw her. Her desire for a moment of brief freedom slowly changed into a desperate need to flee, and all at once she was running. She tore out of the steading yard and raced for the green refuge of the forest. Reaching the trees, she did not stop, but kept going.

The pathway took her to the beach. There she stopped and stared out at the shimmering gray waves, and relief finally found her. Her pounding heart slowed. She had come to this place by the sea, and by the sea she could leave again. She was not trapped here for all eternity.

She walked out on the rocky shoreline, examining the Viking ship grounded a few hundred paces from the water. It was a beautiful thing, the vessel Sigurd called the *Stormjomfru*. Exquisitely graceful, yet durable and strong. In this ship, men dared to take on the power and strength of the sea, to risk their lives travelling hundreds of leagues in a small, seemingly fragile vessel. It amazed Fiona to think that men could build such things, and then have the courage to use them.

The Vikings were brave, of that she had no doubt. As much

as she hated their blood lust and rapacity, she could not help admiring their boldness.

But she was bold, too, and proud. The Norse would not break her. If she had to endure this place for a dozen years, never would she waver in her intent. Someday she would return to Eire; someday she would be free again.

Fiona left off surveying the ship and took a seat nearby on a flat rock in the sun. Here the warmth did not seem smothering, but soothing. She closed her eyes and leaned her head back, feeling the sea breeze on her face like a caress.

The fishing had been good, but Dag was anxious to see Fiona. As soon as the men docked the dinghies in the cove down the coast, he left the others to load the catch in the cart and set out through the narrow band of forest which edged the fjord.

Everything seemed well when he arrived at the steading. Geese and chickens scratched in the dirt around the byres while the huge homefield sow wallowed in a cool dirt bed under a beechtree. There was no sign of the women or thralls, and Dag surmised that they must be busy in one of the workhouses. Fiona would be with them.

He sought out the dairy first, a cool, dark building made of stone where the women transformed buckets of fresh milk into curds, buttermilk, and butter. Seeing no sign of Fiona or Breaca, he went on to the bakery. The small building seemed unbearably hot, and he was relieved to find that Fiona had apparently not been forced to toil there. He was on his way to the sour-smelling brewhouse when Breaca came running toward him. Her eyes were wide with alarm, but she did not speak until she drew near.

"Dag." She spoke in a low, urgent voice. "I can't find Fiona!"

Fear clutched at Dag's insides. Had Brodir or some other man abducted her? Was she even now being raped in some shadowy glen in the forest? He fought for calm, reminding himself that Brodir had been along on the fishing trip and, until a short while ago, far from the steading.

"When did you last see her?"

"She was in the bakehouse," Breaca panted. "When I went there, the other thralls told me she had left. When Ymir asked about her, I lied and said that I had sent her to the brewery to get more yeast. But the truth is, Fiona has vanished."

"You don't think she ran away, do you?" As he asked the question, Dag shuddered inwardly. The punishment for a slave who sought to escape was always death.

"I don't think so. She seemed restless this morning, but I feel certain she understands how hopeless such an attempt would be. Still . . ." Breaca drew nearer and lowered her voice even more. "If she did run away, we must find her before anyone notices she is gone. I've told no one but you that she is missing."

The impact of Breaca's beseeching words jarred Dag. She was asking him to find Fiona and bring her back before her foolishness was known, to cover up an escape attempt. If he did such a thing, he would be in defiance of the laws of his people. Did he care enough for the woman to agree to do something so underhanded?

He considered a moment, then decided abruptly that he did. It was his fault that she was his captive; he was responsible for her.

"Where would she go?" he asked Breaca.

Breaca shook her head helplessly. "The forest . . . the hills . . . I know not."

"Keep looking here," Dag ordered. "I'll search the woods."

Dag's breath kept catching in his chest as he searched, even though he moved slowly enough that he caused himself no real exertion. It was his thoughts which made him gasp with dread. If Fiona were found and accused of fleeing, he would have to argue for her life again, and he likely would not succeed this time.

He swatted violently at an overhanging branch which blocked his pathway. Damn the reckless wench! Why could she not think before she acted?

As he circled back to the far edge of the home meadow, he heard the commotion. Raised, angry voices, a woman's scream—it could only mean one thing.

He raced toward the sound, vaulting easily over the low turf wall and dashing across the open area behind the longhouse. His worst fears were confirmed when he rounded the corner of building and saw the Irishwoman flailing in Balder's grasp, her long black hair unbound and wild around her face. Nearby, Sigurd stood with his hands on hips, regarding the woman coldly.

Dag forced himself to a walk and approached. "What's this? What's happened?" he called, struggling not to sound winded.

Sigurd turned. His blue eyes were harsh, forbidding. "Balder found the woman on the beach. He said she was near the ship, either planning sabotage or intending to hide there until she could escape."

In response to Sigurd's words, the woman shouted something and struggled furiously. Dag was near enough now to see the terror in her eyes, the blind, unreasoning panic. She thought she was going to die.

Dag tried to meet her gaze, to reassure her, but she looked beyond him, as if he were only another of her persecutors. "What does the woman say?" he asked Sigurd.

"She denies the accusation, of course. She said she only needed some fresh air, that the heat of the bakehouse made her sick."

"It seems like a probable explanation." Dag shrugged, seeking to lighten the tense atmosphere. "The woman knows it would be futile to run away. Why would she throw her life away in such an absurd fashion? She has no hope of using the ship to return to Ireland; if she wished to escape, or even hide, she would flee to the hills."

"Panic can make even clever minds useless. Look at the woman now, and tell me that she is not capable of witless behavior."

Reluctantly, Dag glanced at Fiona. She did look half mad. Her eyes were dilated, her fine features distorted. Silently, he cursed her for falling into such an obvious trap. But what would he do, he asked himself, if he faced a terrible death in a foreign land? Might not his composure fail him also?

"Tell me." Dag turned his gaze to Balder. "What was she doing when you found her?"

The barrel-chested warrior gave Fiona's slim arms a vicious squeeze, then answered. "It matters not what she was doing, only her obvious intent."

"Kill her!" Brodir's voice echoed with barely repressed satisfaction. "If naught else, we have reason to believe she cursed the ship. For that alone, she should die!"

"Of all the superstitious, stupid . . ." Dag broke off his angry words as his brother raised his hand for silence. He reminded himself that he must keep his head and make Sigurd his ally. Sigurd might mislike the woman, but he would not allow his feelings to cause him to pass judgment unfairly. "You cannot kill the woman for giving the appearance of trying to escape," Dag reminded his brother. "What law did she break by going to the beach and *looking* at the ship?"

"She cursed it, you fool!"

"Silence!" Sigurd cut short Brodir's outburst with a savage glance. "My brother has asked a reasonable question, and will consider it as such." He turned his penetrating gaze to Balder. "Tell us, Balder, what was the woman doing when you found her?"

Some men would have lied—Brodir certainly would have— but Balder was a loyal oathman and he would not bend the truth he gave his leader. "She was sitting on a rock, looking at the ship. When she saw me, she jumped up and began to run."

"Which direction did she flee?" Sigurd asked.

"The path toward the longhouse. When I caught up with her, she tried to scratch my eyes out." Balder took his sword hand off the woman long enough to gesture toward the bloody gouges on his cheek, and Fiona immediately jerked away from his grasp. Dag reached out and grabbed her, capturing her thrashing form in his arms. She struggled for a time, then quieted. Dag held her in an iron-like grip, determined that she would not slip away again.

"It seems to me that if the woman's intent had been escape, she would not have run *toward* the longhouse," he argued to Sigurd. "More likely she was afraid Balder meant to molest her."

"Once again, your brother defends the little Irish witch." Brodir moved close to Dag, his eyes narrowed in hatred. "It makes me wonder what the woman did to him when they were down in that hole together. I think she has bewitched your brother, Sigurd. If you want him as he was, you'd best kill her before her venomous beauty poisons the rest of his mind."

Dag met his brother's gaze, wondering if Sigurd believed a little of Brodir's accusations.

Sigurd regarded him intently, his eyes dark with displeasure. " 'Tis obvious that my brother wishes the woman's life preserved," he said grimly. "Because there is no clear proof of her disobedience, I will grant his request. But from this moment on, I make him completely responsible for her behavior. If she breaks Norse law, he will suffer as well as her."

"I will go to Knorri!" Brodir howled in outrage, turning to head toward the longhouse. "If you will not punish her, I will see that the jarl does!"

"Nei, you will not." Sigurd's commanding voice stopped Brodir in his tracks. "The incident took place on the beach, near the ship which is under my authority. You will not trouble the jarl with this matter. You will accept my decree."

Brodir stared at Sigurd, then his shoulders sagged with resignation. Dag watched with relief. Despite his hatred, Brodir was obviously not fool enough to defy the man who led him into battle, who guided the ship he sailed on. Then Dag turned toward his brother, and the grinding dread in his belly returned. Sigurd wore an expression which made it clear what he felt about the Irishwoman and Dag's defense of her.

Dag tightened his grip on the woman in his arms. He could not keep doing this, defending Fiona against the wrath of his sword brothers. Somehow he must teach her meekness. Somehow he must impress upon her the futility of defiant behavior.

At Sigurd's abrupt gesture, the crowd of men dispersed. Dag led Fiona toward the longhouse. Breaca met them and gave

Dag a puzzled, worried look. He motioned with his head toward his bedcloset, and the slave girl indicated she would be there soon.

Inside his sleeping chamber, waiting for Breaca, Dag released Fiona and heaved a sigh of aggravation. He had seen the Irishwoman's life spared, but what foolishness would she think up for the morrow? As soon as Breaca arrived, he would have her warn Fiona that she must be an obedient thrall from now on or he would beat her himself.

The woman appear to have collected herself. She no longer trembled, and her eyes held sense once again. Dag was not certain he trusted a rational Fiona any more than a crazed one. He remained blocking the doorway.

There was a faint knock. Breaca entered and rushed to Fiona, examining her for injury. "What did they do to her?" she asked Dag breathlessly. "Did Balder try to rape her?"

"Nei," Dag answered, his voice cold. "She left the steading and went down to the beach. Balder found her there and nearly convinced everyone that she was trying to escape. Her dim-witted behavior nearly cost her her life."

The woman responded to his words with an angry retort. Aggravated that she could not wait for Breaca to translate his explanation, Dag reached out and grabbed Fiona's arm. He shook her lightly, punctuating his next words. "Because of her stupidity, I am to be held accountable for her future actions. Her disobedience will be counted as my disobedience; her punishment will be mine!"

Breaca's eyes widened, then she turned to Fiona and spoke rapidly. The Irishwoman's gaze jerked to meet his. For a moment, there was amazement in her expression, then it gradually froze to anger. She spoke vehemently, then turned her back to him.

Dag looked to Breaca. She hesitated, obviously reluctant to give him Fiona's words. "She says . . . she says she did not ask for your help." Breaca swallowed. "She says you were a fool to save her life."

Fury washed through Dag, blotting out all fear, sympathy, and concern. "Leave us!" He ground out the words to Breaca, not looking at her. She took a sharp breath and scuttled from the room.

He advanced toward Fiona, his hands itching to finish what Balder had begun. When he grabbed her arms and turned her around to face him, fire leapt into her eyes. She jerked away and moved backwards until she could retreat no further, then squared her shoulders and raised her chin. On some level he was aware of how beautiful she appeared in her defiance, how awe-inspiring. No *valkerie* had ever faced an enemy with more spirit and courage. She was a goddess.

He reached out and grabbed a handful of her gown, pulling her toward him. Her chin lifted higher; her eyes seemed to flash green sparks. He sought to tear the gown down the front. She yanked it from his grasp, protesting. Before he could lay hands on her again, she lifted the skirt of the garment and began to pull it over her head. He watched, spellbound, as her naked body was revealed. She pulled the garment free of her tousled hair and flung it aside. Her breasts heaved—with exertion, with excitement, he knew not what, only that he was utterly bedazzled by the sight of her.

Dag felt himself lose control, felt the heavy, intoxicating desire flooding his veins. His anger vanished. He moved toward the bed, half-dragging her onto it. When she lay beneath him, he tore down his trews and mounted her. She moaned softly, but did not struggle. He cried out, overcome with the lush warmth surrounding his flesh, thrusting fiercely inside her. She keened her pleasure with a harsh, animal-like cry. He thrust again, harder, knowing he could make her scream, knowing anyone hearing them in the longhouse would think the cause pain, not passion.

How rough he was! This was what she had expected the first time—not the gentle expertise he had shown her. He was a beast now, a wild, lust-filled beast. But Fiona did not care. It did not hurt; nay, it felt wonderful. To feel his power, his strength, his maleness impaling her body to the edge of her womb. She shuddered and gave in to him, reveling in the tremors that wracked her arms and legs and pulled him deeper inside her. Clutching his shoulders, she reached for the heights, climbing to the very precipice. The maelstrom whirled inside her, inflaming her every sense. She arched her back and cried out. . . .

Spiraling down from her climax, she heard Dag's exultant shout. Some fierce emotion swept over her, a raging, helpless tenderness. *This man had saved her life—again.* The thought astounded her, utterly undid her. She reached to stroke Dag's sweaty skin, murmuring Gaelic love words.

Too late, she realized what she was doing. Her fingers stilled on his cheek, and she looked up into his lust-dilated eyes. Her slowing heartbeat began to race again. Did he guess how close she had come to telling him she loved him?

As he moved off of her, she looked away, embarrassed and disturbed. She did not want to be under this man's power. She had sought to stand up to him, to make him hate her. In the end she had failed.

Dag shifted to lie on his back and pulled her to nestle against him. Again, Fiona felt the lump in her throat, the onslaught of emotion. Why could she not hate this man? He was her enemy. Why must he try to disprove that fact? He insisted on coming to her defense, saving her life. It made her want to weep. She had no shield against his kindness.

Dag must have sensed her turmoil, for he moved his hand to fondle her breast. Fiona felt an answering throb inside her. With a sigh, she gave in to the slow, lazy waves of pleasure lapping at her resolve.

Chapter 18

"Kylling." Breaca pointed to brown-feathered fowl pecking in the dirt.

Dutifully, Fiona repeated the word. Her mind whirled with strange sounds; she wondered how she would ever remember them.

"Ull." Breaca gestured to the bales of raw wool stacked against the wall of the weaving house, Fiona nodded and said the word, then took a seat on a stool to begin spinning. "You must continue with my lessons as we work," she told Breaca. "I would speak at least a few Norse words to Dag this night."

Breaca reviewed the words she had already given to Fiona. Fiona repeated them impatiently, desperate for a grasp upon this elusive tool which might give her access to Dag's thoughts. The lesson was abruptly interrupted by a loud shriek. Young Gunnar came tearing in, his brother Ingolf in hot pursuit. Mina rose wearily and said something in her quiet voice.

Ingolf exploded with a torrent of angry, tearful words. Fiona guessed that his older brother had done something to him and Ingolf had retaliated. Now, Gunnar was out for vengeance.

Gunnar began to shout as well. Mina took a sharp breath,

as if in pain. She looked as if she might faint. Fiona hurried toward her while Breaca shooed the quarreling boys outside.

Fiona helped Mina to the stool, frowning. It was bad enough that Mina had to work so hard, worse yet that her sons were constantly coming to her to settle their disputes. Why could not Sigurd look after the boys for a time if no women could be spared for the task?

Fiona picked up the spindle she had dropped and resumed her seat on the stool. Breaca came back in, still carrying her spindle. Fiona looked at the simple implement, and a sudden thought came to her. Why must the spinning always be done in the weaving house? The spindles were portable, as was the wool. Why couldn't the tedious work be done outside where it was more pleasant?

She pondered the thought, trying to decide how to suggest the idea to Mina. The sound of the boys arguing again gave her the perfect plan. ''Breaca,'' she called softly in Gaelic. ''Why can't we take our spinning outside while we look after Gunnar and Ingolf? We could take them to the orchard and give Mina a respite from their squabbling.

Breaca seemed startled by the idea, but then she nodded and explained the plan to Mina.

Mina assented easily, and Fiona and Breaca gathered up their spindles, distaffs, and wool. The boys raced ahead to the orchard. Breaca followed quickly after them. Fiona took her time as she walked through the sweet-smelling hayfield that bordered the orchard, savoring the warm nostalgia that washed through her. On hot days like this one, Duvessa and she had often found refuge under the boughs of her father's apple trees, spicy rich with fruit ripening in the sunshine. It seemed so long ago. She had been such a child then, no more heedful of the dangers of the world than young Gunnar and Ingolf. How swiftly her life had changed. She had acquired the wisdom of a woman and been made a thrall in one bleak, dark night.

She looked back toward the steading, and a shadow of fear crossed her mind. What if Brodir or the other men accused her of trying to escape again? Nay, surely they would not. Why would she take Sigurd's sons if she meant to flee?

She turned again toward the orchard and willed the rare sense of peace to return.

The boys took turns seeing who could climb each tree the fastest, then made a contest of gathering apples. Finally, exhausted by their competition, they joined the women in the shade and began to munch the tart, still-green fruits. Fiona had Breaca warn them not to eat too much, lest they get a stomachache. They ignored her, and Fiona resigned herself to having to brew some chamomile that night to soothe their bellies.

Not yet satisfied, the boys thought of another game—seeing who could eat apples the fastest. Fiona shook her head at their foolishness and went back to her spinning and repeating the words Breaca taught her.

She was concentrating so intently, she did not realize what had happened until Ingolf grabbed her arm. "Gunnar," he said, his voice high with panic. Fiona turned to see Sigurd's eldest son in the throes of choking. He clutched his throat and tried to cry out, but could not. His face was purple.

Fiona dropped her spinning and leapt up to pound the child on the back. She guessed immediately that a piece of apple had blocked off his breathing passage.

"Run," she told Breaca. "Get Dag, Sigurd, any of the men."

Breaca did not hesitate, but set off at a wild pace. Fiona bent the boy forward and tried to pick him up by his legs. As she feared, she was not strong enough to hold him upside down and pound his back at the same time. She looked desperately toward the steading, hoping Breaca could find someone quickly.

Moments passed as Fiona futilely pounded the child's back. Gunnar went limp. Ingolf sobbed great gulping sobs. Fiona felt like crying herself. She dropped to the ground, then maneuvered the boy's body so it rested over her knees. Again, she struck him brutally on the back. Once . . . twice . . . with a popping sound, the piece of apple flew from his throat.

Fiona took a deep breath of relief, then went rigid as she examined the boy. His face remained bluish and still. *He did not breathe!* Fiona's panic increased. Too late had she jarred the apple loose! Too late! She ran her fingers over the small, perfect, child's face and felt tears flow down her cheeks. Then something took hold of her, a fierce determination

"Nay," she whispered. "You will breathe. You *will!*" She shook the boy, then again thumped him on the back.

She knew not if it were the third or fourth or tenth time she struck him when she was rewarded with a faint gasp. She turned the boy over. His pale-gold lashes fluttered. "Breathe," she whispered. "Breathe." She held her own breath as his narrow chest began to expand and contract with a normal rhythm.

Slowly, the warm flush of life creeped back into his face. Fiona began to weep. It could be her own child she held in her arms, so grateful she was. Her foster brother Dermot might be dead; but this child lived!

When the men came, she was cradling Sigurd's dazed son in her arms, weeping helplessly.

"She tried to kill the child! Anyone with eyes in their head can see that she did something to Gunnar!"

The jarl, seated in his ceremonial chair in the cool of the longhouse, grunted at Brodir's words and turned to Sigurd. "What say you, nephew? 'Tis your son we speak of."

Sigurd shook his massive head. Dag thought his brother still looked ashen. "Ingolf says the Irishwoman saved his brother's life," Sigurd answered. "He said that Gunnar was not breathing and Fio—the woman helped him."

"A boy of five winters!" Brodir's voice rose with outrage. "How can you credit the word of child? The witch might have confused his wits or threatened him if he did not lie to protect her."

"My son does not lie." Sigurd's voice was soft, but all seated at the jarl's table guessed the threat behind his words.

"My apologies, sword brother." Brodir lowered his eyes to the table although Dag saw a muscle twitch in the ugly warrior's jaw. "I did not mean to disparage the boy's honor. But surely his explanation lacks sense. If Gunnar were dead, how could she bring him back to life? I smell witchcraft here. How do we know she did not curse the boy to make him stop breathing for a time?''

''Breaca said that the boy choked on a piece of apple. There is no witchcraft in that. I've seen grown men felled by a lump of gristle in their craw.'' Dag sought to sound as reasonable as possible. He did not fear that his brother would rule against the woman; *nei,* Sigurd was too relieved to have his son alive to question the means by which it was accomplished. But Brodir's constant mention of witchcraft concerned Dag. His fellow warriors were a superstitious lot, and the Irishwoman was so unusual-looking, so fierce and strange in her manner. It did not take much imagination to ascribe supernatural powers to someone like her. Had not even he, in his delirium, thought her a fairy?

''I do not like it,'' the jarl pronounced bluntly. ''Since she has been in our midst, the foreign wench has caused two serious disturbances.'' Knorri raised a gnarled hand to ward off Sigurd's protest. ''Though she may have saved the life of a child of my own blood, that does not dissolve my distrust of her. I must think of the good of the steading.'' He turned to Dag. ''Can't you control the woman? In my day, women thralls did not roam the orchard like lazy geese. We kept them busy in the workhouses or naked and compliant in bed.'' He fixed Dag with a commanding look. ''Beat her, shackle her ankles, deprive her of clothing—do *something* to keep the wench out of trouble.''

''*Ja,* uncle.'' Dag nodded dutifully, but in his heart he knew he wanted to do none of those things.

''What about her evil powers?'' Brodir demanded. ''If she were merely an unruly thrall, that would easily be remedied by thrashing. But we speak of a foreigner, and one who obviously knows sorcery. I say she is a *volva,* and a dangerous one at that. As long as she lives, all our lives are at risk. Your wife—'' Brodir faced Sigurd accusingly. ''—has given the Irishwoman access to her herbs. How do we know the witch will not slip something into the ale and poison all of us?''

Knorri sighed and wiped a withered hand across his brow. ''I tire of this conversation. 'Twas Sigurd's son she treated; let him be the judge of the woman's intent." The jarl closed his eyes for a moment, then opened them and ordered peevishly "Have one of the *hushjelps* bring me a horn of ale, a cold one this time!"

Rorig, seated at the end of the table, rushed to do the jarl's bidding. The young warrior had been the first man to reach Fiona and the boys in the orchard, but no one had asked him for his report and he had not volunteered it. Dag suspected he was still amazed by what he had seen. It had been an odd sight—the small, dark woman rocking the sturdy Norse boy in her arms while the other child clung to her, weeping even as she did. Who would not be touched by such a sight?

Brodir, he thought grimly. He had turned the woman's rescue of the child into an accusation of witchcraft. Calling her a *volva* was certain to unsettle most of the men. *Volvas* were soothsayers, and not so much honored by the Norse as feared. Dag wondered if Brodir really believed his own words or had merely seized upon this clever plan to destroy Fiona.

Sigurd rose from the table. The slowness with which he moved revealed to Dag how drained his brother was. "I will not condemn the woman who saved my son's life," Sigurd announced. "There is no clear proof of her treachery. I would have the whole matter dropped." He paused. "If that is satisfactory with you, Jarl, of course."

Knorri weakly gestured his assent. Dag thought the old man well on his way to falling asleep and that someone should help him to his bed. Sigurd apparently shared his thoughts, for he called out sharply to the blank-faced thrall who brought the ale. "Wench, come and aid the jarl. The warm ale you served him before has given him a bellyache. Help him to bed! Now!"

Fortunately, the thrall was as stoutly built as she was obedient and she had little trouble supporting the jarl as he moved sluggishly to his bedcloset.

The men drifted away from the table after the jarl departed. Sigurd joined his wife and children in their bedcloset; Brodir left the longhouse with Balder and Kalf, still muttering angrily. Dag went to the hearth and stared at the glowing embers of the fire that burned there summer and winter, day and night.

"Do you think the Irishwoman knows magic?" Rorig's tentative voice interrupted Dag's musings.

"Nei, not the kind Brodir speaks of." Dag turned to regard the younger man. "She is quick-witted and resourceful, and I suspect she has trained with another wise woman, but that is all."

Rorig exhaled his breath slowly. " 'Tis a relief. Breaca is so much in her company, and I should not like to bed a woman who is a *volva's* assistant."

"Breaca?" Dag raised a brow.

Rorig grinned sheepishly. "I had not noticed before we left on the Irish raid, but the thrall *is* comely."

"You've bedded her?"

Rorig's smile vanished. *"Nei,* she is always busy, like a little bee buzzing around the longhouse, one that never lights long in one place. I trow she does not even know I exist."

Dag considered his companion's confession. What words of advice did he have for a fellow warrior smitten with a foreign thrall's charms? His relationship with Fiona was rife with misunderstanding and tension. He could hardly pretend to give sound counsel. "I could speak to Breaca," he offered. "I cannot yet converse well with Fiona, but Breaca and I are quite comfortable with each other."

Rorig flushed. "What would you say—that I would like to lie with her?"

Dag grimaced at the other man's obtuseness. *"Nei,* I would tell her that the color of her hair reminds you of the sunset. That you have never seen such beautiful tablet weaving as she does." Poor Rorig, Dag thought. Even *he* knew enough of wooing to realize a man must ply a woman with compliments about her looks and womanly skills before he attempted bedding her.

"You promise to speak for me?"

Dag nodded, touched by the yearning in the other man's voice. Had he ever been so blindly lovesick over a woman? *Ja,* his mind answered, *when you met Kira, you were just like Rorig.* "I will aid you, but you will owe me a boon because of it."

Rorig nodded. "When will you speak to Breaca? I trow I am so hungry for her, I cannot sleep at night."

"Loki help you! Don't be so impatient. I will speak to her this night, but you cannot expect her to offer herself to you on the morrow. These things take time. Women like to think they have chosen you, and they do not always make up their minds quickly!"

Rorig sighed and walked off, obviously mooning over his beloved. Dag turned back to the fire, sifting his own words in his mind. In his disillusionment over Kira, he had hardened his heart against all women, and it seemed to him now that he had been overly harsh with Fiona. Her treachery toward her father still worried him, but less these days. He had seen enough of her consideration for others to know she was not heartless. Surely she must have had some good reason for what she did. Someday he would ask her.

In the meantime, he found himself caring more and more for her. Even the catastrophes she involved him in had not sapped his passion but, instead, had sharpened his admiration. She was proud, courageous, clever. Who would not admire such attributes? His own people, Dag reminded himself grimly. They feared her spirit and willfulness; they sought to crush it. To them she was a thrall, to be subdued and used. To him, she would always be a princess.

He shook off his melancholy mood as Breaca approached the hearth carrying a large platter of fresh loaves. "Breaca," he called. "Put your burden down and come speak with me."

Quickly, the slave girl obeyed. "What is it?" she whispered as she neared him. "What have they decided to do to Fiona?"

"Nothing, for now at least."

Breaca looked toward his bedcloset. "Why don't you go to her and tell her what the jarl has decided?"

Dag shook his head. "I have not the words—remember? You must tell me a few things to say, in Gaelic."

Breaca nodded. "Of course. What words do you wish to learn?"

Dag furrowed his brow as he repeated the phrases Breaca gave him. When he had learned them to Breaca's satisfaction,

he slave girl went to pick up her load of bread. Dag stopped
ier. "There is another thing. You know the young warrior
Rorig? I would have you tell me what you think of him. Later,
after I have reassured Fiona."

Breaca looked surprised, but nodded as she left.

Fiona waited quietly in Dag's bedcloset while the jarl decided
ier fate. She knew no fear. Indeed, she was so filled with
exultation, she could not worry that they might decide to execute
ier. The child lived; that was what mattered. That she had been
able to save Gunnar at least partly made up for her failure to
protect Dermot and the other boys.

She looked down at her hands, no longer fair and smooth
but roughened by the days of work she had endured on the
ship and in the steading workhouses. Siobhan had been right
when she'd promised Fiona had the healing gift. And it was a
gift, too, the gift of life. Someday she would use these hands
to bring babes in the world, to soothe the brows of those who
passed on to the next one.

If she lived. She glanced toward the bedcloset door, wondering when word would come. Rorig had scarce handed Gunnar
to Sigurd before Brodir had begun his ugly accusations. She
had not needed to know the Norse words to tell that he had
accused her of hurting the child. It was unfair, vicious, but
what could she expect from one such as Brodir?

At least Sigurd had not believed the ugly warrior. After Mina
came to get Gunnar, Sigurd had squatted down and questioned
Ingolf himself, listening intently to his childish voice. When
Sigurd had looked at Fiona, there had been gratitude in his
expression. He might never say a word of the matter, but she
knew he acknowledged that he owed her a debt.

She stood, finally growing restless. She had not heard men's
voices raised in anger for some time. Surely they had decided
her fate by now. Had Sigurd and Dag prevailed, or Brodir? For
the second time in a sennight, she faced death.

The door to the bedcloset opened. Fiona went still, expecting
Breaca to come rushing in with the men's verdict. Instead,

Dag's tall form loomed on the threshold. He looked so somber Fiona decided the worst had come to pass. She swallowed fighting tears. How could she say goodbye to this man? They had had so little time to understand one another, to make the long journey from enemy to friend. Somewhere in between they had met as lovers. It was not enough; her spirit yearned for more.

Dag stepped into the chamber, and Fiona sought to memorize his graceful features, the way his hair shone gold-red even in the dim light. She would remember him thus.

"Thank you," he said in Gaelic. Fiona stared at him. The words were so unexpected, she did not know what to think. He must be thanking her for saving his nephew's life.

He reached out and lifted a strand of her hair, smoothing it between his fingers. "Fiona," he said. His deep voice caressed the word.

His eyes were smoky-blue, intent, but they spoke nothing of death or punishment. Fiona realized she'd been again reprieved from the Vikings' wrath. Once more, she owed Dag her gratitude for saving her life.

"Fiona," he said again. He moved close and bent his mouth to hers. After the kiss, he again spoke haltingly in Gaelic. "They do not understand." He motioned toward the main room of the longhouse. His gaze was helpless, but expressive with meaning.

Fiona closed her eyes, struggling with tears once more.

"Storm Maiden," he whispered in Gaelic, calling her by the name of his brother's ship. "You fight for what you believe in—my fierce, lovely storm maiden."

For once, Fiona did not fight the tenderness Dag aroused in her. She wrapped her arms around his broad chest, clinging to him. It did not matter that she did not yet speak his language. There were no words for this, for this moment.

Chapter 19

Dag slipped out of his bedcloset into the early morning gloom of the longhouse. The place was quiet, save for the jarl's oathmen snoring on benches around the hall. But he was not the first one up; Mina leaned over the hearth, poking the fire into life again.

He crossed to where she stood. "Mina, can that not wait? Surely it is too early to begin cooking."

"I could not sleep." She turned, and Dag saw the shadows under her eyes, the pinched look of her features. "I did not want to wake Sigurd."

"Don't be a fool, woman—that man can sleep through fierce sea squalls! Take yourself back to bed."

Mina shook her head. *"Nei,* the boys will wake soon." She reached unconsciously to rub her lower back, and Dag watched a spasm of pain cross her face.

" 'Tis the babe, isn't it? All is not well."

"I don't know what is wrong. I've never felt so uncomfortable this early on."

"You should speak of it with Fiona."

"She examined me some days ago."

"What did she say?"

Mina sighed. "Nothing helpful, only that I should rest more—as if I could sleep when I feel as if a band of trolls does battle inside me. I do not mean to criticize her," Mina added quickly. " 'Tis clear that there is nothing she can do."

"I could wake her, and she could feed Gunnar and Ingolf their morning porridge."

"*Nei,* let her sleep. Since you keep her up most of the night with loveplay, I trow she needs her rest."

"I do no such thing!"

A twinge of a smile curled Mina's lips. "Explain then those screams and moans which come from your bedcloset."

Dag allowed himself to return Mina's half-smile. Fiona was an exuberant and *noisy* bedpartner.

" 'Tis no harm done," Mina added. "Because of her outcrys, half the warriors are convinced you beat her nightly. They are pleased you show her discipline."

"Brodir?"

Mina shook her head. "Nothing but rivers of blood would satisfy that one."

Dag sighed. "He will not cease in his efforts to have Fiona put to death. Knorri has always said a woman should not come between sword brothers; but if I had to choose between Fiona and Brodir, I would not hesitate."

"She is kindhearted," Mina said. Her voice trembled with emotion. "I owe her much."

"I am pleased she has won your concern."

Mina straightened and returned to the fire. "If you wish to help, find Breaca for me. She was not in the thralls' dwelling, and I fear she spent the night with one of the men. Please make certain she has not been hurt."

Dag smiled again as he left the longhouse. *Nei,* Rorig was not like to hurt Breaca—lest you called the rending of her maidenhead an injury!

He easily located Breaca, curled up with Rorig in a corner of one of the byres—a favorite trysting place during the summer. Breaca hastily grabbed for her clothes, but Rorig merely sat up, fully naked, and regarded Dag with lazy contentment. "Do you not have enough to handle in your own bed that you must interrupt the pleasure of others?''

Dag snorted. Ignorant pup! How soon he forgot the one who had aided him! '' 'Tis not you I seek out, but the girl. Mina is not well this morning. Breaca must see to her.''

The slave girl jerked her kirtle over her head, gave Rorig a solemn, unfathomable look, then left the byre without a word.

"You owe me a boon, sword brother," Dag told Rorig.

"*Ja,* I do." Rorig's voice was rich with satisfaction.

"I am amazed that affection took root so quickly between you."

Rorig's smug look turned to puzzlement. "In truth, so am I. I spoke a few words to her in the longhouse last night. A moment later, she followed me outside. What did you say to her, Dag?"

"I told her that you found her fair to look upon. Then she asked me what kind of man you were—whether you were a valiant warrior, if you had won much booty in the Irish raid.''

"Your answers must have pleased her."

"Indeed." Dag regarded the younger man searchingly. "A woman who values a man only for his wealth and battle skill is not one worth having."

"I care not why she agreed to share my bed, only that she was willing and eager."

"Someday, mayhap you *will* care. I warn you, sword brother, I have known women like that, and they are not worth the pleasure they give you."

Rorig smiled. "You worry overmuch."

The younger man began to dress. Dag hesitated, wondering if he should press his point. Nay, Rorig was obviously too young to realize he did not know everything about women yet.

Dag left the byre and walked across the bare, hard-packed yard, thinking of Fiona, sleeping in his bedcloset. He knew she did not value him for his prowess with a battle axe or the plundered riches which filled his sea chest. But what did she feel for him? Was it gratitude that he spared her life and continued to defend her? Hunger for his body and his skill in bed?

He wanted more from her. He wanted her to care for him,

to prize his spirit as well as his body. To take pleasure in the sight of him, in the words he spoke. In short, he wanted her to feel for him as he did for her. How had it come to this—that the Irishwoman had grown so important to him?

It was not a thing a man admitted to anyone. Some warriors, like Sigurd, dared to show fondness for their children in front of all. But to admit love for a woman, and a foreign, captive one—it was unthinkable. And every day she meant more to him. Every time he lay with her, her hold upon him intensified.

Dag frowned. Because of her, the world he had grown up in had begun to seem oppressive, its laws rigid and unfair. To his people, Fiona would always be a foreigner, an outcast. Even if he freed her and made her his wife, there would be those, like Brodir, who would never accept her. They would wait for a chance to destroy her. Even if she ceased her defiant, independent behavior—which Dag's instincts told him was impossible—even then, she would eventually break some Norse law by accident and face punishment.

Frustration rose inside him. He had not asked to care for this woman. He had fought his feelings as fiercely as he could, but the battle was for naught. The woman had captured him. She made him see things through her eyes, suborned his loyalty to his kin and sword brothers, confused his sense of who he was. Worst of all, a nagging voice warned him that there might come a day when he would have to choose between his people and her.

Dag shook off the tormenting thought. He would go mad if he did not stop thinking about the woman. He needed to find some backbreaking labor that would numb his mind and chase away his worries.

Seeing Ranveig, the shipwright, cross the yard with a chopping axe over his shoulder, Dag called out, "Ho, Ranveig. Remember that tall pine you saw in the west forest—the one you thought might make a good mast? Let's go look at it again."

* * *

"What next?" Fiona asked, reaching up to wipe her sweaty face. "The butter is churned, the bread made, the ale brewing—what else does Mina wish us to do?"

"She suggested we might go berrying."

Fiona regarded Breaca with amazement. "Berrying? Truly?"

A smug smile curled Breaca's lips. "That is what she said. There is a patch of ripe whortleberries up the hillside and some blueberries at the edge of the meadow beyond."

Fiona swiped again at her brow. "You mean she does not want us to wear out our fingers spinning or go blind weaving? That she gives us leave to walk out in the sunshine, to feel the cool mountain breeze upon our faces?"

"Berrying can be arduous. There are brambles and thorns to avoid, and your fair skin will get baked in the sun."

"You jest!" Fiona accused.

"Aye," Breaca answered, her smile broadening. "I look forward to the freedom and fresh air as much you do."

Fiona wrinkled her brow. "You're certain this is Mina's order, that it is not some trap of Brodir's? I don't want to be accused of trying to escape again."

"Of course, it is Mina's order. I think she wishes us to enjoy a pleasant afternoon."

"What of her? Does she promise to leave off working and rest herself?"

"Aye. Sigurd has the boys with him, and she said she would try to sleep."

Fiona smoothed her soiled kirtle. "I would fetch a head wrap first; I don't want to sunburn my face."

"And baskets," Breaca reminded her. "We must at least pretend to work."

Fiona giggled and raced Breaca to the longhouse to gather the things they would need.

As they left the forest and climbed up the hillside, Fiona leaned her head back and sighed as the sunlight warmed her face. " 'Tis a beautiful day. 'Twas kind of Mina to suggest we go berrying. I have not done it much since I was a child."

"She's fond of you."

Fiona looked to her companion. "Because of Gunnar?"

Breaca nodded. "Although she cannot openly show her gratitude to a slave, I know she feels beholden."

A twinge of irritation threatened to ruin Fiona's tranquil mood. *A slave.* No matter what she did, she would always be less than human to the Norse.

"Even Sigurd admits he owes you. He loves his firstborn deeply; if Gunnar had died, Sigurd would have been devastated."

Fiona nodded, wondering how far Sigurd's gratitude extended. Would he take her side the next time Brodir threatened her?

"You have done well, Fiona." Breaca paused on the pathway to remove a stone from her shoe. "I would not have thought it possible a fortnight ago when you first came to Engvakkirsted, but you have managed to earn the goodwill of the most powerful men of the steading."

Fiona, pausing beside her companion, poked at the dirt with her shoe. She was not certain the idea of winning the Norsemen's goodwill reassured her. Were they not still her enemies? Should she not be fighting them rather than earning their favor? A part of her felt guilt at Breaca's words.

"Sigurd owes you a boon, and Dag—why the man is clearly besotted with you. I would not be surprised if he decided to give you your freedom and make you his wife."

Breaca's words jarred Fiona even more. "My freedom I might well wish for," she answered. "But not marriage to a Norseman—I would never agree to that."

"But Dag is kind to you; he cares for you. And you—'tis clear you hold him in affection."

Fiona opened her mouth to protest, then realized she could not. It was all true. Dag treated her well, and she did care for him. Fiona swallowed. How had it happened? How had she fallen in love with her enemy?

"I would be grateful if you could tell me how you won his favor." Breaca cleared her throat. "I'm certain much of your appeal for him is your beauty, but there must be other things.

Are you bold with him in your loving? Do you merely agree to do as he wishes or do you offer to pleasure him before he asks?''

Fiona regarded the woman beside her. ''Why do you ask?''

Breaca flushed. '' 'Tis not something any other woman will share with me. The other thralls have not had the opportunity to know loveplay with a warrior. 'Tis different from rape. More subtle . . . more complicated . . .''

''Jesu! Breaca, what are you asking? What have you done?''

Breaca's fair skin flushed vividly.

''Who is he?'' Fiona demanded. ''Did some Viking ravish you?''

''Nay, I was willing.''

''Who?''

Breaca's auburn-lashed eyelids drooped demurely. ''Rorig,'' she answered.

For a moment, Fiona could not think how to respond. Rorig *was* handsome, and Dag spent enough time in his company to suggest the young man might be honorable and kind. But Breaca was so young, so vulnerable. ''What you do is dangerous,'' Fiona pointed out in a shaken voice. ''He could use you and throw you aside, and no one would protest or think anything wrong in it.''

''But he won't,'' Breaca insisted. ''Not if you tell me how to please him. You have won Dag's heart—'tis unfair of you to refuse to share your secrets!''

''My secrets?''

''Aye. All know you have bewitched Dag. How did you do it? Is it mere skill in bed or did you use some potion to weaken his wits and make him love you?''

''Blessed Saint Bridget!'' Fiona cursed. '' 'Tis not like that! I never wanted Dag to care for me, at least not more than was necessary to win his protection. What happened between us is not based on magic or spells! It is just . . . *there*.''

''Rorig said I was comely. Do you think he begins to care for me?''

''Mayhap, mayhap. I don't know!'' Fiona took a deep breath, trying to think what to say to Breaca. Why was the girl obsessed with making Rorig fall in love her? Did she truly desire the man or did she follow what she saw as Fiona's example in gaining the protection of a warrior? She rounded on the young woman. "Do you care for Rorig? Not because he is a good warrior, but because you take pleasure in his company."

Breaca shrugged. "He is pleasing to look upon, and he won treasure in the last raid. Most of all, I decided to bed him because he sought me out. I thought it would be easier to win the favor of a man who already seemed to desire me."

"But what of your feelings? Do you *care* for Rorig?"

"I don't know." Breaca sighed. "If I thought about what I *felt*, I would have perished long ago. Life is harsh. I do what is necessary to survive. I do not *think* about it."

Once again, Fiona was struck by the grimness of a thrall's lot. Would that be hers in a few years? Would she lose her sense of honor, of herself, of her dreams? Would she live from day to day, doing whatever was necessary to endure?

"Will you help me?" Breaca's voice was pleading. "If nothing else, Dag is friends with Rorig. You could find out from him whether Rorig craves me."

Briefly, Fiona considered discussing the matter with Dag. If Rorig did care for Breaca and she sought him merely as a protector . . . Fiona shook her head. This was witless. Why should she care what happened to Rorig? Let Breaca break his heart.

"Men like you to touch them," she told Breaca. "To caress their private parts, to put your mouth on them."

Breaca's eyes widened.

"If the man is clean, 'tis not unpleasant," Fiona added. "Take him to the bathing shed. It makes a good place for a midday tryst."

Breaca's startled look faded, and she nodded calculatingly. A stab of guilt went through Fiona. Had she ever plotted to win Dag's favor by pleasuring his body? Nay, she had always *wanted* to do it. From the first time she had beheld the man, she could not resist touching him. As she had told Breaca, things between her and Dag had never been planned. They had merely *happened*.

But where could her passion for the Viking lead her? She had vowed to return to Eire, and her feelings for Dag only complicated her plan. Even if he cared enough for her to free her as his thrall, he would seek to bind her to him with marriage. And there was the matter of children. As often as they lay together, his seed would surely take hold in her womb. What would she do then? She could scarcely travel to Eire with a child, nor could she bear to leave behind a babe of her body. She might end up trapped at Engvakkirsted forever.

Fiona sighed. She should never have lain with Dag. It was that irrevocable act which had bound her to the Norseman. "Your plan is faulty," she told Breaca as they neared the first stand of berry bushes, lush with gleaming purple fruits. "When you entice a Viking man, you risk becoming entrapped yourself. 'Tis better to endure hardship and retain the freedom of your will."

Breaca's blue eyes met Fiona's with a look of incredulity, and she shook her head. "Fiona of the Deasúnachta—you are ever a fool."

Chapter 20

"We will eat bread this winter even if it is a long one," Breaca said as she loaded another sheaf of rye in the cart at the edge of the field. Seeing Fiona's weary look, she added, "Here the snow piles higher and stays on the ground much longer than in Eire. Steadings that do not have adequate provisions have been known to starve.

"If bringing in the grain harvest is so important, why don't all the men work in the fields?" Fiona cast a hostile glance toward the nearby grove of trees where Brodir and several of the other men lounged on the ground, drinking ale and doing nothing more strenuous than polishing weapons and exchanging stories.

"Many warriors think it demeaning to work in the fields; they believe such tasks should be done only by slaves and women."

"Why does Sigurd allow such laziness?"

"'Tis not Sigurd who condones it, but the jarl," Breaca answered. "He is a man of old ideas. To his mind, being a warrior is enough. He would like the men to go *aviking* and capture more slaves to do the work. But he could not convince Sigurd to take the *Storm Maiden* out again this season."

"Why not?"

Breaca shrugged. "Sigurd said the ship needed some repairs to the hull. In truth, I think he is loathe to leave Mina."

Fiona nodded. Mina's situation had not improved. All feared that she would not make it the last two months until the babe was due to be born.

"If Brodir and the other warriors refuse to do their share of the work, Dag more than makes up for them," Breaca commented. "He toils from morn to eve, doing the work of two men at least. I trow, if I were the jarl's nephew, I would find ways to shirk the more difficult jobs. Dag seeks them out. Chopping firewood, cutting grain, replacing the rushes in the longhouse—he seems to favor the most backbreaking, miserable sort of labor."

Fiona shaded her eyes to look out at the stubble-filled field, easily picking out Dag's tall figure from among the crew of thralls who worked their way across the field, harvesting the last of the rye with huge, curved scythes. She, too, had marked the way Dag drove himself. There was something desperate in it, something restless and frustrated. He was clearly troubled, although Fiona was not certain as to the source of his discontent. She had learned enough of his language to communicate simple things, but they still did not talk much. For all that she surrendered each night to the evocative language of his lovemaking, she had little idea of what went on in his mind. Did he fear the future as she did?

Sighing, Fiona looked down and examined her work-roughened hands. She understood some of Dag's need to work. It made the time go faster and kept her from thinking about how trapped she was, how far from fulfilling her vow.

"How late in the year is it possible to sail?" she asked Breaca.

" 'Til a month after butchering. Then the seas become stormy and treacherous." She gave Fiona a probing look. "I told you that Sigurd would not take the ship out again this season."

Fiona sighed. Summer hastened by; in two months it would be Samhain, what the priests called All Hallows' Eve. A wave of homesickness passed through her. In the Old Ways, that night was considered the end of the year, when the spirits walked the earth and the barrier between the spirit world and the physical world grew weak. Most Celtic-speaking people counted it among the major festivals of the year.

"When you lived in Eire, did your people celebrate Samhain?" she asked Breaca.

Breaca frowned. "I remember them building bonfires to ward away the spirits."

Fiona nodded. "When I was little, my mother always dressed my brothers and me in costumes so the spirits would not recognize us and steal our souls."

"You had brothers?" Breaca asked. "What happened to them?"

"My two older brothers both died of a fever when I was five winters."

"Your father must have been sorely grieved to lose his heirs."

"Aye, he was . . . but not enough to take a concubine. Although my mother could bear no children after me, my father still kept to her bed. He loved her dearly." Pain lanced through Fiona.

"How else did you celebrate Samhain?" Breaca asked.

"We also built bonfires high in the hills. Late at night, the more daring youths would sneak out of the palisade to dance and make revelry in the firelight."

"Did you go?"

"Never. My father would not let us. Last year, Duvessa and I tried to join the celebration. My father caught us leaving the women's house and had an older woman keep watch over us for the rest of the night. We vowed that next year we would go if we had to hide in the forest the day before." Fiona sighed, thinking of how rebellious and irresponsible she had been.

"The Vikings do not really have an autumn festival," Breaca said. "Some steadings hold a sacrifice to Thor or Odin, but Knorri does not believe in it. He thinks the only way to honor the gods is through valor in battle.

"There will be a special feast, though, when the butchering is done. The men will gorge themselves on fresh meat and the skald, Tyrker, will arouse their blood lust with tales of battle and heroes. Then they start planning raids. It begins harmlessly—a few cattle or horses stolen, a byre or shed burned. But inevitably someone is killed or a woman raped. Then, the injured clan swears vengeance and what was once a cattle raid turns to murder and destruction.''

Fiona nodded. The tradition of raiding, of blood feuds and vengeance, sounded uncomfortably familiar. The Irish practiced a similiar sort of warfare. The priests and holy men tried to teach tolerance and reason, but when Irish tempers ran hot, innocent blood was still shed for the sake of warriors' glory. It was an unpleasant similarity between the Irish and Norse way of life, Fiona thought grimly.

The two women looked up as Dag approached them, carrying his scythe. Perspiration streamed down his bare chest and his face was flushed with exertion. Mina had cut Dag's hair recently, and it hung in reddish-gold waves to his shoulders. His coppery mustache had also been neatly trimmed, and his fair skin was glazed ruddy tan by the sun and wind, sharply defining the muscles of his shoulders, chest, and arms.

Fiona watched him carefully place the the long curved tool on top of the full cart, then wipe his hand over his sweat-soaked features. He looked at her and smiled, his teeth white against his bronzed skin. The sight of him made Fiona's heart do a familiar flip-flop. As hard as she fought to keep her emotions aloof from the passion he aroused in her body, she was less than successful. Looking at him now, glorying in his masculine beauty, she wondered how she would ever leave him to return to Eire.

"I trow I smell like a stallion under harness," Dag said. "I must visit the bathing hut before I enter Mina's newly cleaned longhouse. Would you like to join me, Fiona?" His smile widened.

Fiona hesitated, guessing that bathing was only part of his plan. She both dreaded and reveled in their lovemaking. With each tender kiss and enticing caress, her resolve to leave him crumbled a little further. Did he plot to imprison her with love, to use affection to trap her in his northern homeland forever?

"Fiona?"

She looked at Dag and, unwillingly, returned his smile. "*Ja*," she answered, using the Norse words. "I will come."

Before they bathed, Dag took her to the steam room, which Fiona had only discovered a few weeks before. In the small enclosed area, big enough for only two people to stand or sit, Dag poured water on the hot rocks and the soothing steam wafted over them. Fiona sat back on the bench and sighed. The heat and moisture relaxed her sore muscles while the vapory atmosphere reminded her of the mists of Eire.

Sitting beside her, Dag leaned back and closed his eyes, apparently content to do nothing for a time. Fiona closed her own eyes and let her mind wander to thoughts of her homeland. What was Siobhan doing? she wondered. And Duvessa and the other women? Did they still live? Had they fled Dunsheauna and made their home in another settlement? Had there been anything left to salvage after the fires died?

Fiona frowned. In time, other chieftains would surely claim her father's land and anything left of value. If it took too long for her to return to Eire, there would be nothing left. Dunsheauna, her surviving kin, even her father's name might disappear and be forgotten.

She felt Dag's hand rubbing her shoulder, then his fingers moved to her nape as he eased the sore muscles there. Fiona sighed. She did not want to relax and be content.

"Fiona." Dag spoke her name in his deep, heavily accented voice. "What are you thinking?"

She opened her eyes to meet his gaze. The hunger she felt for him made her want to melt into his arms. Instead, she said, "I was thinking of my homeland, of Eire."

His blue eyes grew bleak, and Fiona immediately felt guilty. Anger followed swiftly on regret. She could not help that it hurt him to speak of her homeland. Her vow to her father had to come before her feelings for him—didn't it?

Ja, Dag thought grimly. It was well that she reminded him that they both had responsibilities to others. So easily when he was with her he forgot that she was a foreign slave, forgot everything except how beautiful she was, how desirable.

He looked away; his fingers stilled on her neck. Bringing her to the bathing shed had been a mistake. They might join their bodies in splendid ecstasy, but it did nothing to resolve their problems.

He stood. Beside him, he heard her slight intake of breath. He glanced down at her. She looked troubled, mayhap even disappointed. She had expected him to couple with her; she *wanted* him to couple with her. Dag struggled for control. His body ached for hers as well, but this time he could not give in to his need.

He left the sauna area and went out into the main bathing room and sluiced cold water over his face and body. Wiping water from his eyes, he glanced over his shoulder. She had not followed him or tried to entice him into lovemaking. Resignation settled hard in his gut. She knew as well as he that the differences between them were too great, too irresolvable.

There was a sharp rattling at the door. "Dag, Fiona, come quickly. 'Tis Mina . . . the babe . . . it comes!"

Breaca sounded breathless from running. Dag moved toward the sauna, but Fiona had already heard and come out into the bathing room. She gave him a worried look and began fumbling for her clothes. Dag grabbed his own garments. Fiona finished dressing first and dashed from the bathing hut. He caught up with her and asked, "Do you know what to do?"

"I hope so."

Dag's stomach twisted at Fiona's words. If something happened to the babe or Mina, would Brodir use the tragedy to turn the others against Fiona?

When they reached the longhouse, Fiona stopped to catch her breath. Dag gave her arm a gentle squeeze, then watched her go into Mina and Sigurd's bedcloset. Sigurd stood by the doorway, his face stony and expressionless.

Dag found it hard to meet his brother's eyes. Women often died in childbirth or during miscarriage. What would he say if Sigurd lost his wife?

* * *

Gazing at the pale, exhausted-looking woman in the bed, Fiona's mind raced. It was too soon for the babe to be born. If possible, she must halt Mina's labor.

"Fetch Mina's herbs," she told Breaca. When she had left, Fiona approached the bed. "Has your water broken?" she asked.

Mina shook her head. "*Nei,* but the pains come often."

Fiona could read the fear in the Norsewoman's eyes. She pulled down the bedrobes and quickly examined her. Her heart sank. Labor was well along. As intense as Mina's contractions were, the birth sack could break at any moment. The babe meant to be born this day.

To Ingeborg, the smith's wife, standing beside the bed, Fiona said, "Bring me some goose fat." Ingeborg nodded and went to do Fiona's bidding. Breaca hurried in with the herbs; Fiona shook her head, indicating that it was too late to use them. Then she sat by the bed and waited.

Mina labored silently. Fiona watched her, wondering if the Norsewoman knew how little hope there was. Ingeborg returned. She stood by the bed and spoke in a soft, reassuring voice and wiped at Mina's sweaty face.

A smothered cry from Mina brought Fiona instantly to her feet. She swept back the bedrobes and helped Ingeborg prop Mina up so she could push.

It was an easy delivery, the babe being so small. Holding the wet, fragile infant, Fiona tried every trick she had seen Siobhan use. She rubbed the babe's body with goose grease, breathed into its mouth, even slapped it gently. Nothing worked; the tiny body remained still and lifeless.

Fiona handed the little corpse to Breaca, then turned to Mina, prepared to give her the tragic news. The Norsewoman's face was flushed and distorted, and Fiona quickly realized that she strained to give birth again. In moments, Mina gave another hard push and a second small infant slid into Fiona's hands. This babe took a feeble breath and went limp. Fiona massaged it frantically, struggling to make it breath again. Tears seeped into her eyes when she realized the little spark of life was permanently quenched.

Fiona forced the tears away and returned to her duties. After wrapping the dead infant in rags and placing it on the storage chest with the other, she went to aid Mina as she strained to deliver the afterbirth. When the afterbirth came, Fiona placed the bloody mass on a rag and carefully examined it. She breathed a sigh of relief when she found it intact; if a part of it remained inside the woman, further bleeding was likely, endangering the woman's life.

She disposed of the afterbirth while Ingeborg and Breaca cleaned the bed and made Mina comfortable. When Breaca offered to get Sigurd, Fiona shook her head. "I want to speak to Mina alone before Sigurd comes." Breaca moved to go; Fiona stopped her. "Nay, you must stay. I may need you to translate." Ingeborg also remained in the room. Fiona had grown used to the smith's wife's calm, capable presence, and she did not think it would hurt for the Norsewoman to hear her words to Mina.

Fiona sat beside the bed and spoke in Norse. "You will recover, Mina, but it would be unwise for you to get with child again too soon." When Mina gave her a puzzled look, Fiona grew insecure with her command of the Norse language and had Breaca repeat her words. Mina still looked puzzled. Frustrated, Fiona said, "If Sigurd will not leave you alone, you must take something to prevent conception."

Breaca repeated the words in Norse. Mina's eyes grew wide. "She wants to know how that is done," Breaca reported.

Fiona hesitated. Siobhan always said that preventing unwanted babes was as important a skill as birthing those which were heartily desired. Still, Fiona knew the priests frowned on the practice, as did most men. Was it wise to share her knowledge of such things with this foreign woman? One look at Mina's wan face decided her.

"There are several detections you can take to prevent conception," she told Mina. "You drink them every day until your bleeding time comes. They work by preventing a man's seed from taking root in your womb."

Breaca translated. Mina gazed at Fiona and shook her head. "She would not do such a thing," Breaca said. "Sigurd would not like it."

Fiona gritted her teeth, wondering if Sigurd would like it better if his wife died in childbirth because she had conceived too soon. If he were as arrogant and stupid about having sons as most men were, he probably did not care. He likely assumed he could get another wife anyway.

She shrugged. "Tell Mina that it is only a suggestion. If she does not feel comfortable with the idea, then she should forget it. But I mean to talk to Sigurd myself, to be certain that he understands the risk."

Breaca bent over the bed to convey Fiona's message, and Fiona left the room. She barely had a chance to take a deep breath of the fresher air in the main room before Sigurd grabbed her arm. "How is she?" he asked in Norse.

Fiona turned toward him. "There were two boy babes; they were both born too small and weak to live." Sigurd nodded, his face expressionless. Fiona guessed that Mina had warned him of the likely outcome.

"And Mina?" he asked.

"Things went well for your wife. She should recover." Fiona looked up at Sigurd, searching his massive contenance. For a moment, she thought she saw relief in his deep-set eyes, then his features resumed their formidable outlook. "The important thing is that her body not be burdened with another babe too soon," Fiona continued, switching to the more comfortable Gaelic. "Her womb must heal or there is a serious risk she will miscarry again." She fixed Sigurd with a stern look. "With successive miscarriages, her body will grow less able to carry a child to term. There is risk to her life as well. If you must rut like an animal, whenever you will, find another partner for a time."

Anger flared in Sigurd's face. "Mayhap my wife will be jealous if I stray from her bed."

"Better jealous than dead," Fiona said coldly. She had half-expected Sigurd to act this way, mocking and defiant. No wonder Siobhan held men in such low regard. It was despicable

that a man considered his own pleasure more important than
his wife's health. Would Dag refrain from bedding her if he
knew pregnancy might harm her?

As if her thoughts had called him, Dag suddenly loomed
between her and Sigurd. "Fiona," he said. "You look very
tired. Let me get you something to drink."

Fiona smiled weakly at him, thinking of his concern for her,
his kindness. Nay, she did not think Dag would chance starting
a babe in her body if it put her life at risk.

She let Dag lead her to the hearth and sat down wearily. She
had been tired when they finished bundling up the grain; now
she was half-dead with fatigue. She sat by the fire, drinking
the ale Dag had brought her and half-dozing.

Dag watched Fiona, frowning. She had not been able to
save the babe, but Mina was well. Recalling the conversation
between Fiona and his brother, Dag's frown deepened. They
had spoken in Gaelic, so he could not tell what was said, only
that Fiona had been angry. Had Sigurd lashed out at her for
the loss of his offspring? He would have to confront Sigurd
and find out what had passed between them.

For now, he was reluctant to leave Fiona's side. This day
had reminded him how fragile life was, how precious. 'Twas
a wonder any boy survived to manhood, or girl to womanhood.
Life began so perilously, so mysteriously. He glanced at Fiona
again, imagining her pregnant, her narrow belly swelling with
his child. It was a foolish, witless thought, but he could not
resist it.

He reached out and smoothed a strand of hair away from
her face. If she still wanted him, he would make love with her
tonight. He would not worry about the future, but content
himself with the warmth of her flesh, the silk of her skin, the
glow in her unfathomable eyes.

He leaned over and whispered in her ear. "*Macushla,*" he
said. She turned and stared at him. He met her gaze knowingly.
Breaca had taught him the word for 'darling' in Gaelic, and
he had been waiting for the right moment to use it.

Despite the lack of privacy in the longhouse, he leaned over
and kissed Fiona. "*Macushla,*" he said again.

She smiled faintly. "I'm tired, Dag."

"I know. Sleep." He motioned toward his bedcloset. "I'll join you later."

When Fiona had left, Dag rose and went outside. He took a deep breath of the evening air, filled with the sweet scent of fresh hay. The harvest was almost in, and the days grew shorter. Autumn would be upon them soon, and the whole long snow-season after that. Mayhap during the endless dark hours in the longhouse, his people might finally come to accept Fiona.

A low sigh next to him interrupted his thoughts. Sigurd had come out of the longhouse and also stood looking out over the harvested fields around the steading.

"You've seen Mina?" Dag asked. "She is well?"

Sigurd nodded. "Weak, but recovering."

"Thank the gods," Dag murmured. "I always fear for women in childbed, especially since our own mother died that way." He turned to his brother. "I am sorry for the babe, Sigurd. Fiona told me she feared it would be born too soon.

"There were two babes, both male."

Dag drew a sharp breath. What could he say to Sigurd, knowing that his sorrow must be doubled?

"Mina said that is likely the reason they came too soon," Sigurd said. "Women are not meant to birth twins. 'Tis unnatural."

"I'm sorry, brother."

Sigurd shrugged. "There will be other babes. Although Fiona did warn me that I should not lie with Mina too soon lest she conceive before her womb is healed."

Dag looked at his brother searchingly. " 'Tis good advice."

Sigurd nodded. "Although I did not much like the manner in which she gave it to me, suggesting I had as little control over my actions as a rutting beast." He gave a snort of disgust. "The Irishwoman is so arrogant at times. She forgets that she is a slave."

Dag's insides tightened. Fiona seemed incapable of learning the meekness necessary for her situation. How was he to protect her?

"It might surprise the Irishwoman to know that I've practiced restraint before," Sigurd continued irritably. "I did not take Mina's maidenhead until after we were wed, and our courtship was one of several months." There was a look of challenge in Sigurd's eyes as Dag met his gaze. "It seems to me that the Irishwoman should look to her own situation before she chastises me. If anyone ruts like animals in this longhouse, it is the two of you."

"She is my bed thrall," Dag protested. "From the beginning, on the ship, you encouraged me to seek my pleasure with her."

"I wished you to subjugate her, not fall in love with her," Sigurd growled. "There is a difference."

"What has turned you against her this time?" Dag complained. "Do you hold her responsible for Mina's loss? You admitted that the babes were born too soon to live."

"*Nei*, I do not blame her. Nor have I forgotten that I owe her for Gunnar's life. I merely seek to warn you, as your brother and your future jarl, that I see what the woman does to you and I do not like it!"

Dag faced his brother angrily. "Why must you meddle in something that does not concern you? I have never told you how to manage things between you and Mina."

"Mina is Norse and behaves as a proper wife should. Fiona is a slave. Her independence and lack of meekness is shameful.

"I find no shame in it!"

"*Ja*, that is the trouble." Sigurd's voice grew thoughtful. "I wonder more and more if she has not already corrupted your sense of Norse ways."

"That is absurd!"

"Is it?" Sigurd's mouth quirked bitterly. "Can you swear that you would put the interests of the steading before your concern for the woman?"

Dag opened his mouth to swear before Odin and the other gods, then stopped. Had he not once told Mina that if he had to choose between Brodir and Fiona, he would not hesitate?

"She unmans you, brother," Sigurd said. "I sensed it the first time I beheld you together on the ship. I should have drowned her then and saved us both this trouble."

Sigurd walked off into the twilight. Dag remained, staring

after his brother. Was it true? Had the Irishwoman stolen his Norse soul? He had once thought her a fairy, a supernatural being. Had there been some wisdom in his instinctive fear of her?

He turned, gazing toward the longhouse. Never in the few weeks since Fiona had learn to speak his tongue had he dared to ask her about the first time she had appeared to him in his damp, dark prison. His memory of the incident was blurry, fever-glazed. It was time he knew the truth.

Chapter 21

Fiona tossed and turned restlessly in the box bed. Why did Dag not come? He had said he would. His eyes had promised hours of passion, and at this moment, her spirit craved passion, craved the fierce senselessness that filled her when Dag made love to her. His strong, powerful body reminded her of life, of potency and triumph. She needed something to take her mind from the two small bundles wrapped in rags. That was death and sadness and failure; she needed the warmth and vigor of Dag to replenish her spirit.

For a time she had dozed, but her dreams were unsettling, suffused with images of blood and fire. Her soul seemed filled with death. The two stillborn infants added intolerably to her burden of grief. If all died, she thought despairingly, what was the point of life?

She closed her eyes, wishing she could weep and let the blessed pain wash over her and cleanse her thoughts. Grieving purged her doubts and left her spirit bright with anger and determination. But the tears would not come. She felt empty inside, empty and cold. Oh, where was Dag?

She must have slept again. When she woke, Dag was beside

the bed, calling her name. She sat up abruptly, aware of the serious timbre to his voice. What had happened?

"Mina?" she asked anxiously. "Has she need of me?"

"All is well with Mina," Dag said. "But there is something else—something I must ask you."

Fiona's skin prickled. Dag and she seldom talked more than to share simple information about their days or to exchange endearments; that he woke her to have a conversation sounded ominous.

Dag sat on the side of the box bed, his voice low and thoughtful. "When I was a prisoner, you came to me. I do not understand why. I was your enemy. Why did you try to seduce me?"

Fiona swallowed. She had dreaded this moment. There was no honorable answer to give him, no answer which did not reveal her shame.

He softened his voice. "I am grateful that you did, else neither of us would be here now. But I cannot help wondering why."

Fiona sighed. She might as well speak the words. Mayhap then, things between them would be finished. If he rejected her, it might be for the best. She could get on with her plan to return to Eire.

Her voice rang out clear and strong, revealing nothing of her regret—she would not let him see her humiliation. "I wanted you to couple with me, to take my maidenhead. That way my father could not wed me to a lewd, old chieftain I despised."

Dag was silent for a time. Fiona waited impatiently. If he meant to condemn her, let him do it now, before she fell even more irretrievably in love with him.

"That does not really explain your actions," he said. "When it became obvious that I was too wounded to be capable of what you wished, you could have pursued another plan to thwart your father. Instead, you came back. You tended my arm; you bathed me . . ."

Fiona sucked in her breath. "You were aware? You remember?"

Dag nodded. "I pretended to swoon because I did not understand what you wanted . . . and I feared you."

She felt a deep blush creep up her face. What must he think of her—that she had handled him with such a lack of inhibition?

"I have to know." Dag's voice was harsh, agonized. "Why did you save my life?"

Fiona let herself be swept back in time to those fateful hours in the souterrain with the beguiling Viking prisoner. What had she felt, before the threat of a raid became real . . . when she was just an innocent, curious maiden alone with an enticing, and helpless, man?

"At first, I pitied you. 'Twas no more than anyone kindhearted might feel for a wounded creature. You were a living thing in pain, and a magnificent one at that." She smiled faintly, remembering. "I knew it was witless, that I should be terrified of you. But when you looked at me . . . your suffering pulled at my heart. I suppose I was stubborn as well. Until I left you the last time, I maintained some hope that you would recover and take my maidenhead."

Dag shook his head. "Was there no other way to avoid the marriage? Could you not reason with your father? If you despised the man . . ."

"It seems simple now, but it was not then." Fiona sighed. "My father would not give me his reasons for wedding me to Sivney, and I assumed the worst. I never knew until too late that he hoped to gain warriors to fight off Viking raiders . . ."

Her voice broke. Dag fought the urge to reach out and comfort her. *Nei*, he had to think on what she had told him first. It shocked him that she admitted defying her father so audaciously. In his experience, honorable woman did not rebel against their sire's wishes. But he had never known a woman like Fiona before. She was as bold as a man sometimes, as courageous, too. Was not her fearlessness which he admired?

He rose to leave the bedcloset. "Go back to sleep," he said. She made a sound, half-sigh, half-sob. Pity pulled at his heart, but he did not waver. He would not go to her until he had decided.

He moved past the benches full of snoring warriors and into the half-darkness of the late summer night. The scent of newly cut hay drifted on the breeze, melding with the ever-present reminder of the sea. He breathed deeply, trying to clear his head. At this moment, he wished he were on the *Storm Maiden.* There was nothing like sailing under a clear, star-studded sky— no passion that compared with the dangerous freedom of going *aviking.*

Nei, that was not true. The Irishwoman made his veins throb with a fever as fierce as the thrill of riding a well-made ship over the waves. For her, he was willing to do almost anything. *Even return with her to Ireland.*

The idea had come to him a few days before when he was talking with Ranveig. The old shipwright loved to tell about journeys he had made, places he had seen before his swollen joints had made cold, damp days on a ship pure *hel.* He had mentioned raids made on the northern shores of Albion, the land of the Picts. They had gone back several years, stripping the land of all its portable treasure. Then, finally, a ship of Norsemen had settled there. There was good land they said, and pretty, foreign women.

Ranveig had nodded approvingly, remembering his sea companions' foresight. Most men had to give up *aviking* someday, he said, if they wanted to settle down and breed sons. The wise ones found a choice bit of land in an area exhausted by raids and made their home there.

That was when the image had first come to Dag—he and Fiona presiding over a feasthall built upon one of those strange rounded hills of Ireland. Sometimes it seemed preposterous, an addlepated fancy from one of his fever dreams. Other times, it captivated his thoughts, making his mind whirl with ideas of how to make it come about. He had discussed the matter with no one; he had not dared. He needed Fiona's knowledge of her homeland to have any hope of succeeding, and he did not know if he could trust her yet.

That was the decision he had to make. Could he risk depending on her to aid him? By all rights he was her enemy, but it had never felt that way. From the first time he had seen her, he had been drawn to her. Tonight she had admitted that she knew something of the same. Their spirits, Norse and Irish, seemed bound together more tightly than the affinity they felt toward their own kin. Dag wondered—could ties of the spirit be stronger than those of blood?

"Who goes there?"

Dag jumped as a voice jarred him from his thoughts. " 'Tis I, Dag."

"Thor's balls, but you scared me," Rorig complained, rising up from the shadow of the turf wall. "I had half dozed off when I heard your footfalls.

"What are you doing out here so late?"

Rorig sighed. "Word came yesterday that the Agirssons are raiding. Sigurd believes we should keep watch at night."

Dag felt a twinge of guilt. He had been so preoccupied with his dilemma over the Irishwoman, he had scarce paid attention to anything else. Raids were an ever-present danger to a prosperous steading. Sigurd was wise to set a watch, although a dozing guard was scarcely better than none.

"You should take your responsibility more seriously," Dag chided. "We could have all been burned in our beds before you noticed anything amiss."

"You think the danger is real?"

" 'Tis hard to say. Sigurd reminded me recently that we are distantly related to the Thorvalds. That might be enough to set the Agirsson clan against us."

"Tiresome feuds." Rorig sighed. " 'Twere not for the Agrissons' foolishness, I would be snuggled in a haystack with Breaca."

"It goes well between you?"

"*Ja.* Better than I'd hoped. The little thrall is ... ummm ... more inventive than I'd imagined."

"Have you thought of asking the jarl if you might purchase her for a wife?"

"Why would I do that? I am well pleased with things between us as they are."

"What if she gets with child?"

"I would claim the babe, of course."

"What if the jarl decides to sell her? If you don't own her you have no say in what happens to her."

"Knorri would not do that."

"Knorri will not be jarl forever," Dag reminded the younger man. "If you care for Breaca, you should do something to secure your future with her."

"Mayhap I am not certain if I care for her that much. There is a whole wide world of women out there. I might fancy to sample a dark one next time, or one with a rounder bottom and bigger breasts."

" 'Tis your decision, Rorig. I only suggest these things because I know what it is like to have a woman I cared for decide that she would fare better with another man.

"Breaca would not choose another man over me!"

"She might—if he offered to buy her."

"Has she told Fiona that?" Rorig demanded.

"*Nei*, not Fiona. 'Twas to me Breaca suggested it. She is keen to be under some warrior's protection. If you do not offer her that . . ." Dag let his voice trail off meaningfully.

"Trolls' ears! How could she? What other man at Engvakkirsted is as fine to look upon as me?"

"I do not think your attractiveness is at question, but rather your willingness to secure her future. Women set great store by the comforts and protection a man can give them."

Rorig swore some more and kicked viciously at the turf wall complaining bitterly of fickle, greedy women. Dag walked off pleased that he had at least given the young warrior cause to stay awake this night. A sleeping guard was worthless, after all.

The night air was wet with dew as Dag returned to the longhouse. He had been awake half the night, weighing his decision. His conversation with Rorig had decided him. If a man waited until he was completely sure of a woman, he might wait forever. There came a time when he must reach out and seize his dreams with both hands. If they crumbled to dust in his fingers, he would still die knowing that he had chosen the courageous path.

He crept into the longhouse on tiptoe, fearing to wake the

other warriors and alarm the household. Quiet filled his bedcloset; Fiona must have slept at last.

He crawled into the box bed and drew the furs over himself.
"Dag?" Fiona's sleepy voice whispered through the darkness
and wrapped around his heart.

"*Ja*," he answered.

She said nothing more, but moved close to lay her head on
his chest. Her silky hair blanketed him like the warm, soothing
waters of a dark river.

"Dag!"

Dag sat up abruptly at the sound of his brother's voice.
Instinctively, he reached for a weapon, sensing warning in
Sigurd's tone.

"*Ja*, brother, what is it?" He rose and moved to the doorway,
keeping his voice low so as not to wake Fiona.

"The jarl would speak with you."

Dag dressed hastily, wondering what had happened. From
the sounds in the longhouse, he guessed it to be late morning.
He should not have slept so long.

When Dag left his bedcloset, he saw the jarl sitting in his
carved chair at the front of the longhouse, surrounded by his
oathmen. Dag approached them slowly, his heartbeat quickening. From the serious expression on the men's faces, he
feared something ominous. Had there been an attempted raid
or other threat to the steading?

He took his place next to Sigurd. The jarl turned toward him
and said, "I am banishing the Irishwoman from the longhouse."

When his shock had worn off, Dag looked at his brother
accusingly. "Are you blaming her for Mina's loss? All knew
the babes came too soon—ask any woman in the steading!"

"*Nei*." Sigurd's voice was cold. "I do not blame her for
what cannot be helped. Indeed, I have argued for mercy for
your thrall." He nodded toward Brodir. "There are those who
would have her put to death or sold outside the steading. I
argued that the matter could be settled by keeping her away
from the freewomen."

"Why? What has happened?"

Veland, the brawny smithy, spoke. "Your thrall suggested to Mina that she take some potion to keep a babe from starting in her womb too soon."

Dag was hardly surprised by Veland's words—it sounded exactly like the sort of thing Fiona would do. But he was a little awed by Fiona's knowledge of such things. Glancing around at the other men, he realized that they, too, were astonished, and fearful. Brodir's accusation of witchcraft had already tainted Fiona; this latest situation lended substance to the charge.

"I'm certain Fiona meant only to aid Mina," Dag said, hoping to win at least Sigurd to his side. "She fears that conceiving too soon might endanger Mina's life."

The jarl shook his head. " 'Tis appalling magic—a potion that kills a man's seed. I fear what Brodir says is true. The woman is a *volva,* a sorceress."

" 'Twould be disastrous if a woman could control what man she conceived with," Utgard agreed. "When a man lay with a woman, how could he know that her body was not full of poison meant to kill his offspring?"

"I don't see why this is grounds to banish Fiona from the longhouse," Dag insisted. "She was only trying to protect Mina."

Velund thumped his meaty fist on the table. "We don't want our womenfolk exposed to such subversive, evil practices. If my wife had not convinced me that the Irishwoman had other useful skills, I would argue for her death myself!"

Sigurd spoke in a controlled, quiet voice, "The jarl has made his decision. He expects you to remove the woman from the longhouse as soon as she rises. From now on, she will sleep in the slaves' dwelling and fulfill the duties of a field thrall. She will be allowed to use her healing abilities on members of the steading, but only under close supervision. And she is not to have contact with Mina or any of the other freewoman unless the woman's husband is present."

Dag sighed with resignation. Poor Fiona. Now she was not only a thrall, but a field thrall. He thought of her satiny skin

urned dark and coarse by the sun and wind, her regal posture
wisted to the weary stoop of a field hand, her delicate fingers
gnarled and roughened by constant toil. He had to protect her
from such hardship, to keep his countrymen from ruining her
beauty as Brodir had smashed her enameled gold girdle when
they were on the ship.

He looked up and met Brodir's gaze. The crude Norseman
had said naught during the discussion of Fiona's future, but
the satisfaction on his face was evident. He meant to destroy
Fiona; he would not rest until she was dead.

Dag rose quickly, intending to rouse Fiona and hasten her
from the longhouse before she could see the hatred and fear
in his sword brothers' eyes. He had to shield her from their
misguided loathing.

"Dag." Sigurd stood and motioned his brother away from
the group of men. "I would have told you the news myself,
but I was busy convincing the jarl that the Irishwoman intended
no harm. 'Twas not easy arguing that she be spared. In doing
so, I have paid my debt to her for Gunnar's life. From now
on, the woman is your responsibility, not mine."

"I thank you for your aid," Dag responded stiffly. "Tell
me, though, who carried the tale of Fiona's advice to the jarl?
Was it you?"

"*Nei.* Mina did not mention the matter to me. She counts
Fiona as friend; she would never have betrayed her." He shook
his head. "At this moment, my wife lies in bed weeping for
the injustice done to Fiona, as if she did not have enough to
grieve for."

"Who, then?"

"Ingeborg. She meant no harm either, but she can be simple-
minded at times. She went to her husband with this plan to
wait two more years before conceiving again. After three babes
in three years, she is keen to have a rest from childbearing.
Since they have not yet had a son to train in his profession,
Velund found the idea unacceptable—and Fiona's advice dangerous."

Dag thought of Ingeborg with her yellow braids and her
calm, round face. Why should she be forced to carry another

child when she was already so busy with her three girls? I
was the women who took the risk in childbearing—why should
they not have what control they could over their future? Obviously, he did not share the concerns of his sword brothers. He
would not want Fiona to bear him a child unless she wanted
to.

He thought of that now, wondering suddenly if Fiona had
used such a potion to kill *his* seed. The idea made him slightly
uncomfortable, but he knew he could not condemn her if she
had made such a choice. It seemed heartless to try for a babe
when their own lives were so unsettled and uncertain.

"I'd better go to Fiona," Dag told his brother. "I do not
want her to wander out into the longhouse and unwittingly
incur the men's wrath.

Sigurd nodded and left him. Dag went to his bedcloset,
pausing before the door. He had made up his mind, and the jarl's
recent decree only reaffirmed the inevitability of his choice. He
must get the Irishwoman away from Engvakkirsted. He would
take her back to Ireland, and if possible, start a new life with
her there.

Dare he tell her his decision yet? He had no ship to make
the journey, no means to make his plan come to pass. *Nei*,
better not to arouse her hopes. He might yet fail in his scheme.

Chapter 22

"I would have you hurry," Dag urged. "The men have all left the longhouse. 'Tis better if they do not see you in the vicinity of their womenfolk."

Fiona sighed and began to collect her belongings. When she had woken to find Dag gone, she had not been alarmed. She had dressed leisurely, humming as she did so. For the first time in weeks, she had felt at peace, part of her grief and shame lifted. She had told Dag the truth of their first meeting, and he had not turned from her. Instead, he had held her tenderly much of the night and loved her with a thoroughness that left her body deliciously replete.

But now there was a new difficulty to overcome. As soon as Dag entered the bedcloset, he told her of the jarl's harsh, unfair pronouncement. She was to be driven from the longhouse, banished from contact with the women of Engvakkirsted, excepting the female thralls. She was not only a slave, but an outcast. Angry curses against the Norse race sprang to her lips; but seeing Dag's troubled face, she had not spoken them. She would not blame him for the ignorance of his kinfolk.

" 'Twas not Mina who let slip your advice to her, but Ingeborg," Dag said. "She does not always think before she speaks.

She thought it would be wonderful to be able to plan when her
next child would be born; Velund thought otherwise."

Fiona nodded. She should have heeded the warning voice
which had reminded her that some knowledge was dangerous
to share. At least she knew Mina had not betrayed her. It would
have grieved her deeply to think Sigurd's wife wished her ill.

"I will take you to the slaves' dwelling and speak to old
Sorli myself," Dag said. "The slavemaster is not heartless. He
is something of an outcast himself; he treats the field thralls
with decency, knowing what it is like to be regarded as less
than a man."

Fiona's ears pricked up. "Why is he an outcast?"

"The code of a warrior is a harsh one. To die in battle is
considered the only worthy fate. Sorli is crippled; his shattered
sword arm never healed. Some men consider him less than a
man because he can no longer fight."

Fiona pondered this, thinking it likely that Brodir was one of
those who condemned the slavemaster. The thought of another
disabled warrior came to her mind. "What of the jarl?" she
asked. "He is scarce fit to do battle, yet his word is law at
Engvakkirsted."

"That is Sigurd's doing. All the warriors know that it is
really my brother who rules the steading. But he honors Knorri
and will not see the old jarl's authority usurped."

It was strange to think of forbidding Sigurd as being protec-
tive of a feeble old man. "Why does Sigurd care so much for
Knorri?" Fiona asked.

"Our sire died in a raid when we were boys. There were
those who would have murdered us for Engvakkirsted's wealth.
Knorri protected us until we grew to men." Dag shook his
head. "You cannot know my brother as I do. Like everyone
else, you see only the harsh, rational warrior. But I suspect
when Knorri dies, Sigurd will weep like a brokenhearted boy."

"You brother loves you, too," Fiona said softly. "I think
he would do anything to protect you."

"That is why we must do everything we can to convince
him that you are good for me rather than ill. We need Sigurd
on our side."

Dag's intensity when he spoke of his brother worried Fiona.
The two Norsemen were obviously close. She did not like to
think that she had come between them. Ties with your close
kin were important. She, who had lost so many of her loved
ones, knew that truth.

When she had gathered her few possessions, they set out for
the slave dwelling. "It pains me to think of you dwelling here,"
Dag said as entered the crowded, poorly built structure. "If I
had my way, I would dress you in jewels and silks from Mikel-
gard and have body thralls wait upon you from dawn to dusk."
He smiled at her ruefully. "But all is not hopeless. While the
weather is warm, I will find a place for us to bed down together.
You are still my thrall; the jarl has no authority to keep me
from enjoying one of my possessions."

Fiona smiled back at him. It no longer angered her to hear
him speak of her as his slave. If she remained his captive, she
was a willing one.

"Dag, what word do you have of the Agirsson-Thorvald
feud? I trow I am too busy to learn the latest news." A vigorous
man with skin aged to leather grabbed Dag's arm with his
healthy left one. "I heard that Sigurd set a watch. Is there real
danger?"

"I don't know," Dag answered. "A watch seems a wise
precaution. It has been quiet in the valley for years; I fear the
peace cannot last."

The man—who Fiona assumed to be Sorli—nodded emphat-
ically. "Too many men would rather play coward and burn
out their neighbors in the stealth of night than meet a foe in
battle." Seeing Fiona, the man paused in his philosophizing.
"Is this the Irish wench? I heard she was a *volva.*"

"*Nei,* not a *volva,*" Dag assured him. "I have bedded her;
I would know if she knew witchcraft."

Sorli nodded. "Spooky-looking though, she is. Never have
I seen such black hair, nor eyes so green."

"Well, you'd best get used to her. She's to live in the thrallhouse."

Sorli's eyes widened. "What nonsense is this? I don't need

some cunning-faced vixen distracting the field thralls from their work.''

"She speaks Norse and still enjoys my favor, so you'd best take care in how you talk about her."

"If she enjoys your favor, why are you bringing her to me?"

Dag's face grew grim. "The jarl has banished her from the longhouse. The warriors mislike her foreign ways and fear their wives being exposed to her."

Sorli frowned and looked Fiona up and down, as if expecting to find she had two heads instead of one. "The jarl suspects her of witchery, so he burdens me with the wench," he said sourly. "As if I did not have enough to worry about with the harvest not yet in and the butchering ahead of us."

"She is not a witch," Dag repeated. "Give her a chance, Sorli. She is clever and hardworking, although I would not have her do strenuous outdoor work. Her value lies not in brawn or endurance, but in her quick mind. Find some tasks for her that will not damage her beauty."

Sorli gaped at him. "You want me to protect her? To pamper her like a house thrall?"

"Not only that, but keep her away from the warriors. I fear they might threaten her if they find her alone."

"And why should I do these things for you, Dag Thorsson? What payment will you make me?"

"Whatever you like. Surely there is some comfort or luxury I could provide to sweeten your existence."

Old Sorli frowned and scratched his stubbled jaw. "I would like a new bed. Not merely a soft pallet, but a real box bed with rope supports and a straw mattress."

"Done," Dag answered. Fiona gaped at him, wondering where he meant to procur a bed for the slavemaster. Only Dag, Sigurd, and Knorri slept on box beds; the rest of the steading made do with sleeping sacks on benches or pallets on the floor.

"You may return to your work, Sorli. I will help the woman with her things."

The old man nodded and strode off. Fiona let Dag lead her into the dark, smoky thrallhouse. "Where will you get a bed?" she asked.

"I hope to make an arrangement with Ranveig. He can build other things than ships. If all else fails, I will give Sorli my bed."

"You would do that for me?" Fiona asked softly.

Dag leaned over to kiss her. *"Ja.* That and much more. You are precious to me, Fiona."

Fiona sighed as she stored her belongings under the pallet she had been assigned in the thrallhouse. Things between her and Dag had never been better, but the future still appeared grim. She was an outcast among the Norse, and that would never change. Could she live this harsh, lonely life, even knowing she had Dag? And what of her plan to return to Eire? How could she forsake her vow?

She brought her hands to her temples, trying to ward off the headache her mental turmoil caused. A low, ugly laugh behind her brought her sharply back to her reality. Fiona whirled.

Brodir stood in the low doorway, his brutal countenance livid with hatred. "Murdering wench," he growled.

Fiona went rigid. Where was Sorli when she needed him?

Brodir's thin lips contorted. "You killed Sigurd's babes with poison. I know it, and soon everyone at Engvakkirsted will learn the truth. Then the jarl will order you killed. Before you die . . ." Brodir moved closer, his hot, foul breath scalding Fiona. "I will have you, *ja,* have you for my pleasure."

Her heart had fair stopped. Fiona took a deep breath, then stepped back and tried to get a grip upon her nerves. "I did nothing of the sort. The babes came too early; there was no hope they would live. Mina or any of the other women will tell you that."

"But why did she go to childbed so soon?" Brodir taunted. "Was it not because you have been giving Mina poison for weeks?"

"Nei!"

The Viking smiled a hideous smile. "The women tell me that you made Mina a special mixture to drink each morning. Of course it was poison."

"*Nei,* it was dragonwort, an herb meant to strengthen her body and prevent the babe from coming. It did not work; but with some pregnancies, there is nothing that does."

"Do you expect anyone to believe you?" Brodir sneered. "You are a witch—a devious, corrupt Irish witch. And soon the jarl will know it."

Fiona found herself shaking. There was no way to argue with this man. He twisted the truth into a lie. She could only hope he did not succeed in convincing the others.

"Sigurd does not believe I harmed Mina, and he has told the jarl so. Your threats are for naught."

At the mention of Sigurd, Brodir's face grew even more menacing. "Sometimes Sigurd is a fool, but he will see I am right, in the end. Then he will urge the jarl to condemn you." He moved closer. "You will burn; but before that, I will have you. Your pale, perfect skin will be covered with bruises and welts ere you leave this life."

"What happens here?" a man's voice called out. Fiona jerked away from Brodir as Sorli poked his head into the dwelling.

"What are you doing, Brodir?" Sorli asked. "You know Sigurd has ordered you to keep away from the women slaves. He won't see the jarl's good thralls ruined by your viciousness. And this one . . ." He moved beside Fiona protectively. "She has the jarl's nephew's favor. You will answer to Dag if you touch her."

"Dag is not here," Brodir taunted. "What would you do to me, old man. Would you hurt me with *that?*" He pointed to Sorli's withered arm, eyeing it with repugnance. "You're not even half a man!"

"I serve my jarl well," Sorli answered evenly. "I put food on his table and fill his carts with goods for trade. He remembers that. He also recalls that I fought beside him in a dozen battles. Leave us." Sorli gestured with his good hand.

To Fiona's surprise, Brodir gave her a vicious look, then abruptly left the slave's dwelling. She looked at Sorli, regarding him with new respect. She had seen few men stand up to Brodir as he had done.

"What are you looking at, wench?" Sorli demanded. "The next time you see your master, tell him that I want posts carved with dragons' heads for my bed. I trow, I have earned them."

"Fiona."

She looked up from the tunic she was mending for Aeddan, the youngest of the field thralls. Smiling, she put the garment aside and rose to greet Dag. His impassive expression warned her to refrain from embracing him, but she could not resist moving close, drinking in the sight of him. In the firelight of the thrallhouse, he reminded her again of a sun god—so big and strong and golden.

"Come, walk with me," he said.

Fiona obeyed with delight. Outside in the twilight, she inhaled deeply, then made a face. The thrallhouse was much too close to the cattle byre and the privy for her taste.

"How do you fare?" Dag took her arm and began to lead her toward the turf wall.

"Well enough. For the last two days, my lot has almost been easier than it was in the longhouse. Sorli does not know what to do with me, so he set me to mending. I have repaired all his work tunics and trews, and now he has me sewing for the other thralls. I don't know what he'll have me do when I finish."

"Good, I would not have your skin and hands ruined by field work. I'm pleased that Sorli has kept his part of the bargain."

"And what of your part?" Fiona asked. "Have you made any progress toward securing a bed for the slavemaster?"

" 'Tis complicated, but I am close. Ranveig will make the bed, but only if he can have a new sail for the mast he is making for the *Storm Maiden*. I have bartered with Ingeborg to sew it. She cannot do it unless she has a woman to watch the two youngest of her three girls. Mina had agreed to keep them with her in the longhouse, but only if she does not have the boys underfoot as well. I am taking the boys out hunting and fishing with me. That is why I did not come last night; we did not get back to the steading until late. Then the jarl called a meeting to talk about the raids.'' Dag sighed.

"Jesu!" Fiona exclaimed. "You should have been a merchant. All that bargaining and negotiating to obtain one bed!"

"There have been some other things involved as well. Ingeborg wanted some silk for a girdle she is weaving. I gave her the blue garment you wore on the ship and said she could unravel it and use the thread.'' Seeing Fiona's dismayed look, he added, "I promise to buy you a new gown, even finer, as soon as Sigurd agrees to make a trading voyage to Hedeby.''

" 'Tis no matter. Much of the skirt was stained by salt water on the journey.''

"I see that it grieves you, though.''

Fiona sighed. "The gown belonged to Duvessa, my foster sister.''

Dag nodded. "I will see Ingeborg tomorrow and ask for it back.''

"Nei! You have worked too hard on this arrangement for me to ruin it with my selfishness. I know you do all this to protect me, and I am grateful.''

"Has anyone bothered you?'' Dag asked, pausing on the pathway leading up into the hills beyond the steading.

Fiona hesitated. Should she tell him about Brodir? Sorli had handled the situation successfully, and she did not want to worry Dag. Then she remembered the slavemaster's request for a *carved* bed. "Brodir did come once, but Sorli sent him away. I'm afraid the slavemaster has upped his payment for protecting me. He said to tell you that the bedposts must be carved with dragons' heads.''

Dag's eyes darkened with rage. "Brodir dared to threaten you? I will kill him!'' He jerked away as if he meant to return to the steading and do the deed that moment. Fiona ran after him and grabbed his arm.

"Nei, Dag! Do not fight Brodir! I would not see you hurt, and the jarl will blame me for coming between his oathmen. It will only make things worse!''

Dag took a deep breath. "You are right, although it scarce

tempers my anger.'' He turned toward her. ''I cannot stand this—to see you harassed and intimidated.''

''I am well, Dag, truly.'' Fiona pressed her face against his chest. ''When you hold me in your arms, I forget all else.''

Dag's hands came up to stroke her neck. ''Ah, Fiona, what will become of us?''

Fiona buried her face deeper against Dag's warm strength as tears filled her eyes. What, indeed? Although she struggled to avoid thinking of the threatening future, it remained like a cloud over their lives. Brodir would never leave her in peace, and sooner or later, Dag would be forced into a confrontation with his sword brother.

''I would forget, too.'' Dag's fingers moved lower, from her neck to her breasts. His stroking grew urgent, provocative rather than soothing. Fiona's nipples tingled in response, and a low, fervent heat spread through her lower body. She gasped at the intensity of her desire and swayed against him.

Dag melded his mouth to hers, kissing her with long, deep tongue strokes that left them both shaking. When he began pulling at her clothes, Fiona found the presence of mind to remove his hands. ''Let me undress,'' she whispered. ''I'm tired of mending things.''

Dag nodded, his face intent in the half-darkness. Shivering in the evening air, Fiona pulled her kirtle over her head and bared herself to her lover. Dag groaned. ''A bed—what I would not give for a bed. I would lay you down and . . .''

''I know of a bed.'' A mischievious notion took hold of Fiona. ''There is a meadow just beyond this rise. Meet me there!''

She dashed off, naked, giggling with exhilaration, a girl again, playing games in the magic hours after sunset. But this time it was not Duvessa who chased her, but Dag. She could hear him behind her, following with long, ground-eating strides. Fiona shrieked and quickened her pace. She reached the meadow, breathless with exertion and anticipation. Dag moved toward her and struggled out of his clothes. Fiona watched him bare his long, muscular, breathtaking body in the fading twilight.

She waited, helpless with desire for this beautiful Viking.

"Elusive, bedeviling wench." Dag reached for her, drawing her against him. His jutting erection pressed against her belly. Boldly, Fiona moved her fingers to enclose him. Her breathing quickened. Such a fascinating plaything men possessed. So eager and enthralling, beguilingly silky and rigid. She wanted to kiss him there, to bury her face against him.

Dag had other ideas. He grabbed her hips and lifted her up, then slid her body slowly down his until her thighs met his belly. Fiona moaned and parted her thighs so his shaft slid into her wet, slippery sheath.

Neither moved. "I want you," Dag said. "I cannot be gentle the way I feel."

Fiona nodded against his chest. Somehow he manuevered them both to the ground. She closed her eyes and surrendered.

He loved her with fury, as strong as the wind tearing at a ship's sails or the waves lashing against the shore. He was her Viking god, thundering amid the heavens. She accepted him, loved him, melded into him.

Afterwards, Dag rolled on his back, feeling the grass cold and wet against him. With his sword hand he reached out to touch Fiona's face. The warm wetness on her cheeks alarmed him. "I hurt you?" he whispered.

"Nei."

"You weep!"

"Not with sadness."

"Ah." He felt it, too. Some emotion so powerful it was like a bird taking flight within his breast. "I will love you slow next time. I will be gentle."

"Nei. 'Twas perfect. I will never forget."

Dag stared up at the stars. How far he had travelled to reach this place. He lay naked in a mountain meadow watching the moonrise with an Irishwoman. At this moment he could not even remember what it meant to be Norse. There was only himself . . . and Fiona.

Chapter 23

"A messenger from Ottar's steading just arrived," Sigurd said. "They've called a meeting of the *Thing*."

Dag put down the barrel of salted fish he was carrying to the storage shed and faced his brother. "Because of the raids?"

"*Ja*. Like you, other men think the Agirssons should pay wergeld for the attack on the Thorvald steading. They hope to end the feud before it involves more families and causes more deaths."

"Where will the meeting be held?" Dag took off his sealskin gloves and flexed his fingers.

"At Skogkrasse, a sennight hence."

Dag nodded in satisfaction. He would see warriors from other steadings and feast and drink with them. He would have a chance to discuss his plans with other landless sons. Not only did he need a ship, but men willing to sail with him. The thought of Ireland reminded him to ask, "Who will go?"

"You and myself, of course. The jarl does not feel well enough for the journey, so we will represent him. We will also take a full complement of warriors to watch our backs. In times like these, you cannot be too cautious."

"Brodir?" Dag asked.

"*Nei.* He is exactly what we do not need at a peaceful gathering. The man is always stirring up trouble. He enjoys raiding and bloodshed; he would probably encourage the Thorvald clan to break the truce as soon it was made." Sigurd regarded his brother warily. "Why would you want him along?"

"I fear that Brodir might harm Fiona while we are gone. He has threatened her already. I have asked Sorli to look to her safety, but without my presence to discourage him, I fear Brodir will grow bold."

"You asked the slavemaster to look after Fiona?"

Dag met his brother's eyes with defiance. "*Ja,* I did. She is my property, after all. Why should I not seek to protect her?"

"Brodir would not dare hurt the woman. He knows you would return and exact vengeance."

Dag shook his head. Sigurd did not understand how deep Brodir's hatred of Fiona ran. His passion to destroy her had twisted his mind and made his reasoning dangerously warped. Dag felt certain the warrior was capable of anything.

Anxiety over Fiona plagued Dag as he finished stacking the casks of dried fish in the storehouse. By the time he completed the task, his anxiety had grown until he could not stand it. He must see Fiona and reassure himself that she was well.

Finding the thrallhouse empty, Dag decided Sorli must have set Fiona to work outside after all. He walked down the pathway toward the grainery.

In the area in front of the storage building, slaves busied themselves cleaning out the baskets of rotted grain and debris from the last harvest so the new crop could be stored for the winter. Seeing no sign of Fiona, Dag turned, intending to look elsewhere. He nearly stumbled over a small black-and-white cat carrying a mouse flushed from the grainery. A smile came to his lips as he righted himself and met the feline's wary, amber eyes. While most Norsemen considered cats as bothersome and disgusting as the rodents they preyed upon, Dag admired the lithe creatures. They were such clever hunters, and their knowing, mysterious eyes always made him feel as if their spirit spoke to his.

Dag left the steading complex and headed toward the stubbly fields behind the longhouse. He grimaced as a pungent smell met his nostrils. So, that was where the rest of the thralls were—rendering fat for soapmaking. Although important to a prosperous steading, soapmaking was a disgusting process and always done as far from the living area as possible. Thinking of Fiona working amid such a mess made him angry. He had asked Sorli to look after the Irishwoman, to keep her from the more odious tasks. What if she were burned? The thought of her smooth skin being scarred made Dag walk faster.

Reaching the work area, he waved aside the billowing smoke and scanned the half-dozen grubby thralls overseeing the work. No Fiona.

Torn between relief and aggravation at not finding her, Dag whirled and strode back toward the longhouse. Where could she be? He did not like the idea of her working by herself any more than he favored the thought of her doing the crude tasks the other thralls did. If she were alone, it would be too easy for Brodir to accost and threaten her.

By the time he finally cornered Sorli by the water trough, Dag's temper was running hot. "Where's Fiona?" he demanded of the older man.

Sorli's pale-blue eyes narrowed. Remembering what Fiona had told him about Sorli's defending her from Brodir, Dag softened his voice. "Your pardon, Sorli, I did not mean to shout at you. I'm only concerned for my thrall's welfare."

The bitter look in Sorli's eyes eased. "She should be in the slaves' dwelling. I've set her to cooking meals for the other thralls. She has a fair hand with a cooking pot, for all that she says she has not prepared food much before. Her bread is better than most; her porridge actually quite savory . . ."

"I just looked there," Dag interrupted. "I did not see her."

Sorli shrugged. "She asked for access to the forest to gather herbs. Mayhap she went there."

Dag's heartbeat quickened at the thought of Fiona alone outside the steading, collecting the last of the season's plants. He strode off toward the woods, his stomach tight.

An hour later, he gave up and returned to the steading, sick with helpless worry. He would check the thrallhouse one more time, then go to his brother and demand men to search for her.

A fragrant odor assailed Dag's nose as he entered the low doorway of the building. Fiona kneeled by the cooking fire, stirring something in a cauldron. Dag went weak with relief. He wanted to rush over and crush her slim body to his chest. Instead, he barked, "Where were you?"

Fiona glanced up, her eyes wide with surprise. "What do you mean?"

"I came looking for you some time ago, and you weren't here."

"I went to gather some wild garlic. It makes a nice flavoring with pork."

Dag stood over her. "I was beside myself with worry. You should not go anywhere alone!"

Fiona's eyes lit with resentment. "Am I a prisoner in this place? Dare I even leave to use the privy by myself . . . *master?*"

The sarcasm in her voice enraged him. He had spent nearly the whole afternoon searching for her. *He was simply trying to protect her.* "Always you defy me! I tire of your independence and your stubbornness! Mayhap I should beat you. Then you might learn to mind me!"

Fiona stood. Her head reached barely to his shoulders. "Beat me then, if it soothes your pride, Viking," she taunted. "Act a brute like the rest of your race!"

He raised his hand to give her what she demanded. At the last moment his fingers stalled in midair. He sighed and turned away. "You provoke me, wench. But I get more pleasure bedding you than I would beating you." He turned to face her again. "I have only your welfare in mind. I would not see you hurt."

Her anger appeared to fade as quickly as his had. "I beg pardon, Dag. I know you care for my safety."

He breathed a sigh of relief at her compliance, but could not disregard his worries. "I came to tell you that Sigurd and I must make a journey to attend a meeting of the *Thing*—an assembly of men from different steadings who gather to make and enforce the laws of our people. I fear for your safety while we are gone.''

Fiona nodded. ''Brodir . . .''

''He will try to hurt you, I know it.'' Dag took a deep breath, struggling for a solution. Sigurd was right; Brodir could not go with them. He was exactly the sort who caused problems at a peaceful gathering. But left behind, he was a hazard to Fiona. *Unless she came with them.* He wrinkled his forehead, considering. Although women were welcome at the *Allthing* in the spring, this was not that sort of meeting. The jarls met to forestall war, and few men would bring their wives or families to such a potentially volatile event. If he took her, Fiona would have to remain alone at their camp much of the time. She'd dare not act defiant or haughty.

He gazed at the woman before him. Short of temper, long on pride—she was a volatile creature. But she was sharp-witted, too, and reasonable, for the most part. Dared he trust her to behave herself if explained the circumstances?

He had no choice. Better the dangers they might encounter at the *Thing* than the inevitable disaster of Fiona alone with Brodir at Engvakkirsted.

Fixing her with a stern look, he said, ''I am taking you to the *Thing*. I can't leave you alone with Brodir, but I need your promise that you will behave on the journey. You must agree to act the part of a docile, compliant thrall every moment we are away from Engvakkirsted.''

Fiona nodded slowly, but Dag still felt anxiety. She could not guess how important this journey was to their future—unless he told her. Mayhap it was time he shared a little of his plans. He took a deep breath. ''While we are at the *Thing*, I mean to find a man with a ship who will sail to Ireland. I intend to take you back to your homeland.''

With the area outside the slave dwelling lit only by moonlight, Fiona could scarcely see Dag, and it took a moment for his words to sink in. When they did, her mind reeled. Return to her homeland, see her kinfolk, be free . . .

Dag spoke again, his voice impatient. ''You still want to go, don't you?''

"*Ja,*" she breathed. Of course she did. This was the dream which had kept her alive. Why, then, did she feel so disappointed, so empty? "I am very grateful," she told Dag. "When will we leave?"

"I'm not certain. I hope to sail yet this season, but I must find a man willing to provide a ship for the journey, as well as a crew. At the *Thing,* I will be busy talking to other warriors, finding out if they are willing to join me. I will not have time to keep you out of trouble—that is why your cooperation is so important."

Fiona could hardly focus on what Dag was asking. She forced herself to answer. "Of course, Dag. I promise to do your bidding in all things."

She heard him exhale the breath he had been holding, and his hands came up to stroke her arms. "You are cold, Fiona. We must see about getting you some warmer garments." He leaned over and kissed her. Fiona closed her eyes as the familiar fire burned through her. *How could she bear to give this up?*

The kiss deepened. Suddenly, Dag pulled away. "Ah, Sorli," he said. "I needed to speak with you. The woman will be going with Sigurd and me when we journey to the *Thing.* I trust that you can do without her for the several days we will be gone."

After Dag and Sorli left, Fiona lay down on her hard pallet and stared up at the thrallhouse roof. Dag meant to return her to Eire, to give her back all she had lost. It was everything she had wished for. She would return to her home and resume her role as princess of the Deasúnachta. Her life as a thrall among the Norse would be over, banished as if she awoke from a bad dream.

Why, then, was she so unhappy? Why did she feel as if she had been stabbed in the heart? She squeezed her eyes shut, fighting tears. The thought of leaving Dag made her feel empty inside. He had come to fill the void within her that her father's death had left; now she was to lose him as well. Could she bear to give him up?

The great, yawning emptiness inside her grew. What would

life be like without Dag, without his beautiful, strong body; his warm smile; his courageous, proud spirit? Without him, she would be only a shell of herself, living and breathing, but no longer really alive. It sounded unendurable, but then, so had being a Viking thrall.

Fiona took a deep breath, struggling for control. She had made a vow, and she would keep it. Dag had offered her the chance to be a princess again. It was her duty to accept his gift.

Dag walked back to the longhouse. His plan was taking shape. At the *Thing,* he would surely find men willing to sail with him to Ireland. He savored his dream, fleshing it out. Each time he imagined it, the feasthall on the hill grew larger. Now it had carved timber supports and the defending walls of the fort were of stone instead of wood. Beautiful, swift horses grazed in his fields, and his hall was crowded with strong warriors and fair maids. Fairest of all was Fiona, dressed in a vivid green gown and gleaming gold.

He frowned. She had not seemed as pleased as he had hoped, tonight when he'd announced his intentions. He had expected her to embrace him, her face to light up with gratitude. Why had she been so quiet, so thoughtful? Could it be that she did not feel for him what he felt for her?

He tensed at the thought. Never had they spoken of the future, trying instead to deny the oppression and worries of the present. In his mind, it was natural to see her as his wife, but he could not know if she wished him for a husband. Mayhap she meant to return to her people and wed an Irish chieftain. Anger rose in him. He would not give her up to another man. She was *his,* and he would have the lands she was heir to as well. If necessary, he would fight for them.

He entered the longhouse. Sigurd and the other men still sat up drinking, talking, playing dice and board games. Dag ignored them. Already, he felt distant from his sword brothers. If things went well, he was to embark on an adventure more daring than all the raids and trading journeys any man of his clan had ever taken part in.

He slipped into his bedcloset, his mind still racing. There was so much to plan, so many details to arrange. He needed a crew of at least thirty men and a light, durable sailing vessel. And then there were weapons, foodstores . . .

Chapter 24

Dag reached out and patted the horse's shaggy forelock. He stared into the animal's dark eyes, seeking to communicate with its spirit.

"What do you think, brother?" Sigurd asked impatiently. "Are they worth the price? I'm no judge of horseflesh, but we need some draft animals to pull the supply cart when we journey to the *Thing*. Will these beasts do?"

Dag nodded absently. The horse seemed wary, fearful; it appeared likely it had been abused. "The animals are sound. If properly fed and cared for, they will serve."

Sigurd gestured to the fierce-visaged man standing next to him. "My brother says they will serve. We'll take the pair." His eyes narrowed. "But Thor strike you down, Ottar, if you have cheated us."

Ottar Jokulsson, jarl of the steading, smiled, the movement causing his battle-scarred mien to grow even uglier. "You say your brother can judge a beast's temperament? What a queer skill for a warrior to possess. Can he also predict the weather and which way a battle will turn?"

"*Nei*," Sigurd answered sharply. "My brother is no wizard; he simply has a way with animals."

Ottar greeted this remark with a grunt, then said, "Bring the gold to the longhouse when you are ready to depart. I'll have my thrall hitch the horses to the cart."

Ottar left, and Dag and Sigurd watched a dark, wraithlike slave harness the horses. The horses acted weary and resigned. Dag frowned. He observed no lashmarks on the animals' hides, but they had been poorly fed and neglected.

"You are certain, Dag?" Sigurd asked as the slave moved out of hearing. "The jarl will be angered if I have spent his wealth on beasts too sickly to survive the winter."

"There is nothing wrong with them that a few days of good feed would not set aright," Dag announced confidently. "Indeed, I think they are a bargain at the price. Their spirits are low now, but with proper care, they will be eager to serve their new master."

"Spirits?" Sigurd shook his head. "How could such mute, stupid creatures have spirits?"

"Some animals don't, but these do. It is the wild part of them that speaks in their eyes. They were not always draft animals; once they thundered over the ground with beauty and freedom. That memory is still with them."

Sigurd shook his head again. The slave finished harnessing the animals and began to lead them toward the gate of the turf wall surrounding Ottar Jokulsson's steading. Dag and Sigurd followed. After stepping into the longhouse to pay Ottar his gold, Sigurd departed through the gate with Dag and the horsecart, Dag urging the horses along with a firm hand on the darker animal's harness.

"If we did not take Fiona, we could get along without any cart and we would not have had to make this trip to purchase horses," Sigurd pointed out.

"The animals will be useful for other journeys and tasks. Besides, if I go, Fiona goes," Dag said. "I dare not leave her behind lest Brodir hurt her."

"And I have your vow that she will not act defiantly and shame us before our countrymen?" Sigurd's blue eyes bored into Dag.

"*Ja*, I swear it," Dag answered.

Sigurd gave him another searching look. "By what means do you intend to make certain of the woman's obedience?"

Dag smiled. "I trow she will mind me in all things."

Sigurd's dark brows rose. "You would only promise that if you were very sure of her. What have you done? Have you offered to wed her?"

Dag shook his head, but Sigurd ranted on. "How could you be so foolish! By offering her hope for a life beyond what you have already given her, you increase her dissatisfaction and encourage her to rebel against her lot. Dissatisfied thralls are dangerous, especially ones as clever and determined as the Irishwoman."

"Dangerous? How is she dangerous?" Dag scoffed.

"Can you deny that she considers us her enemies? Why should she not harbor plans for vengeance against us?"

"You have been listening to Brodir!"

"*Nei*," Sigurd answered, "merely observing the woman. I underestimated her at first, thinking she was like the rest of her sex, conniving for comfort and luxury and the petty power of a pampered concubine. Now, I see that there is more to her. She still fancies herself a princess and clings to her past life in Ireland. She has not accepted her lot as slave, and now you encourage her to think of herself as equal to a freewoman."

"She is equal."

"*Nei!* Never! She is a conquered slave; she has no rights!"

"Unless I choose to give them to her!"

Sigurd's eyes widened in outrage. "I fear Brodir is right. The woman *has* bewitched you. You forget who you are, Dag Thorsson."

"And what am I?" Dag demanded. "A landless second son who will live his life always in his brother's shadow!"

The anger in Sigurd's eyes turned to hurt. "Always, I have treated you as my equal, Dag." He shook his head. "I would not have us fight. I would have things between us as they were."

Dag shook his head sadly. How could he tell his brother that such a thing could never be?

* * *

It was well past twilight when they arrived at the steading. Sigurd went to Knorri to make his report. Dag excused himself and went to see to the care of the horses. He took them to an old cattle byre that was half-falling down but still a decent shelter and unharnessed them himself. Then he fetched them fresh water and plenty of hay and even added several handfuls of grain to their feed. After spending a few moments talking to them and stroking their necks as they ate, he left them and headed for the slave quarters.

Sorli was nowhere in sight, and Dag guessed he was probably eating in the small, bare dwelling were he lived. Pushing aside the hide door covering, Dag entered the slave hut. The field thralls were gathered around the cooking hearth, and Fiona was using a bone ladle to dish the stew into wooden bowls. It smelled as delicious as the potful she had been stirring the last time Dag had seen her.

With their senses concentrated on the food, none of the slaves noticed Dag's presence. He cleared his throat. A dozen pairs of startled eyes met his. Dag restrained himself from seeking out Fiona's gaze and focused instead on a dark-haired youngster. "Boy," he said, "what is your name?"

The youth gaped at him, his eyes wide and frightened, then answered, "My name is Aeddan . . . my lord. How may I serve you . . . master?"

Dag felt the tension in the slave house. Obviously, few warriors ever came here, preferring instead to deal through Sorli. Dag's presence had clearly aroused the thralls' dread, and the realization angered him. Did these people live in fear of every Norseman they saw? Was that what Brodir and his ilk had brought about with their cruelty?

Dag spoke abruptly. "The jarl has purchased a pair of horses. I need a boy to tend them. Aeddan, are you willing?"

The boy's mouth opened and closed like a fish out of water. "I . . . I . . . I am willing," he finally managed.

"It will mean sleeping with the animals, cleaning out their

byre, brushing them down every day," Dag warned, his voice stern. "I want these beasts to have constant attention."

Aeddan nodded, a mingled look of disbelief and pleasure crossing his face. "They will want for nothing, I swear it, master."

Dag let himself half-smile, then said, "I will take you to them shortly. Go, gather your things."

The boy hurried toward the back of the dwelling. Dag finally let his gaze rest upon Fiona. He gestured toward the doorway. "Come and speak with me."

She appeared in the darkness beside him. "That was kind of you, Dag. Aeddan does love animals."

"Not kind, merely sensible. A man or boy who enjoys his task does it more willingly. I would have the jarl's horses well cared for."

Fiona's voice was tender with admiration. "You would make a good jarl, Dag. You understand men's ambitions and dreams."

Dag grimaced, remembering his angry words with Sigurd. He had not meant for things to come to this, that he must break with his brother and live without his goodwill.

"Dag!" Sorli came to join them. "Are you back from Ottar's?"

"*Ja.* Sigurd and I purchased some horses for the jarl. I have asked the boy called Aeddan to look after them.

Sorli snorted audibly. "You are a clever man, Dag Thorsson. I have tried for months to come up with a task that the boy won't shirk. Then you decide he will tend horses. I don't suppose you had any inkling that the boy dotes on animals, did you? Of course not. 'Twas merely a lucky guess, wasn't it?"

"I noted some time ago the young thrall's penchant for animals. He could not pass by my hound Ulvi without giving the beast a pat. Here the boy is now," Dag added as a shaft of light peeked out around the hide doorway. "Aeddan, are you ready?"

A small figure scrambled through the doorway. "*Ja,* master."

Dag turned back to Fiona. "I will come tomorrow and help you prepare for the journey." He moved away, the boy following after him. As they disappeared into the darkness, Fiona heard Aeddan's childish voice, "What are the horses' names, master."

Dag answered, low and thoughtful. "I have not had time to consider it. Mayhap you would do me the favor of naming them. We cannot merely call out, 'Hey, horse,' when we want them to go, can we?"

Aeddan's answering peal of laughter made Fiona's insides wrench. Dag sought to better the life of even a lowly slave.

Sorli moved beside her and cleared his throat. "Have you eaten yet, wench? If not, you'd best return to the dwelling and grab a bite before all is gone. I'll not have you out here catching cold. *Nei,* not when you are of such obvious value to the jarl's nephew."

"Of course, master," Fiona answered glumly.

The next day, Dag took Fiona with him to the longhouse. Although he had argued that Fiona should not come when he went to get the clothes, she had begged for a chance to appraise Mina's well-being with her own eyes. Finally he had relented.

Mina rose from her stool by the loom as soon as she saw them.

"Mina, I would have you provide warm clothes for my thrall," Dag said. "She is to accompany Sigurd and me on our journey to Skogkrasse."

Mina gave Fiona a brief, warm smile, then led her and Dag to the main storage closet. While Mina fumbled with the ring of keys on the cord around her neck, Fiona assessed the Norsewoman's health. She had regained a little weight in her face and her complexion was not as pallid. She appeared to be recovering well.

When the door to the closet was opened, Mina gestured for Dag to drag out one of the large storage chests. She searched among the piles of cloth and finished garments, finally locating a plain woolen cloak and tunic. She handed the clothes to Dag, then her gaze met Fiona's.

Fiona's throat ached to exchange some words with her friend, but Dag had warned her that it would not be wise. Although the longhouse was empty of warriors, he wanted no one to interpret Fiona's presence there as an act of disobedience.

Dag accepted the garments from Mina, and they turned to leave. Before they reached the doorway of the longhouse, Mina called out, "Wait!" The Norsewoman hurried back toward the storage area, then quickly reappeared. She held out a pair of tall, sealskin boots to Fiona. "Take them," she said. "They were my sister's. She was small like you. They will keep you warm if the weather turns bad."

Fiona nodded, fighting tears. "Thank you," she told Mina gravely.

After they left the longhouse, Dag took Fiona's arm and gave her a puzzled look. "What is wrong?" he asked. "You seem so unhappy. Do you have doubts about returning to Ireland?"

Fiona shook her head. She would not burden Dag with her turmoil. She had made her decision, and she must keep to it. "I will miss Mina," she told him softly. "I feel as if I said goodbye to her, and I sorrow at our parting."

Dag nodded and led Fiona to the cart by the horse shed. As he stored her new boots among the other supplies, he told her, "We are taking tents for sleeping comfort as well as stored food and cooking supplies. When so many men gather, it is impossible to feed everyone by hunting. You will cook the meals."

Fiona met his glance blankly. Her mind was hardly on preparing food.

"You promised you would behave as an obedient thrall," Dag reminded her. "And cooking is a reasonable task for a woman."

He paused, his eyes searching her face. Fiona looked away, unwilling for him to see her unhappiness.

She heard him sigh softly. "We will leave very early on the

morrow, Fiona, so I advise you to seek your bed as soon as the evening meal is finished.''

She nodded, and Dag walked her back to the thrallhouse. After she had eaten and cleaned up the remainders of the meal, she lay down on her pallet. Once again, her torment began as the desires of her heart fought with the sense of duty she had been born to. The battle raged far into the night until Fiona fell into an exhausted sleep.

They left before dawn. Fiona found herself yawning every few steps. Although she refused to give in to Dag's suggestion that she ride in the cart, she knew she would later be grateful to rest from struggling to keep up with the men's long strides.

She was surprised by how many warriors accompanied them. She had thought it would merely be her, Sigurd, and Dag and perhaps Kalf or Balder. Instead, she found a dozen others would be making the journey. If every jarl brought so many warriors, the ''Thing'' would be a huge gathering.

The day was cloudy and breezy, but not cold. After the sun rose, Fiona grew so warm that she flung back the hood of her cloak.

They stopped for a meal when the sun was high in the sky, and Fiona dutifully served dried fish and dark bread to all. The men ignored her, treating her as if she were simply one of the serving thralls in the longhouse. Fiona ate her own meal quickly, then washed her hands with a little of the stored water they had brought. When she returned to the wagon to put the food away, she discovered Dag by the horses, stroking one of the animals' foreheads. As she neared, she heard him speak in a low voice. She looked around, wondering whom he was talking to, then realized his words were meant for the horses. She paused to watch him.

When he looked up, she could not help smiling at him. ''Do they ever answer you?'' she asked.

A slight flush spread up his neck. ''Sometimes,'' he answered.

Fiona watched him, her throat tight. Dag looked like the

most fierce and deadly of warriors, but his heart could be as tender and sensitive as a woman's. A deep pang of longing and regret went through her. What might there have been between them if she and Dag had not met as enemies?

She turned away; her hands shook as she replaced the leftover fish in a wooden cask in the cart. Tonight, she was to lie with him, to join her body with his. What sweet agony it would be, to experience once again that consuming bliss, knowing that they might have only a few more nights together.

Tears stung her eyes. How could it hurt so much? Mayhap it would be best if she refused him instead. He might be angry, but at least it would spare her suffering in the end.

Dag came up beside her. "Are you tired, Fiona? Would you like to ride for a while?"

"Nei," she answered. "I will not avoid hardship. I need to prepare for the deprivations of the long journey home."

He nodded and moved away. Fiona sighed. She both welcomed and dreaded the distance growing between them. Let him reject her now, before the bond between them deepened— and left her with even more gaping wounds when they parted.

The rest of the day seemed endless. They walked and walked until Fiona's legs and back ached. She embraced the discomfort, hoping it would distract her from the pain in her heart. She also forced herself to make plans for when she returned to her homeland.

Her future in Eire was very uncertain. Even if Duvessa and the other women had survived, they could not rebuild Dunsheauna by themselves. They would need men to help them. Fiona realized she might find herself forced into marriage with a neighboring chieftain in order to protect her people. At the thought that she might even have to wed Sivney Longbeard, she shuddered. Had all she had borne been for naught—her father's death, the burning of her home, these discouraging months of enslavement among the Vikings? Was she fated to marry Sivney in the end?

She wanted to cry, to rage at the gods for cursing her so cruelly. But she dared not give vent to her anger and frustration. Dag would see, and he would be hurt, thinking that she was not happy with his plans. She forced her face to impassivity and kept walking.

At last, they stopped for the night. While Dag unharnessed the horses and Sigurd set up the tents where he and his brother would sleep, Fiona took out the food stores. One of the men built a fire, and she made a stew using dried meat, vegetables, and grain. The warriors each carried a horn cup in their packs, and once the gruel was hot, they used this to scoop out a portion and gulp it down. Then, as Fiona was cleaning up, Rorig and Utgard—who had gone off to hunt—returned carrying two plump ptarmigans they had killed with a bow and arrow.

"Ah, fresh meat," Sigurd exclaimed with obvious delight. He gave Fiona a questioning look. "You do know how to cook game, don't you, wench?"

Fiona opened her mouth to tell him that she did not, then remembered her promise to Dag. She nodded dutifully.

"Tomorrow," Dag said, taking her hand. "Tomorrow, she will cook for you; tonight I have other things in mind."

Fiona followed Dag into the tent they would share. Once inside, she hesitated. Now was the time to tell Dag her decision. Surely, he would understand that lovemaking would only worsen the pain of parting.

"Dag," she began. "I don't think this is wise."

The tent was dark, but she could hear him fumbling with his clothes. "Why?" he responded, still undressing.

She searched for the right words. "I fear the pleasure we share will only lead to more pain in the end."

"You must trust me, *macushla*," Dag said huskily.

Desperation choked her throat. Dared she tell him how she felt about him? Mayhap he did not care for her as she did for him. She would truly feel a fool if she discovered he sought only a few quick nights of pleasure before he was rid of her.

"I . . . I don't know if I can . . ." He silenced her protest by pulling her into a fierce embrace. Fiona shuddered at the touch of his lips. Her resolve wavered. She pulled away and gasped for breath, then lifted her face to his again. It was part of the bargain, she told herself as his tongue filled her mouth.

She had agreed to be his obedient thrall, and a princess of Eire never reneged on a bargain.

Between passionate kisses, he removed her clothes. Fiona trembled at his touch, feeling lost and helpless. Nothing mattered but the hunger that burned between them, this soul-deep craving that blotted out thought and reason.

When they were both naked, Fiona leaned against him, feeling as if she had fallen into an abyss. His fingers stroked her from her neck down to her hips, then swept upwards again. He cradled her neck in his hands and kissed her until she moaned. Her body arched up to his, eager and yielding.

Gently, he lay her down on the bed furs. His shaft was hard against her thigh, but his fingers felt light and caressing. He touched her all over, then let his lips follow where his fingers had roamed. Fiona cried out as he knelt over to nuzzle the back of her knees, then moved his mouth higher. Wantonly, she spread her thighs, urging him to taste her, to use his mouth to ease the tormenting ache inside her.

The harsh skin of his unshaven jaw met her tender flesh, and his tongue fluttered against her wet opening. Her hips moved upward, seeking fulfillment. Fire whirled inside her, but it was not enough. She wanted him to fill her.

Reaching down, she tangled her fingers in his thick wavy hair and lifted his head. "Please," she whispered. "Please."

He raised his body to cover hers, but did not enter her. Instead, he strewed kisses over her breasts, then licked his way up her neck and along her jaw. Fiona whimpered.

At last his lips melded to hers, and with a shuddering groan, he entered her. Fiona cried out, overcome by the wonder of their bodies joining together. Rays and ripples of delight swept through her as he thrust with slow, deep strokes. She hovered at the brink of ecstasy, then fell into the chasm beyond. As the waves of her peak died away, he continued to move inside her. Unbelievably, she climbed the heights again, exploded with rapture, and still felt his relentless rhythm rocking her throbbing flesh.

She heard her own voice rise in rasping, wordless cries. Her nails dug into the skin of his shoulders. Hot, white light filled her, then all was still.

They lay together, their bodies slick with sweat, their hearts beating a frantic tattoo. In moments, Dag fell asleep beside her. Fiona sighed, the tension inside her returning. She reached out to caress his face, feeling his heat and life. He was so precious to her. How could she bear to lose him?

She began to cry, silently at first, then with muffled sobs.

Dag woke. "*Macushla,* beloved—what is wrong?"

Fiona shook her head. How could she tell him what she felt? Even after she returned to Eire and fulfilled her vow, a part of her would always be missing.

" 'Tis nothing," she said, stroking his face again. "Only that you please me so much."

Dag frowned into the darkness. Fiona seemed so unhappy. What was it that troubled her? Did she fear the sea voyage or what they would find when they returned to her homeland? And why had she been hesitant to make love? It worried him, this tension he felt in her. Mayhap he should explain all of his plan—that he meant to claim her father's lands and rebuild Dunsheauna.

But what if she argued against it? He had neither the time nor energy for conflict with her. He must keep his goal clear in his mind and be confident of success or he would never convince other men to take the risk with him. It was as he had said—she would have to trust him.

Chapter 25

The golden light of sunset gilded the surrounding hills and cast long, eerie shadows across the broad valley where the *Thing* would be held. Fiona's breath caught as she surveyed the multitude of men and tents gathered beside the gleaming lake. 'Twas like the fair at Cashel, she thought, only mayhap even bigger.

"How long will the meeting take?" she asked as she walked beside Dag. Sigurd and the other men had taken off down the pathway, obviously anxious to join their countrymen, while Dag remained behind to guide the horses.

"I cannot say. We might reach a decision in a few hours . . . or a few days."

Fiona tensed. Her time with Dag grew shorter and shorter.

Seeing her ill-ease, Dag reached out with his free hand and touched her shoulder. "There is nothing to fear. I won't let anyone hurt you, I promise."

Fiona could not meet his eyes. Dag thought she feared his countrymen. He did not guess that her anxiety and dread came at the thought of leaving him. "I will not forget *my* promise," she said. "I will be the most obedient thrall at the gathering."

They reached the Viking encampment, and Dag guided the

horses around the perimeter to an area where there were several other horsecarts. Fiona helped him unharness the horses and put out feed for them, then he went off to meet the other men.

Fiona gazed around, taking notice for the first time of the other people near their camp. Most of them were young warriors left to care for the animals while the older men held their meeting, but Fiona noticed with surprise a woman sitting in an ornate chair by one of the carts. Around her hovered two young thralls. As Fiona watched, the seated woman sent first one thrall, then the other, scrambling for something in the cart. They presented the items to their mistress with a bow, then backed away.

Fiona stared as the woman took down her long braid and began to comb out her honey-colored hair, grooming herself as nonchalantly as if she sat in her own bedchamber.

Shaking her head, Fiona turned away. When Dag returned, she would ask him about the woman. For now, she must see to preparing a meal.

It took her a long time to find enough wood for a fire, then even longer to light it with a flintstone. Her back ached and sweat trickled down between her breasts by the time she had fetched water from a spring that fed the lake and gathered foodstuffs from the cart to make a stew. Despite her fatigue, a sense of satisfaction filled her when the men of Engvakkirsed returned and she was able to offer them something hot and tasty to eat. She had fulfilled her role as a dutiful thrall.

The men talked animatedly as Fiona cleaned and put away the cooking utensils. They obviously considered a gathering of the *Thing* an exciting event. In between discussions of political alliances, she heard mention of goods being traded and contests of skill that would be held before the assembly was over. She decided that the *Thing* was indeed much like the fairs of her homeland, although women played a more important part in the activities there. When the clans gathered in the summer at Cashel, tents were set aside for the women, competitions held for weaving and embroidery skills, and many merchants catered almost exclusively to women's tastes.

With surprise, Fiona realized that the exotic woman and her

attendants appeared to be the only other females at the gathering. Her curiosity about the woman returned. Who was she, some wealthy jarl's wife?

Abandoning her tasks for the moment, Fiona sought out Dag, who was helping Rorig set up the tents. "When we arrived, there was a woman over there." She pointed to where she had observed the female grooming her hair. "She sat in a carved chair, and there were thralls waiting on her. Do you know who she is, Dag?"

He looked up. "What did she look like?"

"She has beautiful hair—the color of well-aged mead. I saw her combing it, acting as haughty as a queen."

"Ah, that is Lygni's bed thrall."

"She is a thrall?" Fiona asked in astonishment.

"Lygni's first wife died last winter. I'm sure he means to wed the woman as soon as she bears him a son."

"Why did he bring her? I've seen no other women here, excepting those who serve her." Fiona said.

"Mayhap she wanted to come or Lygni thought to impress the other jarls that he possessed such a beautiful concubine."

"You think she is beautiful?" Fiona felt a sudden stab of jealousy.

Dag turned toward her, and in the fading light she could just barely make out his teasing grin. "*Ja,* she is beautiful—and a sharp-tongued shrew. Believe me when I tell you that I don't envy Lygni his woman."

Fiona was silent, wondering how often Dag's countrymen had referred to her with similar words.

When the tents were finally arranged, Dag led Fiona inside the one they shared. He leaned down and kissed her. "I must keep company with the other men this night. Sleep well, Fiona."

She reached for his tunic, pulling him down for another kiss. "Do you have to go?"

"*Ja.* Much of the business of the *Thing* will be settled by men talking in small groups around the fire. This is my opportunity to find a crew for our journey."

Fiona released him and sat back with a sigh. He left the tent and she heard him talking to the other men. Gradually the sound of male voices receded in the distance. Fiona removed her outer tunic and snuggled under the bed furs.

Without Dag's warmth, the bed was chilly. She wriggled, trying to generate some heat. She felt restless and edgy, torn by her conflicting emotions. For the thousandth time, she reminded herself of her responsibility to her people. She was a princess and heir to Donall Mac Frachnan. She had a duty to return to her homeland.

Turning onto her back, she stared glumly into the darkness.

Dag walked back to camp, tense with frustration. Thor's fury! He had not thought it would be so difficult. *Ja,* other young Norsemen were eager to go to Ireland—to raid and burn! He had gotten nowhere when he mentioned settling there. Why could not other men see the real wealth of Ireland was not in the gold and jewels that could be plundered from her monesteries and settlements, but in the isle's rich green fields and gentle climate, her good harbors and favorable sea currents? His countrymen were fools if they could not imagine the possibilities.

Mayhap he would have had better luck if he had approached one of the wealthy jarls. A man with several ships might be more willing to risk one on an unknown venture. But he dared not go to most of the older men for fear they would betray his plan to Sigurd. He did not want to share his dream with his brother until all was settled; he dreaded the thought of Sigurd's disappointment and hurt at his defection.

Dag sighed as he reached the group of tents which marked their campsite. Tomorrow, he would try again. After the games and contests and an afternoon drinking ale, men would be zealous and primed for adventure. He would seek out the warriors with the most to gain and the least to lose—younger men, landless men—and convince them of the merit of his plan. He would find the crew he needed, and the use of a ship.

Quietly, he crept into the tent he shared with Fiona. He would not wake her—not when he had no good news to give her.

* * *

When Fiona opened her eyes, it was morning and Dag was struggling into his clothes.

"You're leaving again?" she asked sleepily.

"The formal meeting of the jarls is today. Both Sigurd and I will attend."

"Why can't Sigurd go alone? He will be jarl after Knorri, not you." Fiona knew she sounded peevish, but she could not help herself. If Dag succeeded in his plan, they did not have much more time together.

"Sigurd wishes for me to accompany him," Dag answered. "Two men can better represent Knorri's interests than one could." He leaned over and kissed her warmly. "After this meeting, the gathering will turn to fun and entertainment. There will be contests between warriors this afternoon, then feasting and competition between skalds tonight. We will be together then."

Fiona nodded, feeling unpacified. They had so little time; she wanted to spend every moment with Dag.

With the men gone, Fiona had few duties this morning, and she took advantage of the fact, lying in the tent until the sun was well up, then dressing lazily. After washing in the spring, she went to the cart and found some bread in one of the packs. She nibbled on a piece and surveyed the nearby campsite.

Lygni's thrall sat on her carved oaken chair, grooming her gleaming hair in the sunshine. Fiona watched her for a while, then decided to approach. She could not help being curious about this thrall who conducted herself like a queen.

Reaching the woman, Fiona cleared her throat and greeted her in Norse. The woman did not pause in her task, although her topaz-colored eyes flickered briefly to Fiona's face.

"My name is Fiona," she continued. "I am here with Dag Thorsson of Engvakkirsted." The woman remained silent. In exasperation, Fiona said, "Since it appears we are among the only women at this gathering, I thought it might be pleasant to become acquainted."

The woman finally focused her gaze on Fiona. "Dag Thorsson—is he a jarl?"

"*Nei,*" Fiona answered.

The woman sniffed disdainfully. "Then you are a common thrall and it is beneath me to have speech with you."

Fiona went rigid. She would not stand for this sort of treatment. "I was a princess back in Eire!" she retorted hotly. There was a glint of interest in the woman's smoky-gold eyes. Fiona continued. "I intend to return to my homeland as soon as Dag finds a shipowner willing to transport me there."

The woman laughed. "Is that what your master told you? How amusing." A hard look came over her face. "I would wager my best jeweled comb that by the time your generous master finds a willing shipowner, your belly will be swelled with his babe and he will never agree to let you go."

Fiona's indignation intensified. "Dag brought me here to the *Thing* for the purpose of arranging my transport. I expect to leave within a fortnight."

"A fortnight!" The woman threw back her head and laughed uproariously. "Stupid Irish wench! Do you really think your master will let you go?"

Fiona glared at the woman. "Of course he will let me go. Dag is a man of honor. He would not make a promise he did not intend to keep."

The woman leaned over the side of the chair. "Obviously you have lost favor with your master and he means to sell you off." She tsked sadly. "The life of a bed thrall is harder than it looks. You must keep your wits about you if you want to keep your master interested and accommodating. Some women make the mistake of appearing too eager and subservient, but men soon tire of that. 'Tis better to be scornful and difficult."

Fiona blinked, startled by the woman's unasked-for advice. The woman continued, "Forget your notion of returning to your homeland. You will never be a princess again. But you can be *treated* like a princess if you are clever. Get with child if at all possible. If you bear a girl, don't even bother to let your master see it. Strangle it or give it to one of your women

Your milk must dry up so you can get pregnant as soon as possible. Bearing your master a son is the only certain way to secure a comfortable life.''

''I have no need for your counsel on how to ensorcel my master,'' Fiona said firmly.

'' 'Tis clear you know nothing about men, Princess Fiona. Your master has no more plan to return you to Ireland than mine has to return me to Brittany. More like he has tired of your whining about your homeland and means to sell you off to another master. Mayhap that is where he is now—arranging for a buyer.''

''*Nei*,'' Fiona said stubbornly. ''Dag would not lie.''

The woman shrugged, and a faint smile played over her lips. ''I have found that it is when you are most sure of a man, your hold over him is in the most danger of slipping away. Heed my advice; secure his affections with a babe before it is too late.''

Fiona turned away from the woman, keeping her expression controlled. She would not listen to this. The woman did not know Dag.

She walked back to their camp and went to the cart. Searching in a pack, she found her comb and began to redo her braid. She would ignore Lygni's thrall; she was obviously a manipulative, conniving person and not to be trusted. Indeed, she should never have let the woman goad her into losing her temper.

Suddenly, Fiona realized how unwise she had been to reveal Dag's intentions. Although he had never told her so, she understood implicitly that Dag did not want Sigurd to be aware of his plan. It was easy to guess Sigurd might try to prevent Dag from returning her to Eire.

Anxiety began to gnaw at Fiona's insides. She would have to tell Dag of her indiscretion. He would know if Lygni was friendly enough with Sigurd to pose a threat. She glanced again at the haughty, exotic thrall. She could only hope the woman would say nothing to her master.

* * *

It was past midday when Dag returned to camp. Fiona sought to speak with him alone, but he dismissed her request impatiently. "The contests have begun. I would not miss them."

He took her arm and led her rapidly through the disorderly camp. They finally reached an open area in the center of the encampment where a pair of huge, bare-chested Vikings grappled. "This is the final wrestling match," Dag announced. "Then come the footraces and the axe-throwing contest."

Fiona glanced at Dag, noting his heightened color and the intense look in his eyes. He obviously took a great interest in the games. With a sigh, she turned her gaze toward the contest of agility and strength before them.

The two Viking athletes circled, assessing each other with taut alertness. One was tall, with brown, curling hair, reminding Fiona of Sigurd. The other, a fair-haired man, was slightly shorter, but his body was as broad and sturdy as a bull's, his arms like gnarled branches. Observing the man's enormous size and watching his massive muscles flex, she wondered if even the strongest of Irish warriors would be able to best him.

The tension built; the crowd shouted encouragement. At last, the taller of the two men lunged forward. So quickly it was difficult to observe, he grabbed the other man's leg and jerked him off balance so he tumbled to the ground. Then, again using the advantage of speed, he whirled behind his fallen opponent and grabbed his shoulders. The shorter man strained in his grasp, grunting fiercely, using sheer muscle power to resist.

The two men writhed and struggled, stirring up the dust. Sweat shone on their fair skin and darkened their hair. Those watching erupted with cheers and shouts, and even Fiona felt a tingling exhilaration.

Unconsciously, she chose the taller man as the one she wished to win. She bit her lip and tensed as the fair, broad man suddenly broke free, then rolled to knock his opponent into the dirt. The tall man's shoulders hovered perilously close to the ground, then he regained control and, with a stunning reversal, pinned the other man beneath his body.

At the victory of the man she favored, an exuberant cry broke from Fiona's throat, mingling with the roar of the other spectators. She flushed, realizing how easily she had become caught up in Viking ways, and turned to Dag, expecting him to be as excited as she was. To her surprise, he appeared distracted. Instead of watching the wrestlers, he perused the crowd around them as if searching for someone."

She pulled on his arm. "Dag . . ."

He shook his head and walked away, striding toward a warrior with striking silvery-blond hair and light-gray eyes. In contrast, the man's tanned skin appeared almost brown.

When she caught up with Dag, the other man was thumping his shoulder heartily. "Dag Thorsson, you clever bastard, how did you know Einar would win? Anyone could see that Bjarni is bigger and stronger."

"Ah, but not as fast," Dag answered, grinning at the man. "What say you—would you like to wager on the footrace as well?"

The man surveyed the contestants thoughtfully. "A bunch of striplings!" he said derisively. "Nothing like what you and I were like when we ran races. I trow we could still beat these puny boys."

Dag laughed. "Not with your knee."

The man looked down ruefully at his leather-clad legs. "*Nei,* you are right. A few battles may harden shoulder and arm muscles and sharpen a man's reflexes, but war plays havoc with legs. But what of you, Dag?" The man looked up expectantly. "Why aren't you participating in the contests this year?"

"I took a blade in my sword arm this summer; it still isn't back to full strength."

Fiona looked at Dag in surprise. She had not guessed the wound still troubled him.

The man nodded genially and turned away. "If you don't mean to wager with me, I must find other quarry."

As the man disappeared into the crowd, Fiona moved closer to Dag. "Who was that?"

"His name's Ellisil. We used to compete in these contests together. At one time, he was unbeatable in the footrace, but an axe blow smashed his knee a few years ago. He's fortunate he can still walk, let alone run."

Fiona shivered at this reminder of war. "Is it true your arm still bothers you?" she asked accusingly. "You told me you were completely healed."

Dag shrugged. "I am healed, enough for battle anyway." He again scanned the men around them, frowning. "I'm sorry, Fiona, but there is something I must do. Stay close to Sigurd. I will be back shortly." Fiona gaped in surprise as Dag disappeared into the mass of brawny warriors.

Chapter 26

Dag caught up with Ellisil and grabbed the pale-haired man by the arm. "Take a moment from your wagering to speak to me, sword brother. I have not seen you since the beginning of the sunseason. Did you go *aviking* this year?"

Ellisil smiled. "*Ja,* we raided the coasts of Albion. The plunder was good and the women pleasing . . . though nothing like that black-haired thrall I saw you with. Celt, is she?"

Dag nodded. "*Ja,* an Irishwoman. I captured her in a raid last spring. Indeed, that is what I meant to speak to you about. I would like to make another journey to Ireland, but my brother feels it too late in the season. I seek a ship and a crew to sail with me. What say you—does the thought of some autumn *viking* make your blood run hot?"

Ellisil glanced back toward the contest area. "Are there more women there who look like that one?"

"*Ja,* I suppose so," Dag answered, thinking it was probably a lie. There could only be one Fiona. "Are you only interested in women, Ellisil? Would not the thought of land of your own also appeal to you?"

"I suppose it is expensive to keep a woman like that,"

Ellisil mused. "Such a delicate, soft-skinned creature cannot be expected to toil as a stout Norsewoman would."

"I fear the harsh climate of our land is damaging to such beauty," Dag agreed. "The land of Eire has a gentle climate and a bounty of food and comforts. " 'Twould be a better place to settle if you wished to keep a woman like mine."

Ellisil frowned thoughtfully. "And you say you plan to go there now, not even waiting until spring?"

"Why wait? Why spend a lonely winter in the longhouse with naught but smelly, rude warriors for company when you could bed down in a cozy hall with a comely Irishwoman?" Dag held his breath. Ellisil was near the first man he had found who had some interest in Ireland beyond a quick raid.

" 'Tis an appealing thought, but I will have to talk to my father. Skirnir gives me the use of his ships, although my brother will, of course, be jarl after him."

"Is Skirnir here?"

"Nei, he sent me in his stead," Ellisil answered. "Mayhap you should come back with me to Ferjeshold and talk to him."

Dag considered Ellisil's offer, feeling torn. He could hardly expect Skirnir to offer his ship without receiving a detailed account of Dag's plan, but what of Fiona? He could not take her with him to see Skirnir, and the only alternative was to leave her with Sigurd. She would have to understand that this was necessary if he meant to return her to Ireland. He weighed his decision hurriedly. "When do you leave for Ferjeshold?"

"Early on the morrow. My brother plans a trading expedition to Hedeby, and he is eager for me to return so I can sail with him."

Dag nodded. "I will meet you at dawn. Tell me where your camp lies."

Dag shivered as he walked back to the assembly of Norsemen. The sun had vanished behind thick clouds, and a few raindrops fell, hissing on a nearby fire. He would speak to Fiona first, then find Sigurd. Could he trust his brother to keep Fiona safe while he was gone from Engvakkirsted? He would have to.

He breathed a sigh of relief when he found Fiona standing

close to Sigurd, observing the axe-throwing contest. He took her arm, then spoke to his brother, "I'm taking Fiona back to camp. I will speak with you later."

Sigurd nodded and returned his attention to the contest.

"What's wrong, Dag?" Fiona asked as they walked away from the circle of Norsemen. "You have scarce watched the contests, nor spent a moment with me."

"There are many things to arrange if I am to return you to Eire yet this season."

Fiona opened her mouth, ready to tell Dag that she no longer was certain she wished to go. Dag forestalled her with his intense, commanding words. "On the morrow, I am going to Ferjeshold, Jarl Skirnir's steading. If luck is with me, he will provide the ship and crew I need. I'm leaving you in Sigurd's care while I am gone. I will make him swear to protect you from Brodir."

"You're not returning to Engvakkirsted?"

"*Nei.*" Dag stopped walking and pulled her around to face him. "You must trust me, Fiona. If I make him vow to it, Sigurd will keep you safe. He is a man of honor, and he cares enough for me to heed my wishes."

Fiona felt sick inside. It was happening so fast. Already, Dag was leaving her. "Why can't I go with you?" she asked. "If I came to the *Thing,* why cannot I journey with you to Skirnir's steading?"

"I'm afraid your presence there would cause too many difficulties."

"You mean you fear I would shame you! Tell me, have I not been obedient on this journey? I have done everything you asked, conducted myself with meekness. . . .''

"Hush, Fiona, I would not fight." Dag pulled her close. "I do not wish to leave you, but it cannot be helped. Do you never consider how fraught with difficulty this journey is? I must find a man willing to trust me with his ship, then gather men and supplies, all in the short space of weeks before the weather turns foul and the seas too rough to sail. I scarce have time to think of anything else." He sighed heavily.

Fiona chewed her lower lip. Dag had worked so hard to

make this journey to Ireland possible. How could she tell him of her doubts? "If it grows too dangerous to sail this late, could we not wait until spring?"

Dag shook his head. "You cannot spend the winter in that shabby slave dwelling. 'Twould break my heart to see you thus." He tightened his arms around her.

Fiona closed her eyes against the threat of tears. Dag cared enough for her to give her back her freedom. How could she not be touched by his selflessness? If only she could accept his gift without feeling despair.

I love you! her heart screamed as he kissed her tenderly. *I cannot bear to leave you!*

Dag released her, and they continued their journey to camp. Once there, he helped her into the tent. "I must go," he told her as he put on warmer clothes. I have to speak to Sigurd tonight, to seek his promise to see to your protection."

As soon as Dag left her, Fiona buried her face in the bed furs and cried with great racking sobs. In time, she calmed and, brushing away her tears, lay back on the bedplace. It did not seem fair that she must love Dag only to give him up. But life was not fair. She must do her duty to her kin, even as Dag expected. She had forgotten her responsibilities when she defied her father, and her failure had brought disaster upon Dunsheauna. This time she would act as a princess should and choose her people over the yearnings of her heart.

Sigurd gazed after his brother thoughtfully. He did not understand Dag's sudden plan to go with Ellisil. He would have thought Dag unwilling to be parted from the Irishwoman for any reason, yet now he left to go on a trading voyage to Hedeby. Sigurd shook his head. 'Twas utterly unlike Dag.

"Shall we walk back together?" Jarl Lygni approached Sigurd, his heavy gold neck-collar and armbands clanking as he walked. "I weary of the *skald* contest, and our camps are close. I would not mind a friendly ear on the journey to my tent. I'm certain I will not find such a thing when I arrive.

Sigurd laughed. "Is your foreign thrall still bedeviling you! Thor's thunder, Lygni—why do you endure the wench?"

Lygni looked sheepish. "I hope to get a son of her. With her sharp tongue and cunning, I trow that a warrior of her blood would be a man to reckon with." He sighed. "But sometimes I wonder if 'tis worth waiting 'til her womb quickens. If only I could find a way to silence her complaints. Always, she bends my ear with tales of other men who treat their women better, as if I did not pamper her like a queen. Why, just this day she spoke of your brother and how generous he is to his Irish thrall!"

"Dag?"

"*Ja.* Although I could scarce credit her story, Eleni says Dag is so besotted with the woman, he actually means to return her to her homeland."

"What?" Sigurd asked harshly.

Lygni nodded. "Eleni vows he cares so much for his thrall that he intends to restore her to her people. It may have been a lie—Eleni often exaggerates. I certainly can't imagine a sane man doing such a thing. If he loves the woman, why would he give her up?"

Because he is a soft-hearted fool! Sigurd's jaw tightened. Damn Dag for his ridiculous affection for the Irish wench!

Lygni's bushy brows rose. "You think it is true?" he asked incredulously. "What is Dag thinking of? I am fond of Eleni, but never would I forget what she is—a valuable piece of property. I would no more return her to her kin in Brittany than I would hand over my neck-ring."

"I fear it is true," Sigurd answered bitterly. "My brother has strange notions regarding women, and I fear the Irishwoman has aggravated his confusion."

"Do you intend to aid him in this nonsense?" Lygni asked.

"*Nei,* I will find a way to stop him, if I can."

They reached the area where their tents were spread. Sigurd gazed thoughtfully at the one which belonged to his brother. Fiona was there, alone. Dag had told him that he made camp with Ellisil this night since they intended to leave so early. Sigurd flexed his fingers. How easy it would be to snap the

Irishwoman's neck and rid his brother of her once and for all. But *nei,* he could not. He had promised Dag; he was honor-bound to protect her.

"Beg pardon, Lygni, I would ask you to join me for a drink beside our fire, but I must find my brother. I have a notion that he means to leave early to seek out men and aid for his absurd plan. I would speak to him ere he goes."

Lygni nodded. "Do what you can. Other men with restless women thralls depend upon you to keep Dag from this ill-conceived venture.

"Turgeis and his men have settled in the north, but we could control the south." Dag spoke intently, so on fire with his plans he scarcely noticed the rain falling on them as they walked. With the storm coming, he had convinced Ellisil not to wait until morning, but set out for Ferjeshold immediately.

"Think of it, Ellisil, land of your own, and a fair Irish maiden like Fiona. I trow, such a prospect seems to me worth dying for!"

"I have heard it is a forbidding isle, Ireland is," Ellisil responded. "Their dead sleep uneasily, and the place is overrun with supernatural beings. I'm not certain I want to dwell there, even as jarl of my own steading."

"For land of my own I would be willing to dwell among a band of trolls," Dag retorted.

"Do you know the language? Did the woman teach you to speak her tongue?"

"I learned enough to converse with her about commonplace things. Fiona knows the territory and the other chieftains in the area. That will making settling there much easier."

"And she has agreed to help you?"

Dag hesitated. He and Fiona had never discussed the details of the expedition. Would she be willing to aid him in subduing her people and gaining control over her father's lands? Even if he took her to wife and made her his queen, would she accept his rule over Dunsheauna? His jaw tightened. She must; it was the only way they could be together and both retain their freedom and their pride. "The woman would be a princess of Eire again," he answered. "She wishes to return to her land and recover her inheritance. I offer her the opportunity to do so.

Ellisil sighed. " 'Tis a bold plan, but for every warrior who succeeds in settling in a foreign and hostile territory, dozens of others die trying. I wish I had more time to think on it. Could the journey not wait until spring?"

"If we wait, it may too late. Other Norsemen will soon realize Ireland's vulnerability as we have. If we hesitate, they will take the best land."

Ellisil did not respond. Dag grew impatient. Dare he ignite the old competition which had been between them since they were boys? If he goaded Ellisil, he might make an enemy for life. But he was desperate to make the other man see his viewpoint. "I cannot believe this." He made his voice cold with disgust. "You are afraid of the Irish!"

Ellisil jerked to a halt beside him. "Are you calling me a coward? Do you suggest that I am a soft, weak man to be left behind while others challenge the boundaries of the Norse world?"

"Nei, I suggest no such thing. I know you are a brave and fierceless warrior. That is why I would have you with me." Dag held his breath.

Ellisil laughed. "You have learned tact and persuasion in the years since we were boys. I trow, you will manage to beguile my father with your silky words and he will demand I go. He wishes to see me settled and wed—so I do not trouble his conscience that he has no land to give me. Your plan will fit perfectly with his."

"If Skirnir provided a ship and some of the men, we would share our profits equally with him. Eire is a rich land; we could make him wealthy.

"Think of it, Ellisil," Dag continued. "We would live in a fortress on a soft green hill within a stout palisade, mayhap even a wall constructed partly of stone—there are stones everywhere on that isle. We would have cattle, sheep, and horses—and hounds, big fluffy-coated beasts like my old dog, Ulvi. On winter nights, we would let the dogs into the feasthall to warm themselves before the fire while the *skald* performed. Fiona says that many Irishman play the harp as well as telling tales, *bards* the Irish call them. The hall would with ring with music and the clink of horns and beakers as the warriors drank and boasted. And there would be women, smooth-skinned, graceful women.''

Ellisil laughed. ''You have almost convinced me, Dag. But tell me more about the women.''

''We would find you a princess, sword brother. One fearless and beautiful. Her skin would be as white and fair as the mist, her voice as soft and seductive as the wind through the reeds, her body as gently rounded as the Irish hills and as supple as a silvery stream. You would breed great warriors upon her body.

Ellisil groaned. ''Curse you, Dag! You should have been a *skald*.''

Fiona struggled to escape the tendrils of her dreams. Even as she woke, she was aware of a sense of loss. She instinctively reached out for Dag. Her eyes snapped open as she found cold, empty space beside her. She sat up, remembering. Dag had left her to find a ship and men. He had asked her to trust him.

She rearranged her clothes hastily, tidied her braid, then left the tent to go out in the rain. Nothing remained of their camp except the tent she had slept in. She looked around uneasily. Spying the cart, she hurried toward it. The horses were already harnessed to the vehicle, and the cart was piled high with supplies. Sigurd came up, grunting as he loaded his rolled-up tent.

Fiona snapped at him. ''Why didn't you wake me? Did you mean to leave me behind?''

Sigurd's cold, blue eyes flicked to the tent she had just left. ''I would not desert a valuable tent, and you were inside it.''

Fiona bristled at Sigurd's implication that she was less than baggage. Then she remembered that Dag had asked Sigurd to look after her. It might be wise to temper her hostility and seek Sigurd's favor. ''Is there any way I can help?'' she asked.

"Nei, I think you have done enough already."

Glancing at Sigurd, Fiona was suddenly aware of the rage in the huge man's face. The sight sucked the breath from her body.

"If I could choose," Sigurd continued in a slow, deliberate voice, "I'd leave you here, my gift to the men gathered for the Thing—*all* of them."

Fiona flinched. What had Dag done—leaving her under this man's protection?

Sigurd stepped back, as if the sight of her disgusted him. "Unfortunately, my brother made me promise to see you safely back to Engvakkirsted, and I must honor his wishes. Get your things together—quickly, quietly. I do not need any excuse to discipline a wench who has subverted my brother's loyalty."

Feeling as if she had woken to a nightmare, Fiona scurried to obey.

Chapter 27

The journey back to Engvakkirsted took twice as long as anticipated. The storm followed them, slowing their progress as the heavy cart foundered in the mud. The wind whipped the rain against their faces, and their garments grew sodden and heavy. Fiona trudged along listlessly, overwhelmed by the struggle to keep warm, to keep walking.

The second day, the mud grew even deeper, the rain colder. After Fiona stumbled and fell several times, Sigurd, swearing, finally allowed her to ride in the cart. She climbed among the barrels and sacks of supplies and sank down into a deep, empty sleep.

When she awoke, she was lying on a pallet in the slaves' dwelling. Breaca leaned over her, a beaker of hot liquid in her hand. "Drink, Fiona. 'twill warm your blood."

Fiona drank, then choked as memory returned. She was back at Engvakkirsted, and Dag was gone. Tears filled her eyes.

"Fiona, what is it?"

She looked up at Breaca's young face, scrunched up with worry. "Oh, lass, I don't know what to do. Dag means to take me back to Ireland."

"But that is what you wish, isn't it?"

Fiona shook her head. "No longer do I know what I wish. I can't deny that it breaks my heart to think of leaving Dag."

"You must speak to him," Breaca said. "I'm certain Dag won't make you go if you don't wish it."

"I will. *If* I see him again. Dag has gone to another steading to secure the use of a ship and a sailing crew. He has left me in Sigurd's care, and I worry I will survive 'til he returns."

"That is nonsense. Sigurd would not kill his brother's thrall. Besides, he owes you a debt for saving Gunnar's life."

Fiona shook her head grimly. "I fear Sigurd has learned of Dag's plans and blames me for driving his brother away."

"How could Sigurd know?"

"I foolishly boasted to another woman thrall that my master meant to return me to my homeland. I'm certain Sigurd found out my words from the woman or the woman's master." Fiona sighed heavily. "I am doomed. Even if Sigurd does not order my death, Brodir means to kill me and Sigurd has little reason to stand in his way."

"I cannot believe Dag would leave you unprotected."

"He tried. He went to Sigurd and obtained his promise to keep me safe. Dag could not know that Sigurd would learn of his plans and blame me."

"Sigurd is a man of honor. If he made such a promise to Dag, he will keep it, no matter how much he might despise you."

Fiona shook her head again. "I would like to have faith in Sigurd's honor, but my heart is cold with dread."

" 'Tis only that you are tired and ill," Breaca soothed. "Drink the rest of the broth, then go back to sleep. You will feel better soon."

Fiona lay back, so exhausted she could not keep her eyes open.

Almost a day later, she awoke. As it might heal a fever, sleep had burned away the worst of her anxiety. If she could avoid the notice of Sigurd and the other men, they might ignore her until Dag returned.

She rose unsteadily, looking for Breaca. The slave dwelling was deserted. A cauldron of pottage sat near the fire. Fiona stuck a finger in the congealed broth and licked it. She made a face. No wonder the other thralls had been so appreciative of her cooking skills; she would resume her duties as soon as possible.

She returned to her pallet, searching for her warm clothes. They lay beside the bedplace, neatly folded. Fiona picked up the fur-lined tunic and lifted her arms to put it on. A stale, unpleasant smell wafted to her nostrils.

"Saint Bridget, but you stink!" she said aloud. She looked down at the dirty kirtle she wore. All those days of travelling, and no opportunity to bathe properly. At the *Thing,* what with dozens of men around, she had been unable to do more than wash her face and hands. Now she sorely needed a bath.

She bent over her pallet, searching beneath the straw mattress for a change of clothes. There was only one clean linen undershift left from the days when she'd slept in Dag's bed-closet. She would have to wear that under her tunic until her kirtle could dry.

Grabbing the clean shift and a bone comb, Fiona walked cautiously toward the bathhouse. She breathed a sigh of relief when she found the slave portion of the dwelling empty. Slipping inside, she firmly latched the door, then stoked the fire. While she waited for the hut to heat, she undid the plaits of her hair and undressed. Memories crowded her mind. What pleasure Dag had given her in this place, what awe-inspiring lovemaking they had shared.

She shivered at the thought, then began to wash. As soon as she was clean, she dressed and sat down on one of the benches to work the snarls from her hair. Her hands stilled in her damp tresses as her gaze rested on the wooden bench she sat on. Never would she forget the feel of Dag's skin against hers, the glow of his blue eyes in the firelight. Her golden god—impaling her body with his own until they were joined in ecstasy.

She closed her eyes. How could she leave Dag? He was her soul, as dear to her as her own self. If she gave him up to do her duty, she would live the rest of her life as a ruined, empty shell.

Resolution filled her as she opened her eyes and gazed at her surroundings. She could not leave Dag. It would be better to suffer the humiliation of remaining a Norse thrall than to give up her lover, better to forget her heritage than to destroy this chance for happiness. Her parents had married for love—so would she. She would follow the instincts of her heart.

She sighed deeply. If Dag returned and the gods blessed her, she would soon conceive. And once she bore Dag's child, nothing else would matter. She would find happiness—even in this grim, lonely land.

She smiled as she looked around the bathing hut. She could scarcely wait for Dag to return to tell him of her decision. He need not struggle to put together this expedition to Ireland. She would stay with him, by his side, until the last breath left her body.

She got up slowly, picking up her dirty clothes, and went out of the bathing hut. The cold, raw air assaulted her damp hair and skin, and some of her euphoric mood faded. When would Dag return? He had made no mention of how long his mission would take. Would he be gone days, or weeks?

She quickened her pace, abruptly realizing how alone and helpless she was. She was nearly to the thrallhouse when something caught at her hair, drawing her up short. Fiona twisted around to free herself and met Brodir's mocking face.

She stared at him wildly, her mind sifting through the possibilities for escape. There were none. Brodir had hold of a thick strand of her hair. If she tried to pull away, he would be on her in seconds. His slit-like eyes glittered with triumph; his thin lips stretched into a mirthless smile.

"I could have you now," he said, his voice low and disturbingly soft. "I could take you into the woods or to one of the byres and use you until you begged for death."

Fiona forced herself to take a shaky breath. She must remember to breath normally or she would never be able to run if she had a chance.

"But I've thought of a better way." He smiled again, his ugly face like a death's mask. "You won't escape, witch woman. I will see you die a horrible death."

He released her hair. Fiona stared at him, unable to believe he meant to let her go. Then she whirled away.

By the time she reached the slave dwelling, her teeth rattled in her head with cold and fear. She sank down before the fire close to weeping.

"Fiona?"

She looked up to see the boy, Aeddan, the one whom Dag had assigned to care for the horses.

"Where is Dag?" Aeddan asked. "Why didn't he come back with you?"

Another bolt of fear shot through her. "He's visiting another steading. You'll have to see to the horses by yourself."

"When is he coming back?"

In the boy's stark, anxious gaze, Fiona saw her own dread. "Soon," she said firmly. "Soon."

"The jarl would like to hear of your raid of the Irish coast." Ellisil gestured to an older man whose pale hair and eyes mirrored his own coloring.

Dag settled himself politely on a bench across from his host. "Of course, Skirnir, I would be pleased to tell you of our adventures. 'Twas my brother's idea to sail so far. A few years ago, he wintered at the Norse garrison called Dublin. He became convinced that much of Ireland is ripe for the taking. The chieftains are forever making war with each other; they have as yet not learned to stand together to repel invaders . . ."

As Dag related his story, Ellisil, Skinir, and the other men listened raptly. With every eye on him and the crowded longhouse quiet except for a fussy child and the click of a loom in the corner, Dag felt almost like a *skald* spinning a tale of adventure and heroism. The men shook their heads and grimaced in sympathy when he told how he had been wounded and thrown into the souterrain, then edged their benches closer when he described Sigurd leading the Norsemen in an ambush of Donall Mac Frachnan and his guard.

"Hold, Dag, there seems to be a piece of the story missing," Ellisil interrupted when Dag began to tell about the booty found within the Irish chieftain's private chambers. "You tell of the torching of the fortress as if you were there, but you have yet to explain how you escaped the chieftain's prison."

"The chieftain's daughter aided me." Dag stared at the startled faces of the men around him and felt a twinge of worry over telling Fiona's part in his rescue. Would they think her a traitor to her people, as he had at first?

"Ah, the black-haired thrall." Ellisil smiled with sudden comprehension. "She is a princess of her people," he told the gathering. "And one of the most beautiful woman I have ever seen—hair as black as night, flashing green eyes, and a slim, supple body like a cat's. She carries herself like a queen, too.

"What made this woman aid you, her father's enemy?" Tongstan, Ellisil's brother, asked.

"Mayhap she fell in love with his handsome face," Ellisil gibed.

Dag gave his friend an irritated look before answering. "The woman was angry with her father and desired to thwart his marriage plans for her."

Skirnir nodded. "And now you mean to take this woman to wife and claim her lands?"

"*Ja.* As her husband, I will have the right to her inheritance."

"And if her people resist, you will enforce your claim by might." Skirnir nodded again and pushed away the platter of pork before him. "It seems a worthy expedition, with much potential profit. I would be willing to lend one of my ships to such a venture, but you would have to raise your own crew. 'Tis a pity that most of the warriors who might join you have already agreed to travel to Hedeby with Tongstan."

"Why could Dag not come with us?" Ellisil suggested eagerly. "We could obtain supplies in Hedeby, then return to Ferjeshold and outfit the ship for the Irish voyage."

Dag repressed a sigh of protest. He did not want to go to Hedeby. Every moment away from Fiona, he felt sick with worry.

* * *

"The warriors gather at the longhouse."

Fiona nodded at Breaca's words and went on with her spinning.

"If only the Agirssons had agreed to abide by the decision of the *Thing*," Breaca complained. " 'Twas a fair decision, Rorig says. They broke the law, and they should pay. Instead, they commit worse atrocities, until even Sigurd believes they must be stopped."

"And how does he plan to do that?" Fiona asked.

"Sigurd has met with Ottar, jarl of the closest steading. They intend to join their men and go out looking for the Agirsson brothers. When they have found them, they will take them to the Thorvald family for justice."

Fiona stood up, carrying the spindle with her. The slave dwelling felt small and closed in, like a prison. She paced the length of it, then returned to the hearth where Breaca sat patting dough into loaves. "If Rorig sees fit to share the men's plans with you, he must trust you," she told the younger woman.

"But he has not spoken of going to the jarl about purchasing me."

"Mayhap he does not have the hacksilver to meet your price."

Breaca nodded. "When they go to the Agirsson steading to capture them, they might search for the family's treasure trove. If they find it, Rorig would have a share. Then, he might have enough to buy me." She frowned. "But I can't help worrying. What if he is hurt or killed? Who will care for me and the babe?"

"Babe!" Fiona exclaimed. "You have conceived? Why did you not tell me?"

"You have been so anxious over Dag, I feared to worry you with my own troubles."

Fiona sighed guiltily. She had been selfish, moping over her problems and thinking of no one else's. Without Breaca's company, she would have gone mad long ago. "How do you feel?'' she asked the younger woman. ''Does your belly churn?''

Breaca nodded. ''I have lost my meal these past three mornings.''

''Go to Mina and ask if she has any willow leaves so I can make you a brew to ease your discomfort.''

''I'm afraid she will not know willow from the other dried plants. Mina has little knowledge of herbs.''

Fiona frowned. ''Mayhap after the men leave on the raid, I could dare to go to the longhouse and find what we need in Mina's herb basket.''

Breaca's eyes widened. ''You would do that for me?''

Fiona gathered Breaca's slim form in her arms. ''Of course, Breaca. I would not see you suffer.''

''By the saints, not again!'' Breaca moaned.

Before Fiona could reach her, Breaca stumbled to the hearth and, falling to her knees, began retching into a cooking vessel. Fiona found a rag and took it to Breaca. ''Are you fevered?''

Breaca shook her head as she wiped her mouth. ''Nay, 'tis the babe.''

Fiona regarded Breaca with concern. Sickness in the morning was common for a woman with child, yet it worried her. She knew how dangerous pregnancy could be, especially for one as young as Breaca. Quickly, Fiona decided. ''We *must* go to Mina and seek the aid of her herbs. With the men gone after the Agirssons, there is no one here to prevent me from seeing her.''

Breaca nodded. ''Let us dress and then we'll go.''

As they walked to the longhouse, Fiona noticed Breaca's gloomy, preoccupied mood. ''You are worried about Rorig, aren't you?''

Breaca sighed. '' 'Tis not all fear for my babe's future. I have come to care for Rorig. I would miss him if he did not return.''

Fiona smiled. ''I am pleased. I had hoped the two of you would come to share a little of what Dag and I have.''

"But it hurts," Breaca complained. "I did not want to fall in love, to care!"

Fiona patted her arm. "You said the men would not be gone long, only a few days. And if Rorig succeeds, he will be able to purchase you. You will be a free woman."

A tremulous smile broke through Breaca's gloom. Fiona felt an answering warmth inside her. For all the anxiety it could bring, love was what made life worth living.

When they reached the longhouse yard, Fiona spied Brodir practicing with his weapons. She froze and watched uneasily as the warrior flung his battle-ax blade first into the dirt. He retrieved the weapon and repeated the motion. Taking a deep breath, Fiona turned to Breaca. "What is he doing here? I thought you said all the warriors had gone with Rorig."

"Someone had to stay behind and guard the steading. Apparently, Sigurd chose Brodir for the task."

Fiona cursed softly. "I'll wager he half-hopes Brodir kills me while he is gone. That way he would be rid of me without having it on his conscience."

"What do we do?" Breaca asked. "Do you wish to return to the thrallhouse."

"Nay." Fiona squared her shoulders. "We have come to see Mina, and so we shall. I'll not let that ugly Viking rule my life." She turned to Breaca. "Is there another man at the steading who could watch as we spoke to Mina?"

"There is Veland. The smith did not go on the raid either."

"Run and find him," Fiona said. "He can verify that I did not speak of anything unseemly to Mina."

Breaca returned with Veland. He gave Fiona a wary look when she explained what she wanted, then accompanied them inside the longhouse. Fiona squinted in the dim light and saw Mina at the loom in the corner. Nearby, two house thralls busied themselves spinning while young Gunnar and Ingolf shelled hazelnuts near the hearth.

Mina left her weaving as they approached. "Breaca—are you well?" were the first words from her lips.

Fiona answered, "Nothing appears amiss, but her belly is

queasy in the forenoon. If you have some willow, I would like
to make her a soothing draught.''

Mina nodded. ''I'll get my herbs.'' She gave Fiona a searching glance before turning and heading toward the back of the
dwelling.

She returned shortly with the basket of dried herbs for Fiona
to inspect.

''I need a lamp,'' Fiona said, bending over the basket. ''So
many plants look alike when they are dried.'' Breaca lit a lamp,
and Fiona searched until she found what she desired. ''Your
supply of dragonwort is almost gone,'' she warned Mina as
she closed the lid.

''I know. We are short of medicines,'' Mina answered. ''I
meant to remind Sigurd to ask Ottar's wife if they had any to
spare. They are fortunate to have a wise woman living at their
steading.''

Fiona met the other woman's gaze. There were so many
things she wanted to ask Mina, but she could not speak freely
with Veland watchng.

''Have a care,'' Mina said to Fiona, her gaze flickering
toward the entrance of the longhouse. It was clear she also
feared what Brodir might do.

Fiona nodded. ''And you as well.''

When they left the longhouse, Brodir was gone. Breaca and
Fiona looked around uneasily, then raced back to the slaves'
dwelling, heads bent against the wind.

*No escape. Fiona ran, desperate, terrified. Flames were
everywhere, licking furiously, vicious tongues of gold and
orange. Smoke billowed up and smudged the night sky. At every
turn, the massive silhouettes of Viking warriors stalked the
blaze-filled corridors of the palisade.*

*She turned back, running into the wild strobe of fire. Smoke
sucked into her lungs, a burning beast that tore at her insides.
She breathed in deeply. Once. Twice. The gasp that woke her
turned into a scream. . . .*

Sweat dripped down her face as Fiona stared around the

quiet dwelling. Beside her, thralls stirred. One of the women lifted her head and asked, "What's wrong?"

Mutely, Fiona shook her head. It had been a dream, only a dream. She lay back down again and tried to slow her frantic breathing. The uneasiness would not leave her. She could not shake the terror.

Again, she rose to a sitting position. Swiping at her damp brow, she shivered as drafts of air swirled through the openings in the flimsy structure sheltering her. A windy night, mayhap blowing in another storm.

Restless, she crawled from her bedsack and went to the doorway. The hide covering trembled and shook in the wind. She pushed it aside and peered out. Nay, not a storm. The air did not smell damp. It smelled like . . . smoke.

Fiona's nostrils flared in recognition. She had dreamed of her father's palisade burning, but that was thousands of leagues away and a dozen sennights. Now she dwelt in the land of the Norse; the scent of death-tinged smoke could not follow her here. And yet, it had. The odor was unmistakable.

She took a deep breath and ran outside.

The longhouse was heavily ablaze when she reached it. Fire ringed the oblong dwelling, trapping those inside. Fiona stared in horror. Mina, the children—oh dear God, it could not be happening again!

She began to scream, although her plaintive cries scarcely rose above the roar of the flames. She cried out for Mina, for Sigurd's sons, for her father and kinsmen. Beating her chest, she shrieked her agony to the pitiless wind.

"Witch! Irish witch!"

Fiona whirled at the low snarl beside her and met Brodir's hate-filled gaze.

"I hear how you curse them," he said. "It is because of you they die!"

Fiona bared her teeth at her enemy, but he approached her, his boar-like eyes wild. "You made the fire. You are evil. Knorri should not have let you live!"

"Odin have pity!" Sorli limped up, his seamed face grotesque in the firelight. "The murdering bastards have fired the longhouse!"

"Who, Sorli?" Fiona demanded. "Who?"

"Raiders, of course," the slavemaster answered. "Who else would do such a wicked thing?"

"Who else, indeed?" Brodir sneered. " 'Twas this witch. I heard her screaming her incantation. She brought down this calamity upon our heads. *She* is guilty!"

To Fiona's eyes Brodir appeared as mad as a slavering dog, but her hatred was too strong to hold back. She lunged at him, aiming for his face, clawing at his skin.

Strong arms dragged her away. "Cease your struggles, wench," Sorli hissed in her ear. "Do you want to be put to death for attacking a warrior?"

Fiona forced herself to go limp, her breathing to calm.

"Why weren't you at your post, Brodir?" Sorli snarled. "And where is Utgard? Did the raiders get him?"

"*Nei,* not raiders. It was *she* who caused the fire." Brodir grabbed Fiona's arm and shook her until her teeth rattled. Fiona jerked away. Mayhap she should run and hide. Sorli seemed to believe in her innocence, but there was no reason others would.

Brodir cursed her, low and fierce. Sorli gazed in dismay at the flaming longhouse while Fiona looked into the darkness behind the ruined dwelling and considered her escape. Her eyes widened as she saw figures moving through the haze of smoke.

"Blessed Jesu! They're alive."

They all stared in disbelief at the dozen women staggering toward them. Mina and a house thrall clutched Sigurd's sons to their chests. The others carried children or heavy casks.

Fiona rushed to Mina and took the child from her arms. "The jarl," Mina breathed. She bent over, coughing, then turned stricken eyes to Sorli. "Please, go after the jarl."

Sorli glanced at the inferno of the longhouse. "How?"

"There is a tunnel beneath the storeroom which leads through the ground to an entrance outside. Knorri showed us where it was. Then he went after the hacksilver. I thought he was behind us, but when we reached the outside opening, he was gone."

Sorli gripped the arm of one of the stouter thralls. "Show me."

As Sorli and the woman disappeared into the night, Fiona embraced Mina. "Thank God you are safe."

Mina stared at the longhouse. "If it were not for the old jarl, we would all be dead. Everyone was asleep when he came and pounded on the bedcloset door. He led us right to the tunnel. Said he'd had it built in case of a raid. We all grabbed something and went down into darkness. We begged the jarl to come with us, but he would not listen. He wanted to go back for the treasure." She took a gulp of air. "We had to feel our way along the stone walls. The smoke followed us. I'm afraid it caught Knorri." A sob broke from her throat.

"You must not think of it," Fiona soothed. "You are alive, and you saved the children. If Knorri does not live, then at least he died bravely, like a warrior."

It seemed only moments before Sorli and Brodir came from behind the longhouse, bearing the limp form of the jarl. When Sorli shook his head, indicating that Knorri was dead, Mina fell to her knees and began to tear at her hair in grief. The other women joined her.

Fiona stared at the dead man and grieving women, reliving her own loss. Then she heard a panicked shout and turned to see a half-dozen men running toward them. By the firelight, she recognized them as freeholders and craftsmen who lived in their own dwellings outside the longhouse. They had finally smelled the smoke and come to help. The first word on their lips was "raid."

Brodir answered them, his voice thick with hatred. " 'Twas not a raid. The Irish witch . . ." He pointed at Fiona. "She did this!"

Chapter 28

Fiona backed away from the wild-eyed men encircling her. *"Nei,* I did nothing! I was asleep in the slaves' dwelling—ask any of the thralls!"

"And why should they not lie for her?" Brodir taunted. "They are slaves like her, and she has put them under her spell. I tell you, I arrived at the fire to see her cursing in her foul tongue and waving her hands. She caused the fire with her evil sorcery."

"I was grieving!" Fiona cried, half hysterical. If these men believed Brodir, they were like to throw her into the fire now and think about it later. "I wept for the children, the women. I feared them all dead!"

"And where were *you,* Brodir?" Sorli asked sharply. "Sigurd left you to guard the steading, and you failed. The jarl is dead, our longhouse destroyed. I think you cast blame on the Irish thrall to save your own skin."

Brodir's face contorted. "I cannot fight sorcery! No warrior can!" He moved toward Fiona as if he would grab her.

Veland, stepped between them. "On the morrow, there will time to settle this. For now, we must tend to the jarl's body and find shelter for the women and children."

At his reasonable words, the other men came forward to aid Mina and the others. Within a short time, the survivors of the fire were led off to temporary beds in the dwellings of the freemen living near the steading. Breaca appeared out of the darkness and took Fiona's arm. They began to walk toward the slaves' dwelling.

"Seize the witch! She's getting away!" Brodir shouted.

Fiona turned and met Sorli's eyes, begging him to intervene for her. Sorli shook his head at Brodir. "You've lost your wits, man. Loki's name, she's only a woman. She couldn't hurt anyone." He gestured toward the eerie, orange-edged skeleton of the longhouse, still burning furiously. "That fire was set by men, by raiders. If I were you, Brodir, I'd think up a better excuse to explain to Sigurd why you failed to guard the long-house. These lame tales of sorcery and spells are unworthy of a Norse warrior."

Fury flashed in Brodir's eyes, and he took a step toward Sorli. Fiona held her breath. At last, Brodir turned and stalked off into the night.

"Thank you," she whispered to Sorli.

The gnarled-faced man gave her a fierce look. "I spoke naught but the truth, but I would not vow to it if Sigurd sees things differently. You'd best hope they find evidence of raiders when they search on the morrow. Sigurd's no fool, but he might not pass up this chance to rid himself of you. He's sore grieved over his brother's going away, and now he must face another loss."

Fiona swallowed. Sigurd would return to find his home burned and much of his wealth destroyed. Would he blame her for his misfortune? If naught else, he might have her put to death to silence Brodir.

Panic beat through her veins. She could run away, but where? As Breaca once pointed out, she was certain to perish if she fled outside the steading. Besides, if she ran, she would appear guilty of Brodir's accusations. She could not allow Mina and the others to believe she had set the blaze. And Dag—she thought desperately. If he believed her guilty of burning out his kin, he would be beside himself with remorse. He would grieve over his mistake for the rest of his life.

She shuddered. Even if it meant her life, she would not flee. Never would she allow Dag to suffer the damnable torture she had known the last few months.

She reached for Breaca's arm. "Come, let's go back to the slave dwelling."

Breaca spoke glumly as they walked. "I did not realize what it was like, how horrible a raid could be. I never considered that innocent children might perish."

"It could have been much worse. No one died but the jarl, and I imagine he was proud to go to his death defending his home rather than dying quietly in his bed. The Norse prize death in battle as the height of glory. The jarl's struggle to get the women and children out and his wealth to safety was a battle of sorts."

"I am not thinking of this raid," Breaca said. "I am thinking of what Rorig and Sigurd and the others meant to do to the Agirsson steading. I was . . . so greedy. I thought only of myself, of Rorig's securing hacksilver so we could be wed. I did not think of how others might suffer."

Breaca began to cry, and Fiona drew the weeping woman to her breast. The bitterness of Breaca's guilt reminded her of her own. But was it not merely human to think of one's own interests and forget the price that must be paid by others? "Pray, Breaca, do not carry on so."

She led Breaca to the slave dwelling and helped her lie down. Two thralls rescued from the longhouse had squeezed in among the rows of pallets, and the small building was more crowded than ever. Finding her own pallet occupied, Fiona snuggled up to Breaca and tried to sleep.

Although her body felt drained and exhausted, sleep eluded Fiona. The images of the fire and the jarl's scrawny body lying still on the ground would not leave her. What if it were Dag who had been caught in the poisonous smoke? How could she bear to go on living if Dag no longer walked the earth? A sharp pain caught her in the chest. Oh, how she loved that fierce, stubborn Viking!

A sudden thought struck her, and she jerked upright. Surely Sigurd would send word to Dag of the jarl's death. Close kin as they were, Dag was certain to come home for Knorri's funeral. Hope suffused Fiona's weary body. To be held in Dag's strong arms again, to hear the thud of his brave heart beneath her ear, to smell the enthralling musk of his skin—the thought of it nearly stole Fiona's breath away. She clutched herself tightly and tears stung her eyelids. *Blessed Bridget, please let me live long enough to tell him I love him!*

The day dawned gruesomely cold. Despite the many bodies huddled together, the chill sweeping through the cracks in the daub-and-wattle structure woke everyone early. Sitting up stiffly, Fiona surveyed the crowded dwelling. The other thralls were quiet as they went about their personal tasks this morning. They were clearly shocked by the news of the fire and apprehensive about what the disaster meant for them. Fiona sought to shut out their anxiety and concentrate on her slim hope. To see Dag again . . . to speak to him . . .

A groan from Breaca brought Fiona back to gloomy reality. "Oh, Fiona, find me a pot. . . . I'm going to be sick!"

Fiona hurried to the storage area by the hearth, stumbling over several thralls as she did so. By the time she reached Breaca, it was too late; the young woman was bent over, retching onto the dirt floor between the pallets.

"Ohhhhh," she moaned as she straightened. "Now there is no more willow to make a soothing draught for my stomach. All Mina's herbs burned in the fire." Realizing how much else had been lost, Breaca began to weep again.

Fiona planted her feet and decided that the time for coddling Breaca was past. "Nay, Breaca, you must not cry any more. 'Twill make the babe sickly and weak." She turned her glance to the rest of the thralls. "It is grim, aye," she said. "But no lives were lost, save the jarl's, and he would not have lived many more years anyway. Rebuilding the longhouse will take a great deal of work, but at least the foodstores are safe. We will not starve this winter."

"Well spoken, Irish."

Fiona looked around to see Sorli standing in the doorway. His expression was dour, as always, but Fiona thought she recognized the glint of admiration in his eyes.

He stepped into the room and spoke brusquely. "There is much to be done. Food must be prepared for the jarl's household, and Mistress Mina wants the men to go through the ruin of the longhouse and search for anything that can be salvaged. The larger timbers still smoke, but some areas can be cleared."

At Sorli's words, the thralls quickly dispersed, the woman to find food stores, the men to begin the filthy task of scavaging among the rubble.

"I can cook for Mina and the children," Fiona suggested.

Sorli shook his head. "Until Brodir's accusations are disproved, you will not go near the new jarl's family."

Jarl. Sigurd was jarl now. The thought banished Fiona's optimistic mood. When Dag returned, would Sigurd even allow her to see his brother? "Was there any sign of raiders?" she asked.

"Some," Sorli grunted. "The fire was clearly started by human hands, not sorcery. We found an empty cask of fish oil near one of the turf walls. I believe someone doused the outer timbers of the longhouse and set them ablaze."

"Are you convinced now that Brodir is mad?"

Sorli shook his head. "I tell you the facts as I see them, but I will not contradict Sigurd if he decides otherwise. 'Tis for the jarl to decide your fate, not I."

Fiona shivered. What if Dag did not come back in time? "When will Sigurd return?" she asked.

"I've sent one of the freemen to Ottar's steading to seek out the jarl. Unless Sigurd and his warriors are still chasing after the Agirsson brothers, the message should reach them in a day. I would look for the jarl to arrive by dusk tomorrow."

"And Dag?" Fiona asked breathlessly. "Have you sent word to him? Knorri was his uncle. He should know of his kinsman's passing."

"Do you hope that the jarl's brother comes and speaks for

you?'' Sorli shook his head sadly. ''That Dag cares for you does not reduce Sigurd's hatred, but increases it.''

''What should I do?'' Fiona asked. ''How can I prove my innocence?''

''If you appear a dutiful thrall, that might sway Sigurd in your favor. You must keep busy. Cook for the other thralls, as you have been doing. And spin. Except for what is on our backs, there is scarce a scrap of cloth left at Engvakkirsted.''

''Is there another loom?''

''I'm sure one of the freeholder's women has one. Can you weave?''

''I was taught to weave as a small child,'' Fiona answered tartly.

''You never know about princesses. I'll fetch the loom for you.'' Sorli gave her a wry smile and left the dwelling.

Fiona turned to her domestic tasks with a sigh. A tremor of grief ran through her as she thought of the piles of woven linen and wool stored in Mina's supply closet. It would take a household of women nearly a generation of spinning and weaving to replace such a wealth of fabric. Now it was reduced to ashes, not by an unchancy spark from a cooking fire, but by the destructive hands of raiders.

Damn men for thinking up war!

Sigurd arrived the next day. Fiona was alerted by the eager shouts that carried through the thin walls of the slave dwelling. She went out and watched as Sigurd and his oathmen entered the steading yard. Women and children, slaves and freeholders all gathered to welcome their new jarl, their cheers desperate with relief.

Fiona watched stonily as Sigurd greeted his wife with a solemn nod, then swept his children up into his arms. For a moment, her animosity lessened as she saw intense emotion sweep across Sigurd's broad face. The man obviously loved his children; she felt sure he prayed his thanks to Odin for sparing them.

Then Sigurd's expression once more grew harsh and stoic.

He dismissed the women, children, and thralls and began to question the men he had left behind to guard his home. Half-hidden behind one of the storehouses, Fiona watched intently. She heard Brodir voice his vicious accusations. Sigurd listened briefly, then silenced him with an abrupt gesture. The jarl turned to Utgard and questioned him.

Fiona strained her ears to hear what he said. Utgard had been the other warrior guarding the longhouse on the night of the fire. He could not be found that night, but the next day he had stumbled into the courtyard with a story of being struck over the head, tied up, and left in the woods. Fiona was not certain she believed him, although she had seen the raw places on his wrists. It seemed very odd to her that the raiders had not killed him, but had merely shackled him out of the way.

But no more odd than the story Brodir had finally given Sorli. He claimed the ale he had drunk that evening was drugged and he had fallen into a deep sleep, not waking until he "heard the witch's screams." Fiona could not fathom Brodir's mind. Did he imagine that casting the blame on her would save him from Sigurd's wrath? Or did he really believe that she had drugged him and set the blaze with magical incantations?

Now Sigurd spoke to Sorli. Fiona held her breath, praying that the slavemaster would be able to sway the new jarl with his practical explanation for the source of the fire. She knew Sigurd respected the old warrior. Surely he would accept Sorli's word over that of a raving, self-serving lunatic like Brodir.

Sigurd looked thoughtful as Sorli made his report, but his thick fists clenched and unclenched in an impatient rhythm. Fiona's dread intensified. Finally, he spoke. Fiona could hear his deep voice boom across the courtyard. "Bring me the woman."

She wanted to run and hide, but she would not. She had faced Sigurd before and survived. Of course, she reminded herself, those times Dag had intervened. Now he was not here, nor would he be, mayhap, until it was too late.

Trembling, she stepped out from behind the building and walked to face her fate.

Sigurd regarded her as she approached. His eyes were full of hatred. Fiona straightened her shoulders, standing tall, like a queen. She wished she wore something finer than the soiled tunic she had worn to the *Thing,* but there was no help for that now. Sigurd had never responded to her as an attractive female anyway, at least not since the first time he had seen her and tried to ravish her.

She reached him and bowed slightly. "Jarl."

His eyes, darker and less blue than his brother's, swept over her contemptuously. She guessed he noted how small she was, how frail. In a physical contest with him, she had as much chance as a lamb facing down a full-grown wolf.

"Fiona of the Deasúnachta—you have been accused of treachery and murder."

Fiona's heart skipped a beat, and she watched Sigurd intently.

"Sorli argues for your innocence," Sigurd continued. "And for all you have shamefully manipulated my brother, I have marked that you have a kindness for woman and children. I don't believe you would murder my family while they slumbered in their beds."

Fiona released her breath.

"But—" Sigurd eyes glittered suddenly. "—'twould be an easy way for me to be rid of you and I cannot say that the thought of your death displeases me. You have cost me much by subverting my brother's mind with your bedevilments. I must think on this matter. Even now, Utgard rides to deliver the tragic news of my uncle's passing to Dag. I judge that I have less than two days to decide whether it would be wiser to greet my brother with your corpse or your living body."

Fiona closed her eyes and swayed.

"No word of Dag's arrival?"

Breaca entered the doorway and shook her head. Fiona cursed and began to pace the small building, her body as tense as a water-soaked skin left out to dry. Any moment she expected Sigurd to enter the tiny doorway of the dwelling and condemn her. That he had not only worsened her ordeal.

"What could be keeping Dag?" Fiona demanded. "It's been two full days since Utgard left for Skirnir's steading. Surely

Dag would not decline to come back for his uncle's funeral. If he does refuse to return—sweet Jesu, save me—Sigurd will have me put to death for certain!''

"The weather has worsened," Breaca reminded her. "That might have delayed him. Or it could be that Dag was not at Skirnir's steading when Utgard arrived. They might have gone off on a journey."

"Where?" Fiona whirled to confront Breaca. "If the weather is chancy, why would they travel? I fear the worst, that Dag has declined to come. He may not even know what danger I face."

"This is foolishness. Of course, Dag will come. He would not do something so ignoble as missing Knorri's funeral. The Norse gods willing, Dag will be here."

"Even if he comes, I do not know if he can stop Sigurd from killing me." Fiona chewed her lower lip furiously. "Sigurd does not understand what Dag and I share. He thinks that I have bewitched Dag and undermined his loyalty to the Norse. Sigurd especially hates me for making his brother plan a journey to Ireland."

"Dag can convince his brother to spare you, I know it. He will return and set things right with Sigurd."

Fiona sat down on a stool by the fire, exhausted. "I keep hoping you are right. Yet with each hour that passes, my hope grows fainter."

"Mistress! I have news!"

Fiona sprang up again as Aeddan came flying into the room. The youth paused to compose himself, then bowed faintly to Fiona. She winced inwardly. Try as she might, she could not convince Aeddan that she was a thrall like him and deserving of no special consideration. He persisted in calling her "mistress" and observing absurdly respectful behavior in her presence.

"What is it?" she asked.

"Utgard has returned."

"With Dag?"

The boy shook his head. Fiona bowed her head and turned away.

"Tell us." Breaca demanded. She grabbed the boy's arm. "Did Dag refuse to come?"

"Nei, Dag was not there. He had gone somewhere with Skirnir's sons."

Fiona turned slowly around. "Did Skirnir say where?"

The boy looked sheepish. "I did not hear. After Sigurd received the news, he walked away, angry. Utgard was busy with his ale, and I could not ask him the rest of it."

"I'm finished," Fiona whispered. "Even now, Sigurd plans my execution."

"Nay!" both Breaca and Aeddan cried.

"Ja," a rumbling voice responded.

Fiona raised her gaze to the huge man blocking the doorway.

"I've chosen a fitting punishment for a woman who does not know her place," Sigurd said. "I'm sending you with the old jarl—as his slave and concubine in the otherworld."

Breaca gasped. Fiona's throat closed up.

Sigurd continued his pronouncement, " 'Tis customary to send a great jarl to the otherworld with an accompaniment of his wealth—fine clothes stuffs, utensils, armaments, and jewels. The fire has stolen much of the riches of our steading, but I would not have Knorri go on his journey without gifts appropriate to his standing. We will send him on his proud ship, accompanied by a woman to tend to his needs. You will be the woman, Fiona. The jarl desired you in this life; now he will find satisfaction with you in the realm of the dead."

Her thoughts disordered by shock, Fiona wanted to laugh hysterically at the irony of Sigurd's decree. She had once feared that Knorri would make her his concubine. Now she was to be bound to the ancient Viking in death; the bed they shared would be a funeral pyre.

"You cannot do this!" Breaca stared up at Sigurd, her blue eyes wild. "You cannot kill Fiona! She has done nothing to deserve death!"

Sigurd regarded the young thrall with narrowed eyes. "You forget yourself wench, to speak to me so. I am jarl now. I can do anything I wish. As for the fairness of my pronouncement—" He swung his gaze to Fiona. "—'tis considered an honor for a young woman to serve a great warrior in death. I honor you, Fiona of the Deasúnachta."

A muscle twitched in Sigurd's jaw. Fiona wondered briefly if he mocked her. But if Sigurd were amused by the cleverness of his vengeance, he hid it well. His eyes were grim and bitter.

Fiona took a deep breath. She must argue for her life, and she had only one weapon to use. Although she had feared to bring up Dag before this, now she had nothing to lose.

"And what will your brother say?" she asked boldly. "Do you not fear to lose your brother's regard altogether if you murder me?"

The muscle in Sigurd's lower cheek jumped again. "He might be grieved at first, but in the end, he will thank me. I do him a favor by disposing of you in such an appropriate fashion."

"Nei," Fiona protested. "Dag loves me! He will be sorrowed by my death."

Sigurd shook his head. "He will come to his senses and remember who he is. A Norseman—a proud, valiant warrior who would never lose his heart to a woman of foreign blood."

Fiona felt numb. She forced herself to meet Sigurd's cold eyes. "Your brother does not plan to attend his uncle's funeral?"

"The messenger could not reach him." Sigurd's voice was taut. Fiona knew better than to think he lied merely in order to torture her. She accepted the truth. Dag could not be found. He would not return in time to save her.

Sigurd nodded to her curtly, then left the dwelling. After a moment, Fiona went to the doorway. Pushing the hide covering aside, she came face-to-face with a stony-faced Viking named Kalf. "Get back inside," he ordered in gruff Norse. "Sigurd says you are not to leave this dwelling until the day the old jarl is sent on his journey to the otherworld."

Fiona retreated inside the building, trembling. Breaca took her arm, leading her to a stool by the hearth. "We'll think of something," Breaca reassured her. "Dag will get the message and come and save you, I know it."

Fiona shook her head. "The messenger came back without delivering his message, and Sigurd will not send another. By the time Dag returns, there will be naught left of me but ashes."

Breaca began to weep.

Chapter 29

"For now, the jarl's body lies in a temporary grave, with food and drink and his weapons beside him," Breaca said. "When the funeral pyre is ready, they will dress him in what finery they can devise—since the fire destroyed so much—and place him in a tent on the ship."

"And me?" Fiona asked. "What will they do with me?"

Breaca's mouth quivered as she answered. "You will be taken to the ship and placed in the tent with Knorri's corpse. There will be feasting and celebration. The warriors will toast Knorri's memory and the *skald* will tell tales of his bravery." Another tremor passed over her face, then she continued. "Before the actual cremation takes place, the closest of Knorri's oathmen will come and lie with you."

"Lie with me? You mean . . ."

Breaca nodded stiffly. "To honor Knorri. After he lies with you, each man will ask you to convey his regards to the dead jarl. 'Tell your master that I do this only for love of him,' they will say." Seeing Fiona's appalled look, she added, "By this time, you will have been drugged by the wise woman; you will not even know what is happening. They say there is no pain; that you will feel peace and even happiness."

"The wise woman—who is she?" Fiona demanded. She must focus on the facts; that was why she had asked Breaca to tell her exactly what Sigurd planned. If she knew every detail of the Viking funeral rites, she could discover some route of escape.

"Sigurd has sent for the old wise woman from Ottar's steading. For the funeral, she will play the role of the 'Angel of Death.'" Breaca grimaced. " 'Tis she who will oversee your execution."

"You mean I am to be killed before the fire is lit?"

Breaca nodded. "A cord will be tied around your neck, and you will be strangled and stabbed to death at the same time."

Despite her resolve to be calm and dispassionate, Fiona shuddered. The worshippers of the old gods of Eire had once performed similar sacrifices, but most of her countrymen were Christian now. The Viking funeral rite seemed barbaric in the extreme. What horrified her the most was the thought of coupling with Knorri's warriors. In her worst nightmares she had imagined being raped repeatedly by Vikings; now, if Sigurd had his way, such a fate would be hers.

Wrapping her arms around herself, Fiona gazed desperately at the doorway. How was she to escape? The entrance to the slave dwelling was guarded day and night, and she would scarcely have any more freedom once she was placed on the ship. She would be in the care of this wise woman, this "Angel of Death." The horrible creature would surely guard her prey carefully.

Fiona shivered again. She could only hope that the drug the woman gave her banished her awareness of what was happening. If she were not able to comprehend what they did to her, it would not be so bad. Nay, it would be worse. To go helplessly, meekly, to her death—it was a shameful thing. Better to end her life herself and cheat the Vikings of their ugly, evil plans. Fiona glanced around the small building again, searching for a knife or other weapon.

Breaca saw Fiona's questing glance, and immediately guessed her goal. "Nay, Fiona," she said quietly. "They left no weapons for you to use against yourself or them." The young woman shook her head, sympathetic tears blurring her eyes. "I will try to find some poison for you, if you wish it. I know Mina would help, but her store of herbs is gone."

"Mina!" Fiona looked up, surprised out of her blind terror. "You think Mina would help me?"

"Aye, I do," Breaca answered, moving close to Fiona so that she might whisper. "Mina thinks what Sigurd plans is wrong. She argued with him to spare your life, to forget his murderous scheme for burning you with Knorri."

"And?"

"He would not listen. Sigurd has made up his mind, and he sees it as a sign of weakness to back down. He will not heed the advice of anyone, even his wife."

"Do you think Mina would contrive to help me escape?"

Breaca shook her head. "As much as she disapproves of Sigurd's plans, she would not defy him openly. Nay, the most we could hope for is that she might secure some poison from one of the other women so you could end your life ere Sigurd puts his wicked plan in motion."

Poison. Fiona wrinkled her brow in thought. Would it be more noble to seek her end that way? In the past, she had considered choosing death a coward's decision; now, she was not certain. Why should she endure the degradation and pain Sigurd had planned for her if she had the means to avoid it? The image of Brodir coming to rape her flashed into her mind, and Fiona decided quickly.

She took Breaca's arm. "Ask Mina," she whispered. "Ask her if she would do this for me."

Breaca nodded and left the slaves' dwelling. Fiona sighed and sat by the fire. An image came to her, taking shape among the flickering flames—Dag's proud, handsome face, his blue eyes glowing with passion, his wavy hair a wild nimbus around his features, his body strong and hard. Fiona's soul reached out for the compelling vision, drawing it into her heart. She would think of Dag when she took the poison. She would send him her spirit as she died. In death she would be joined with him, even if they had failed to join their spirits in life.

A sob broke from her throat. She was not ready to die! She

had not said goodbye to Dag nor had the chance to tell him how much she loved him. She had not borne him a child of her womb. How could she leave him now, with so much left unfinished between them?

She choked back another moan of grief and stood up and began to pace. There must be some way out of this trap, some means of escape she could not see. Mayhap the wise woman could be bribed. At the thought, Fiona paused in her restlessness. Breaca had said that Rorig had returned with treasure, enough hacksilver to buy her freedom and more. Would Breaca consider asking her lover for a portion of his wealth, enough to tempt the wise woman? Fiona exhaled in relief. It was a clumsy plan, but a plan nonetheless. While there was breath in her body, she would not yield. She would fight for her life until the cincture closed around her throat and her vision went black.

"Fiona would be very distressed to learn of your plan," Breaca said.

"Do not tell her," Aeddan responded. "If Sorli knows of it and promises not to speak, what have I to fear?"

"But you are a thrall—thralls do not carry messages to other steadings. You don't even know the way to Skirnir's holding."

"I cajoled directions from Gudrod; he's been there once. Besides, I am taking Brudhol; the horse will find Dag."

"That's absurd. A dog might be able to trail its master, but a horse, never. They are naught but stupid beasts."

"Do not speak ill of Brudhol!" the boy responded angrily. "She is a fine animal with a stout heart and willing spirit."

Breaca shook her head in consternation. Aeddan meant to go after Dag, to make one last attempt to save Fiona. A reckless, foolish plan, but how could she fail to help? If there were anyone who could turn Sigurd from his horrifying scheme, it would be Dag. If only Aeddan could find him in time . . .

She drew breath sharply. "If you insist on going, I will find you some provisions. And you'd best take grain for the horse; this time of year there is not much fodder."

* * *

"Would you speak to her? Please?" Fiona stopped her pacing and gestured beseechingly to Breaca.

Breaca gave a mournful shake of her head. "It won't work, Fiona. Even if I offered the wise woman gold, she would not free you. Creatures like her . . ." She hesitated. "She enjoys her role as Angel of Death. One of her assistants told me that she goes into an ecstatic trance as she wields the dagger. She loves to see blood shed."

"But you will approach her?" Fiona insisted. "You will at least try?"

Breaca sighed. "Of course. Rorig has agreed to give me part of his treasure for the bribe. I will do what I can."

Fiona started to pace, but Breaca grabbed her arm and drew her near. She cast a swift, surreptitious glance at the doorway, then fumbled beneath her cloak. With her back turned to the two thralls who sat spinning in the other end of the room, Breaca held out a small packet. "The poison," she whispered. "If nothing else works, there is always this. Mina says it takes some time to take effect. Don't wait too long to put it to use."

"How will I ingest it?" Fiona whispered.

"Ask for ale when Sigurd orders you put on the boat. As soon as you receive the drink, pour the poison into the ale and swallow it down."

Fiona nodded and reached for the packet. Breaca shook her head. "You will be stripped and bathed ere you are placed in your ceremonial funeral garments, and the poison would surely be discovered. Mina will sew it in a flap at the entrance of the tent. I merely wanted you to know what it looks like so you can find it more easily when you search for it."

Fiona pulled her shaking hand away. "When will they come for me?" she asked.

"Sigurd has decreed that the funeral rites will take place at sunset on the morrow."

Although it was difficult to ascertain the time of day from within the slaves' dwelling, Fiona guessed it to be near sunset now. One journey of the sun across the sky, and her doom would be upon her. Dread, heavy and thick, closed over her. If only she could breath fresh air once again and feel the breeze in her hair. If only she could see the green hills of Eire one more time.

She choked back a sob. Her rebellious nature had brought her to this pass. She had sought to please herself and ended up destroying all. Now she was to end her life in a foreign, barbaric land, her disgrace complete. Desperately, she thought of Siobhan. Her aunt was said to have the gift of sight. Why had she not warned Fiona of her woeful fate? Siobhan had encouraged her to aid the Viking prisoner. Had her aunt's hatred of Donall compelled her to urge Fiona on this destructive path?

"If you cannot sleep, Mina has given me something for that as well," Breaca said gently.

Fiona shook her head. She had little enough time in this world; she would not waste it in sleep. "Do you think, if I asked him, Sigurd would allow me a boon before I die?"

Breaca gestured uncertainly. "I know not. Mayhap. It would depend upon what your request is."

"I would like to climb the the hill behind the steading and watch the sun rise one last time," Fiona answered. "Sigurd can send a dozen men to guard me if he wishes."

Breaca nodded. "I will ask him."

Again, Fiona paced the narrow dwelling; impatience swept over her. If Sigurd waited too long, she would not get her wish. Already the other thralls rose from their beds and prepared to begin their work. Sunrise came late in the month of the Blood Moon, but it could not be much longer.

"Fiona." Sorli appeared in doorway and nodded solemnly.

Fiona hastened to pull her heavy tunic over her head and put on the fur boots, then followed the slavemaster outside. She paused to take a deep gulp of fresh air before hurrying after Sorli. Already, the darkness thinned in the east. If she meant to observe the sunrise, they did not have much time.

Sorli set a brisk pace along the pathways of the steading. Fiona half ran to keep up, her nerves dancing with excitement.

Pulling beside the man, she said, "I can scarce believe Sigurd sent only you as my guard. Does he not fear I might run away?"

"I have given him my word that I will return you to the steading ere the sun reaches midpoint in the sky. I trust that you will not force me to break my vow."

Fiona took a deep breath. Sorli had been nothing but kind to her; she would not compromise his honor in a futile attempt at escape.

They were past the turf wall of the steading now and climbing upwards. Sorli's pace slowed, and Fiona guessed that his old, battle-scarred legs pained him. She slowed as well, no longer in a hurry. She meant to savor every moment of these last hours of freedom. To memorize the feel of the cold, moisture-laden air upon her skin, the crunch of the half-frozen ground beneath their boots, the smell of the sea wind blowing in over the valley. This place was not Eire, but there was beauty here as well, a harsh, dazzling loveliness. Fiona could imagine the valley swathed in glittering snow, ice crystals winking in the sun. And she had memories of the landscape green and gold and lush with the bounty of summer and a sky overhead so blue that it nearly hurt the eyes.

This wild land of the North had its own enchantment, its own ancient gods. They were deities of the sky, of thunder and lightning, of stone and oak and things unyielding and powerful. And the men of this place were equally fierce and stalwart, men like Dag.

Fiona felt the memories assault her mind. She remembered Dag as she had first seen him—wounded, bloodied, weak, but so unearthly handsome and well-made it seemed a crime against the gods to let him perish. He had looked at her with those stunningly blue, fever-glazed eyes and something inside her had answered. *Such a man would sire valiant sons and proud daughters,* her woman's instinct spoke. *He is for you,* the gods whispered. *Save him, heal his wounds . . . love him.*

Fiona shuddered. She and Sorli had reached a little ridge above the steading. They turned toward the east. The sky brightened expectantly, but she watched unseeing. Her mind was filled with dreams and memories more real than the sunrise.

She blinked, forcing herself back to the moment, to reality. Her last sunrise. Her last hours in the world of the living. She watched ribbons of lush pink and mauve unfurl across the sky. Then, suddenly, the vision altered. The rugged Norse landscape vanished, and she stared instead at the sun rising over one of the green hills of her homeland. A man stood on the crest of the hill, his hair long and gleaming gold, his stance strong and proud. Fiona gasped as she recognized Dag. She felt his spirit reach out to her, drawing her toward him. The bounds which connected her to the earth unraveled. She was free, her soul released from the constraints of her flesh. . . .

Slowly, the sensation faded. The sun rose, and the world became ordinary again. Fiona turned—expecting to see Dag beside her. She saw only Sorli standing there. Yet, she knew. Dag had not abandoned her. His love was with her still.

"Fiona?" Sorli's voice was awed, uneasy. She met his gaze. His hand quickly went to the Thor's hammer amulet he wore around his neck as a charm against evil. "Thor, save us," he whispered. "Dag was right. You are a wise woman—a *volva!*"

"A what?"

Sorli swallowed. "A *volva,* a seer, someone who can see the future. For a moment there, when I looked in your face, I knew . . ."

"Knew what?"

The old warrior shook his head. "Sigurd is a fool if he does not see it. Your death will bring the wrath of the gods down upon us. Dag is right; we should return you to your homeland before it is too late."

"What's happening, Sorli? Why are you afraid of me?"

Sorli shook his head again and would not answer.

They waited on the outcrop for a time, then slowly made their way back to the steading. The calm and strength she had found as she'd gazed out at the sunrise remained with Fiona. Even knowing what was to come, she felt peace. Dag had not forsaken her; he loved her. Their spirits would be together, even if she no longer walked the world of the living.

At midday, the Angel of Death came for Fiona. She was an old crone, broad and immense of body, with blackened teeth

and gnarled features. The sight of her should be enough to
frighten her victims to death, Fiona thought wryly. The wise
woman was accompanied by two younger, less repulsive assistants. It was the younger women who took Fiona to the bathhouse and bathed her and washed her hair. They fussed over
her as if she were a bride, as she supposed she was in a way—
the bride of a dead man. They oiled her skin until it gleamed,
arranged her hair in an elaborate coiffure of braids around her
head, then helped her into a snow-white linen shift and an
exquisite overtunic of scarlet silk trimmed with fur. The tunic
was not fashioned in the normal style for a woman, and Fiona
suspected it had been made over from a man's garment.

When Fiona tried to put on her fur boots, one of the women
snatched them away and told her that she would not need them.
Indeed, she had scarcely stepped out of the bathing hut when
she was picked up by the warrior Kalf. As he carried her through
the steading, Fiona was surprised to find the place near-deserted.
Then, they reached the end of the path that led to the harbor,
and Fiona realized that the Norsemen, their families, and even
the thralls were already gathered around the grounded ship.
Huge piles of timber and brushwood surrounded the graceful
hull. Fiona inhaled sharply, thinking of bright flames consuming
the abundant kindling and then racing upwards to devour the
ship.

Do not think of it, she told herself. *You will be dead or
insensible by then.*

The crowd was silent as Kalf strode up. Then Sigurd and
old Ranveig lifted their burden, and those gathered began to
wail and cry out in grief. Old Knorri lay on a plank of wood,
wearing a long tunic that nearly matched the one Fiona wore.
After five days of death, his corpse appeared gray and shrunken,
the more so because of the bright attire.

Fiona shivered. She did not want to be placed in a tent with
a dead man. She looked around frantically. Kalf still held her
tightly, and they were surrounded by grieving warriors. She
closed her eyes, searching for the peace which had eased her
spirit earlier.

There was a rancid smell. Fiona opened her eyes to see the

Angel of Death standing before her. She held out a beaker. "Drink," she said, her eyes glittering. " 'Twill ease your passage to the otherworld."

Fiona stared at the woman, then knocked the beaker from her hand. The woman cursed her, her mouth gaping open in a toothless sneer. Fiona gathered saliva in her mouth to spit, but before she could, Kalf began moving again. He carried her to the ship as Sigurd and Ranveig had done with Knorri. Kalf's booted feet trod heavily on the plank leading up to the ship, then Fiona heard the creak of the ship's timbers. She gritted her teeth.

Kalf jostled her roughly as he entered the tent, then bent down and deposited her on a soft surface. Fiona turned her head and supressed a scream at the sight of Knorri's corpse a mere arm's length away.

Chapter 30

The dead jarl was propped up on cushions, and his flesh had sunk into his bones until he looked more like a skeleton than a man. Despite the spices used to preserve his body, the putrid odor of decay filled the tent. Fiona edged away from the corpse and examined her surroundings. Beside the pile of rugs and furs she lay upon was a large beaker of ale. She lifted the beaker, examining the frothy dark contents, then replaced the beaker on the ship deck and crawled to the tent entrance to search for the poison.

She found it neatly sewn into the edge of the tent flap. Carefully she took it out, then opened the leather packet and stared at the white powder within. This, then, was her means to an easy and painless death.

The light of day was still visible at the tent entrance, and in the distance, she could hear the voice of the *skald,* clear and true, celebrating Knorri's bravery and wisdom in life. She glanced toward the shrunken corpse sharing the tent and sighed. Poor old Knorri. Was a part of him aware of how his people honored him? She did not think so. Knorri's spirit was gone; the ceremony outside was for the living, to ease their grief and validate Sigurd's authority as the new jarl.

The poison is slow acting. You must not delay in taking it.
Breaca's words filled Fiona's mind, and she looked again at
the packet clutched in her hands. It would be so easy to mix
it in the ale and drink it down. By the time the first of the men
came for her, she would be beyond caring.

Dag dug his boots into the horse's side, urging his tired
mount faster. *Sigurd means to burn the Irishwoman with the
dead jarl.* The young thrall's words rang in his head, igniting
a panic so intense Dag could scarcely breath. Thor's fury! What
madness had come over his brother? Dag knew of the ancient
rite of burning a deceased man's concubine or wife with him
so she might serve the warrior in the underworld, but he had
not known it done in his lifetime. Nor did men of his era
ordinarily burn perfectly sound ships with their dead jarls.
Sigurd must be mad, so beside himself with grief and anger
that he wanted to destroy everything around him.

"Slow down," Ellisil remonstrated from behind Dag. "We
won't get there any sooner if you kill your mount with your
breathless pace."

Reluctantly, Dag eased up on the reins. His friend was right.
The horses represented their only chance of reaching Engvakkirsted in time. Gratitude filled him as he glanced back at Ellisil.
Aeddan had arrived at Skirnir's steading just as they'd returned
from the trip to Hedeby, and Ellisil had not wasted time asking
questions or wondering at the oddness of a young thrall serving
as messenger. Instead, hearing of the crisis, he had immediately
secured one of his father's fine horses for Dag to ride, then
compounded his generosity by offering to accompany Dag and
show him the fastest route home.

Dag took a deep breath, trying to calm himself. He would
not let his impatience cause harm to the horse he rode. Unlike
the plodding beasts he and Sigurd had purchased from Ottar,
Skirnir's horses were sleek and beautiful, with deep chests and
long legs. If he were not so worried about Fiona, he would
greatly enjoy the thrill of riding such a magnificant animal. It
was like gliding on the wind.

But the stallion was only a flesh-and-blood creature, Dag reminded himself. They could not drive the beasts endlessly. At some point they must stop and rest. He jerked his head around to call out to Ellisil, "How much farther?"

Ellisil scanned the rugged terrain before them. "I believe Engvakkirsted lies over the next range of hills. We should reach it by nightfall."

His friend's words struck a chill in Dag's heart. By custom, funeral pyres were lit at sunset so the glow of the flames could be seen clearly in the gathering darkness carrying the dead man's soul to Valhalla. If they arrived by nightfall, they might be in time, or hopelessly late. Once the flames of the pyre reached the pitch-soaked ship, there would be no chance of rescuing anyone caught in the inferno.

The rocky, narrow pathway forced them to walk the animals for a time, then they set off again at a steady, ground-eating pace. Dag scanned the sky impatiently. On such an overcast, gloomy day, it was difficult to guess how soon twilight would creep over the land.

"The boy slave who came with the message—did you teach him to ride, Dag?" Ellisil asked.

"*Nei.* He must have learned on his own."

"I'm amazed he was able to coax that old nag such a distance," Ellisil continued. "And how he found his way to my father's steading—he's little more than a boy. The woman must mean a great deal to him that he would venture so far alone. Is she kin of his?"

"*Nei.* They did not even know each other until Fiona went to stay in the slaves' quarters."

"Sigurd vows to kill her. . . . You and the boy risk your lives for her. I wonder that the Irish wench is not some supernatural being after all that she arouses such strong feelings in those who know her." Dag gave Ellisil a helpless look, and the Norseman continued. "Mayhap this desperate journey is unnecessary. Such a powerful creature may be impossible to kill. They say witches don't burn."

Dag tried to find comfort in his companion's words, but could not. The wrenching fear in his gut told him that Fiona was naught but flesh and blood like him. Fire would reduce her beauty to ashes, just it would destroy Knorri's proud dragonship. Another pang of anguish swept through him. Would that he were in time to save the *Storm Maiden* as well! That proud vessel did not deserve a fiery fate any more than Fiona did. He shook his head at Sigurd's madness. Knorri would not have wished for a funeral that beggared his people. Without the *Storm Maiden,* Sigurd would not have the means to go trading, nor raiding either. His brother's extravagant expression of grief could doom the Thorsson clan to poverty for years to come.

As if echoing his thoughts, Ellisil asked, "Was Sigurd so fond of your uncle that he must make such a display of mourning on his behalf?"

"Knorri was like a father to us. But *nei,* that does not explain Sigurd's actions. I've never known him to lose his reason before. It was always he who restrained me from impetuousness. . . ." Dag broke off, the sick feeling in his gut deepening. His world seemed turned upside down. Was there anything he could be sure of? *The Irishwoman,* his mind answered. His love for her felt clear and strong—if only he could keep her safe.

They reached a familiar rise, and Dag urged his horse faster. They slowed as they moved down the incline and saw the valley spread out before them. Dag drew rein and stared. The sight of the burned-out longhouse struck him like a blow to the belly. The dwelling he had been born in, then passed from boyhood to manhood in, had been reduced to blackened ruins. He had the sense of the solid ground shifting beneath his feet.

"I see the ship, but no fire yet. I trow we have arrived in time, sword brother."

Ellisil's words took a moment to register. Finally, Dag shook off his shock and answered, "I would like to arrive unnoticed, if possible." He met Ellisil's questioning gaze. "I'm not certain I can dissuade Sigurd from his senseless plan. We may have to rescue Fiona by stealth."

Ellisil made a motion of assent, then smiled grimly. " 'Twill be like a raid, with the woman as plunder."

Dag nodded and gazed down at the steading—his home, now utterly changed. He considered several plans, discarding each one in turn. They could not wait until dark and sneak into the steading; it would be too late by then. They would have to lead their horses down the slope and leave them behind the main cattle byre. They would circle around behind those gathered for the *skald's* final tribute to Knorri. Ellisil would go and speak to Sigurd, bringing Skirnir's respects to the dead jarl and greeting the new, thereby creating a diversion so Dag could make his way unseen to the other side of the ship. He would climb the planks and have Fiona out of Sigurd's murderous clutches before anyone was the wiser.

He quickly explained his plan to Ellisil. "After the fire is set, slip away and meet me again behind the cattle byre. We'll leave at once. I don't want to linger."

"I could stay with the woman while you spoke to Sigurd," Ellisil offered.

Dag shook his head. "It might be difficult for me to get away if Sigurd knew of my presence. Besides, I have no desire to see my brother." He sighed. "I'm not certain I know the man any longer."

"There is nothing else you wish to rescue from your home?"

" 'Tis my home no longer. What possessions I had burned in the fire. All I want now is the woman." He gazed intently at his companion. "Now that I am near destitute, are you still willing to join me in the expedition to Ireland?"

Ellisil shrugged. "You have convinced me that it is a risk worth taking, and we will have supplies and support from my father. I will go with you, Dag."

Dag smiled and reached out his sword hand to grasp Ellisil's. "Thank you, brother. You make me proud to be a Norseman." Releasing Ellisil, Dag gazed again toward the valley. "As my brother has made me ashamed," he added softly.

The slow journey down the hillside was agonizing. But as much as Dag longed to hurry, they could not risk discovery yet. They reached the cattle byre and left their horses there, then went on toward the beach. They crept to the very edge of the underbrush and paused to listen to the sounds coming from the funeral gathering.

The *skald* had finished now, and there was the soft keen of women weeping. As Dag heard men arguing, a chill ran through him. If Sigurd observed the ancient ritual, Knorri's closest oathmen would take turns lying with Fiona before the fire was set. The thought of it made Dag's blood run cold. Fiona would be drugged and near insensible, but still, what would it do to her to endure one man after another rutting upon her body? *Nei,* he must rescue her before that happened!

He put his hand on Ellisil's arm. "Go, announce yourself to Sigurd." Ellisil moved out of the woods, and Dag listened for the men's reaction to his arrival. Sigurd would surely halt the proceedings to greet a representative from another steading.

Hearing Sigurd welcome Ellisil, Dag inched to an opening between the trees and tried to determine his route to the ship. The *Storm Maiden* was beached crosswise to the shoreline, with the funeral gathering on the starboard side. If he could make it safely across the open area between the forest and the vessel, he could board the ship on the port side without being seen.

He crept forward. No one seemed to notice him as he moved past the mourners; the men were gathered around Ellisil and Sigurd, the women too intent in their weeping to observe him. He wondered if the women wept for Knorri or for Fiona. Nearing the ship, he dashed behind it, and almost cried out in surprise when he saw Breaca. She knelt on the ground behind the ship, her eyes red from weeping. As her gaze focused on him, her despair turned to horror.

He was too late! The frantic thought beat in his brain, but he refused to accept it. "I've come for Fiona," he told Breaca. "Is she on the boat?"

Breaca nodded mutely, her eyes miserable. Sick with fear himself, Dag asked, "What is it?"

"Poison . . ." she croaked out. "Mina gave Fiona poison so she would not have to endure rape and violent death. I told Fiona to take it as soon as she was placed on the ship. That was hours ago. . . ."

Breaca's voice trailed off in a whispered sob. Dag closed his eyes. Poison! Fiona had taken poison! He stood, stunned, despairing. Then he opened his eyes and glanced toward the ship. Even now, Fiona might be dead or dying. Could he bear to see her thus?

If only they would get it over with. Fiona clenched her hands into fists, listening. The *skald's* tale was finished, but still, nothing happened. She gripped the dagger more tightly in her right hand. Stupid fools, to have left a ceremonial weapon strapped to Knorri's belt. Did they think that she, a woman, would not have the courage to use it? Let the Viking bastards come for her—they would see!

A grim smile touched her lips as she adjusted her sweaty fingers on the dagger hilt. The first man would be easy. She would wait for him to free his member and climb on top of her, then she would slash his throat. When the second man came, she would be waiting inside the tent entrance. He, too, would be sent to the crude Viking underworld with a swift stab of the blade.

Of course, sooner or later, the other Vikings would come looking for their companions. Then they would kill her, but she would die vindicated. If luck were with her, Brodir would be the first one to the tent, and the first one to fall. How gratifying it would be to send that arrogant swine back to the foul *hel* from whence he came!

There was a rustling noise at the entrance of the tent. Fiona regarded the tent opening through slitted eyes and adjusted her body on the cushiony furs.

A man thrust through the tent opening. In the dim light, Fiona could only make out broad shoulders and hair too light to be Brodir's. Disappointment swept through her as she realized her nemesis would not be the first to die. Then the man approached her, and Fiona's nerveless fingers dropped the dagger among the furs and rugs.

"Dag!" His name was torn from her throat in a gasp of surprise and incredulous relief. Her gaze drank in her lover's blue eyes, his handsome features, the reassuring bulk of his shoulders and chest. He leaned over her, and his hand reached out to touch her cheek.

"Fiona," he whispered. "Am I too late? Does the poison already stir in your veins?"

"Poison?" Fiona shaped the word with dry lips, and, for a moment, she could not think of what he spoke. Then the memory came back to her. "*Ja*, I mean, *nei*. I did not take it. I could not bear the thought of going meekly to my death." She fumbled among the furs and retrieved the knife. "They left Knorri's ceremonial dagger on his belt. I was going to use it on the men when they came to lie with me."

Dag exhaled softly, and some of the tension in his face eased. "No man will ever lie with you but me, I promise you." He cast a dismayed look at Knorri's corpse.

Giddy with relief, Fiona let loose a small chortle. "The old jarl is not bad company, excepting he smells a bit. I trow I would rather share a tent with him than Brodir."

Dag's eyes gleamed with something like amusement, then he grasped her arm. "Can you walk?"

"Of course."

"Keep close to me. We'll creep around the back of the tent and go over the side.

Fiona nodded and got to her knees. Crawling to the tent entrance, she followed Dag outside. It grew dark, and Fiona shivered in the evening chill. Dag looked at her elaborate but impractical attire. He pulled his own fur tunic over his head and handed it to her. "Put this on."

Fiona obeyed, inhaling deeply Dag's warm, male scent as she pulled the garment over her head. Harsh, excited voices carried across the beach, making Fiona's heartbeat quicken. At any moment, Sigurd might give the order for the men to draw lots to couple with her. Indeed, that was likely what they argued about. She heard Brodir's guttural voice raised in anger, then Sigurd's rumbling answer.

She followed Dag to the far side of the ship and watched him climb down and brace himself on the planks supporting the hull. He held out his arms and caught her as she slipped over the side. He scrambled nimbly down the timbers, still carrying her, then set her on her feet.

"Fiona!" Breaca's gasp of relief made Fiona turn. Wordlessly, the women hugged each other.

Dag interrupted their embrace with a whispered warning. "We must hurry!"

Breathlessly, Fiona released Breaca and took Dag's hand. Her bare feet flew over the cold, hard beach as if they had wings. Once they reached the cover of underbrush screening the harbor, Dag paused. Fiona waited beside him, aware that he listened to Sigurd and Brodir argue. The Norse words rose and fell on Fiona's ears, but she could not quite catch their meaning. She touched Dag's shoulder imploringly. "Why do we wait?"

"Sigurd has decided to forego the bedding ritual." Dag's voice sounded shaky and relieved. "Mayhap he finally realizes what evil he does."

"He will still send the Angel of Death to the tent to kill me. When he does, she will discover I am gone. Come!" Fiona urged desperately.

Dag took her hand and led her swiftly through the trees and among the deserted buildings of the steading. He paused to stare at the gutted longhouse, then hurried on. Behind the cattle byre waited two horses Fiona had never seen before.

"Where did you—" she began.

Dag did not wait for her to finish, but lifted her up on one of the animal's broad back. "The horses belong to Ellisil, a sword brother of mine. Can you ride?"

Fiona nodded. "Where are you going?" she asked when he made no move to mount the other horse.

"I must talk to Sigurd. I must convince him not to burn the ship. It is my nephews' future he squanders with this absurd act of mourning." He looked up at Fiona, his eyes intense and commanding. "Ride, Fiona. Ride as if the demons of your dreams followed you. There is a *shieling* beyond these hills— a summer dwelling for the herdsmen. You remember it?"

Fiona nodded, recalling that they had passed it on the way to the *Thing*.

"Wait there. I will meet you."

"When?"

Dag gestured helplessly. "I'll take no more time than I have to. If Sigurd persists in his stubbornness, I'll leave him to his folly. But I have to try. I can't bear to see the whole steading suffer because my brother's wits are disordered."

"But what if . . ."

"Nei, he won't detain me. Even once he knows I have set you free, Sigurd will not lay hands on me or order other men to take me prisoner."

"How can you be certain? You said yourself that Sigurd's wits are disordered!" Fiona reached out and clutched Dag's tunic.

Dag disengaged her fingers and brought them to his lips. "I vow I will not desert you, Fiona. Upon my honor as a warrior, I will meet you at the *shieling.*"

Tears filled Fiona's eyes. She curled her fingers around Dag's strong jaw and stroked his whisker-roughened cheek. Damn his honor and his sense of responsibility to his people! She could not bear to lose him now.

"Dag, please . . ."

Her entreaty whirled away on the wind as Dag slapped the horse's flank and the beast jerked forward. "Ride," Dag ordered harshly.

Clinging to the horse's mane, Fiona twisted her body so she could catch one last look at her lover. The startled horse gained speed, and staying on its back required all Fiona's attention.

At last the animal slowed and she was able to retrieve the dangling reins. She allowed herself one miserable glance behind her, then urged her mount in the direction Dag had pointed.

Dag warily approached the gathering on the beach. Despite his confident words to Fiona, he was not certain what his brother would do when he saw him. He could not imagine Sigurd taking him captive, but then he had hardly imagined his brother planning to kill Fiona and burn the ship, either.

Dag paused as he made out the eerie, torchlit scene ahead

of him. Sigurd stood by himself, scowling. Across from Sigurd, Ellisil and the steading smith, Veland, restrained a furious Brodir. It was obvious that Brodir felt provoked to violence by Sigurd's decree. Dag felt a stab of hope.

Moving into the torchlight, he called his brother's name. The crowd of men and women went silent. Sigurd recognized him and stepped forward. "Brother," he said.

Dag nodded curtly but made no move to approach. "I mourn our loss as much as you do, brother, but I cannot agree with your plan to destroy all that Jarl Knorri Sorlisson built over his proud and honorable lifetime." He motioned to the ship. "Are you so vain that you must shout your grief to the world with this outrageous display? 'Look at me, I am Sigurd Thorsson. I am such a great jarl; I will burn my only ship to prove I can soon build another!'"

Dag saw a muscle twitch in his brother's jaw, but it was Brodir who broke the frosty silence. "Don't listen to him, Sigurd. The Irish witch has filled his mind with lies. You must kill her . . . now . . . before she destroys the rest of us!"

"The woman is gone." Dag gestured again toward the ship. "Search and see. Naught but the body of our revered jarl lies on the deck of the *Storm Maiden.*"

A hush settled over the beach, then a huge, ugly woman stepped forward. "You cheated me!" she accused Sigurd. "You brought me here for an execution and made me wait and wait. Now the victim is gone. I will curse you for your foolishness!"

The crowd backed away. She must be the Angel of Death, Dag thought. A twinge of fear swept across his mind as he wondered if she had any real power, then he banished his foreboding. "Go," he ordered her. "You are not needed here."

Her grotesque features contorted with hate and rage. "I will curse you as well!" she sputtered. Slumping to her knees, she began to screech strange, blood-chilling words.

Dag hesitated, dread prickling along his spine. Then anger swiftly overtook his anxiety. This foul, twisted creature had meant to kill Fiona! He stepped forward and pointed at the woman. "Where are her handmaidens?"

Two young, unattractive women silently appeared in the torchlight.

"Take her from our sight," Dag commanded. "She has no power here. She is naught but an evil, old creature, jealous of all youth and beauty."

The two women looked at him hesitantly. He met their stares with cold, ruthless command. Fear and awe crept over their faces, and they went to the wise woman and hurriedly helped her to her feet and led her away.

The crowd was utterly still. Dag faced at his brother and was startled to see an awed look on Sigurd's face.

"So, the boy has become a man at last," Sigurd said. "Do you come to challenge me as jarl, brother?"

Dag took a deep breath. *"Nei,* brother. I intend to build my own steading, in Ireland."

Sigurd's smile vanished. "You will not swear to me as oathman?"

"Nei."

Sigurd stared at him, his mouth working. Finally, he said, "Come and share a horn of ale with me. Tell me of your plans." He gestured toward the steading. "My longhouse is no more, but we will find a warm hearth to sit beside."

Dag hesitated, thinking of Fiona, fleeing blindly into the darkness. He could not be certain she would be able to find the *shieling* on her own.

Ellisil's voice came to him from behind the other men. "I will go after the woman, Dag. I will see that she is safe."

Dag met Ellisil's eyes. Dared he trust the other man to see to Fiona's safety? His heart urged him to forget Sigurd and his kin and go after Fiona. His mind reminded him of his duty. Ellisil might not be able to convince Sigurd to forgo torching the ship, but Dag felt he had a good chance of it. Even though he meant to leave them, he owed his people, and he would respect himself less if he failed to aid them in this crisis.

"Go after her," he said to Ellisil. "She rides to a *shieling* beyond the eastern ridge." Then to Sigurd he said, "I would be pleased to drink at your hearth, jarl."

Chapter 31

Fiona reined in her mount and surveyed the hillside, straining her eyes in the deepening twilight. She had some idea where the *shieling* stood, but feared to miss it in the dark. If she did, she might ride in circles all night among these frost-covered hills.

A wolf howled in the distance, and fear prickled down her spine. She had been saved from rape and certain death, but her future was by no means assured. Once she reached the *shieling,* she must wait there for Dag, hoping Sigurd did not decide to detain his brother.

Fiona sighed. Despite her frustration, she understood why Dag had remained behind. He was the only one who could reason with Sigurd, the only one who could sort out the disaster which had befallen Engvakkirsted.

But what if Sigurd took Dag prisoner and prevented him from leaving? A tremor of fear made her stiffen on her mount, and the horse started at her sudden movement. Fiona eased her grip on the reins and spoke soothing words. As she leaned forward on the animal's neck, a shape—lighter than the surrounding landscape—caught her eye. The *shieling!*

Fiona heaved a sigh of relief. She had almost missed the

small building, situated as it was in a hollow. She urged the mare toward the shelter. Another wolf howled, closer this time. The horse snorted and tossed her head in alarm.

Fiona calmed the horse, then guided her mount near the small timber structure and dismounted. She winced as the sharp rocks of the hillside dug into her bare feet and gingerly led her horse to the *shieling*. There was a lean-to built next to it. Fiona settled the horse into the flimsy shelter, then opened the door to the main building.

Pitch darkness met her eyes. Shivering, she felt her way into the room. She stumbled over the fire pit and banged her knee on a raised platform at one side of the chamber. Her outstretched hands encountered musty furs and blankets on the platform. At least she had a place to sleep. Now for some food.

A thorough search of the rest of the dwelling yielded utensils and implements for cooking, but no food stores. Fiona gritted her teeth at her growling stomach and climbed onto the bedshelf. She closed her eyes and tried to sleep.

It was no use. She had not eaten anything since the forenoon hence, and her hunger would not let her rest. What she would not give for a piece of fish or bread! A sudden thought came to her, and she sat up so quickly she hit her head on the sloping ceiling.

Dag would not have set off without provisions—there must be a supply pack on the horse. Barely controlling her excitement, she climbed off the bedshelf and proceeded cautiously to the door. Outside, it felt even colder, and Fiona shivered as she entered the lean-to. The horse knickered a greeting and allowed her to feel her way along its shaggy neck. Her hands found the pack behind the saddle and frantically searched.

Success! Not only had Dag thought to bring bread and some dried meat, there was a full skin of water as well. Fiona clutched the precious food stores to her chest and moved past the horse. As she reached the doorway, the mare whinnied wildly. Fiona froze, and the hair stood up on the back of her neck. Something was out there!

Shifting the food to her left arm, she used her right hand to search for a weapon. She touched the side of the lean-to, testing

the ancient, spintered wood. Finding a loose board, she brok
off with a creaking sound. Splinters dug into Fiona's finger
as she hefted the makeshift club, and her heart thundered i
her chest. Was Dag out there? Or some unknown enemy? Sh
called Dag's name, then waited. The only answer was the sa
of wind through the lean-to cracks.

Fiona swallowed. Should she risk making her way to th
shieling or remain with the horse? She thought of her exhaus
tion, the bone-numbing chill of the wind. Nay, she could n
bear to spend the night here. There was no place to lie dowr
lest the horse step on her. She would have to make a dash f
it.

Still clutching her weapon, she inched through the lean-t
door and crept out into the darkness. The moon had slippe
behind a cloud, and she could scarce see the shape of her ow
hand before her. She took two steps, paused, and listened.
rustling sound in the underbrush sent her heart thudding int
her throat. She looked up helplessly at the sky, begging th
clouds to shift. Slowly they did, and a half-moon peeped ou
illuminating the landscape around her.

She took another step, and froze as she saw two pairs c
yellow eyes glinting in the darkness. Blessed Bridget—wolve
Fiona's mind raced as she tried to sort out a plan. If she gav
in to her panic, she would die. Gripping the club, she considere
lunging at the wolves and trying to frighten them away. Sh
might spook them a little, but she doubted she would make
to shelter. Then she thought of the food. Fumbling in the sadd
pack with one hand, she found the chunk of dried meat. Sh
waved it in the air, hoping the wolves would catch the scer
of it. A low growl came from one of the predators. She threw th
meat toward the glowing eyes and dashed toward the *shielin*
without looking behind.

Reaching the rickety door, she dropped the club and tor
inside, then slammed the door shut and barred it behind he
She leaned against the door, breathing hard. Outside, she coul
hear the snarling of the wolves as they fought over the mea
It would not occupy them long. Fiona thought of the mare i
the lean-to and anguish filled her. The horse could fight o

two predators, but if more arrived, drawn by the scent of food . . .

She shook off the disturbing thought. Surely Dag would come soon. With trembling hands, she fumbled in the pack and found the waterskin. She drank deeply, then began to eat.

"Tell me of your plans for this Irish trip." Sigurd's voice was calm as he settled his bulk on a bench by the fire in the smith's turfhouse.

Dag gazed thoughtfully into his beaker of ale. Now that he was alone with his brother, he did not know how to begin. The funeral party was still gathered on the beach, anticipating the torching of the ship, and Fiona and Ellisil waited for him in the hills. He raised his eyes to Sigurd's. "I would rather speak of the raid and the fire."

An anguished look crossed his brother's face. "I should not have left them," Sigurd said sorrowfully.

"Surely you assigned someone to guard the longhouse while you were gone."

Sigurd nodded. "Brodir and Utgard. But whoever led the raid easily disarmed them. They were both struck over the head from behind. Utgard was found tied up in the woods the next day."

"And Brodir?"

"Was able to wrest off his bonds. He was nearly the first one to the fire . . . after the woman." Sigurd's gaze met Dag's, his eyes bitter. "Brodir said she was dancing around and shrieking to the heavens when he found her, as if casting a spell."

"You think Fiona set the fire?" Dag asked incredulously. "How can you believe such a thing?"

"She hates us."

"Fiona may hate Brodir, but she does not wish ill upon any of the rest of our people. And she would never kill women and children."

Sigurd's jaw grew tight. "She has destroyed everything, just as Brodir said she would. Because of her, you sail to Ireland, abandoning your kin, your home."

With sudden comprehension, Dag realized why Sigurd had condemned Fiona to die. He did not really believe she had set the fire, nor did he condemn her because she was a threat to Norse law and convention. Sigurd hated Fiona because he blamed her for damaging the bond between them as brothers.

"Sigurd . . ." he began gently. "It would have come to this someday even if I had not captured Fiona. I must move out of your shadow and seek out my own lands, my own destiny."

"I would have helped you." Sigurd's voice was anguished. "I would have given you the use of the *Storm Maiden* for your journey. But you did not ask me . . ."

"Do you not see, brother? Some things a man must do on his own. If I risk Skirnir's ship, it is because he believes in me. If you give me yours, it is because I am your kin. 'Tis not the same."

Sigurd sighed and was silent.

"Do you still mean to burn the ship?" Dag asked after a time. If he could not make his brother understand his plans, he would at least pursue his other goal of saving the *Storm Maiden*.

Sigurd's features twisted with grief. "I owe Knorri a worthy funeral. He was like a father to me . . . and I . . . I failed him."

Dag took a deep breath, searching for the right words. Always before, it had been Sigurd who had soothed *him* and made him see reason. Now, the roles were reversed. "But did not Knorri die a hero?" he asked. "He saved the women and children and much of the treasure—was that not a deed worthy enough to send his spirit to Valhalla?"

Sigurd did not answer. Dag took another breath and continued. "After his valiant struggle to save your sons, I can't think that Knorri would want you to beggar them by burning the *Storm Maiden*. Without the ship, you will have no means to go raiding. Without plunder, it will be difficult to purchase the skilled labor you need to rebuild the longhouse."

"I am finished with raiding," Sigurd said harshly. "I have not the heart for it."

Dag nodded. Because of Fiona, he had learned to view raids through the victims' eyes. Sigurd, through his own tragedy, had experienced that sickening awareness as well. "But what of trading?'' he asked. ''You'll need a ship to take your goods to market at Hedeby.''

''We can build another ship.''

''When? Next sunseason you will be busy rebuilding the longhouse. Can you go a whole turn of the seasons without trading?''

''I'll pay another jarl to carry my goods to market.''

''With what? I trow, it will take near all your wealth to rebuild the longhouse and furnish it once again.''

Sigurd was silent, his broad jaw set like a stubborn child's. ''I have announced my intentions,'' he finally said. ''I will not go back upon my word. 'Tis bad enough that you freed the woman so I cannot punish her. Now you ask me to break another of my vows.''

'' 'Tis not a sign of weakness to admit you erred. Except for Brodir, I think your oathmen will be relieved to learn that you do not mean to burn the ship.''

Sigurd's look was swift and sharp. ''You talk like a follower of that damned White Christ. Because of the woman's influence, you forget true Viking ways!''

''Ah, true Viking ways—what do you mean by that, brother?'' Dag's voice rose in the low-ceilinged dwelling. ''Do you mean mindless bloodshed? Raids that beget more raids? Barbaric funeral rites that impoverish the living? *Ja*, brother, I have turned from those things, but it is not the woman's doing. I simply no longer wish to indulge in such stupidity!''

Dag held his breath as blood fired Sigurd's face and his blue eyes blazed. He had gone too far. He had insulted his brother gravely.

Sigurd clenched his huge hands into fists. Then he relaxed them and threw back his massive head and laughed. ''Thor's fury, but you are changed, brother. Where is that puny, freckle-faced boy I used to tease?'' He poked Dag in the shoulder and laughed again, making the small timber dwelling nearly tremble with his mirthful outburst.

Dag exhaled and smiled with relief. His brother had not changed so much after all; beneath his burden of guilt and grief, Sigurd could still find humor in life.

They finished their ale, talking finally of Dag's plans, then together they walked down to where the mourners waited. The women were dry-eyed now, pale and exhausted; a few held sleeping children. Nearby, the grim, silent warriors kept watch over the ship.

Sigurd stepped into the crowd. His deep voice boomed out, echoing across the torchlit beach. "Since the woman is gone, there is no reason to burn the ship. We will make a funeral pyre of the wood we have gathered and send Knorri to Valhalla with his weapons and armor. With his brave heart, he will need naught else to secure his place in the hall of heroes."

A soft gasp rippled through the crowd, and Dag guessed it to be an expression of relief as well as surprise. Although their grief for the old jarl was genuine, the people of Engvakkirsted were undoubtedly concerned about their future without a ship. Except Brodir—how disappointed he must be that the woman had escaped her gruesome fate.

Dag looked around, suddenly realizing Brodir's absence. A chill moved down his spine. He reminded himself that he had sent Ellisil after Fiona; his sword brother would protect her. The thought brought him little peace of mind. Brodir seemed capable of anything.

"Sigurd," Dag called out, interrupting his brother as he led the other men in moving the oil-soaked timbers away from the ship. "I'm sorry, Sigurd, but I must leave. The woman awaits me."

A look of bitterness crossed Sigurd's face, but all he said was, "You will come back, brother—before you leave for Ireland?"

"I will come back," Dag promised.

"Woman! Fiona! Open the door!"

The loud male voice jerked Fiona out of her fitful sleep. She sat up. *Wolves!* was her first thought, then she realized that wolves didn't yell.

"Dag sent me. Let me in!" the man hollered.

Fiona climbed off the bedshelf and crept closer to the door. "Who are you?" she asked in a quavering voice.

"My name is Ellisil, son of Skirnir. I am sword brother to Dag. I rode with him to rescue you."

Fiona took a deep breath, trying to decide whether to believe this man who so harshly demanded that she let him in. She did not know his voice. How was she to be certain he was not someone sent by Sigurd to drag her back to Engvakkirsted?

"Damn it, woman, I'm cold and weary and the wolves are circling closer. If you don't let me in, I'll get my horses and ride off."

"Those are your horses?"

There was a slight hesitation. "They are my father's horses, although I have had the care of them since they were foals. Skirnir agreed to let Dag and me ride them so we could reach the steading before Sigurd put you to death."

Fiona made up her mind and went to unbar the door. The mare had been well-cared for and expertly trained. A man who took such an interest in animals was more likely to be a friend of Dag's than Sigurd's.

She only had a glimpse of the man's silhouette before he joined her in the blackness of the *shieling*. Other than the fact that he was smaller than Dag, she had no idea what he looked like.

Ellisil shut the door. "Thor's hammer, I am half-froze. Have you no flint, woman, with which to make a fire?"

"There may be some in the horse's pack, but I did not take time to look. After I found the food, I heard the wolves. . . ." Fiona's voice trailed off in a horrified gasp. "What if the wolves attack the horses?"

"My horses are trained to fight. Any wolf who ventures into the lean-to will get his skull smashed. It is not so late in the season that the wild creatures are desperate for food."

Fiona relaxed slightly, acknowledging the wisdom of his words. She heard rustling sounds as the man opened a pack of some sort and fumbled inside. A flint flared near the hearth. In moments, Ellisil had a fire going.

He added wood from a pile by the door to the growing blaze,

then rubbed his hands together over the flames. Fiona shivered and moved forward, suddenly realizing how cold she was, even with Dag's heavy fur-lined tunic. Her bare feet were the worst, so numb by now that she could scarcely feel them. She lifted the ornate kirtle and stuck one foot close to the blaze.

Ellisil turned toward her, and she recognized him as the man she had seen Dag talking to at the *Thing*. His gaze moved over her, lingering for a moment on her leg bared to the fire's warmth. Unease replaced her relief. The warrior's eyes returned to her face; there was awe in his expression, and a hint of fear. "Are you really a *volva?*" he asked.

Fiona lowered her leg and covered it with the flowing skirt of the kirtle. "What's a *volva?*"

"A woman who can foretell the future and cast spells."

"You mean a wise woman?"

"Nei. Most steadings have a healer, but the ability to do true magic is rare."

"Did Dag tell you I was?"

Ellisil shook his head.

Fiona sighed. "If I knew magic, do you think I would have bungled things so badly that Sigurd almost had me executed?"

Ellisil stared at her, then laughed, banishing the tension between them. The Norseman dug inside his pack again and took out a skin. He offered it to Fiona.

She shook her head. "We should save it for Dag." Thinking of her lover, alone at the steading, her grinding fear resumed. "Do you think Sigurd will listen to Dag?" she asked.

"I do not think Sigurd will imprison his brother, if that's what you ask. Whether he will hear the sense in Dag's words is another thing. I do not know Sigurd well enough to say."

"Dag told me that you knew each other as boys," Fiona said.

Ellisil nodded.

"Were you and Dag close?"

Ellisil smiled and shook his head. "Not so you would notice. We met every year at the *Allthing* and fought constantly, as boys will. Always we were rivals, vying to beat each other in races, wrestling, battle practice, every sort of skill. Then Dag grew bigger than I, and except for footraces, I could no longer beat him. I almost hated him then.'' He laughed again. ''But now we are men, planning a great adventure. I am pleased Dag asked me to make this journey to Ireland with him. It seems almost too good to be true—to have land of our own.''

''What do you mean?'' Fiona's throat felt dry. Did Dag plan to claim her father's lands? The thought startled her.

Ellisil gave her a curious look. ''Dag said you had agreed to help us.''

''*Ja,* of course I will.'' Fiona could not decide if she were elated or angry. Dag did not mean to return her to Ireland and then sail away, but instead, intended to conquer her people and set himself up as chieftain. It was a bold, audacious plan, and she could not help but admire it. Even so, she was hurt he had not discussed the matter with her. He arrogantly assumed she would be delighted to hand over her inheritance to him.

''Dag is the ideal leader for this voyage,'' Ellisil enthused. ''A superb seaman, valiant warrior . . . and he knows the Irish language and terrain as well. If anyone can conquer the Irish, it is he.''

Fiona gritted her teeth. She had not been conquered! She had given her love freely; if Dag did not understand the difference . . .

There was a thudding sound at the *shieling* entrance, and a voice spoke, low and urgent, ''Fiona? Ellisil?''

Ellisil jumped up to unbar the door and let Dag in. Fiona remained seated, staring into the flames.

Dag ducked through the doorway, his tall form filling the small shelter to bursting. Fiona tried not to look at him, but she could not help it. One glimpse and her heart turned over.

''Fiona,'' Dag said huskily. He stepped awkwardly around the hearth, then knelt beside her and pulled her into his arms.

Fiona exhaled in a gasp. Nothing mattered but to have Dag hold her. She could not resist this man. He possessed her, stole her soul. No matter what he did, she would not stop loving him.

''Fiona. *Macushla.*'' Dag sighed against her hair. ''I will never let you go.''

Chapter 32

Dag climbed onto the bedshelf and pulled Fiona close to his chest. She had hardly said a word to him since his arrival. No doubt she was still in shock. Stroking his fingers through her tangled hair, he listened to Ellisil's soft snoring and tried to relax. Although he had saved Fiona and his brother's ship, threats still clouded the future. Brodir, mad with hatred as he was, could strike at anytime.

Fiona touched his face. "Dag, why do you not sleep?"

Dag gathered her more tightly against his chest. "I was thinking about all that is ahead of us."

There was silence, then Fiona asked, "Is it true you mean to claim my father's lands?"

Dag took a deep breath. He could not tell from her voice what she thought of his plan. Would she agree to aid him? "*Ja*, I do." She made an indigant sound and sat up. "And you assumed I would help you. You did not even bother to *ask* me!"

Dag felt his heart begin to pound. "I . . . I had hoped you would approve of my plan. If you wed me, my claim to the land might have weight with the other chieftains."

"Wed you! Who said I would agree to wed you? You have not even asked!"

His heart seemed to shrivel and grow cold. Had he been wrong to think she cared for him?

"Men!" Fiona's voice rose in exasperation. Dag knew Ellisil must surely be awake and listening. "They never think to explain their reasoning," she fumed. "You treat me as if I were a little child! If only you would share things with me, Dag, ask for my help . . ."

"I *am* asking," Dag said desperately. He saw his whole dream crumbling before his eyes.

"Asking what?"

"I am asking you to wed me! To aid me!"

"Why?"

"Why?"

"*Ja,* why do you do this? Why do you want my aid?"

Dag took another deep breath. "This is the only way we can be together, Fiona. I have my pride as well. I cannot give up everything for you—my home, my people—without having a plan for the future. I won't live in exile or start over again as oathman to another jarl. I want to be master of my own lands, my own hall."

Fiona was silent for a moment. When she spoke, her voice was soft. "I love you, Dag. I would not want you to be less than you are—a warrior, a trader, a seaman, a *leader.* I think you will make a fine chieftain."

"You *will* wed me?" Dag asked, half incredulous. "You will validate my claim to your father's lands?"

"*Ja,* Dag, you had only to ask."

He pulled her down next to him, burying his face in the warmth of her neck. "Ah, Fiona, how I love you."

Ellisil raised his head from his pallet on the floor. "Odin's fists, Dag, will you go to sleep? Between your bickering and your love prattle—I trow I have a headache from listening to you!"

Fiona giggled and snuggled closer. Dag sighed contentedly and whispered, "I have waited long to hear you speak of love."

" 'Tis true. I do love you, Dag."

"As I love you, Fiona."

"Viking and Irish—we will go back to Eire and found the dynasty my father dreamed of."

Dag closed his eyes. With Fiona at his side, he could do anything.

The journey back to Skirnir's steading took all of the next day, but no one minded. They were busy discussing plans for the journey to Ireland. The ship was ready; now they had merely to pack provisions and armaments and gather warriors to accompany them.

"Who of Sigurd's oathmen will want to join us?" Ellisil asked as they rode among the steep hills, Fiona riding astride in front of Dag on the stallion.

Dag shook his head. "I would have a care whom I took. I do not mean to rob Sigurd of the men he needs to rebuild the longhouse. I would sail with only younger, unmarried warriors who have lesser ties to Engvakkirsted. Rorig, Utgard, and Gudrod, perhaps."

"Rorig means to wed Breaca," Fiona reported."

"Truly?" Dag asked in surprise. "Where did he get the wealth to buy her?"

"In the last raid. Sigurd and the others where not there when the longhouse burned because they went to hunt down the Agirssons. Apparently, they received a reward from the Thorvald family for capturing the outlaws and Sigurd gave Breaca to Rorig as his portion."

"And what happened to the Agirsson brothers?" Ellisil asked.

"I did not hear." Fiona shuddered. "In truth, I did not want to know."

"I will ask Rorig to come with us," Dag decided. "And bring Breaca to keep you company. Although I mislike taking Breaca away when Mina needs her services."

"As Breaca is breeding, she will not be able to do as much this winter as she once could."

"She is with child? When does it come?"

"Not until sowing time, I believe," Fiona answered. "I did

not ask Breaca much about it. I was preoccupied with my own troubles, and I admit to being jealous as well.''

''Jealous?'' Dag asked in surprise. He grasped her shoulder gently and turned her around until her eyes meant his. ''You wish you carried my babe?''

''*Ja*, Dag.'' Fiona smiled.

The blue of his eyes deepened until they gleamed like the fairest of summer skies. ''I vow, I will give you a babe.''

She blushed and looked toward Ellisil.

Dag leaned close to whisper in her ear, ''We will begin tonight, Fiona.'' A hot thrill went through her, making her ache. How she had missed Dag's loving!

''Would you purchase the thrall named Aeddan from your brother?'' Ellisil asked, ignoring their intimate conversation. ''He seems a likely boy, and that he rode so far to warn you of Fiona's plight speaks well of his loyalty.''

''*Ja*, I would have one such as him to tend my animals, when I have them,'' Dag mused. ''I wonder if any of Donall's horses escaped the flames.''

''How could they?'' Fiona asked. ''Penned in the palisade as they were, they surely succumbed to the smoke.''

''*Nei*, I freed them.''

This time, Fiona jerked around to face Dag. ''When?''

''After I rescued you from my brother. A fool thing to do, wounded as I was, but I could not help myself. Never I could I bear to see beasts suffer.''

Fiona stared at Dag, amazed.

''You are pleased?'' Dag asked, his mouth quirking.

''Of course I am pleased. Do you fish for words of praise for your brave deed?'' she teased.

''We do not know that the horses live,'' Dag reminded her. ''They might have been trapped by the flames and perished.''

''If the chieftain's horses remain alive, that would aid us greatly,'' Ellisil said. ''But it will not feed us this winter. What of other livestock and grain? 'Twas it all destroyed in the raid?''

Dag shook his head. ''I told Sigurd not to fire the grain supply, and he did not. Dunsheauna's cattle and sheep were also left untouched, although they were likely scattered and are now claimed by other chieftains. We may have to purchase stock to survive through the winter.''

''Or raid for it,'' Ellisil suggested, his eyes gleaming.

''Nei, I'd not make enemies of my neighbors so soon. If we are to be accepted as settlers rather than raiders, we must not fight except to keep what is ours by right of Fiona's inheritance.''

''But we will raid,'' Ellisil insisted. ''If not this winter, then the next. Our food supply will be secure by then, and we will take what we want.''

Fiona felt Dag stiffen behind her on the horse. She guessed that he no longer shared Ellisil's taste for raiding, but declined to speak of it to his companion. A shiver of unease went through her as she considered that many of the warriors who accompanied them to Eire might be eager to make their fortunes rather than peacefully settling the land. Could Dag hold them in control or would they someday foreswear their allegiance to him and become enemies?

Dag and Ellisil's conversation turned again to provisioning the ship, and Fiona allowed her mind to wander. She thought of Siobhan and wondered if she still lived. Now that her father was dead, her aunt was her closest kin. She longed to speak with her of Dag and his intent, to gain Siobhan's aid and goodwill for their plan.

She sighed. There was much to be done ere they even set sail for Eire. Dag meant go back to Engvakkirsted to gather men and say farewell to Sigurd, and she worried that Brodir would harm him. Her fear was no longer for herself, but for Dag. She loved him so.

''Macushla, are you still awake?''

Fiona struggled to stir from the comfort of the bedfurs. She had fallen asleep almost as soon as she lay down upon the soft bed in the chamber Skirnir's wife had bid her to when they arrived at Ferjeshold. Now her fatigue ebbed at the thought of being alone with Dag.

"*Ja,*" she whispered. "And how is it with you? Are all the arrangements made with Skirnir?"

"I'd not speak of that now." Dag slid in beside her, then reached out and pulled her toward him. She gasped at the feel of his warm skin, and immediately her body tingled with desire. She lifted herself to her elbows and leaned over to touch his face, tracing the graceful lines of his brow and cheeks, then caressing his mustache and the harsh skin of his unshaven jaw below.

"Uhhh," Dag groaned. "I vow I am so fatigued I could sleep for a sennight."

Fiona felt a faint disappointment. Dag needed his rest; it was selfish of her to seek to couple with him ere he slept. She withdrew her fingers from his face.

"Rub the back of my legs, please," Dag murmured as he turned over to lie on his chest. "I am unused to riding a horse, and my legs ache fiercely."

Fiona pulled back the bedfurs and began to massage Dag's thighs. Beneath her fingers, his skin felt warm, his muscles tight and hard. He groaned again, then sighed. "I do so like it when you touch me, Fiona. It reminds me of when I was a prisoner and you tended my wounds. You have such a pleasing touch. When you bathed me, it was near torture to endure your caresses and pretend to be unconscious."

"You told me once that you pretended to be in a swoon that day because you feared me. Why?"

"If I tell you, Fiona, will you promise not to laugh?"

"*Ja,* I promise."

"I thought you were a fairy."

"A what?"

Dag sat up, the movement faintly visible by the glow of the brazier that warmed the bedcloset. "A fairy—a supernatural being. I feared you meant to steal my soul."

"The fever," she suggested. "It made you imagine things."

"*Ja,* it was partly the fever, but it was you as well. You were so unearthly beautiful. When you first came, I thought you meant to kill me, but then you began to undress. . . ." Dag's hand moved to cup one of her breasts. "What a vision

you were. Your hair loose and wild, your strange green eyes—
a shade I had never seen before . . . your perfect body . . ."
His voice trailed off, and Fiona sighed as his fingers found
her nipple and gently teased. "I wanted you desperately," he
whispered. "But I was too sick and frightened to take you. I
feared to couple with you, lest you steal my soul and trap me
in fairyland forever."

Fiona closed her eyes and let herself melt at Dag's touch.
"You must have thought me a wanton, that I fondled you while
you lay helpless and in pain."

Dag laughed huskily. "If you would know the truth, I scarce
noticed my injuries then. I was on fire for you, but something
kept me from taking you."

"Your fear."

"*Nei,* not only my fear. I also recognized your innocence,
that you had not known a man before. I was beholden to you
for tending my wounds and aiding me. I did not think it right
to take you like that. I would have frightened you, and likely
hurt you as well."

"But I wanted it," she protested. " 'Twas my purpose in
aiding you, that you might couple with me and save me from
my father's marriage plans."

"*Nei,* you thought you wanted that, but you did not. You
were but a silly maiden then."

"Silly?"

"*Ja,*" Dag answered, his grin visible in the brazier's glow.
"Not a fairy, but a silly maid."

"You said you were afraid of me," Fiona reminded him.

Dag's smile vanished. "Sometimes I fear that you *have*
stolen my soul, Fiona."

She felt her chest tighten with emotion. " 'Tis not enchantment, Dag, but love. If the truth be known—" She leaned
forward so her face was close to his. "—I feel the same for
you."

Dag brushed her hair back and kissed her deeply.

"You are tired," she whispered, pulling away. "You must
rest."

''Not so tired,'' he murmured, his hand coming up to fondle her breast again. ''And I will rest better when I am inside you.''

Fiona gasped and smothered a moan as Dag's hand moved between her thighs. ''Sweet Bridget, but the things you make me feel!''

Dag swiftly reversed positions, pushing her down on the bed. ''I have only begun.''

She groaned as his mouth found her neck and moved lower. Her body felt afire. She wanted this man, wanted to feel his hardness inside her. Arching her hips, she reached for him.

''Such a greedy wench,'' he murmured as he fitted himself within her. ''Always you have rushed me.''

Fiona hardly heard him. Her thoughts dissolved as he found a slow, steady rhythm. The intense pleasure built and built until she felt she would burst from the pressure welling up inside her. Her lips formed wordless, desperate sounds as Dag coaxed her body over the edge. At her climax, she screamed, the sound echoing in the tiny bedchamber. Dag followed her seconds after, his groan of completion a husky counterpoint to her wild cry.

They lay in a sweaty tangle for a few moments, then Fiona lifted herself from beneath Dag's still-heaving chest. ''By the Saints, I've done it again. Skirnir and the others will think you're murdering me!''

'' 'Twould be fitting punishment for such an ill-tempered wench.''

Fiona gasped and struggled to sit up. ''Ill-tempered! Me? If I am ill-tempered, it is because I was provoked by a wretched lout of a warrior!''

Dag grinned at her. ''I like your fire, storm maiden. 'Tis part of what beguiles me.''

Fiona's anger faded, and she smiled back. ''We are well-matched, Viking,'' she said as she smoothed a lock of his wavy hair away from his sweat-glistened face. ''Together, we shall be invincible. No warlord dare stand against us, not even Sivney.''

Dag's face sobered. ''Sivney Longbeard I do not fear, but Brodir haunts my thoughts. Although I tell myself that you will be surely safe here at Ferjeshold, I am still reluctant to leave you to say farewell to Sigurd.''

"Take me with you."

"To Engvakkirsted? *Nei,* I'll not agree to such foolishness. Sigurd nearly had you put to death already, and Brodir is like to cut your throat the first chance he gets!''

'' 'Twill be easier or you to keep me safe if I am at your side than if you leave me here among strangers who might be bribed by Brodir. Besides, I would say goodbye to Mina and the others."

Dag shook his head in negation, but even as he did so, he could not help considering Fiona's suggestion. He *would* feel better with Fiona at his side, and for all that he trusted Ellisil, he was not as certain of the other men of Ferjeshold. He had seen some of them cast lustful eyes in her direction.

"If you came with me, you would have to remain in my sight at all times," Dag began cautiously. "We could not be parted for even a moment."

"I would guard your back, and you would guard mine," Fiona enthused. "We could protect each other like sword brothers.''

"You fear for me?" Dag asked in surprise.

"Ja, Brodir hates you almost as much as me.''

Dag nodded. There was sense in what she said. Brodir might well see Dag's bond with Fiona as a betrayal of their clan. "There is another advantage," he mused. "If we sailed to Engvakkirsted rather than riding, it would save us a day or more of travelling time."

'' 'Tis settled then,'' Fiona said, cuddling next to him. "As soon as the ship is ready, we'll leave on our journey."

Dag pulled her close and inhaled the clean scent of her freshly washed hair. Tenderness filled him as he felt the caress of her silken skin against his body. Fiona feared for him; she would fight for him as he would for her. The thought touched him deeply. Other women had desired him for what he could give them, status or wealth or pleasure. But with Fiona it was different. He felt that she cared for his spirit, his self.

Sighing deeply, he stretched out and slept.

Chapter 33

"Freya help me, but my stomach tosses and pitches with every wave." Standing beside Fiona at the edge of the ship, Breaca clutched the gunwale and groaned.

Fiona patted her companion's shoulder, then turned to watch Dag and the other men adjust the sealskin ropes which controlled the huge red-and-white sail. "You will grow used to it," Fiona said. "This ship is smaller than Sigurd's and seems to ride the waves more roughly. The sea also seems choppier this journey."

"Things went well at Engvakkirsted, at least," Breaca answered. "There was no sign of Brodir, and even if Sigurd and the other warriors ignored you, the women wished us well."

Fiona paused, remembering her tearful goodbyes to Mina and the other women. "Parting was easier because I knew you were coming with me," she told Breaca. "And it helped that Dag stayed at my side, never wavering in his loyalty, even when Sigurd acted as if I did not exist."

Breaca suddenly wiped at her sweat-beaded brow. "Fiona, forgive me, but I must lie down."

Fiona helped the younger woman to the tarpaulin-covered portion of the deck so she could crawl into a warm bedsack.

After settling Breaca in, Fiona resumed her watch at the side of the ship. A cold wind blew through her heavy fur tunic, making her shiver, and a vague, nagging sense of unease accompanied the chill. She struggled to shake off the mood, reminding herself that they were on their way to Eire—she should be brimming with happiness.

Turning from the prow, she watched the Norsemen try to control the whipping sail. Only thirty-two men, counting thralls, manned the ship, and Fiona knew that Dag worried if it were enough. Not only had he voiced concern that such a slim crew could keep the vessel afloat if a storm struck, he also had doubts about what would happen if they encountered a strong defensive force when they reached Ireland. Ellisil had suggested that Irish defenses were so inferior to Norsemen as to be unworthy of consideration, but Fiona knew Dag thought otherwise. Last time, the Irish had been unprepared for a raid, he said, but those who survived would not make the mistake again. They must be ready to fight as soon as they beached the ship.

Tugging an errant wisp of hair into her braid, Fiona shivered again and turned to duck the wind. Nay, it was not fear of shipwreck nor an attack of her countrymen which gnawed at her thoughts. It was a deeper, less reasonable sense of foreboding. Her thoughts turned to Brodir—she could not get over the fact that he had made no attempt to attack her or to prevent this voyage. His hatred for her was so strong, so violent; it did not seem possible he had given up all thoughts of revenge.

But he could not hurt her now, she reminded herself as she looked out at the foaming, gray waves. In a matter of days, she would be back in Eire among her countrymen.

Dag moved past her as he made his way to take over the tiller, and she noted his harassed expression. "Damned landsmen," he muttered. "I could teach a herd of sheep to sail better than these fools."

Fiona could not help feeling amused by his grumbling. "Not every man has your multitude of skills, Dag," she chided him. "Warrior, sailor, horseman, lover—is there anything you do not excel at?"

"I have no skill at tasks that require patience, as well you know," he answered. "My father's uncle was a smithy who tried to teach me his trade. He gave up when I ruined everything I set my hand to. If you want a man who can fashion a fancy brooch, forge a weapon, or carve a bowl, do not look to me."

"I think you are quite good with your hands." Fiona gazed at him suggestively. "I have no complaints of being unsatisfied."

Dag stared at her, then leaned over to nuzzle her neck. "Thor's hammer, but you are a distracting wench. What if we all drown because you keep me from taking the tiller?" he whispered in her ear. "Do you even care?"

"*Nei.*" Fiona lifted her face to return his kiss. "Sigurd always said I was an *undine,* luring Norse sailors to their doom."

Dag kissed her back a moment, then gently pushed her away. "Well, I have no desire to end up on the bottom of the sea quite yet. I mean to get you back to your enchanted isle first, fairy queen."

Fiona smiled as she watched Dag gracefully make his way among the jumble of sea chests and supplies cluttering the deck. She loved him so much, sometimes it scared her. He was brave and strong, but then, so had her father once been. The thought made her smile fade as she made her way to the cargo hold to see about food for the exhausted, hungry crew.

The rest of the day passed uneventfully, and by night, the sea calmed. Dag was able to leave Rorig at the tiller and seek his rest. Fiona lay beside him, not sleeping but listening to the reassuring sound of his rhythmic breathing. She dozed for a time, then woke with a start and reached out for him. He mumbled slightly at her touch, but did not wake. Fiona sat up and looked around. By starlight, she could make out Rorig's tall form near the tiller. She lay down again and tried to sleep, but she could not rest. Her chest felt tight, her muscles tense. Mayhap it was the discomfort of sleeping on a hard deck which bothered her.

She turned over restlessly, then her heart caught in her throat as a shadow moved a few feet away. Straining her eyes in the dim light, she tried to ascertain who it was. Could it be Breaca, too seasick to sleep? Nay, the shape appeared too large for Breaca.

The hair on the back of her neck stood up, and without puzzling further, Fiona reached out and felt for the dagger Dag wore at his belt. Usually he took it off to sleep, but tonight he had been too tired to bother. Fiona grasped the hilt of the weapon and gently disengaged it from Dag's belt. She thought of waking him and decided against it. If she was wrong about the danger, she would feel terrible for interrupting Dag's badly needed rest.

Gripping the dagger in sweaty fingers, she waited for the dark shape to move again. As moments passed and nothing happened, Fiona began to feel foolish. Why would someone on the ship try to creep up on her and Dag? All the warriors had been handpicked by Dag and Ellisil, and they had sworn as oathmen to one man or the other. She was being ridiculous.

She closed her eyes again and relaxed her grip on the weapon. Breathing in the sea air, she sought to calm herself. An acrid, unpleasant scent permeated the tangy odor of the ocean, reawakening memory. Fiona opened her eyes and saw a dark silhouette looming above her. She had only a second to grasp the dagger and thrust it upwards with both hands.

There was a harsh cry as the dagger tore through flesh, and the dark figure staggered backwards. Fiona froze in fear, but Dag jerked out of a dead sleep and, shielding her with his body, rolled them both beneath the hide covering which sheltered this part of the deck. "My knife," he breathed, groping at his belt.

"I used it," she answered.

"On who? What's out there?"

"Brodir."

"What?"

"It's he," Fiona gasped. "I recognized his smell."

"Thor's thunder!" Dag threw off the tarpaulin and stood up, bellowing, "Brodir, you cowardly bastard, I'll tie you to the prow and let the sea creatures eat you! I'll deny you water, make you beg for my mercy!"

"Nei! I'll die like a warrior," Brodir challenged. "You'll have to take me in honest battle. If you can still fight—you coward, you man who hides behind a witch woman for protection!"

Fiona scrambled from beneath the tarpaulin. It was so dark, she could scarcely make out either Dag or Brodir. Frantically, she realized that Dag was without a weapon. If Brodir attacked, Dag might be wounded before anyone could come to his aid. She groped across the deck, making her way to the nearest sea chest. There would be weapons inside, wrapped in cloth to protect them from the corrosive sea air.

" 'Tis you who will die a coward's death," she heard Dag say to Brodir as the two men faced off near the prow. "Never will you reach Odin's hall. Never will you see your battle companions again."

"I'll die a hero for trying to save my people from the witch woman." Brodir's voice sounded strained, and Fiona realized that the wound she had inflicted must pain him. "If only you hadn't interfered in my plan."

"What plan?" Dag demanded.

"I set the fire," Brodir taunted. "I thought she would be blamed for it. If only Sigurd had believed me."

"You burned the longhouse!"

"Better that a few women and children should perish than the whole clan succumb to the woman's evil."

"What about Knorri?" Dag asked. "How dare you kill the man you were sworn to! For that alone, you deserve to die a gruesome death."

"The fire killed Knorri, not I," Brodir answered stubbornly. "He was old anyway. He should have stepped aside years ago and let Sigurd become jarl."

"Do not argue with him!" Fiona called to Dag. "I fear he uses this time to scheme."

As if in answer, Brodir laughed, a chilling, murderous sound. Fiona recalled Brodir's battle prowess; he had a weapon and Dag did not. Desperate, she searched the sea chest until her fingers closed around the long, slim shape of a sword. She yanked it from its cloth covering and rushed to Dag. She thrust the sword hilt toward him.

"Nei, I will not use it." Dag pushed the weapon away. "I will not ease Brodir's passage into the otherworld by giving him a warrior's death."

"Please, Dag," she begged. "I would not have you hurt."

"This craven wretch does not have the courage to hurt me."

Fiona glanced behind them and made out vague silhouettes. Dag's oathmen had risen from their sleep to aid their leader. If only they could reach Brodir before he attacked Dag!

A glint of light flashed through the darkness. Dag dodged the weapon, and it rang harmlessly against the deck. Another object whistled through the air. Fiona could made out Dag's quick movement, and then the two men grappled in a blur of shadows on the foredeck.

"Someone help Dag!" Fiona begged the men around her.

It seemed too late, for all heard a bloodcurdling shout and then a splash. Fiona rushed forward. "Dag!" she screamed.

He came to her out of the gathering sea mist. "Fiona," he murmured, wrapping his arms around her. "You are safe. Brodir is no more."

"You killed him?"

"Nei. When I laid my hands upon him, he pulled away and jumped overboard. As I thought he would, he chose a coward's death."

Fiona breathed a sigh of relief as she allowed Dag to lead her back toward their sleeping area in the stern of the ship. "Oh, Dag," she murmured, clutching him. "I am so glad you are safe."

Dag cradled her in his arms. " 'Tis over now. Brodir will not trouble us again."

"Odin's fury, but that was close," Rorig called from the tiller, where he tried to steer while holding a trembling Breaca. "Brodir must have hidden in the underdeck before we set sail. I trow he meant to murder you both while you slept."

"What woke you, Dag?" Ellisil asked from nearby. "I am ashamed to admit, I heard nothing until the fight was joined."

" 'Twas not I who roused," Dag said. "Fiona was the one."

Ellisil came closer, his voice full of awe. "Though Dag says you do not have magic powers, I wonder. How did you know there was danger when all the rest of us slept peacefully?"

Fiona gave a shaky laugh. " 'Twas not magic which alerted me, but smell. Brodir has no fondness for bathing, and a distinctive odor follows him wherever he goes. Even with the scent of the sea and all the smells of the crew and supplies, nothing reeks like Brodir."

"Ah, Fiona, once again you saved my life," Dag said softly. "One would think you wished to keep me always in your debt."

"What is between us has nothing to do with honor or debt. I love you, Dag. I will do whatever I can to keep you safe."

Dag guided Fiona back to their sleeping place. At least it was dark, and the other men could not see the fiery blush on his face which Fiona's words aroused. She was but a woman; it was not her responsibility to defend him. Even so, her avowal of love pleased him. What other man could boast of having such a fierce warrior-woman to guard his back?

Settling down into his bedsack, Dag smiled into the darkness.

" 'Tis very green," Ellisil commented to Dag as the two men stood side by side at the tiller, gazing upon the shoreline to their port side.

"*Ja.* I have often wondered what the color of the place reminds me of. I think it is emeralds, the bright green jewels a Norseman I know once brought back from a year-long trading expedition to the Eastern city Constantinople. When the sun shines in Ireland, the hue of the hills is fair blinding."

" 'Tis a wonder more Norsemen have not thought to settle here."

"They will," Dag answered. "As ambitious younger sons leave Norseland and sail out to plunder, more and more will discover this place. We must expect to fight off our greedy Norse brothers as well as Irish chieftains who would increase their lands. We must have a strong fortress and keep a constant guard. Fiona's father chose a good location for his palisade, but his men were unprepared to defend it. We will do better."

"Making plans?" Fiona asked as she joined them.

"*Ja,*" Dag answered. "Can you advise us if there is a place to land where we could hope to remain unseen? I would not risk being forced into battle ere we even reach Dunsheauna."

"There is a shallow area upriver from my father's lands where we could beach the ship and make our way through the woods. I do not think our arrival would be noted there."

Dag nodded. "We will take down the sail now and wait until dusk before rowing in."

Beside them, Ellisil gave a little shiver. "I can't forget the stories I have heard." He turned toward Fiona. "Are there spirits in your homeland we should fear?"

Fiona cocked her head, thinking of Siobhan's insistence that ancient spirits dwelled in every rock and stream and tree of Eire. Had Fiona not felt them herself sometimes when she walked alone, heard them whispering to her?

"There are forces, very old ones, which sometimes still hold sway over men," she answered thoughtfully. "Legend tells of a race of men who knew magic; they were called Tuatha De Danaan, and they ruled the isle for many years. Other men came and conquered Eire, and the Tuatha De Danaan went to live underground. Many say they survive there still, guarding the land from intruders."

Fiona saw that Ellisil's eyes grown wide. She smiled at him. "To my mind it seems more prudent to fear the men of Eire rather than the spirits. Although I am not certain how Irish spirits perceive Norsemen, I know that Irish *men* with stout spears and swords hate them."

"That is why we must not travel upriver until night comes," Dag said firmly.

Fiona excused herself to see to Breaca, who suffered from another bout of seasickness. After she left, Ellisil moved closer to Dag. "Tell me truly, sword brother, do you not fear the spirits of this place a little?"

"Mayhap I do. But with Fiona at our side, I believe we will be safe."

"All along you have denied her powers; now you say you depend upon them. What is the truth? Do you believe Fiona possesses magic or not?"

"I don't know," Dag answered. "If she has powers, she is not aware of them, and I do know that she would never use them for evil. She is not like that cruel woman of Ottar's steading who poses as the Angel of Death to prey upon bound and helpless victims."

"So, you knew the old wise woman was false. I wondered how you were brave enough to order her away even as she sought to curse you. I'll admit that impressed me. I would not have dared to speak so to a woman reputed to be a *volva*."

"*Volva!* That one was no more a seer than I. Merely a sour, old woman who hates those younger and more appealing than her and kills them when she has a chance."

"It seems you had the right of it, Dag. And of Brodir, too. I heard him admit that he started the blaze which burned the longhouse. What a treacherous wretch he turned out to be." Ellisil shook his head.

"*Ja*," Dag answered. "It will satisfy me greatly to someday tell my brother that he was wrong about Fiona—and even more wrong about Brodir. But for now—" He flexed his shoulders restlessly. "—now we must concentrate on reaching Dunsheauna."

The *Wind Raven* glided up the Shannon. Fiona closed her eyes and listened to the men dip their oars gently in the water. A drizzly rain fell, dripping off the hood of her cloak and glazing her bare face with moisture. She stuck out her tongue and tasted the sweetness of Irish rain. As the men spoke in low voices around her, Fiona's chest tightened with anticipation. The dragonhead prow of the ship had been removed to disguise the ship, and the men were all garbed in full battle attire beneath their cloaks. Whatever met them at Dunsheauna, the Norsemen would be ready.

Dag appeared beside her. "Are we near the place, Fiona?"

Quickly, she scanned the mist-shrouded shore off their starboard side. She had not realized they had travelled so far already. Could they really be near the shallow cove above the curve of the river where her father's palisade had once stood?

"I can scarce tell in the dark," she answered. "But I think . . . *ja,* it is only a little farther."

Dag gave a quiet order to the rowing men, and the ship's progress slowed. Fiona squinted at the ghostly dark shape of the shoreline, suddenly afraid. Once she had known every rise and curve of the river, but that was months ago. What if she made a mistake and the ship ran aground or put in too soon to arrive at Dunsheauna undetected? Dag trusted her so much; what if she failed him?

"There!" She pointed to a place where the river widened and the alder trees grew a little ways back from the shore.

Slowly, gracefully, the ship glided in. There was a groaning sound as the keel of the *Raven* met the river bottom. In seconds, the men had thrown down their oars and begun to scramble over the sides. Fiona watched as they pushed the ship through the shallows and up onto the beach.

"Fiona."

She rushed to the side and jumped down into Dag's arms. Nearby, Rorig helped Breaca onto land.

Fiona looked down at the squishy ground beneath her feet. Eire—she had thought never to see it again. She wanted to bend down and kiss the mud!

Dag's firm hand on her arm interrupted her foolish musings. "Come," he said.

They walked silently through the forest. Around her, Fiona could feel the tension of the men, the way they clutched at their sword and ax hilts. Once they left the rush of the river behind, there was little sound except the faint hiss of the rain. Fiona and Dag led the way, Dag's left hand supporting her elbow. They paused after a bit, listening, and Dag turned toward her. "Guide us, Fiona. Show us the best way through the woods."

She led them single file down the pathway she had taken so many times. When they passed the thicket where her aunt's small hut was hidden, she hesitated, then went on. Even if

Siobhan still lived there, she did not want to frighten her by bringing a group of warriors to her door. After they saw the remains of Dunsheauna and knew what had happened there, she would return to see how her aunt had fared.

The forest thinned, and they ventured out on the plain below the hill fort. Points of light glinted within the boundaries of the ruined palisade, indicating that people still dwelled there; but from this distance, they could not guess how many and if friend or enemy.

"Fiona and I will go ahead," Dag announced. "The rest of you wait here. If we do not return within a short while, come after us prepared to fight."

Ellisil and the others made sounds of assent, then Fiona felt Dag's hand on her shoulder, guiding her forward.

The sight of the blackened timbers of the palisade wall made Fiona's stomach tighten, and horrible memories of torch-carrying Vikings darkened her thoughts. Beside her, she could sense Dag's tension. He moved with silent caution, like a cat stalking prey.

They both started as a white shape loomed ahead of them. There was a low growl. Fiona's heart leaped into her throat, then she gave a jubilant laugh. "Tully! It's Tully!"

The huge hound sniffed her carefully, then went to investigate Dag. "Careful, Dag," she cautioned. "Tully does not like strangers."

Dag reached out his sword hand, palm up, and spoke in a low, soothing voice. Within moments the hound was licking his hand and whining in a submissive way.

Fiona could only stare. "How did you do that? I swear, I have never seen Tully greet a man so easily before, especially one in battle gear."

" 'Tis a way I have with animals. They know I am a friend, that I would not hurt them."

"Still, it is amazing." Fiona shook her head as the dog came back to her and allowed her to scratch behind his ears. "Never would Tully allow any man but my father to touch him. Only women would be tolerate. Look here," she added as she ran her hand along the curly fur of the animal's back. "Someone has groomed and fed him.'' She raised her eyes to the firelights winking in the darkness ahead of them. ''I wish he could speak and tell us who dwells here now.''

''But since he cannot speak, we must not tarry,'' Dag reminded her. ''If we do not return soon, Ellisil and the others will come prepared for battle.''

They moved through the fort entrance, noting both destruction and renewal. Beside the blackened shape of the burned-out feasthall, a vegetable plot had been planted, and sounds of domestic animals came to them from the pens at the far edge of the fort. Smoke issued from the roofholes of several huts which appeared to be constructed of timbers salvaged from the remains of other buildings.

Fiona and Dag paused beside one of the huts. ''Make yourself known, Fiona,'' Dag said. ''That we have come so far without meeting any guards must mean that only survivors of your clan live here now.''

Fiona nodded and went to the hide door of the hovel. She pushed it aside and called out, ''Hullo, is anyone within?''

''Who goes?'' called a frightened woman's voice.

'' 'Tis I, Fiona, daughter of your old chieftain.''

There was silence, then a rustling sound. Fiona stepped back as a woman appeared in the doorway. ''Fiona, is it really you?''

''Nessa!''

The two women fell upon each other and embraced exuberantly.

''You live, thank the saints!'' the woman sighed as Fiona released her. ''We thought certain the Vikings had killed you or sold you off as a slave.''

Fiona could only nod. Tears streamed down her face. ''Duvessa and the rest of the women—did they survive as well?''

''Aye, we were quite safe in the souterrain, as you said we would be. But by the time we dared leave, the fires had destroyed almost everything. We had a little grain from last season and what livestock we could round up, but it was near impossible to plant much this year without the men.'' Neesa's voice choked slightly, and Fiona remembered that Neesa's husband had been one of the men cut down with her father. "The boys tried to do the work, but they are still too young and none of them were much good with the plow animals."

"The boys?" Fiona asked excitedly. "Who else lives?"

"Your foster brother Dermot as well as Niall, Achlin, and Murrean. And Dubhag survived his wound, although his mind is not right yet. The boys hid in the woods, and the cursed Vikings did not take time to hunt them down. They were too busy stripping the fort of anything of value and burning everything. . . ." Nessa voice trailed off as she noticed Dag. "Who is this man with you, Fiona?" she asked, backing away. "Surely you did you not bring Vikings with you."

Fiona struggled for words to explain. It had taken her months to accept that Dag was not her enemy. How to convince Nessa, who must live in terror of all Norsemen?

"Nessa, this is Dag Thorsson," she answered firmly. "Although we have not yet said Christian vows, I honor him as my husband."

Nessa's eyes bulged out, and her mouth opened and closed like that of a fish out of water. "Your h-h-husband?" she stuttered.

"Aye." Fiona turned to Dag. "Meet Nessa, wife of Brennan, one of my father's oathmen."

Dag bowed slightly. "I am honored, lady. From what I heard of it, your husband met a warrior's death."

"He . . . he speaks Gaelic!" Nessa's hands frantically twisted the skirts of her kirtle.

"Aye, he speaks Gaelic," Fiona answered. "I taught him myself. That way he will be able to communicate after he takes over his new position of chieftain of the Deasúnachta."

If possible, Nessa's eyes widened even further. Fiona, growing impatient, said, "Go, Nessa, gather the other women. I want to explain my plan to all of you."

After staring at Dag a moment longer, Nessa turned and ran.

Chapter 34

"I was prepared for warfare, but not this blind, unreasoning terror," Fiona said, turning to her companion with chagrin.

" 'Tis not all bad," Dag assured her. "It appears they will submit easily, and I can save my men's strength for rebuilding rather than fighting."

"But what of Sivney?" Fiona worried. "I forgot to ask Nessa if he has come to claim lordship of Dunsheauna."

"That he posts no guards to defend the place speaks clearly of his lack of interest."

"He may not concern himself with Donall's lands now, burned and impoverished as they are, but he will as soon as he hears Norsemen have come to settle."

"We will deal with him then. For now, we concern ourselves with building more shelters and stockpiling food for the winter. How is the hunting in the forests near here?"

"It has always been good," she answered distractedly.

Dag went back to tell his men that they had met no resistance while Fiona waited for the other survivors to appear. In time, they came, bearing torches, and Fiona embraced each of them in turn. There was much weeping, and even more questions. Fiona refused to answer any but the most basic queries until Dag came. Finally, he returned with Ellisil, Aeddan, and two other Irish thralls who had travelled from Norseland. With the men flanking her, Fiona began to speak.

She told of her abduction the night of the raid, of the anger she had felt towards the Vikings for burning the palisade and killing her father, of her vow to return and avenge him. Then, she told them of the months she had spent among the Norse and how she had come to appreciate that they were not so different from the Irish and how, over time, she had realized that it was better to go on with her life than to dwell on the past and plot revenge.

"I cannot bring my father back," she told them tearfully. "Nor can I bring back your dead kin. But we can rebuild Dunsheauna and make it something like it once was."

She glanced around, searching the faces of people she had known all her life, wondering if they thought her a traitor. To her own ears, she sounded unconvincing, yet she believed what she said with all her heart.

Gesturing to the men behind her, she continued. "I know you may be shocked to learn that I have taken a Norseman as my husband and that I ask you to accept him as your new chieftain, but I promise you, on my honor as a princess of the clan of the Deasúnachta, that these are good men, that they come not to kill and destroy, but to settle and make their homes here."

There was silence for a time, then young Dermot came forward. His face looked pinched and thin in the firelight, but he had grown tall over the sunseason and his blue eyes blazed with a ferocity that belied his eleven winters. "You are only a woman, Fiona, with a woman's weakness. Although I do not blame you for submitting to the Norseman, I cannot accept him as my chieftain. His people and ours are enemies, and thus it will always be. You may have no heart for vengeance, but I cannot not forget those who died at these men's hands."

Fiona drew breath, considering her response, but it was Dag who answered. "Consider your princess's words carefully, boy, for I will back them up with my sword arm. You may not wish me as your lord, but I am here and you need me. You require men to rebuild your fort and plant your fields; but most of all, you cannot do without warriors. The northern lands swarm with men greedy for plunder, and it is only a few days journey by dragonship to the rich shores of your land. Without my men to defend you, Dunsheauna will soon be ravaged again.

"My brother led the last raid against you, and he was generous, leaving your grain supply and livestock untouched. The next Norseman who attacks this fort may not have my brother's magnanimous nature. He might well slaughter every living thing and burn every building and field. Without a strong leader, I promise you, the future of the Deasúnachta is numbered in weeks and months."

Dag's ominous proclamation was greeted with shudders and furtive whispers, and Fiona knew they remembered that terrible night when the darkness shone with flames and "Death walked on the night wind." She held her breath, wondering what their reaction would be. Did they trust her judgment? Would they accept Dag, albeit grudgingly?

"You speak fine words," Dermot retorted, "even as you admit that our disastrous weakness is the fault of your own kin. Why should we trust you, a man whose blood clearly makes you our enemy?"

Dag shrugged his broad shoulders. "You have no choice."

"There is Sivney Longbeard." Dermot's smile was grim. "He promised to rebuild our fort and take us under his protection."

"Where is he?" Dag glanced around, as if searching for the absent Irish chieftain. "I see no bold hero come to defend you. I see only a group of fearful woman, and boys who would be men."

Even by firelight, Fiona could see Dermot's face color. She wanted to warn Dag of her foster brother's pride, but she feared to interfere with Dag's authority. The Viking was magnificent this night, both intimidating and reassuring at the same time. Fiona had no doubt he would win the women's acceptance, but she was less certain of the young men. Dermot, especially, was an arrogant, stubborn sort.

"Sivney will come," he now announced balefully. "He was betrothed to the princess ere she was abducted, and he still honors that betrothal. Soon he will come to kill you and take Fiona for his queen!"

Dag shook his head in negation, but Fiona felt a chill run down her spine. Sivney might well try to do such a thing.

Suddenly, a woman stepped forward, her long, dark hair visible in the torchlight.

"Siobhan!" Fiona cried.

Her aunt nodded. "Aye, child. I am returned to my rightful place. When the Christian holy man died in the fires, the survivors of Dunsheauna remembered me. They recalled my prophecy of years ago—that Donall's reign would bring them pain and suffering." She moved toward Dag, looking up at the Norse warrior who towered over her. "Is this the man whose life you saved?" she asked in a quiet voice meant only for Fiona's ears.

"It is."

Siobhan gazed steadily at Dag. "You owe your life to this woman, Norseman. Do you intend to honor your debt?"

Dag smiled, displaying both his strong, white teeth and his formidable charm. "Nay, I owe Fiona for *two* lives. She saved my life again on the journey here."

Siohban gave a musical laugh. "I like this warrior," she said loudly. "He is not so prideful as to forget his debt to a woman. I believe the agreement he offers us is fair."

"He is our enemy!" Dermot protested, his youthful voice shrill with outrage.

Siohban turned toward him, her voice softening, "For a hundred generations, invaders have come to Eire. They come to plunder and to settle; but in the end, the land itself conquers them and makes them her own. If Fiona bears a son to this Viking, he will not be half-Norse and half-Irish, but merely Irish. That is the power of this place." She faced Dag again. "Are you prepared, warrior, to surrender yourself to the spirits of Eire?"

Dag felt a tremor of fear run down his spine as he gazed

into the wise woman's gray eyes. He could feel the power of Eire pulling him in like a lodestone drawing iron. He had feared this moment since the day he set foot on this spirit-infested isle. Did he have the courage to abandon his former life and face the future as an Irishman?

He turned to look at Fiona, remembering how he had once feared her, feared the hunger and longing she aroused in his soul. He had dreaded that she would trap him here in fairyland for all eternity—and so she had. But it was not so terrible a fate; indeed, he had never known such contentment. "This place has conquered me already," he answered. "I will devote my life to defending the land and breeding up sons who will do so after me."

A sigh went through the crowd, and Fiona knew they were pacified, all except Dermot, who bristled with fury and frustration.

The gathering broke up, the women whispering together in small groups, the boys lingering near Dag and Ellisil as they discussed the task of rebuilding that lay ahead of them. Fiona watched Dermot stalk off into the darkness beyond the torches.

"There is always one," Siobhan said, coming to stand beside Fiona. "One fool who seeks to defy the pattern the gods have woven."

"And you believe that the gods will it that Dag shall rule?"

"If not Dag, then another foreigner. I predicted this long ago when Aisling wed Donall. I told her that her husband would bring suffering to her people, that her grandson would be of foreign blood."

"But my father ruled here nigh on twenty years," Fiona protested. "And the suffering came not because of Donall, but because of the Vikings."

"You are still loyal to him." Siobhan sighed. "There is much of your mother in you."

Fiona shook her head. For all that her aunt could see the future in some ways, she was very blind in others. Fiona would not see her father's life as a failure. Nay, she would not let it be so. She and Dag would rebuild what was destroyed; and if she bore a son, he would carry Donall's name into the future.

"Come inside where it is warm and dry." Duvessa appeared beside Fiona. "We have much to talk about." There was an odd shyness to her foster sister's manner. Fiona wondered if she had changed so much that her own kin no longer felt comfortable with her.

Before they could reach the hut Duvessa indicated, Breaca ran up breathlessly. "Ellisil says we are to bring supplies from the ship. Do you want me to bring you anything, Fiona?"

"Nay, I need nothing tonight. Do you know where you and Rorig will sleep?"

"On the ship. Ellisil says it must be guarded constantly until we have a chance to unload it."

"See to Rorig then, and sleep well, Breaca."

They embraced. Fiona saw Breaca give Duvessa a curious glance, then the slave girl hurried off."

"I think we must look very like," Duvessa mused as she and Fiona entered a small mud-and-wattle hut. "Does she act like me as well?"

"Oh, aye," Fiona answered. "She scolds me terribly and calls me a fool just as you always did." Then, seeing Duvessa's uneasy look, she added, "I don't know what I would have done without her all those months in Norseland. She kept me from making even worse mistakes than the ones I made."

Duvessa smiled tentatively. "Was it very awful, being a Viking prisoner?"

Fiona cocked her head. "Well, it could have been, but there was a sort of understanding between Dag and me from the beginning. You see, Dag was the Viking prisoner my father captured and imprisoned in the souterrain. I tended him and saved his life. Because of that, he owed me a debt, and he did not treat me cruelly." She met Duvessa's eyes, wondering what her foster sister would think of her now. Would she blame Fiona for aiding their enemy? Would she hold her responsible for the Viking raid?"

Duvessa smiled, the skin crinkling merrily around her blue eyes. "I guessed long ago. You left your things behind in the souterrain, and I found them before we left our hiding place.

'Twas obvious someone had nursed the prisoner and then freed him.''

"I did not free him, although I had half made up my mind to do so. He was able to break his shackles and escape. He found the rest of the Vikings, who were already planning to raid the palisade. Because of my care, he urged his brother, their leader, to deal lightly with our people. That's why they did not fire the grain supply, nor search too hard for the women and children, nor kill all the livestock.''

Fiona spoke the words carefully, finally believing them herself. At last, she could let go of her guilt. She had not caused her father's death, nor defied her destiny. Indeed, she believed now that she had been guided to the souterrain to save Dag's life because he was her fate.

Duvessa shivered. "I would never have dared to go down into that hole to face an enemy warrior, even if he were bound and sorely wounded.''

" 'Twas not bravery, but foolhardiness. You have often said that I act before I think, and 'tis true. My impetuous nature caused me a great deal of trouble when I was in the Norselands.''

"In spite of that, you have found a fair, strong warrior for a husband. I am very relieved that the others agreed to accept Dag Thorsson as their lord. The words he spoke were true; we are desperate for men to defend us, to build and plant crops. Dermot and the other boys try, but they are just that—boys.''

Fiona marked the wistful look on her friend's face and said, "If you could find a man among Dag's oathmen that pleased you, would you wed with him?''

"Of course! With my dowry burned in the raid, I cannot hope for a match with an Irishman, at least not one of noble blood.''

"Remember that the Norsemen are pagans," Fiona warned, "And not all of them as gentle-natured and considerate as Dag.''

"The silver-haired one who stood at Dag's side—what is he called?''

"His name is Ellisil." Fiona considered. "In truth, I know

him little, although he seems loyal to Dag . . . and ambitious.
In time, I think, he will leave Dunsheauna and seek land of his
own.''

"He is not as big as Dag, which reassures me. And he is
certainly fair to look upon. I have never seen hair of a such a
color—neither white nor gold. It glows like starlight.''

Fiona sat down on one of the crude pallets. Weary from the
journey and the tension of the confrontation, she was not
anxious to discuss Ellisil's appearance. She was more concerned with whether her people really meant to accept Dag. ''I
was surprised to see Siobhan speak as your leader,'' she said.
''Never have I seen her take such interest in the affairs of
Dunsheauna.''

"Siobhan was a great help to us after the raid. When we
finally dared leave the souterrain, she was already busy tending
the wounded and giving orders. It was she who directed us in
retrieving the men's bodies and seeing to their burial. We had
not the labor to dig a cairn to bury them in, so we wrapped
them in what finery we could find and lowered them into the
souterrain and sealed it with stones. I hope that does not distress
you, Fiona. It seemed fitting that the dead lie safe in the place
that sheltered us.''

Fiona thought of the souterrain with its ancient stone walls,
its aura of past mysteries. ''You did right, I think, Duvessa.
The souterrain was a tomb ere it was a prison or a storage
chamber. My father will rest peacefully there.''

"Dermot did not like it. He thought that we should have
exhausted ourselves digging a barrow. But I tell you, we did
not have the strength. There was so much to do if we were to
survive at all—shelters to build, food stores, utensils and bedding to salvage.''

"If Dermot wished to build a barrow, he should have done
it himself,'' Fiona said sharply.

"Dermot and the other boys did not even venture out of the
woods until after the burial had taken place. With the priest
dead, there was no one to perform the rites. Siobhan stepped
in; she knew what to do—how to wash and dress the bodies,

the words to say to comfort our spirits. It was almost as if she had been waiting for this disaster.''

''Mayhaps she was,'' Fiona murmured.

Duvessa went on. ''Dermot was very angry when Siobhan took charge. He insisted that he, as oldest male of the line, should be the leader.''

''But Dermot is not even of my father's blood!''

''Yet, as foster son, he might be recognized as heir.'' Seeing Fiona's startled look, Duvessa continued quickly. ''Myself, I do not accept his claim as valid, even if he is my brother. The harsh truth is that he is too young to act as chieftain. 'Tis almost laughable, except in his eyes.'' Her face grew sorrowful. ''I wonder what will become of him now. He cannot stand against Dag, but I doubt he can be forced to swear allegiance to a Norseman either.''

Fiona chewed her lower lip thoughtfully. She was as troubled by Dermot's attitude as Duvessa. Could Dermot not see that his cause was futile? Would he dare to challenge Dag? A boy could not stand against a grown warrior, certainly not one like Dag. Dermot must be made to see reason; if he would not, Dag must banish him. A strong leader could not allow a rebellious boy to gainsay him at every turn.

''I think we should be more concerned with Sivney Long-beard's intentions than Dermot's,'' she said, pushing thoughts of her foster brother aside. ''Is it true that he has claimed Dunsheauna for his own?''

Duvessa shook her head. ''There has been no word from Rath Morrig that I know of. I think Dermot's insistence that Sivney means to honor the betrothal agreement is merely wishful thinking.'' She sniffed disdainfully. ''Now that our wealth is gone, Dunsheauna is no enticement to a greedy, lazy man like Sivney. If he claimed the place, he might have to provide gold and men to rebuild it. Nay, he will wait until we are prosperous once again before he remembers his agreement with your father.''

Fiona breathed a sigh of relief at these words. By the time Sivney again cast covetous eyes at their lands, Dag would have see to it that the place was secure and well-defended.

She yawned extravagantly. So much had happened since they'd rowed up the river; it must be near to the middle of the night by now. "I should find Dag and seek out the ship," she said, rising. "We have much to do on the morrow."

"Nay, you must sleep here," Duvessa protested. "There is no need for you to return to the ship."

"But Dag . . ."

"You have been with your Viking lover for months now; please stay the night with me, Fiona. I have been so lonely."

Fiona submitted to Duvessa's entreaty. After all, she would see Dag on the morrow. Indeed, if she had her way, she would never sleep apart from him again. "I should at least send someone to him with word of where I am."

Duvessa hurried to the doorway. "I'll see to it."

She ducked out for a moment, then returned. But if Duvessa sought to converse more that night, she was sorely disappointed. By the time her foster sister settled herself on the pallet beside her, Fiona was too groggy to do more than mumble goodnight.

The rain had ceased and a thick mist settled over the hills by the time Dag left the ruined palisade and headed down the pathway to the cove where the *Wind Raven* was beached. The night was well nigh half over, and fatigue seemed to seep into every bone and muscle. He walked gingerly, feeling rather than seeing his way through the eerie haze of moisture. If not for the sound of the river, he would have been unable to find his way at all. As it was, he walked with his hands stretched out in front of him, fearing that he would crash into a tree and knock himself senseless.

The sheets of fog shifted, enticing him with an almost clear view of the pathway, then descended again. He cursed loudly, wondering if he should start back toward the palisade. Ahead, one of the men standing guard by the ship spoke to another. He sounded so near, Dag decided to continue on.

He had taken two more steps when a sudden foreboding came over him, very like the dread he had known his first night on the isle. His heartbeat quickened and the clammy dampness of sweat mingled with the moisture already beading his skin. He wanted to run, to throw himself into the river and escape the malevolent forces he felt all around him. He moistened his mouth to call out, then stopped himself. He would not yield to this superstitious panic. A few more paces and he would be at the ship.

Abruptly, he heard the crack of a branch on the path behind him. He whirled around and pulled his battle-ax from his belt with one smooth motion. "Who's there?" he called.

There was no answer. The hair on his neck prickled. He waited, scarcely even breathing. When nothing happened, he turned and took another step. A sharp pain lanced through his back as the knife went in. Gasping, Dag spun around and struck out with the ax. An agony-filled scream rent the night as the weapon met flesh and bone and a spray of warm blood soaked his hand.

Dag staggered backwards. "Thor's fury! Who's there?"

The only answer was a horrible gurgling noise. Dag froze. He had killed his attacker, whoever he was, and the wounded man's spirit struggled to free itself from his body.

Dag dropped to his knees and moved toward the chilling sound. He reached out a trembling hand and followed the trail of warm blood to its source. He jerked his hand away when he touched a body, then forced himself to reach out again. Finding an arm, still pliant and warm with life, he traced it upwards, past the horrible bleeding gash in the man's throat to his face. An anguished groan broke from Dag's throat as his fingers felt the smooth, slender cheek of his attacker.

Chapter 35

Dag slumped forward on the wet ground. The knife wound in his shoulder throbbed, but the pain was nothing compared to the torment in his heart. He had killed the boy—Fiona's foster brother. She would never forgive him.

"Dag?" Ellisil's voice echoed in the distance.

Dag groaned again, unable to speak.

The sound of footfalls, faint in the damp grass. Someone leaned over him. Ellisil cried out in alarm, "By the hand of Odin! Dag—who did this to you?"

"The boy," he answered.

Ellisil shone the torch wide, and Dag heard him suck in his breath as he examined Dermot's body. Then the warrior bent over him again and pulled the knife free. Dag grunted at the pain, but did not attempt to rise.

"Are you wounded elsewhere?" Ellisil asked, his voice heavy with dread. "What is it, Dag? Why do you not get up? The wound in your back is not serious compared to some of the blows you've taken in battle."

Wearily, Dag pulled himself to a sitting position. The mist had almost disappeared, and Ellisil's torch clearly revealed the boy's body lying twisted in its death throes. Dag stared at the slender corpse, beyond weeping.

Ellisil shook his head. "Of all the foolishness—to attack you with a puny dagger like that. What was he thinking?"

"He was only a child, but I cut him down with my ax. I couldn't see!" Dag's voice trailed off hoarsely.

"He stabbed you in the back. You were only defending yourself."

Dag shook his head. "Fiona. She loved him. He was her foster brother."

"Would she have rather you died?" Ellisil asked incredulously.

"I don't know," Dag said. "I fear it may be so."

Fiona slept deeply, buried under the weight of a dream so terrifying it seemed to crush her. She was down in the souterrain. All was dark except for a multitude of glowing eyes that leered at her out of the murk. As she shrank away, the eyes followed her, and suddenly she knew they belonged to the dead. A torch flared and she saw that the chamber was lined with corpses, rotting corpses that danced on mangled, bloody limbs and reached out for her with hideously disfigured arms. She pushed them away, but they fell on her, burying her in putrid, oozing flesh.

She sat upright, choking on a scream, and the pain on Duvessa's face as she bent over her told Fiona that the nightmare had not ended. "Dag," Duvessa croaked. "He wants you to come."

Fiona leapt up from the pallet like a panicked animal. "Where? What's happened?"

Duvessa shook her head. "He said you must hear it from him."

Outside the hut, Ellisil waited for them, torch in hand, his face grim. He shook his head when she questioned him. "Dag will not let me say."

"He is well? Please tell me that he is well!" Fiona begged. Ellisil nodded.

They walked silently, like a funeral procession. The forest seemed impossibly far away; then when they entered the woods, the trees were endless. When they reached Dag, Fiona saw that he was seated on the ground. Siobhan crouched next to him, apparently tending his back.

Fiona rushed to him. "Dag, Dag—what is it?"

He lifted his head to look at her. Fiona's blood went cold at the look of despair on his face. "By the saints! What's happened?"

"Dermot is dead. I killed him."

Fiona swayed on her feet. *Nay! This could not be happening.* Behind her, Duvessa began to weep.

" 'Twas an accident." Siobhan rose and put her hand on Fiona's arm, steadying her. "Dermot tried to kill Dag. He came up behind him in the dark and mist and stabbed him in the back. Dag did what any warrior would have—he pulled his weapon and fought his attacker."

"I struck blindly, never knowing. . . ." Dag's voice bled with grief.

"I want to see him," Fiona said. It surprised her how calm her voice sounded.

"Nay." Dag's answer was harsh, decisive.

" 'Tis my right!" Anger filled her. How dare Dag prevent her from seeing her foster brother!

"It might be well if you did not," Siobhan said softly. " 'Twas not an easy death."

Fiona gasped at the pain the words brought her. "I will see him," she insisted. "I will say goodbye. Never did I get a chance to say farewell to my father. I will at least give Dermot that."

Siobhan nodded and took her arm. "He's in my hut."

"She will curse me," Dag said softly. "Then she will curse herself for bringing me here."

"Get up, Dag," Ellisil ordered impatiently. "You'll take a chill," Numbly, Dag rose. He was surprised to see Duvessa clinging to Ellisil's arm, tears streaming down her face.

"Dermot was my brother," she said brokenly.

Ellisil held the torch out to Dag. He accepted the flaming brand and watched Ellisil gather the little Irishwoman to his chest. As she wept, Ellisil soothed her with soft words and a gentle hand upon her thick wavy hair. A stab of excruciating longing went through Dag as he watched his sword brother comfort the woman. Once he had held Fiona thus, eased her pain, and vowed to protect her. Instead, he had brought her more grief.

"Can you walk?" Ellisil asked Duvessa. When she nodded, he gestured to Dag that he should lead the way to the ship. Dag began to walk. His legs felt leaden, his insides like ice. When they reached the grounded ship, Ellisil reached for the torch again. "I'm going to take Duvessa back to her hut."

Dag handed over the torch and turned away. The elegant prow of the *Raven* loomed above the river, gilded silver in the moonlight. He stared at the ship a long while, then waded in and climbed over the side. Rorig greeted him sleepily. Dag chastised him for not being more alert, then sought out his own bedsack.

He closed his eyes and beseeched the gods to bring him sleep. Slowly, warmth crept through him, bringing with it a kind of dull resignation. He was alive; his spirit had not fled his body on that mist-shrouded pathway. He had done the only thing he could do. If Fiona could not forgive him, he would have to live his life without her.

"Dag! Dag!"

He could hear Fiona's voice. She sounded worried. He opened his eyes—and the memories of the night before flooded back to him.

"Fiona." She looked terribly weary. Her eyes were red; her face pale. It hurt him to see her suffering.

"You must get up, Dag. You must let Siobhan examine your wound. She scarcely treated you last night. It might yet fester."

Dag sat up. "Do you care?" he whispered. "Do you not wish I would die as Dermot did?"

Her eyes widened. *"Nei!* You think I wish you dead?" She leaned over, kissing him quickly on the jaw. " 'Twas not your fault. Dermot did a foolish thing—cowardly, too. I grieve for him, but I would not trade his life for yours. Never!"

Dag sighed and drew Fiona down to him. His back hurt fiercely, but he did not care. The pain in his heart was gone.

"Jesu," Fiona suddenly gasped. "You're burning with fever."

Dag nodded and closed his eyes, sinking down into oblivion.

Over the next few days, Fiona did not leave Dag's side save to relieve herself. She stared fixedly at his flushed face or sometimes leaned her ear to his chest to hear the thready heartbeat that whispered there. She cursed herself a thousand times for not having insisted Siobhan tend his wound that night. It had seemed a shallow wound, but it had festered quickly. Now he burned with fever, and this time, Siobhan's healing herbs did not seem to work.

Helpless anger made Fiona's aching body tense. She and Dag had come so far on their journey to understanding each other. He could not leave her now! He could not!

"Peace, little one. As long as he breathes, there is hope."

Siobhan's soothing words made Fiona bite back tears all the harder. "He cannot die! I won't let him!"

" 'Tis not up to you," Siobhan reminded her. "He walks among the spirits now, and it is their will whether he returns to us."

"I have prayed," Fiona said. "To the Christian god and all the others. How can I make them listen?"

"You cannot. The gods do what they will."

"But you told me that Dag was the one, that he was meant to rule Dunsheauna!"

Siobhan nodded. "I thought he was." Her gray eyes appeared dull this day, slate instead of silver.

Fiona choked back another outburst. She would not curse the gods yet, not while Dag still breathed. She reached out to touch his heated skin. Her fingers stroked his whisker-roughened cheek as she murmured love words. Closing her eyes, she willed him to live. Her spirit reached out to his, searching for the filament of love that bound them together. She concentrated, putting all her ebbing strength into her endeavor.

Frustrated, she opened her eyes. " 'Tis no use. I can't reach him. I don't have the healing gift, or mayhap my spirit isn't powerful enough."

"How do you know?"

Fiona waved her hands impatiently. "I can't feel him. 'Tis as if his spirit has already left me."

"That you cannot feel his spirit does not mean he does not feel yours. How do you know you do not strengthen him each time you reach out to him?"

"He does not stir; he does not acknowledge any of it."

"Do not give up hope, Fiona. You must be brave."

Fiona took a shuddering breath. "I keep thinking of my father. I still feel I failed him somehow, and now . . . now I fear I have failed Dag as well."

"Why?"

"I was so caught up in my grief for Dermot; I should have seen that Dag's wound was tended."

Siobhan nodded. "I also should have insisted that he let me clean it. But he seemed well enough." She sighed.

Fiona released Dag's hand and stood. Tully moved from his place on the floor beside her. He, too, had kept vigil at Dag's pallet since the night he'd followed her down from the hill fort to find her fallen lover.

"If only I had known . . ."

"You could not know," Siobhan observed sharply. "Life can only be lived forwards."

Fiona sighed and settled herself on the stool again.

Near dusk, Duvessa and Breaca appeared. Standing next to each other, they looked to Fiona like siblings who had shared the same birth sack, so close in color was their coppery hair, so similar their diminutive figures—although Breaca's midsection had begun to swell with her growing babe.

They each took a place on either side of Fiona, and she immediately sensed a conspiracy.

"We've come to take you to eat," Duvessa said.

"I've eaten already."

"You will come," Breaca insisted. "You are weak, and there are two of us."

Confronted with such conviction, Fiona stood. She let them lead her toward the doorway. She paused again on the way out. "What if he wakes and I'm not here?"

"What if he wakes and sees what a frightful bag of bones you've become? I trow, he will faint in horror, and it will be an even longer while before he rouses again."

Fiona let them guide her through the doorway.

The nothingness thinned and faded, and all at once he was back. His spirit rushed into his body. It was a useless, pitiful husk of a body, but nevertheless, it was his.

He struggled to open his weighted eyelids. The light seemed unbearably bright. A shape floated into view. A few paces away, a woman with dark hair and weathered skin sat by the fire. Fiona? Nay, this woman was old! Yet she reminded him so much of Fiona. Had he slept through years and awakened to this?

The woman spoke, mumbling as she poked the fire. He puzzled the sound of her foreign words. Once he had known this language; now it eluded him. Had it really been so long ago?

He shifted his head to gaze around the dwelling . . . a tiny, cluttered hut, filled with strange things. Dried plants hung on every inch of wall space. What furniture there was had been fashioned in minuscule form.

He looked to the woman again. She was small and dark . . . and old. Her flesh had begun to shrink into her bones. She must be a fairy, he thought, then drew back, shuddering. Fairies did not age, only mortals did. Unless he was in fairyland and the pattern here had been reversed—he stayed young and his captors grew old.

The woman had heard him rouse. She rose from the stool.

He raised his eyes to hers, terrified he would find Fiona's unmistakable green gaze staring back at him.

The woman's eyes were gray! Dag breathed a sigh of profound relief. Although he still did not know where he was, at least he had not slept through his time and awakened in the future.

She approached the pallet and leaned over him. "Dag," she said. He stared at her, trying to puzzle out how she knew his name.

"Where am I?" he asked.

She frowned, and he guessed she did not know his language. Foreboding filled him again. "Fiona?" he ventured.

Recognition flared in the woman's eyes. She spoke rapidly, gesturing toward the door. Dag's befuddlement and fear eased. If he found himself in an unfamiliar place, at least Fiona had been here. He said her name again. The woman smiled. She placed a soothing hand on his brow and whispered soothing words. The ache in his head seemed to ease although he still felt a fierce burning in his back. He had been wounded again, but how, he could not remember.

"Water," he croaked. The woman looked at him, again puzzled. Dag searched his mind, finally remembering the Gaelic word. *"Uisce,"* he said.

The woman hastened to the hearth and returned with a beaker of water. He drank greedily. His thirst was so great, he felt he could drink a lake. After he had finished, his head fell back against the pallet. The world spun dizzily around him, and he let himself sink once more into the timeless, thoughtless void.

The next time he woke, Fiona was there, sitting on a stool beside the fire, stirring something in a wooden vessel. He said nothing, only watched her. Her hair was unplaited and disheveled, her face pale. She was dressed in a simple, unadorned kirtle. But that scarcely diminished her beauty. She looked as he remembered her, wild and haughty. A warrior-woman—his storm maiden.

She looked up and met his gaze. Unfathomable green eyes stole his soul even as memory rushed back.

''Dag!''

Her hand felt cool against his skin. Her lips touched his tenderly. He kissed her back, his eyes fluttering closed with the effort. The pain and fear vanished. She would heal him.

He reached out to feel the softness of her flesh and sighed with contentment.

Epilogue

Fiona gathered up her skirts and ran. She could not be late, not on this day of all days—Beltaine, the ancient celebration of summer.

Surely they would not begin without her, she reassured herself as her hide sandals squished in the wet grass. Expectation welled up in her, making her half-dizzy with buoyant happiness. Ducking into her aunt's hut, she dug hurriedly in the leather-bound chest in the corner. Triumphantly, she lifted up her treasure. She gazed at it a moment, then whirled and left the hut.

The forest was heady with warm mist and the sweet scent of flowers. Fiona did not pause to savor the sunshine gleaming through foliage, to remark upon the extraordinary fairness of the day. Her thoughts were fixed on another image, one more beautiful to her than any other.

Leaving the woods, she raced up the grassy slope to the freshly hewn walls of the palisade.

Duvessa met her at the gateway. "Where have you been? Siobhan has been searching everywhere for you," she scolded.

Fiona did not answer, only smiled and fell in step beside her friend as they walked to the center of the palisade. Under a canopy of leather, three long, board tables and benches were arranged. There was no great hall, not yet. Dag had insisted that rebuilding the fort walls was more important than the hall. If they had to, they could sleep another winter in their temporary shelters.

Fiona slowed her pace as she remembered the exquisite kirtle she wore and decided she should have a care for it. Fashioned of green silk and embroidered with gold thread, the kirtle was the finest garment she had ever worn. Dag had brought the fabric back from Hedeby after his early spring trading voyage, and Duvessa and Breaca had wasted no time in using the fabulous material to make her a gown fit for a princess.

Fiona smiled, thinking of the hot gleam in Dag's eyes when he had first beheld her in the garment. "In truth, you look like a fairy queen," he had said, his breath catching. "I trow, the only time I have ever seen you look more beautiful is when you are naked."

Could a man be beautiful, too? Fiona wondered as she approached the feasting table. Surely, in her eyes, Dag was the most glorious sight she had ever seen. Standing behind the head table, he wore a short tunic of snowy linen banded with saffron and crimson silk. Fitted in the Irish fashion, the garment bared his powerful neck and muscular arms. With his long, reddish-gold hair, coppery mustache, and ruddy skin, he glowed like a sun god.

She wanted to go to him, to pull his face down to hers and drown in his fiery kiss. But this was a day for ceremony and formality. Around them, dozens watched—her kinsmen and his oathmen—all resplendent in their finest tunics and kirtles, the women's hair neatly plaited, the men's beards and mustaches combed.

This day would seal forever the bond between Irish and Norse. It had been a long time coming. Dag had not recovered from his wound until almost the Yule season. Then they had been busy, so busy, making tools, rebuilding storehouses and shops, rounding up cattle and horses which had strayed since the fire, hunting and fishing to supplement their meager food supply. When the first shoots of new green appeared on the hillsides, they had all worked—man and woman, Norse and Irish—side by side. planting in the fields.

They had scarcely finished the planting when Dag had said it was time for a trading voyage. Although they had little produce to barter with, Dag still had a cache of hacksilver and other booty—his share of the fortune Knorri had saved from the fire. Fiona had also been able to contribute. In their haste, the Vikings had missed a fair share of her father's wealth; and after the fires were spent, Siobhan and the other women had scavaged among the ashes and discovered metalwork and jewelry which had not burned and a whole wicker casket of glassware, silks, and other luxury items.

Although Fiona had wept to see him go, Dag had insisted that trading was different from raiding. They would take no risks, keep to the safest sea route, and be back within a fortnight. He had kept his word, and Fiona had welcomed him back with a passion she hoped would entice him to remain forever at her side. Of course, she knew that the sea and travelling was in his blood, just as the land was in hers. And one of Dag's greatest skills was his ability as a trader; he was able to drive a hard bargain and win men's goodwill simultaneously. In time, he hoped that word would spread and Dunsheauna would become an important trading center.

Looking at her proud, regal husband, Fiona did not doubt that he could accomplish anything he wished. They had been wed as soon as he was recovered enough from his wound to stand, both in a traditional Norse ceremony and then by a Christian priest who happened to pass by in early spring. Siobhan had protested the Christian ceremony, but Fiona felt better afterwards; she wanted her bond to this man to be recognized by every god—Norse, ancient Irish, and the Christ God as well. Her instincts told her that Siobhan's prejudice against the Christian priests was as limiting as Dermot's implacable hatred of the Norse.

Thinking of her foster brother, Fiona tore her eyes from Dag and looked around the gathering. Many of the widowed Irish women had found companionship with Dag's oathmen. Fiona did not doubt that during the next full turn of the seasons there would be a whole crop of Norse-Irish babies born at Dunsheauna. Such a thing would have horrified Dermot.

Poor Dermot, Fiona thought sadly. He had not lived long enough to learn the truth. Between a man and a woman, blood and traditions did not matter as much as that their spirits touched. Why, there was Rorig, a broad smile on his face as he looked down at Breaca and their new, auburn-haired babe. And farther down the table, Ellisil bent his silvery head to whisper to Duvessa and make her laugh. Who was to say that they should not be together because their peoples had once been enemies?

Realizing that everyone waited, Fiona again sought Dag, and she walked to take her place beside him. He smiled at her, his blue eyes soft and melting, then cleared his throat to speak to those assembled. Fiona stopped him with her hand on his arm. "Wait, Dag," she whispered. "I forgot something."

She took an object from the folds of her kirtle, then stood on tiptoe to place it around Dag's neck. An excited whisper passed through the crowd as the sun caught the gold of the massive torc encircling Dag's neck.

" 'Twas my father's," Fiona told Dag shyly. "Now you truly look an Irish chieftain."

As if expressing his approval, Tully sat back on his haunches at Dag's feet and began to bark.

The sun shone bright on the timber-ringed fort perched upon the vivid green hillside, and the sound of laughter floated into the moist, enchanted air.

Author's Note

I enjoy taking my readers on voyages into the enthralling past. I also enjoy hearing their comments on my books. Please write me at P.O. Box 2052, Cheyenne, WY 82001. A self-addressed, stamped envelope is appreciated.